GOBLIN WARRIOR!

The thing was humanoid in form, but resembled an ape more than a man. The face was framed in short, bristly hair and had a leathery appearance. There was no true nose—rather, the thing had a long, leathery snout, like a baboon's. Also like a baboon's, that snout was filled with long, vicious-looking fangs. If Steve had seen it at the zoo, he wouldn't have looked twice.

At the zoo, however, it wouldn't have been wearing leather or carrying a crossbow. . . .

A TWO-EDGED SWORD

The exciting new fantasy
adventure by Thomas K. Martin

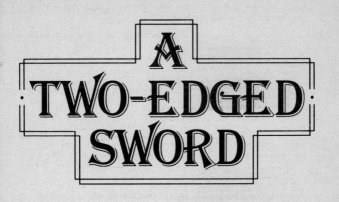

A TWO-EDGED SWORD

THOMAS K. MARTIN

ACE BOOKS, NEW YORK

This book is an Ace original edition,
and has never been previously published.

A TWO-EDGED SWORD

An Ace Book / published by arrangement with
the author

PRINTING HISTORY
Ace edition / January 1994

ISBN: 0-441-83344-6

ACE®
Ace Books are published by The Berkley Publishing Group,
200 Madison Avenue, New York, NY 10016.
ACE and the "A" design are
trademarks belonging to Charter Communications, Inc.

PRINTED IN THE UNITED STATES OF AMERICA

10 9 8 7 6 5 4 3 2 1

This book is dedicated to all of the friends, both old and new, who helped to make it a reality. The list is too long to include here, but you all know who you are. It would have been much more difficult without you.

Dramatis Personae

Delvir:

Tsadhoq: Captain of the Delvan Royal Guard.

Morvir:

Belevairn: Sorceror and one of the twelve Dread Lords of Delgroth.

Daemor: The member of the Twelve commanding the war in Olvanor and Erelvar's former liege and mentor.

Jared: The Dread Lord in command of the war in Umbria.

Nymrans:

Artemas Zelotes: Master sorceror and distant cousin to Theron Baltasaros.

Theron Baltasaros: Priest of Lindra, former centurion of the Veran Guard and cousin to Solon Baltasaros, Regent-Emperor of Nym in exile at Validus.

Olvir:

Adhelmen: War-Master of Olvanor.

Arven: King of Olvanor.

Delarian: Younger brother of Prince Laerdon in service to Erelvar.

Laerdon: Prince of Olvanor and heir to the throne of Olvanor.

Quarin:

Aerilynn: Glorien's shield-maiden and *felgae*.

Erelvar: Champion of the Temple of Mortos and self-proclaimed Lord of Quarin.

Glorien: Wife to Lord Erelvar and the only woman to be recognized as a warrior.

Morfael: Erelvar's liege-man and friend.

Steven Wilkinson: American college student and reluctant apprentice to Lord Erelvar.

Umbrians:

Aldric ap Botewylf: Son of Morcan Botewylf and future chief of clan Botewylf.

Arthwyr ap Madawc: An Umbrian warrior in service to Lord Erelvar who befriends Steve.

Morcan Botewylf: King of Umbria.

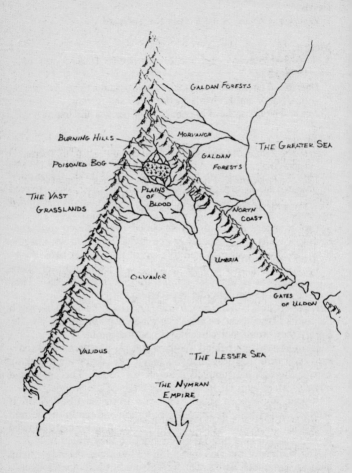

GALDAN FORESTS

THE GREATER SEA

BURNING HILLS

MORVANOR

GALDAN FORESTS

POISONED BOG

PLAINS OF BLOOD

THE VAST GRASSLANDS

NORTH COAST

UMBRIA

OLVANOR

GATES OF ULDON

VALIDUS

THE LESSER SEA

THE NYMRAN EMPIRE

Chapter
-------- **One** -------------

IT REQUIRED ALL his skill to avoid the branches as his
horse galloped through the ruins of the once-burned forest.
Relentlessly the muffled hoofbeats of the Morvir followed—
he mustn't let them catch him. He leapt a fallen, vine-covered
tree and turned his mount to the left. New saplings whipped
his horse's flanks as he charged ahead.

Unfortunately the dead, ivy-shrouded trees offered little concealment while still impeding his progress. He could not imagine
how the Morvir had managed to conceal themselves here.

He risked a glance behind, catching a brief glimpse of ebon-
armored riders racing past on the trail he had just left. They
wouldn't be misled long, he was certain.

He circled back to the east, toward Quarin. If he could but reach
the limits of the forest, he would be within sight of the city's walls.
Surely they would not pursue him past that point. . . .

Horn-blasts from behind told him that his pursuers had discovered their error. He leapt another fallen tree, desperately seeking
a path through the jumbled ruins of the forest. The chase had
already driven him far from familiar areas of the woods.

Ahead, however, a small ridge rose from the forest floor. It
seemed clearer than the surrounding terrain and ran in the desired
direction. They would undoubtedly realize that he had followed
it, but it might take him far enough before they found it.

The warhorse stretched into a full gallop along the ridge, foam
coating her golden flanks. The horse wouldn't last much longer—
he hoped she would last long enough.

It was not the horse, however, that betrayed him. As he topped
a small rise he saw, with horror, that the ridge ended in an abrupt
drop to the forest floor. Without thought he threw himself from
the saddle—his only chance.

1

The breath burst from his lungs as he struck the stony ground of the ridge. He tumbled several yards before falling down a steep slope. Desperately, he attempted to slow his plunge down the side of the ridge.

He came to rest amid a shower of gravel. The screams of the wounded horse told him that she had not fared as well in the fall as he. If that didn't bring the Morvir, nothing would. He had to kill the horse and escape before they followed her screams to him. Surely, he must not be too far from Quarin.

He pulled himself to his feet, using the steep, earthen wall of the ridge for support. For a moment the world spun about him. He took a few deep breaths and allowed his senses to settle back into place.

He looked up quickly when the horse's screams came to an abrupt end. One Morva stood by the dead animal, wiping his sword with a cloth. The young warrior doubted that the Morva had slain the horse out of mercy. More likely, the screaming had irritated him.

Five others sat astride their mounts. The breath caught in his throat—he wasn't ready to die.

Grimly, he clenched his jaw, regathering his courage. He would die well. He owed Erelvar that much, at least. Slowly he drew his sword and retrieved his shield from the ground. He doubted that he would be given the opportunity to use either.

Then again, perhaps he would. With some surprise he watched as the other five Morvir dismounted. Their steeds, superbly trained, stood where the reins had been dropped as if hitched there. The six men approached him, slowly and cautiously, as he placed his back against the ridge.

They stopped in a half-circle well beyond sword reach. For a moment they merely observed him, silently.

"Will you surrender to us?" one of them finally asked. So . . . they wanted him alive.

"To Morvir?" he said. "Hah! I might as well fall on my sword."

Two of them stepped forward. He blocked a powerful side-swing with his shield as he used his sword to deflect a thrust aimed for his throat.

They gave him little chance for attack. The opponent on his shield side maintained a rapid, battering barrage of blows that threatened to numb his arm, while his sword was kept busy defending against his second opponent. Eventually one of them would penetrate his guard if he could not gain the initiative.

His sword-side opponent seemed to prefer the thrust. Very well, he could work with that. His other opponent had already settled into a monotonous, bludgeoning rhythm. Now if he could just match the other to that . . .

Slowly, he maneuvered his opponent into the rhythm; thrust, parry, return—thrust, parry, return. Once satisfied that he had lured him into the trap, the young warrior allowed the point of his sword to drop, ever so slightly.

As he had hoped, his opponent was skilled enough to notice the slight falter in his defense. The Morva replied with a vicious thrust to the side, but was met with more speed and strength than he expected. The momentum of the thrust embedded the Morva's sword deep in the earthen cliff.

The warrior thrust into the gap beneath the Morva's arm. The light chain protecting that weak spot gave easily to the strong, Delvan blade. His other opponent landed another heavy blow on his shield, still locked into the fatal rhythm.

He absorbed the blow with his shield high, but, instead of allowing the shield to be driven in as he had before, he slammed it down and to the side, catching the Morva in the midriff. The Morva's sword glanced from his helm, most of its force spent.

He pulled the blade from the armpit of his first opponent and spun quickly to the left, thrusting his sword through the Morva's visor. He felt the blade bite into bone before his second opponent fell.

He continued the spin, barely bringing his shield around in time to catch the blow aimed at him by yet a third of the Morvir, stepping in to fill the vacancy he had just created. He heard the remaining Morvir laughing.

They appreciated skill, or perhaps the laughter was merely derision for their former colleagues' clumsiness. He didn't care which, only that he now had two fresh opponents to face.

He swung low, at the legs of his newest opponent, exhausting the last of the momentum from his spin. It was blocked easily. Once again he found himself trapped between two enemies.

These were more cautious, refusing to fall into rhythm. He had gotten lucky with the first two—his new opponents were not going to allow that.

So he would simply have to make his own luck. With all his strength, he threw himself against the next blow that landed on his shield. His less than conventional tactic had the desired result; the Morva ended up flat on his back.

He didn't take the time to dispatch his downed opponent, however. Instead he broke from the cliffside, running for the ground-tethered horses. He could hear the other Morvir pursuing him. Whatever lead he had gained from surprise was likely to be lost when he reached the horses.

He hurled his shield directly behind him and was rewarded with some unintelligible Morvan curse and the sound of crashing armor. The others were after him as well, but his lead was too great. With ease that would have made Erelvar proud, he vaulted the leanest horse's back to land smoothly in the saddle.

His feet instinctively found the stirrups as his hands gathered up the reins. Viciously, he kicked the horse in the ribs, eager to be away from the approaching Morvir.

The beast squealed in anger and bit at him, refusing to move. Shocked by this unexpected development, he kicked again. The horse snorted, derisively it seemed, as strong hands grabbed him by the elbows.

He struggled in vain as the Morvir hauled him from the saddle. He began to curse as they pinned him to the ground and brutally removed his helmet. The words died in his throat. . . .

Before him, filling his field of vision, a horse's shank ended in a cloven hoof. A thin wisp of smoke curled up where the hoof touched the ground.

"Greetings, Master Wilkinson," a dry, rasping voice said.

"What do you want of me, Belevairn?" He knew who that voice belonged to. Already he could visualize the mummified, skull-like face and the burning eyes that hid behind the jewelled demon-mask. He would rather face an army of the Morvir than the undead monster that sat before him on its demon-steed.

"As if you did not know," came the chuckling reply. "Bind him."

The Morvir hastened to obey. Soon he was firmly bound to stakes driven into the forest floor, stripped of his armor and clothing. He watched, horrified, as the Dread Lord filled a small, brazen bowl with various leaves, powders and oils. This he placed near Wilkinson's head. With a snap of desiccated fingers, the contents of the bowl burst into flame. The thick, sweet smoke from the bowl enveloped Wilkinson's face.

The surviving Morvir left, taking up positions about the small clearing. It seemed that they were more than happy to have nothing to do with the proceedings.

Runes were drawn in paint on Wilkinson's chest and forehead. He shuddered at the touch of Belevairn's oil-covered fingers. The smoke from the brazier seemed to sap his will, and he found himself unable to offer the slightest resistance.

Apparently satisfied that the preparations had been completed, the undead sorceror knelt behind him and briefly placed his hands on either side of Wilkinson's face. He leaned over, locking his gaze with the young warrior's.

Wilkinson could not look away. The red, burning eyes held his like a bird's helplessly locked in the gaze of a viper. He was vaguely aware of a black, polished dagger in the monster's hand, but the eyes seemed to fill his vision completely.

A guttural chant weaved through his drugged mind as the burning eyes expanded to fill yet more of his vision. Suddenly, he was aware of a burning in his chest as the red orbs engulfed him, drawing him into a twisted and evil presence. He began to scream in horror. . . .

A cold December wind blew across the darkened campus. Steve stared up at the Life Sciences building momentarily. He hoped Frank knew what he was talking about—this dream-research thing still sounded hokey to him. Still, he needed the money, and, with Dead Week just a few days away, and finals right after that, he didn't need the hassles of a full-time job.

He slammed the door shut on his Firebird—the chief cause of his current financial problems. Perhaps he should just let the bank come and take the damned thing away. . . .

He hurried toward the building, anxious to get out of the cold wind. The normally busy campus was deathly silent. Stark shadows lurked at the corners of the building. He quickly stepped inside.

The glass door closed behind him, sealing out the cold. With a shiver he removed his gloves to let his fingers thaw in the warmer air.

He glanced up the darkened halls. Only the lights at the entrance were lit, casting the rest of the building into half-lit gloom. Where had those stairs been? They had actually been easier to find earlier, when the building was full of students.

He found them again, though, and soon was on the second floor. Doctor Engelman had told him that they were going to set up in room two-oh-three. That turned out to be easier to find than the stairs, however—it was the only room on the second floor that was lit.

"You're early," Doctor Engelman said approvingly as Steve walked into the lab.

"Yeah. I wanted to make sure I got here on time."

"My assistants aren't here yet. If you like, though, I can go ahead and get you hooked up."

"Sure. Here are your forms."

"Hm? Oh, yes." Doctor Engelman took the forms from him and glanced through them. Steve still couldn't get over how young the professor was. When he had first come to sign up for the project he had expected some distinguished-looking, old scientist.

Instead, Doctor Engelman was almost young enough to be a student himself. In fact, the professor had only received his doctorate last year.

He wore his light brown hair at the same just-below-collar length that Steve did. His build was only moderately heavier than Steve's own slight frame, and his blue eyes still had a youthful spark in them. If someone had seen the two of them drinking in the campus bar together they might have mistaken them for brothers.

"You've had nothing to drink for the last five hours now, correct?" Doctor Engelman asked, as if reading Steve's mind.

"That's right," Steve lied. In truth, he hadn't drank for a little over four hours; it was easy to lose track of time around Frank. However, half an hour shouldn't make much difference.

"If you'll step over here, please," Doctor Engelman said.

"Sure," Steve replied. The professor led him over to three cots and instructed him to lie down. Steve watched as Doctor Engelman prepared a small array of test instruments.

There was an electrocardiograph to monitor his heart, an electroencephalograph to record his brain activity and a REM counter to track his eye movements. Doctor Engelman explained the function and purpose of each as he attached them to Steve's person.

"Comfortable?" he finally asked.

"Oh, sure," Steve replied. "I always sleep wired up like a Christmas tree."

"Well, this ought to help," Doctor Engelman said, smiling as he inspected a syringe.

"What's that?"

"Just a little something to help you sleep and make you dream. Didn't you read the forms?"

"Yes. They didn't say anything about shots, though. I thought you were going to give me some pills to take."

"I'm afraid not. It doesn't bother you, does it?"

"No . . . of course not," Steve replied.

"Good."

Steve winced a little as the needle penetrated his arm. At least the medicine didn't burn.

"All done," the professor said, laying the empty syringe on the tray. "You'll start to feel a little drowsy. Don't fight it, just relax and you'll be asleep before you know it. You'll probably have some very vivid dreams."

"Okay."

"Well, looks like I've got another one to prep," Doctor Engelman said as another student walked into the lab. "I'll be back to check on you in a few minutes."

Steve nodded. The injection was already making him drowsy. Sleepily, he watched as the professor and his recently arrived assistant wired up another victim. He didn't remain awake long enough to see the end of the preparation.

The professor glanced over at Steve once subject two was prepped; he was already asleep. Doctor Engelman frowned—the drug should not have worked quite that quickly.

He stepped over to the instruments. Everything appeared normal; pulse, respiration, brain activity. Oh well, most students kept themselves in a state of near-exhaustion this close to Dead Week. Maybe he'd just been tired.

His third and final subject arrived. He left Steve in order to attend to the new arrival. He'd check back again when he was finished.

By the time he returned, Steve was already in REM. He glanced at his watch. It had only been half an hour since he'd administered the injection. The subject should not be in REM for some time yet. He scribbled a note on his clipboard prior to leaving for the observation room.

"Well, Mister Wilkinson," he said softly, "you're full of surprises tonight, aren't you?" The sleeping student gave no response.

"Where are we?" Susan demanded.

"We're . . . uh—I don't know," Steve replied. Susan snorted disgustedly. Great. He'd been trying to get her to go out with him all semester and, now that he'd finally succeeded, something like this had to happen.

The funny thing was, he couldn't quite remember how they'd gotten here—wherever "here" was. There were no signs to tell him the way back to familiar territory. There didn't seem to be any houses either.

"Are you sure you're really lost?" Susan asked suspiciously.

Steve felt his face flush. Before he could answer, his headlights illuminated something on the road ahead of him. The figure quickly resolved into a man on horseback. Salvation!

"Maybe we can get directions," Steve suggested desperately. He stopped the car and rolled down the window. Ahead, the horse began to canter toward them, its eyes eerily reflecting the glow from the headlights.

The lights finally illuminated the man's face. However, it was no man. Empty eye sockets glared out at them from a death's head covered with taut skin stretched into a permanent leer. Susan screamed beside him—the horse began to gallop.

Steve threw the gearshift into reverse and pushed the gas pedal to the floor. The roar of the engine and the squeal of tires did not quite drown out the sound of Susan's screams.

The Firebird roared backwards down the narrow country road. The galloping horse followed, sparks flying from its hooves as they struck the pavement. Ever so slowly, the Firebird left the nightmarish rider behind.

Steve didn't see the bend in the road behind them until much too late. The car flew backwards over the narrow ditch beside the road and flipped as the rear end struck the ground. Steve, too, began to scream.

He awoke lying on the ground. At some point he must have been thrown from the tumbling vehicle. By the light of the burning wreck he could see Susan lying face-down on the ground. Of the rider, there was no sign.

He crawled over to where Susan lay, unmoving. The flickering firelight cast odd shadows over her. God, he hoped she was all right.

"Susan," he said weakly. "Susan, are you okay?" He gently rolled her over. Green, catlike eyes gleamed up at him from a face hidden entirely in shadow. Steve's breath caught in his throat.

"Who is the Dreamer?" a husky, feminine voice asked. "Which way shall his Sword strike?"

Steve leapt back, away from what he had thought to be Susan. She rose gracefully, cloaked in shadow despite the flickering glare of the burning car behind her. She held out a darkened hand to him. He screamed and fled into the woods behind him. Her laughter seemed to follow him forever. . . .

Steve had no idea how far he had run. He leaned against the rough bark of a large tree, gasping for breath. The silver moonlight filtering through the branches above lent a dreamlike quality to the forest.

This whole experience had been like a bad dream; a nightmare. Perhaps he would wake up and—he blinked in surprise at the thought. Perhaps he would wake up and Doctor Engelman would tell him that the experiment was over, that he could go home now.

He slid to a sitting position. He leaned back against the tree, sighing in relief. It *was* just a dream—nothing more.

He glanced up suddenly. Had someone called him? There it was again. A . . . call. But he had heard nothing. Slowly, he stood, his back pressed against the tree. Maybe it was *her*. He shuddered.

"Just a dream," he told himself, "just a dream."

The other two subjects had not yet entered REM sleep. Doctor Engelman sat down by the monitors for subject number one again. He took a sip from his coffee and glanced at the EEG monitor.

What he saw made no sense at all. He glanced over at the REM counter. It was still dutifully recording Wilkinson's sleeping eye movements. The EEG, however, showed what appeared to be a conscious brain-wave pattern. A glance through the observation window into the sleep room verified the presence of the rapid eye movements. Perhaps the device was broken?

He sat the coffee down and examined the printout. The transition point was about a minute back on the tape. The alpha, beta, delta and theta waves had changed from REM proportions to a conscious pattern within one second. One second! Meanwhile the REM counter continued to report eye movements. The cardiac and respiratory monitors also reported data consistent with REM sleep. Only the EEG claimed otherwise.

"Mary," he said.

"Yes, Doctor?"

"Help me hook number one up to another EEG. This one may have gone bad on us."

"Yes, Doctor." As she walked away to get another monitor, Doctor Engelman absently scratched his chin. He hoped they hadn't lost several hours' worth of data here. If these readings were accurate, however, subject number one was proving to be very interesting.

Steve stood against the tree, listening. He heard it again—a muffled sound similar to a horse snorting. Had the rider returned? The small night sounds of the forest abruptly died away. In the sudden silence he could hear the sound of leaves crunching from somewhere behind him.

He decided that he didn't want to know what it was, dream or not. Cautiously, he stole from his hiding place to the shelter of another tree. A twig cracked loudly underfoot and he froze into immobility.

The sounds of movement behind him stopped as well. Steve could imagine the ghostly rider casting about for another sound, waiting for Steve to reveal his position. After a brief silence the sounds behind him began again. Steve released his held breath as quietly as possible and made his way to another tree.

A small game trail wound past the other side of the tree, disappearing into the thick forest ahead and behind. Steve debated following it. The rider might assume that Steve had taken it and pursue him. However, Steve could move much more quickly and quietly on the trail.

He stepped onto the packed dirt of the narrow trail. Which way should he go? Left seemed a better direction, although he wasn't certain why. He began a silent, slow-paced trot down the trail.

The trail gradually widened as he followed it until there was almost enough space for two people to walk side by side. Or one horse. Again, Steve questioned the wisdom of following this trail.

He had almost decided to leave the trail for the greater cover of the forest when he saw the shack. Ahead, in a small clearing, stood an old, dilapidated house. In the moonlight the house looked as white as it had probably once truly been. An old, decaying barn in even worse repair stood behind the house.

Should he try to hide here? Or, perhaps he should hide in the barn? No, there was something about the house that suggested safety. Besides, it was probably safer than the crumbling barn.

He ran quickly across the small clearing to the wooden front porch. Cautiously, he climbed the rotting steps. The front door stood wide, inviting him to enter. He stepped into the house. The room seemed empty, filled only with decaying furniture. With one last look out at the clearing to insure that he had not been seen, he closed the door.

The old-style deadbolt lock still worked, thank God. He breathed a sigh of relief and turned to survey the room again. A fireplace sat on the back wall, by an open doorway. Something long and slender leaned against the wall by the fireplace. It almost looked like a rifle.

He walked over and picked up the object. It was a shotgun— twelve-gauge pump like the one his father owned. Steve ran his hand along the blue, steel barrel. It felt slightly oily.

A quick glance in the breach showed that it was loaded. What was it doing here? Perhaps it was here because he wanted it to be. He glanced at the stock, near the butt. In the moonlight he saw his father's initials etched into the wood. The hair at the nape of his neck prickled. *Just a dream. . . .*

Steve glanced over to the black doorway. Perhaps he should check to see if there was a back door and if it was locked, too. He slowly approached the doorway.

The blackness of it was absolute. No stray beam of moonlight penetrated into it. It seemed colder near the door, too, but it was not really a physical coldness. If a door were back there, open, he would see it from here.

He found he could not turn away from the door. Some yearning, some . . . fascination seemed to hold him there. Some . . . *thing* wanted him to enter its lair.

Frightened, he took a step back, leveling the shotgun toward the door. After a few more steps he found he could finally turn away.

"Just a dream," he whispered. If the clearing were empty, though, he would leave. The house no longer seemed the haven it had before. He turned toward the front door.

Green, catlike eyes watched him from the darkness in the corner of the room. Steve gasped, aiming the shotgun at the eyes.

She rose from the rotting chair she had been sitting in. As before, he could see nothing of her but her eyes.

"I . . . I'll shoot," he stammered.

"What is the power of the Dreamer?" she asked, stepping forward lithely. Her voice lured him toward her even as he tried to step away.

He pulled the trigger. The shotgun roared and kicked against his shoulder, forcing him back a step. Her hair blew, as if in a gust of wind, and the window behind her exploded outward in a shower of shot and glass.

The front door crashed open. Framed in the silvery portal was the rider, now afoot, his empty gaze aimed at Steve. They both advanced toward him.

Again he pulled the trigger. The blast drove the rider backwards, out the door.

"Which way shall his Sword strike?" the woman asked, taking another step forward. Her outstretched hand caressed his bicep.

With a cry of horror he turned and leapt through the doorway that had terrified him so earlier. Darkness and cold engulfed him as he realized there was no floor beneath him. He screamed as he began the long fall into the bottomless abyss.

Doctor Engelman glanced sharply at the EEG. All four lines on the paper record had just gone to zero magnitude. His eyes widened in surprise.

The second EEG showed the same impossible data. Subject number one showed no brain activity whatsoever. Heartbeat and respiration were still present, albeit reduced; REM had stopped. Brain activity *should* be present if the heart and lungs were still working.

Two EEGs weren't likely to simultaneously fail in this manner, however. For some reason, subject one had become comatose.

"Mary!" he said.

"Yes, Doctor?"

"Call an ambulance!" he shouted as he ran into the sleep room.

Chapter
-------- Two -------------

THE BAND OF riders crested the hill. Lord Erelvar raised his hand, signaling a brief halt as he turned his ebon mount to survey the land behind them.

The barren terrain offered almost no concealment. Through the shimmering heat-haze he saw the cloud of dust that marked their pursuers. It was, at most, two miles behind them.

"The horses are beginning to tire, my lord," Morfael said. "We cannot hope to maintain our lead."

"And, if we abandon them this far to the north we shall never survive the journey home," Erelvar finished. He sat for a moment studying the dirty cloud that hid their enemy.

"Magus Artemas," he said, turning to the only unarmored man in the party, "can your magics not carry us to safety?"

"Of course, your grace," Artemas replied, smiling sardonically. "I shall require a quiet location in which to work and, for a ritual of such magnitude, approximately two hours of preparation. Unless you wish to take the horses as well, in which case it shall take much longer."

"We do not have that much time. The *galdir* shall be upon us long before then."

Artemas nodded. "I know. Had your grace allowed me the time to prepare a few scrolls before dragging me days outside of civilization, we could take our dinner this evening in Quarin. Unfortunately, time was all-important and we had to leave immediately with no time to spare for 'unnecessary' delays."

A short, stunned silence followed. Morfael's hand moved instinctively to the hilt of his sword. It was stayed by Erelvar's.

"Lord Erelvar," Theron said into the uncomfortable silence, "allow me to apologize for my cousin's . . ."

Erelvar raised his hand, silencing him as well. "No apology is

13

necessary, Prince Theron. Magus Artemas has simply reminded me, as well he should, that the blame for our current predicament is mine alone. Perhaps a charm to hide us?"

Sadly, Artemas shook his head. "No, your grace. I have magics that would hide us, but not our scent, and a *galda*'s nose is keener than any hound's."

Erelvar looked again at the cloud that hid the pursuit. It had not moved noticeably. Erelvar knew, however, that it was indeed moving. Only the horses had enabled them to gain the lead they now enjoyed, but this rugged terrain was not easy on them, as Morfael had noted. The swift-moving *galdir* were certain to overtake them before sunset.

"I suppose, then, there is nothing to do but press on and pray for the best," he said.

"Perhaps not, your grace," Theron said.

"Oh?"

"Artemas cannot take us to safety, but perhaps he can send word ahead of us. Then we could be assured that our news had been received."

"Even if we are lost," Erelvar agreed. "Can you send such a message, Magus?"

"*Certe*. If you pen a message, I can cast it on the winds to your very castle."

"Good. How much time would you require?"

"The ritual will take approximately the second part of an hour to prepare. The message should arrive in Quarin near sunset."

Erelvar looked back to their pursuit. The cloud of dust had moved noticeably now.

"That much we can spare," he decided, "if we can find a defensible site."

"Perhaps the ruins of yon tower," Morfael suggested, pointing toward the west.

Erelvar looked in the direction indicated by his liege-man. A thin spire rose from atop a hill a few miles distant. Erelvar had assumed it to be a natural formation, but it was, as Morfael had said, the ruins of a tower.

"That should serve our needs," Erelvar decided. "Assuming it is not now the den of yet another band of *galdir*." He spurred his mount and rode down the side of the hill at a gallop.

The tower was, in fact, abandoned. The stone walls were smooth and glassy, as if they had been partially melted at one time. Erelvar felt a chill pass over him.

This tower was *old* and, had the stones of its walls not been fused together by Daryna's wrath, should have long since fallen. As it was, the ruins seemed to be in fairly good condition. The battlements were intact with only a narrow ledge to stand on, the roof having collapsed as a result of that ancient holocaust.

"Morfael, take watch from the battlements," Erelvar ordered. "Aldric, Delarian, chase the horses away."

"Why?" Aldric asked. "Perhaps they will kill a few goblins before they die."

"Take the saddlebags, but leave the tack and harness," Erelvar added. "The rest of you begin piling rubble in front of the doorway."

"You think we have a chance of survival, then?" Theron said once Aldric and Delarian were out of earshot.

"A small one," Erelvar replied. "If we do, we shall have need of the horses."

"Of course."

"My apologies, Prince Theron."

"Apologies? For what?"

"I had not intended to bring you and Magus Artemas here to die."

"Nonsense. Artemas knew the risks, as did I. It was fate that failed us, Erelvar."

Erelvar turned away without reply. Theron smiled ruefully at his back as Erelvar watched Aldric and Delarian chase the horses away. He had not yet fathomed much of this strange man, but he had learned one thing—like any good commander, Lord Erelvar drove himself twice as hard as the men under him.

"I had best start on the message that Artemas is to send," Erelvar finally said, turning from the empty doorway.

Erelvar folded the parchment in thirds and sealed it with a droplet of wax from a small candle. His ring, pressed into the cooling wax, completed the letter's seal.

As he rose he saw that Artemas had completed his initial preparations for the ritual. A clear space on the ancient stone floor was marked with strange patterns and symbols. The magus himself stood by the ruined doorway watching the *regir* erect a rubble barricade across it.

"To whom shall it be sent?" he asked when Erelvar handed him the parchment.

"Glorien," Erelvar replied.

"Of course."

Erelvar turned to the battlements. "Morfael! How far are the *galdir*?"

"No further than twenty minutes, my lord. Perhaps less."

"You must begin the ritual immediately, Magus."

Artemas nodded and stepped to the center of his chalk markings. Erelvar watched for a moment as the mage began the spell that would send his words through the air back to Quarin. After a moment he glanced away, to the crude barricade his men were building.

He estimated that it would rise to about mid-thigh once complete. That would be about waist-high for the *galdir*, which was adequate. Still, the tower could not be held indefinitely. Barring a miracle, they would all die here today. Thank Mortos he had forbade Glorien from coming. . . .

"Enough," he finally said to the *regir*. "A few more stones will make no difference. Hie to the battlements and fire each arrow as though it were your last. Morfael! Join me!"

Erelvar glanced toward Artemas. The smoke from several candles whirled about him in a miniature cyclone as he chanted and gestured. To all appearances, the sorceror had not even noticed the sudden commotion.

"And I?" Theron asked.

"Stay here," Erelvar replied. "If either Morfael or myself should fall, you shall be needed to aid in holding the doorway."

Theron nodded solemnly. "As you command," he said.

Erelvar glanced at him curiously before taking his self-appointed post in the tower's door. Theron smiled behind him.

Does it surprise you to hear a Nymran priest speak as a soldier, Lord Erelvar? he thought. *Or did you simply not expect such deference from the Regent's cousin?* In either case it was of no importance. Gaining Erelvar's confidence, and alliance, would soon no longer be Theron's concern. For now, he was merely a soldier, not an emissary.

The *thrum* of bowstrings began above him. His hand strayed to the hilt of the short sword at his belt. It had been several years since he had last served in the legions, but the old skills were still there, waiting faithfully against the day he should again have need of them—against today.

Mere heartbeats since the first arrow-shot, a sea of goblins surged about the tower. The crude barricade before the doorway proved its value as Erelvar and Morfael began the bloody work of buying time for Artemas. The two warriors could not hold that doorway indefinitely, however.

The distinctive sound of metal against stone reached Theron's ears. The goblins that could not gain the doorway were taking their weapons to the tower itself! Given time, the stupid creatures might actually succeed in leveling the structure. The defenders would, most likely, have fallen long before that.

Theron's lips moved silently in prayer as he watched Erelvar and Morfael hew through the bodies of the goblins before them. No sooner was one slain, however, before another would take its place. There seemed no end to them.

A cry from the battlements drew his attention from the doorway. One of Erelvar's men fell into the tower, a quarrel embedded in his shoulder. Theron stepped over to the fallen warrior. The wound was not fatal, but the fall had been.

He was one of the Umbrians, Theron noted—an Aldwyn. He signed a benediction over the body. How much longer would it be before they all fell to the goblins?

A rush of air passed behind Theron, and his ears popped painfully. He turned to see Artemas surveying the situation, apparently finished with his rituals.

"Were you successful?" Theron asked.

"Yes, the message is away," Artemas replied. He closed his eyes briefly, concentrating.

"It seems that Lord Erelvar may have been correct," Artemas announced.

"Concerning what?"

"We have slain roughly two score of the beasts thus far. Let us see if singeing their filthy hides will hasten them away."

Artemas began chanting again, his hands weaving through intricate gestures and dipping into the large pouch at his side. Theron again took his place between his cousin and the doorway. Perhaps they might survive this after all.

Erelvar was not yet showing any signs of fatigue, as though he could, indeed, hold that doorway against the goblins forever. Morfael, however, was another matter. The younger warrior's reactions were already slowing. It might be best if Theron could relieve him before he was wounded.

A stone fell in from the wall before he could do so. The goblins had actually broken through! Apparently, the tower was in worse condition than it appeared. A hideous goblin face filled the opening and Theron thrust the blade of his sword into it.

With a scream the creature fell back, slain or wounded Theron could not see. Immediately, a spear was thrust into the hole by another. He kicked the shaft, snapping it, before turning to seize his own spear. As densely packed as the goblins must be, any thrust through the breach would be certain to strike something.

Before he could return, a quarrel flew through the breach, striking Artemas in the chest. The magus's eyes widened in pained surprise and, with his last conscious act, he flung his hands, palms outward, toward the opening. The ball of fire that had been growing between his hands erupted into a cone of flame.

Theron flung his shield between himself and the tower wall. Even behind its protection the heat was almost unbearable. The fire quickly expended itself and Artemas collapsed to the stone floor. Where the breach had been was now a cooling section of half-molten rock.

Theron dropped his shield, now too hot to bear, and rushed to his cousin's side. A rhythmic sucking sound issued from the wound. The quarrel had pierced a lung. Fortunately, the wound was high enough that he need not worry about injuries to the liver or other organs. Artemas would live—if Theron acted quickly.

Carefully, he cut the head from the protruding bolt and gently withdrew the shaft. The sucking sound grew louder. Removing his gauntlets, he placed his hands over the wound and began chanting.

Theron felt the Power flow into him where it was directed, through his hands, into the wound in Artemas's chest. As the Power flowed into Artemas, so too did Theron's senses. He could "see" the damage done by the arrow as it had pierced Artemas's body.

Not only had the lung been punctured, but the great artery feeding it had been nicked, as well. Theron willed it to heal and the tissues reknitted, sealing the injury.

He healed each such injury, working from the innermost outward. Finally, Theron mended the breaks in the chest wall itself and released his hold on the Power. He sat back, eyes closed, trembling from the exertion.

A hand laid on his shoulder, and he opened his eyes to see Morfael kneeling beside him.

"Will he be well?" the young Olvan asked.

"Yes," Theron replied. The goblins had apparently retreated for the moment. In his effort to heal Artemas, Theron had not noticed the sudden quiet that had heralded their departure.

"Are they gone?" he asked.

"Only below the next range of hills," Erelvar said. "They await reinforcements or the night. Which, I am not certain."

"I saw a small band travelling on to the north," Delarian said. "They may have been messengers."

"Then they can possibly expect reinforcements by sometime tomorrow," Erelvar said. He walked over to the body of the fallen warrior.

"Llwyd ap Aldwyn," Erelvar said softly to the corpse, "your clan chief is not going to be pleased with me." For a moment he simply stared at the lifeless warrior.

"Are there any other casualties?" he finally asked.

"None, my lord," replied Morfael.

"And the message?"

"It is safely on its way," Theron said.

Erelvar nodded in approval. They had survived—for the moment.

The sun sank toward the horizon as the afternoon wore on. The defenders sat within and atop the tower, waiting. Occasionally, one of the *galdir* would be sighted risking a glance over a hilltop, but Erelvar forbade firing at such unpromising targets. The arrows were too precious to waste frivolously.

"It will be dark soon," Theron observed.

"Yes," Erelvar replied. "Hopefully they will attack as the sun sets."

"Hopefully?"

Erelvar nodded. "If we slay enough of them, we may be able to break free of here before their reinforcements arrive."

"And what of Artemas?"

"Once *galdir* run, they run far," Erelvar replied, smiling. "We should be able to escape with Artemas."

"Reinforcements!" Delarian shouted from atop the tower. Erelvar turned and ran up the ancient stairs to the narrow battlements. About a mile distant another group of *galdir* could be seen approaching the tower.

"I would say that band is more than a hundred strong," Theron estimated.

"At least," Erelvar replied grimly.

Glorien stood atop the battlements, looking out over the Plains of Blood as the sun settled in the west. Her hand rested idly on the hilt of the longsword at her belt. The dying rays of the sun made the polished Delvan steel of her armor shine blood red.

She could feel the eyes of the guards on her as she looked out over the battlements. Would they *never* accept her? How many times must she prove herself before they would grant that she had the right to the armor she wore and the sword at her side?

Probably never, she thought. *No doubt they would all rather see me on my back in something* much *less protective than armor.* Her beauty did nothing to help dispell such thoughts. Helmetless, her golden hair spilled down the back of her armor, and her eyes, gray with just a touch of blue, had caused more than one man's breath to catch when he had met her gaze.

Even the armor itself did not hide her beauty as she had once hoped it would. The Delvir had been too painstakingly careful to capture the curve of her bosom and the flare of her hip for that to work. If anything it *heightened* her womanhood—throwing it into sharp relief against the armor's true function.

So, as always, there was nothing to do but ignore the eyes she could feel on her back. She sighed as she continued to scan the Plains, searching for the source of the strange unease that had possessed her. She feared, however, that it was no threat to Quarin that unnerved her. That was a distraction she would almost welcome. She feared the threat was against something far more dear to her.

Over a sennight ago Erelvar had departed for Delgroth. The mere thought of that fortress of evil was enough to cause her to shudder. Scouts had brought back word of increased *galdan* raids on Olvanor and Umbria. Erelvar had decided the matter required further investigation and, as was his way, would not assign the task to another.

She had been fearful, even then, and had persuaded him to take ten of the *regir* with him. He had agreed to that, but had insisted that she remain behind at the castle. She had, reluctantly, bowed to his will. Now she doubted the wisdom of her calm acquiescence.

At least he had taken Theron and Artemas with him, at their request. Of course, it was hard to deny the value of a sorceror or a combat-trained healer on such a mission. Another warrior would not have been as helpful.

A faint breeze stirred her hair, and Glorien could almost swear that with it came the stench of the Poisoned Bog. The breeze, unlike the other fitful winds that stirred during this season, did not abate. As it grew she realized that the stench had not been her imagining, after all.

What meant this ill wind? Unconsciously, her hand gripped the hilt of her sword more tightly. Along the wall she could see the guards become more alert. They, too, found the unnatural wind disturbing.

Something appeared in the air before her. It was a folded piece of parchment, borne upon the wind. A guard near her reached out to grasp it, but the wind carried it out of his reach, almost as if it were eluding him. The wind carried it back to her, and Glorien reached for it.

No sooner had she grasped the parchment than the wind that brought it began to die. She glanced down and saw that it was actually a letter, sealed with wax. At the sight of the seal the blood froze in her veins—it was Erelvar's.

"What is it, my lady?" the guard asked.

"A message from my lord," she said. "The magus must have sent it." Clutching the note, she hurried to her chambers.

Theron watched as the shadows marched up the side of the hill toward the tower. Soon night would fall and the goblins would renew the attack with their increased numbers.

He heard his name called, weakly, from behind him. Turning, he saw that Artemas was sitting up, supporting himself on his elbows.

"You should not be trying to sit," Theron said. "You have bled much."

"Get me some water," Artemas said. Theron did so and watched as Artemas took a long draught from one of the waterskins.

"Now lie back," Theron said.

"No time for that. Give me my saddlebags."

Theron sighed and helped his cousin sit against one of the tower walls. He watched as Artemas rummaged through the saddlebag and finally removed an ivory tube. The magus carefully withdrew a roll of parchment from the tube.

"I thought you had not prepared any scrolls for this trip," Theron noted.

"I always have one scroll, cousin. Now leave me to concentrate on this." Artemas perused the scroll for a moment and then began a chant in the rhythmic tones Theron had learned to associate with sorcery.

To Theron's untrained ear the chant sounded smooth and unbroken—Artemas knew better. Twice he faltered over brief passages in the lyrical language of the scroll. Nothing untoward seemed to happen, though, and he continued on.

Finally, it was finished and a black rectangle, roughly three feet wide and seven tall, appeared near the back of the tower. The magus collapsed back against the tower wall, exhausted.

"Is it a way out?" Theron asked, cautiously approaching the portal. A numbing cold radiated from it.

"Hardly," Artemas replied. His voice was broken, shaky. Theron glanced at him sharply.

"I can think of many more . . . pleasant ways to die than by stepping through that portal. Including being cut to pieces by goblins."

"Then what is it?"

"If we are fortunate, something benign and powerful will come through to aid us."

"And if we are not?"

"Any number of things, including . . . nothing, could . . ." The last words were lost as Artemas returned to unconsciousness.

Theron knelt by his cousin and gently laid his fingers on the sorceror's throat. The pulse was faint, but steady. Theron gently laid Artemas into a more comfortable position.

"And if something inimical uses this portal?" Erelvar asked behind him.

"Artemas would have considered that," Theron replied, rising. "I trust his judgement."

"They come," Morfael announced behind them. Anxiety and eagerness mingled in the young Olvan's voice.

"Then they shall die," Erelvar replied, joining Morfael in the doorway. This time, however, the goblins in the back ranks began the attack with a crossbow volley. In unison, Erelvar and Morfael raised their shields. The missiles rebounded harmlessly from the Delvan steel.

Before another volley could be readied, the goblins gained the tower. Theron noted, with bitter humor, that this time the monsters did not take their weapons to the tower itself.

In the doorway Erelvar and Morfael fought like unchained demons. With each stroke of the longswords, a goblin died. Even so, it was simply a matter of time before everyone in the tower fell before the overwhelming numbers. Theron glanced up toward the battlements. None of Erelvar's *regir* had yet fallen.

A sudden cry, as of terror, came from behind him. Fearing for his cousin, Theron turned to rush to Artemas's side just as a man fell into the tower through the ebon portal. The magical doorway vanished as Theron swiftly drew his sword.

"Friend or foe?" he demanded of the intruder. The stranger was dressed in odd, blue trousers and carried what seemed to be a crossbow stock with a length of hollow metal rod attached. He sat back, away from the weapon, if such it was, and spread his hands wide, speaking timidly in a tongue Theron did not recognize. He seemed no threat.

Another cry sounded behind him and he turned toward the door. Morfael had been wounded by one of the goblins. Theron went to help Morfael away from the door as Aldric stepped in to take his place. Theron glanced up at the battlements. The other *regir* were coming down as well, their arrows spent. Theron smiled bitterly. Their chances of escape had just dwindled considerably.

Steve felt that he had been falling forever as the dark void attempted to draw all the warmth from within his body. Without warning, the darkness came to an end and he was thrown forward onto a stone floor.

Before he could orient himself someone shouted at him. Steve looked up and blinked in surprise. Standing over him was a man dressed in Romanesque armor.

He briefly considered using the shotgun, but the guy was too close. Besides, he might actually be friendly. Steve slowly sat back and held out his hands, palms outward.

"Uh, I come in peace?" he said. Despite their lack of novelty, his words seemed to have some calming effect. Steve was about to try saying something else when another shout took the Roman's attention. With a single, sharp glance back at Steve, he turned and headed toward a doorway.

Steve could see two men standing in the doorway. One in black armor was holding the doorway against some unseen enemy. The other, in silver armor, was clutching his side as the Roman helped him away from the battle. Another man, in a bronze breastplate, joined the Black Knight in the doorway.

I'm still dreaming, he thought. At least the ghost rider and his spooky girlfriend were nowhere to be seen. This he could handle—sort of.

He was apparently in a ruined tower. Several other people were gathering on the tower floor from above. Half seemed to be wearing bronze breastplates over leather. The other half, taller and more slender than the others, were wearing what seemed to be mail.

Lying on the floor near Steve was a dark-haired, bearded man. Steve was wondering if the guy was dead when he noticed a *completely* blanketed form lying nearby. *That* one was dead.

Steve looked back toward the tower door where the defenders fought. He could only catch brief glimpses of who they were defending against. Reclaiming his shotgun, he stood up, trying to peer past the men in the doorway.

A shout drew Steve's attention back to the group. One of the men in mail fell to the floor, an arrow protruding from his chest. Steve looked up to the battlements. He blinked, not certain if he should believe his senses.

The thing was humanoid in form, but resembled an ape more than a man. The face was framed in short, bristly hair and had a leathery appearance. There was no true nose—rather, the thing had a long, leathery snout, like a baboon's. Also like a baboon's, that snout was filled with long, vicious-looking fangs. If Steve had seen it at the zoo, he wouldn't have looked twice.

At the zoo, however, it wouldn't have been wearing leather or carrying a crossbow. It obviously knew how to use the crossbow, too, for it was clumsily fitting another bolt into it.

One of the men in mail was bounding up the stairs even as Steve raised the shotgun to his shoulder. Its roar was deafening in the small confines of the tower. The ape-man was slammed against the battlements and into another who had been climbing over. Both tumbled over the battlements to fall outside.

Steve ran up the stairs past the stunned warrior. If these ape-men were climbing in, then his shotgun made him the most qualified to keep them out.

Sure enough, the baboons were climbing up all sides of the tower, using no equipment other than their natural ability. Steve thrust the barrel through an opening near the bottom of the battlements and pulled the trigger. The entire section of wall below him was swept clean of the ape-men.

He moved over and cleared away another section of wall. The noise and muzzle-flash seemed to be having more effect than the actual shot. He fired three more times, clearing the invaders from the tower.

By then the monkeys seemed to have lost their desire to fight. They began scattering in all directions, radially out from the tower. Steve sent three more barrelfulls of shot after them to hurry them on their way before he ran out of shells.

He set the shotgun down and leaned against the battlements, trembling as reaction to the encounter set in.

"I swear to God," he muttered, "I am never going to watch *Planet of the Apes* again."

He turned to go back down where the others were and stared at the narrow, treacherous-looking steps. Had he actually *run* up those? With a shudder he slowly began descending toward the tower floor.

Theron watched as the stranger gingerly made his way down the tower stairs. Artemas had been right to summon the portal; something benign and powerful *had* come to their rescue. But where had this person come from? His features were almost Nymran but his build, tall and slight of frame, seemed more Olvan.

"Did he say anything intelligible?" Theron asked Delarian. The Olvan warrior had been the only person on the battlements with the stranger.

"No," Delarian replied, "not in any tongue I could recognize. That weapon, though! Never have I seen its like!"

"Sorcery. But unlike any I have ever seen."

"We must take this opportunity to escape," Erelvar interrupted. Theron nodded solemnly. They could all use a night's rest, but they dared not rest here.

"We must fashion a litter for Artemas," Theron said.

"We can use your shield," Erelvar replied. "What of our benefactor?"

"I suppose we shall have to take him with us. He seems a normal man."

"True. That ... weapon of his could be of use should we encounter another band of *galdir*."

"I think its magic is spent," Delarian said.

"Why do you say that?"

"He tried to ... use it at the end and it did nothing."

"Thank Mortos the *galdir* did not realize that."

"They were intent on fleeing at the time," Delarian said, smiling.

"Hm," Erelvar said, turning as the stranger reached the bottom of the stairs and approached them. The newcomer looked at Delarian curiously.

"I do not believe he has ever seen Olvir before," Theron noted, chuckling.

"Truly?" Delarian said. "From his height I would have guessed there to be Olvan blood in his lineage."

"That is a good point," Erelvar said. "Do you think Llwyd's armor will fit him?"

"I am not certain . . ." Theron began but was swiftly interrupted.

"Lord Erelvar!" Aldric said, shocked. "Would you defile Llwyd's corpse by stealing his armor for this stranger?"

"It will be returned, Aldric ap Botewylf," Erelvar replied. "Or do you mean to call me a thief?"

"N-no, my lord. But surely no good can come from wearing a dead man's armor."

"And do you, then," said Theron, "think to tell the Champion of Mortos how best to deal with death?"

Aldric glared at Theron. "I suppose not," he finally said. "By your leave, lord," he said to Erelvar before joining the other *regir* in salvaging arrows from the bodies of the fallen goblins.

"I believe Llwyd's armor will serve," Theron said once Aldric had left. "The Aldwyns are taller than most Umbrians."

"Good. Morfael, assist our . . . friend into Llwyd's armor."

"At once, my lord," Morfael replied, taking the stranger gently by the arm and leading him away.

After a short time Morfael led the stranger, now dressed in Llwyd's armor and leathers, back to them. Theron noted that the young man walked as if unaccustomed to the weight and restrictions of the armor.

"Let us begone," Erelvar ordered, "lest the *galdir* find their courage and return."

They marched off, four *regir* carrying Artemas, four carrying Llwyd ap Aldwyn's body. Theron smiled wryly. A legion would have buried, or burned, their dead here and marched on—especially when in desperate straits such as these. If an army encumbered itself with corpses on a march it would soon not be marching at all.

Theron also noted that the stranger was not carrying his odd weapon. Apparently, Delarian had been correct in assuming it expended. At least *this* person was pragmatic enough not to haul useless baggage with him on a march. Theron turned and joined the others in the long trip south, toward the Poisoned Bog.

To Steve the few hours they had walked seemed like days. The heavy armor made the unusual exertion even less tolerable. Still, if one of those ape-men popped up to take a shot at him, he'd rather have sore feet than die.

At one point Caesar, as Steve had nicknamed the Romanesque warrior, had tried to speak with him, apparently trying several different languages. None of the words had made sense to Steve.

Whoever these people were, they seemed human enough. Half of them were fairly short, about five and a half feet or so. The others, as well as the two in full armor, were taller even than Steve's five-foot-ten.

Caesar and Sleepy, the unconscious man Steve had noticed back in the tower, were both dark-complexioned and clean-shaven with close-cropped black hair. The short warriors, actually taller than the Romans, were fairer than them and wore beards. Their hair tended toward light brown and red.

However, the tall warriors were lighter still, to the point of pallor, and looked as though they'd never had to shave a day in their lives. If it weren't for their height Steve would have guessed them to be about sixteen or younger. That fairness and their almost silken hair, which ranged in color from light red through blond, gave them an almost unearthly appearance. The one who had helped Steve with his armor actually had *silver* hair.

The group's commander did not seem to match any of the three racial groups Steve had noted. The Black Knight, as Steve had nicknamed him, was as tall as the tallest of the fair warriors. Where they were slight of frame, however, he was as stocky as the shorter warriors and he was as dark-complexioned as the two Romans.

That he was in command, there was no doubt. When he spoke, people listened—and obeyed. Even the White Knight, who seemed to belong to the same race as the tall warriors, deferred to him without question.

Well, whoever was in command, at least they weren't going to abandon him to freeze to death. From what he could see of the terrain in the light of the half-moon, however, freezing would be the least of his worries once the sun rose.

The hills they travelled through were as barren as the back side of the moon. Not so much as a tumbleweed could be seen. There was water here, though. Steve had glimpsed a river from the crest of a hill, its waters inky black in the moonlight. Nothing grew along its banks, which he thought odd.

Steve glanced up at the stars. He recognized none of the constellations. That, in itself, was not too surprising; he'd never really known that much about the stars, anyway. Still, he ought to be able to find the Big Dipper. . . . The unexpected sound of hoofbeats drew his attention from the sky.

One of the tall warriors was returning on horseback. Behind him followed what seemed to be a whole herd of horses, already saddled and ready to ride. That was a little too convenient to believe, even in a dream.

The thought of not having to walk any further was a relief, though. It wasn't until Caesar handed him a pair of reins that it occurred to Steve that he had never ridden a horse in his life.

Mounting wasn't too difficult, even with the bulky armor. He clumsily felt around with the toe of his right foot until he found the stirrup. Now what? Steve cautiously took the reins, one in each hand. That couldn't be right—how were you supposed to use a sword if it took both hands to steer the thing? The horse shifted underneath him impatiently.

Caesar rode up beside Steve, taking the reins from him. Holding them with one hand he pulled them to the left as a unit. The horse obediently began to turn and Caesar pulled the reins back to the right. The horse turned back.

Steve took the reins back and nodded his thanks. He pulled the reins to the right and the horse performed as expected. Caesar nodded, smiling, and spurred his horse back to the others. Steve's mount immediately began following.

Surprised, he jerked back on the reins—the horse stopped. When he didn't release the tension it began to back up. Not knowing what else to do, he dropped the reins. The animal turned an accusing eye toward him.

"Sorry, boy," he said. "This is going to take a little getting used to for both of us, I think." He gathered up the reins and kicked the horse gently in the ribs. It started forward at a slow walk and fell in behind the other horses.

After they had ridden for almost two hours, the barren hills began to flatten out into an equally barren plain. In the moonlight, he could see the river to their left. It had begun splitting into smaller branches upon reaching the plain. The party bore slightly to the right and continued riding.

A stray breeze from the direction of the river made him gag. It smelled as if ten different chemical plants had been dumping raw waste into it. No wonder nothing lived along the river; the fumes from it had actually brought tears to Steve's eyes.

The others didn't seem to enjoy it very much either. The party turned further to the right to avoid the river. After riding another half-hour they stopped. Steve was so tired that he almost fell from the horse as he dismounted.

Someone threw a bedroll down in front of him and he clumsily began to unroll it. He removed the heavy armor and slipped between the blankets. The soft, sandy ground felt like the most comfortable bed he had ever slept on.

Funny, he thought as he drifted off to sleep, *I've never been tired in a dream before.*

Chapter
-------- Three -------------

THE MISTS PARTED before Belevairn, forming a window back to reality. He urged his demon-steed forward, emerging above the ruined tower. The carrion birds fled his presence as his mount set its cloven hooves firmly in the air. All was as the *galdir* had described—once one allowed for exaggeration.

From his lofty perch he slowly surveyed the carnage, the gold-inlaid demon-mask hiding any reaction. Nearly six score *galdir* lay scattered about the tower. Many of those on the eastward side were charred and blackened. He pressed his heels into the flanks of his mount, leaning forward. The beast began walking downward.

He could detect the lingering traces of magic in the area. He dismounted and walked into the tower itself; it was empty. Only some dried blood on the floor revealed that anyone had taken refuge here—that and the lingering Power that still suffused the ruin.

Belevairn began to speak in a harsh, guttural tongue, gesturing slowly in rhythm with the words. An unnatural stillness fell over the area as he worked his magic. What few creatures that had dared remain now fled.

As the ritual was completed, images formed about the tower. Mounted warriors rode up, their horses lathered from hard riding. A figure in black, Morvan plate dismounted and entered the tower—his shield bore the symbol of Mortos, Lord of the Dead.

Belevairn hissed angrily. The traitor himself had been here, and the *galdir* had allowed him to escape from under Daryna's very nose. Others entered until a total of fifteen men occupied the tower. Fifteen against more than two hundred *galdir*! None should have survived this battle.

The shades silently reenacted the confrontation as Belevairn watched. Belevairn started in surprise as the image of an ebon portal blinked into existence. This could explain much.

Within moments the figure of a man fell through the gateway to sprawl on the tower floor. With a gesture, Belevairn froze the image to study the newcomer. The stranger was clad in unusual garments; at his knees lay a strange device. Its grip was similar to that of a crossbow, but a length of hollow metal rod replaced the bow.

Belevairn gestured again, satisfied with his examination of the stranger. The tableau proceeded anew. Belevairn watched as the stranger joined the battle, clearing the battlements with the power of his sorcerous weapon.

This did not bode well for the coming war. A sorceror of such power could well alter the outcome of the planned invasion. Steps must be taken to counter this unexpected threat.

The shadows of the invaders were preparing to flee as the stranger gingerly made his way down the steep tower stairs. Belevairn noticed, with some surprise, that he no longer carried the fire-staff. Had it been left above?

Belevairn hastened up the stairs as the shades continued their ghostly reenactment, negligently passing through the image of the alien wizard. Above he found the fire-staff leaning against a merlon. He carefully reached out to touch it.

Yes, it was still there. He lifted the staff, leaving only its image behind. With a wave of his hand, the images vanished. They held nothing more of interest.

By now Erelvar and his party must be in the Bog. Daryna would decide what further action to take against them once he had given his report.

The swamp was unlike anything Steve had ever seen before. The first few miles were barren, foul mud rife with the stench of the polluted river that emptied into it. Before venturing into it, his companions had wrapped some type of oilcloth around their own feet and the hooves of the horses. Steve could understand why; God only knew what was in that mud.

After about an hour of travel, signs of life had begun to appear, although twisted and deformed. Dandelions with white, fluffy heads the size of basketballs—creepers imbued with thorns that would strangle a plant and drain it of life. Occasionally these had to be forcibly deterred from doing the same to the travellers.

How his companions were able to find solid ground beneath

this muck was beyond Steve. As it was, they had to double back twice when a path played out.

The vegetation gradually became thicker, presumably as the water lost some of its contamination. Steve's companions cast frequent, worried glances skyward. He wondered what they sought there. Flying ape-men, perhaps? *Wizard of Oz* stuff. It would fit; everything else about this dream was that bizarre.

Another hour's travel brought them to the first tree. It resembled a cypress—roots supporting the main bulk of the tree well above the standing water. Even the trees didn't want to touch the water in this place. Although Steve was certain the increased vegetation was a sign that the water was becoming less tainted, the stench seemed to increase among the trees.

Sleepy seemed to be having some trouble with the foul air. Caesar walked alongside the ailing man's horse, supporting him as much as possible. Sleepy was the only person riding. The others, including Steve, walked; the horses sank far enough into this muck already without carrying passengers.

As the canopy filled in overhead, the worried glances toward the sky diminished. Gradually, they travelled into a form of twilight as less and less light penetrated the dense foliage.

Lunch, when it was finally taken, was eaten on a small island rising out of the mud. Steve was too tired to eat. They had been walking since before dawn. He glanced at his watch after collapsing onto the relatively firm ground. It had been over seven hours since they had set out this morning.

The respite was all too brief; in less than half an hour they were on the march again. Steve could barely keep up with the others, occasionally leaning against the neck of the horse beside him for support.

He stumbled and fell to his knees with a splash of foul water. For a moment he simply knelt there, head bowed, resting. A large horse nose snuffled into his field of vision. Steve grasped the horse's neck and pulled himself erect.

"What's this?" he asked the animal. "You like me now?"

Steve caught a glimpse of motion out of the corner of his eye, back among the shadows of the trees. There was nothing there when he turned to look, however—just moss and trees.

"This place is giving me the creeps," Steve muttered to himself. A hand clasped his shoulder, making him jump. It was Caesar; he gestured up to Steve's saddle.

"Yeah, right," Steve replied. With some assistance from the

pseudo-Roman he climbed into the saddle. It would be good to ride for a little while.

The deeper they ventured into the bog, the darker it became. Thin shafts of sunlight penetrated to the foul waters, but these were generally far from the trail, as the trees grew more thickly on the more solid ground the party followed. The general solidity of their surroundings seemed to be increasing, overall.

Again, Steve thought he saw movement in his peripheral vision. This time, however, the movement was close enough for him to spot the source. An old cypress stump had just planted one of its roots into the murky water of the bog.

"That stump moved!" Steve yelled, pointing at the thing with his sword, which had somehow found its way into his hand. The "stump," its guise penetrated, charged the group of travellers. Particularly, it was charging at Steve, who was unfortunate enough to be the closest.

Shocked into immobility, Steve watched the horror rush toward him. It had eight leg-roots ending in splayed, webbed feet. Two eyestalks had emerged from the top of the "stump" while two scimitarlike mandibles had slid out from the front of the trunk.

An arrow struck the "wood" just beneath an eyestalk, snapping Steve out of the trance he had fallen into. He slashed downward with the sword, severing an eyestalk and embedding his sword in the top of the monster.

What was left of the eyestalk popped back into the "stump" as the mandibles closed on his leg. The bronze greaves gave some protection to his leg, but the mandibles cut deeply into the side of his horse.

The horse shrieked and reared, dumping Steve into the swamp. Fire flared along his right leg as his wound was soaked with the foul water.

The horse fled, leaving Steve to face the hideous creature looming over him. He thrust his sword toward the only vulnerable area he could see—the mouth.

With the strength of desperation he drove the blade almost to the hilt in the monster's mouth. Ochre fluid pumped out of the mouth as the mandibles snapped shut, piercing his upper arm just above the elbow. Both he and the monster screamed in agony before it fell still, half atop him.

Dazed with pain, Steve stared at the mandibles where they pierced his arm. Why didn't he wake up? He'd never been in such pain in his life.

Two black-gauntleted hands gripped either side of the mandibles and slowly pulled them apart. Other hands under his arms dragged him away from the dead thing. Why wasn't he waking up?

They lifted him out of the muck and laid him across the mossy roots of a cypress. Darkness gathered at the edge of his vision, spreading to envelop the world. Thank God; maybe he would wake up now.

Erelvar slowly pried the sword out of the trunk-spider's mouth. The stranger had managed to wedge it in deeply. He examined the blade; it was unharmed. Good. He wiped it off with some moss as he walked to where Theron tended the stranger's wounds.

"How is he?"

"The wounds are healed," Theron replied. Erelvar noted the ashen color of the priest's face. Theron had been fatigued before exerting the Power.

"They were not as serious as they first appeared," Theron continued.

"Good. Will he be able to ride before long?"

"I'm not certain. The wounds were not overly serious, but they were contaminated with the waters of the Bog. You know what that means."

Erelvar nodded. "Poison. Can you cleanse it?"

"Some," Theron replied. "What I could, I already have. Some of the poisons in this place resist the Power, however. The rest is up to him."

Erelvar frowned. Strong men could sometimes succumb to waters of the Bog. This stranger was anything but strong.

"What of the horse?" he asked, turning to Delarian.

"Dead, lord," Delarian replied. "It was sorely wounded."

"Damnation!" They would have need of *all* the horses once they left the Bog.

"We could abandon the corpse," Theron suggested quietly.

"No. I have no desire to explain to chief Aldwyn why I left his son's body in the Bog. Let us be off; I would be quit of this place by sunrise tomorrow."

Belevairn waited impatiently in the hallway outside Daryna's audience chamber. True, the Morvan guards feared him, but they feared their dark mistress more. The guard that had been sent with word of his presence finally returned.

"She will see you, Dread Lord," the Morvan told him.

Belevairn gave no response as he stepped forward. The guard held the massive, gilt door open for him as he entered. Once within the throne room itself, however, all pretense of superiority vanished as he abased himself on the marble steps to the throne.

"What have you learned?" a soft, husky voice asked him.

Belevairn timidly looked up at the golden throne and the shadow-shrouded woman who sat upon it. The form beneath the shadows suggested great beauty, but only Daemor and Jared had ever seen Daryna revealed—or so they claimed. Her bright, green eyes transfixed him. Belevairn lowered his gaze.

"There are indeed spies within our lands, Mistress," he replied.

"This I already know, Belevairn. Who are they?"

"They are commanded by Erelvar, great one."

The form on the throne stiffened. "Erelvar, the traitor? Here? In my domain?"

"Yes, Mistress. Worse still; in his company are Theron Baltasaros and a Nymran sorceror."

"Baltasaros? The Regent's cousin?"

"Yes, Mistress."

The form on the throne was silent a while.

"Where are they?" she finally said. Belevairn cringed from the cold fury in her voice.

"Why do their corpses not lie at my feet?" she continued.

"The *galdir* fled sorcery, Mistress."

"Do the *galdir* now fear sorcery more than me? They shall learn otherwise!"

"M-mistress," Belevairn said.

Daryna fell silent for a brief moment. Belevairn attempted to abase himself more fully on the marble steps.

"Yes, Belevairn?" she finally said, coolly.

"Mistress, the *galdir* fled the power of an alien sorceror summoned by the Nymran." Belevairn thought he heard a faint gasp from the figure above him. Surely, he was mistaken. . . .

"An alien sorceror?" she said. "Tell me, did he bear a sword?" The unexpected question confused Belevairn.

"N-no, Mistress," he replied. "The stranger bore no sword, but he did bear a staff of fire. I have . . ."

"Enough."

Belevairn instantly fell silent, pressing his forehead to the floor. He heard the light sound of her tread on the stairs as she descended to him; felt the feather-light touch of her fingers on his temples.

Her presence flowed into his mind, enveloping his consciousness. Warm fire flowed along long-dead nerves as she moved through his mind, sifting the memories of the images he had seen.

"You have done well, Belevairn," she purred, remounting the steps to the throne.

"Thank you, Mistress." He drew himself to his knees, glancing up toward her. She held the fire-staff across her lap, gently stroking it.

"This is not sorcery, Belevairn."

"Mistress?"

"However, neither is it of this world. Its origin lies in the realm of dreams. The Nymran sorceror has summoned a dreamer from his sleep."

She rose from the throne and, once again, descended the steps toward him.

"Summon the others," she said. "Command them, in my name, to search the southern border of the Bog for the invaders. Slay all but the Dreamer and bring him here, to me."

"Yes, Mistress!" Belevairn bowed his face to the floor a final time before rising to leave.

Once the great doors to the audience hall had closed behind her chief sorceror, the shadowed goddess retired to her private chambers. Silently, she strode to a marble pedestal and gently opened the leatherbound tome that lay upon it.

"Then did the Arm of Death reach into the Burning Hills and draw forth the Dreamer. And the Dreamer bore a Two-Edged Sword, for his was the power to destroy both the Arm of Death and the Palace of Evil.

"And the Seven did cry aloud saying, 'Who is the Dreamer?' and 'Which way shall his Sword strike?'

"And he that sat on the throne did say, 'None may know until the appointed day.' "

She absently closed the book, her eyes focused far beyond the confines of her chamber. The final pieces of the prophecy were falling into place. The Arm of Death had indeed reached into the Burning Hills to draw forth the Dreamer. In doing so, however, it had also reached into a trap—the jaws of which would close before this time tomorrow.

* * *

They had not covered the distance Erelvar had hoped they would by this time. Night came early under the dense foliage of the Bog; already it was growing dark.

Erelvar would almost prefer to take his chances with the Bog in the dark. Lights would give them away to the *Kaimordir*, whom he was certain were searching for them by now. Unless . . .

He handed the reins of his horse to Morfael and made his way back along the column to Theron and Artemas. He noticed that the stranger was conscious again, sitting up in the saddle instead of draped over it.

"How is he?" Erelvar asked, gesturing toward the stranger.

"Better," replied Theron. "He has recovered more quickly than I would have expected."

"And Magus Artemas?"

"I am quite well, thank you," Artemas interrupted before Theron could answer.

"Good. I need you to . . ."

"He is not that well," Theron said.

". . . provide us with some unobtrusive light. Are you capable?"

"Something approximating swamp glow?"

"Exactly."

"Yes, I should be able to manage that. I shall need to dismount for a short time."

"Of course."

Steve looked up when the column halted. Were they stopping for the night? Tired as he was, he wasn't certain he enjoyed the prospect of camping in the swamp.

He wasn't certain he could keep riding either, though. Even though his injured leg and arm weren't hurt anymore, in some ways he felt worse than when he'd passed out. His stomach and bowels cramped continuously, and he was probably running one hell of a fever since he was cold and sweating at the same time.

Next to him Caesar began helping Sleepy dismount. Surely they couldn't camp here? He could see no dry ground anywhere.

Caesar led Sleepy over to one of the trees where he climbed up onto the roots, out of the water. Caesar seemed poised to catch him. The poor guy looked like he didn't feel much better than Steve.

The Black Knight handed his sword to the invalid. Steve

watched curiously as Sleepy sprinkled some kind of powder over the blade. He held the blade out across his two hands and began chanting in a strange, not-quite-Latin.

A dim, green-tinted glow began to emanate from the sword. The glow brightened until it was almost the intensity of a chemical light-stick. Apparently Sleepy was some kind of wizard or something.

Caesar led Sleepy back to his horse after the Black Knight had retrieved his phosphorescent sword. Once Caesar had gotten the wizard back onto his horse, Steve noted that Sleepy seemed even more unsteady than he had earlier.

They began moving again, more slowly than they had before. As they travelled on, it grew darker and darker until the only light at all came from the Black Knight's sword.

No, that wasn't right. Off in the swamp Steve could see faint, glowing patches—green, yellow-green or blue. Great; on top of everything else the damn place was radioactive. Actually, it was probably just phosphorescence, but he still didn't like the looks of it.

He had almost managed to doze off on the horse when, hours later, they began to emerge from the swamp. It was a gradual thing at first; the ground became slightly more firm and the water slowly receded from their path. Eventually, the vegetation began to thin and more moonlight penetrated the gloom.

Only it wasn't moonlight—it was early, predawn sunlight. Steve must have dozed in the saddle longer than he had realized. They had been travelling for over twenty-four hours.

Eventually the bog all but vanished and they travelled across slightly soft ground latticed with many shallow streams. As the ground firmed, the rest of the party mounted. Steve saw that the Black Knight glanced toward the sky more and more often as the vegetation thinned.

The day slowly brightened, and Steve felt some of the fatigue vanish with it. Hopefully they would make camp soon. He could use some rest.

The Black Knight shouted from up ahead. Before Steve could look to see what was wrong, two columns of fire writhed down from the dawn sky. One struck the ground, narrowly missing the Black Knight. The other struck one of the tall warriors, incinerating both horse and rider in a heartbeat.

"Holy shit!" Steve yelled, now completely awake. He dug his heels into the sides of the horse. Around him the rest of the column broke into a gallop. Ahead, he saw a horse flying through the air.

It wasn't really flying, though. It was running, as if the air it travelled through were solid ground. As the hooves came down they "struck" sparks while smoke puffed from the nostrils of the beast with each breath. Steve couldn't see the rider very well—but then, he didn't have to.

He had seen this coal-black horse with the red, burning eyes before. Then, however, he'd had a car to outrun it with; now he must rely only on the speed of the horse beneath him.

All trace of fatigue had vanished with the attack. This was apparently true for his horse, as well, for it ran like the wind. Even so, he kept flogging the animal with his heels, yelling like he'd seen them do in old Westerns.

Ahead of him the sky opened briefly and another rider emerged from the rip in space. Two of them! The newly arrived rider threw a bolt of fire at the rest of the party somewhere behind Steve. Steve's heart rose to his throat when the thing then turned to pursue him.

He began to turn from this new threat but found his retreat to the left blocked by the other rider, now aground. The death's head was hidden beneath a golden mask. Only the red blaze of the eyes was visible behind it. Its "horse" snarled at Steve, revealing a set of teeth that any shark would have been proud to own. Steve's own mount whinnied in terror, rolling its white-rimmed eyes.

Steve felt a scream building in his own throat as he pulled his horse to the right. *God, let me wake up, please!* he thought. This was the worst nightmare he could ever remember having.

The rider was beside him again, this time on Steve's right. As Steve began to veer to the left, however, he found that the second rider had pulled up beside him as well.

He pulled back on the reins and the two riders shot past him. Of its own volition Steve's horse reared and wheeled about as he desperately tried to remain in the saddle. Steve needlessly kicked it hard in the ribs as the horse completed its turn and leapt into a gallop.

With effort Steve turned the horse around toward the rest of the column. His only chance was to rejoin the others.

Unfortunately, the riders behind him realized that as well. Steve's horse screamed as, unseen behind him, one of the hell-horses sank its fangs into the animal's haunch. Steve was thrown forward, out of the saddle, as his horse was literally hauled to a stop. The rapidly approaching ground was his last conscious sight.

Erelvar's horse leapt to the left, dodging the *Kaimorda*'s hellfire. He began to set himself for the monster's charge when it unexpectedly turned to the right. Who lay that way?

Erelvar looked to see the stranger separated from the others and already pursued by another of the *Kaimordir*. It made no sense. One of the Dread Lords should easily outmatch him. Especially when the stranger could apparently do no more than flee.

Still, the man had saved them all back in the Burning Hills. Erelvar spurred his mount and rushed to aid their alien benefactor. As he watched, the other *Kaimorda* rode up beside the stranger. Unexpectedly, the stranger's mount wheeled and began galloping back toward Erelvar.

Erelvar smiled—Llwyd's horse had always been the best trained. The smile changed to a frown as one of the *goremkir* bit deeply into the horse's haunch, crippling it.

The stranger was thrown from the saddle as the horse collapsed. Erelvar's horse leapt over the man's body as the two Dread Lords finally saw him.

Erelvar's sword rang against the shield of the first. The monster was poorly set to receive the charge and was thrown from its mount. Erelvar plunged his blade into the *goremka*'s flank as he passed. It fell with a blood-chilling scream.

"Well done, Moruth," said a rasping voice behind him. Erelvar's head jerked about at the unexpected name.

"But then," the Dread Lord continued, "Heregurth never was much of a swordsman."

"Daemor," Erelvar said from between clenched teeth, reining his horse about to face the *Kaimorda*.

"Ah. And I had feared the pupil had forgotten his master."

"Master no longer, Dread Lord."

"We shall see. Come, Moruth—it is time for your final lesson."

Erelvar charged, bringing his shield up to catch Daemor's thrust. Daemor's steed bent down to sink its fangs into Erelvar's horse—he was forced to lower the shield to protect his mount's flank. His own level cut was easily blocked by Daemor's raised shield.

The *goremka* continued to occupy Erelvar's shield, leaving him only the sword for defense. Daemor's sword wove a lethal dance of death against him, moving like a thing alive. All of Erelvar's skill was barely enough to deter that shining blade from drinking his blood.

Erelvar raised his shield to block Daemor's next cut, simultaneously cutting at the *goremka*'s eyes. The demon-steed shied from the consecrated metal of the blade as Erelvar nudged his horse forward, thrusting at Daemor's suddenly exposed back.

"Well done!" Daemor said, his sword intercepting Erelvar's seemingly without effort. The Dread Lord wheeled his mount to face Erelvar directly. Erelvar was again forced to defend.

From the corner of his eye, Erelvar saw Heregurth carrying the stranger's body from the field. Why did he not simply slay the stranger? For some reason the Mistress must want this man alive. Erelvar did not know why, but the mere fact that she wanted him meant that she must not have him.

Parrying another blow, Erelvar spurred his mount forward, hoping the unexpected retreat would catch Daemor unawares. It did—Erelvar's horse galloped unhindered toward Heregurth. The unmounted *Kaimorda* turned at the sound of the hooves, dropping the stranger's body.

Heregurth blocked Erelvar's wild swing but the shock of the blow sent him sprawling. A man would have been sorely injured, but the only wound Heregurth had taken was to his pride. The monster rose to face the source of his shame as Erelvar guided his horse to stand over the body of the stranger.

"Away from him, Heregurth," Daemor commanded. Erelvar smiled beneath his helmet. He had hoped that Daemor's arrogance would protect him from the second Dread Lord.

Erelvar deflected Daemor's charging thrust with his own blade, interposing his shield, once again, between his mount and the *goremka*. Daemor charged past to wheel about and come at him again.

Daemor knew that Erelvar was now trapped in his defensive position over the stranger's body. Erelvar pivoted his horse to face Daemor's next charge—a flat cut which forced him to defend with his shield.

The shield was driven solidly into him by the force of the impact. It was obvious that Erelvar could not long withstand such punishing blows. He began to turn to face Daemor's next charge when a blow to his helmet from behind sprawled him forward in the saddle.

The *goremkir* were not normal steeds and Daemor's skill with them was unparalleled. No other could have halted his charge that quickly.

Erelvar's horse continued its turn as he desperately strove to regain his balance. He somehow managed to catch another blow on his shield as he righted himself, hurling a desperate thrust at his opponent.

"Your skills have grown during your absence, Moruth," Daemor said. "They will not be enough to deny us the Dreamer, however."

The Dreamer? Erelvar blocked an overhand swing with his blade. A snap of his wrist sent his own flying in a level cut at Daemor's neck. It was easily blocked by the *Kaimorda*'s shield.

"Even now, Belevairn comes with an army," Daemor continued. "Do you not hear the hooves of their horses?"

Erelvar did indeed hear the beat of distant hooves. Very well; if they were lost, he would ensure that Daryna's prize was lost to her as well.

Suddenly heedless of his own defense, Erelvar hurled a vicious cut at Daemor. The *Kaimorda* found himself unexpectedly on the defensive as Erelvar hurled seemingly mindless attacks at him. Once he had forced Daemor's mount back a few paces, he reared his own steed. He would see how valuable this Dreamer was to the Mistress with a crushed skull.

Just as the horse was about to fall on the unconscious stranger, a horn-blast cut through the sound of battle. He knew that horn! He desperately pulled the horse to the right, narrowly missing the stranger's body.

"Not your army, Daemor," he shouted. "Mine! Do you not hear the horns, Dread Lord?" He urged his horse toward the *Kaimorda* but Daemor's steed was already ascending into the air. Heregurth was mounted behind him.

"This meeting falls to you, Lord Erelvar," Daemor said. "When next we meet, however, *that* day shall be mine." Daemor turned his mount and vanished into a rift in the sky.

Erelvar turned his gaze from the now-empty space as Glorien's cavalry arrived.

Chapter
-------- Four -------------

THE RIVER THEY had followed for the last few days split ahead
of them. Centered in the fork, a sheer bluff loomed more than fifty
feet above the grassy plain. No other hills competed with its sole
domination of the landscape.

The thirty-foot wall that capped the bluff was nearly as impres-
sive. Sitting almost flush with the sheer precipice, no gate penetrated this northern side.

However, a massive gate sat in the northwest wall of the bluff
itself, a long, narrow bridge connecting it to the land. From this
side Steve could see another narrow bridge crossing the opposite
fork of the river—a thin stone ribbon from this distance.

As they rode along the northwest side of the bluff, Steve could
see that the entire top was walled off. He let out a low whistle—
this thing had to be at least a mile long.

They finally reached the causeway—nearly a quarter-mile of
narrow, unrailed stone bridge. It was barely the width of a two-
lane country road. Steve could see yet another such causeway
about half a mile to the south. Apparently this entire bluff was
riverlocked.

The water coursed under the bridge fifteen feet below them
as they rode, double file, across it. The carved battlements of
the gatehouse towered more than thirty feet above them as they
approached. Steve noted, with fascination, that a drawbridge com-
prised the last twenty or thirty feet of the causeway.

The column rode through the open gate, the clatter of their
hooves muting briefly as they crossed the heavy, wooden drawbridge. As the last riders passed through the gatehouse, the iron
bars of the portcullis began lowering behind them. Steve glimpsed
movement through the narrow slits lining both walls of the gatehouse. Archers, no doubt.

43

Just beyond the gatehouse the tunnel ended, branching to the left and right. Steve followed the others to the right, noting the dim, unwavering lights that sparsely lined the corridor. Chemical light, perhaps?

The hoofbeats echoed loudly in the confined space. Arrow slits, dark unlike those at the gatehouse, pierced both sides of the corridor. Steve briefly wondered how many men it would take to fully man this place.

After passing another gate they came to a large octagonal chamber. Directly across from them, more than one hundred feet away, another tunnel entered the chamber. To the left sat a massive double gate. Guards paced the battlemented walls flanking the gate. The ledge they occupied was roughly twenty feet above the party, the arched ceiling another twenty feet higher.

Steve stared, open-mouthed, as his horse carried him through the cavernous chamber. Now he knew where they'd gotten the stone for the bridges and that huge, miles-long wall atop the bluff. Had all this been done by hand?

Just a dream, he reminded himself, feeling more than a bit dwarfed by his surroundings. They passed through the gate and Steve found himself in a steeply sloped tunnel. Sunlight streamed in from the other end of the tunnel, almost two hundred feet away. They emerged atop the bluff and Steve looked about, blinking in the bright sunlight.

The party stood in a broad plaza surrounded by crenelated walls. To the north, yet another gate stood ready to bar their path. The party rode toward this gate, which began to slowly open before them.

Beyond the gate was nothing save the barren, windswept top of the bluff. Large piles of loose stone competed for space with the few, stunted trees that somehow managed to subsist atop this rock. After the grandeur of the underground construction, Steve found this bleak vista disappointing.

Workers moved about the hills of rubble like scurrying ants tending to their nests. Between the mounds Steve glimpsed a smallish castle. The castle sat behind yet another wall—whoever was building this place was paranoid.

The bustling crowd at the castle gate parted to allow the company to pass through unhindered. Beyond the gate sat an entire town of tents and crude shacks, flanking the castle that rose above them.

Fortress was a better word; distance had made it seem small—

up close it was monstrous. It was surrounded by an inner wall, roughly thirty feet high. The keep itself was another ten above that, with towers rising yet another twenty feet.

They entered the castle yard. Stables and other wooden structures lined the inner wall. Young boys ran up to take the horses as the troop dismounted. Once afoot, Steve leaned against the side of his horse as the muscles of his legs threatened to knot up. His legs weren't the only problem, however; he probably wouldn't be able to sit properly for weeks.

He straightened and began to follow the others into the castle. Maybe they would give him a room with a real bed in it—maybe even a bath. Or, better yet, maybe when he woke next he wouldn't even be here. With a brief, searching glance skyward he entered the castle.

Erelvar sent the last of the pages away on their errands. The company was tired from the forced march. Baths and meals would be necessary before anything else could be accomplished.

The *regir* had already departed for their own quarters and baths. Only Theron, Artemas and Morfael remained. Erelvar glanced about quickly, finding that the stranger had discovered a nearby bench to collapse upon.

"Morfael," he said.

"Yes, lord."

"Take our guest and see that he is bathed and bedded."

"At once."

"Post a guard outside his room. I am to be informed the moment he awakes."

"That may not be until the morning," Morfael replied, smiling. Erelvar smiled back briefly.

"If that soon. Report back to me once you yourself have washed."

"Yes, lord." Morfael left, helping the stranger to his feet and away.

"Theron," Erelvar continued, "I should like to confer with you and Magus Artemas later as well, if possible."

"Of course," Theron replied.

"Good. I shall send a page when I am ready."

"We shall await your summons."

Erelvar left for his own quarters, begrudging the time that would have to be spent recovering from the journey. There was much to be done. . . .

*   *   *

The bright, morning sunlight woke Steve early. If his stupid roommate had left the window open again, Steve would kill him. Irritated, he rolled over and buried his face in the pillow. The feathers tickled his nose, however, making it even more difficult to go back to sleep.

Feathers? He did *not* have a feather pillow. He sat up, rubbing his nose.

He was lying in a canopied bed. On the stone wall opposite him stood a large fireplace. The same dream? He vaguely remembered a bath and crawling into the large bed, but he had been too tired to remember last night clearly.

No—that couldn't be right! A person didn't get tired, go to sleep and wake up all in the same goddamn dream! He leapt from the bed and ran over to the shuttered window. He was going to get to the bottom of this, by God.

Morfael stood in the hall, speaking with the guards posted outside the stranger's room. It was early yet; Erelvar had not yet summoned him and Morfael's first thought this morning had been of the stranger.

Of course, Erelvar had left their guest in Morfael's care, so . . .

An unexpected scream of anguish issued from the room. Without conscious thought, Morfael had crossed the hall and hurled the door open before either of the startled guards could react.

The stranger stood by the open window, his hands pressed firmly against either side of his head. He screamed as though the Twelve themselves stood without. Morfael bolted across the room, grabbing the stranger's wrists and pinning his arms to his sides.

The man began thrashing about, as if in a fit. Morfael threw his arms around the stranger in a bear hug and bore him to the floor. He saw nothing outside the window that should make the stranger react so. Perhaps he was sleepwalking?

"You are safe!" Morfael shouted over the man's screams. "You are safe! Awaken, my friend; you are safe!"

Gradually, the screams quieted, replaced with shuddering, gasping sobs. Morfael constantly repeated his litany, calming his tone as the fit passed. He glanced behind him—a crowd of curious faces peered in the open doorway. The two guards dutifully allowed none to pass into the room.

"Close that door," Morfael ordered. "And inform Lord Erelvar that our guest is awake."

* * *

By the time Erelvar arrived the stranger had quieted completely. He was seated in the room's only chair, slowly sipping a goblet of wine Morfael had ordered for him. Morfael himself stood by the open window, idly watching the activity of the workmen below.

He turned as the door opened and Erelvar entered with Theron and Artemas. The stranger glanced up at them and back down to his wine, muttering something incomprehensible.

"How is he?" Theron asked.

"Better," Morfael replied. "I thought the wine would help calm him."

"How much have you given him?" Artemas asked. Morfael thought his tone sounded harsh.

"Merely a goblet, and he has not finished even that."

"Good. Bring him." Before Morfael could ask the sorceror why, Artemas had left the room. He glanced to Erelvar, who merely nodded. With an inaudible sigh, he gestured for the stranger to follow him.

Morfael was not surprised when Artemas led them to the tower rooms the sorceror shared with his apprentice. The center of the circular room had been cleared, making the normal clutter of the place that much more obvious. Tables laden with glassware and huge, leatherbound books had been shoved aside to make room for two pairs of concentric circles drawn on the floor in some type of colored chalk. Inside one sat a small, high-backed chair.

"Have him sit there," Artemas ordered. Morfael coaxed the stranger onto the stool, giving Artemas's back a questioning look. The sorceror seemed even more bellicose than normal, if that were possible.

The stranger seemed suspicious of the proceedings. Morfael did not blame him—he wasn't comfortable around sorcery himself. However, this was apparently being conducted with Erelvar's approval. He patted the stranger's arm and gave what he hoped was a reassuring smile.

Artemas gave the stranger a goblet of some foul-smelling brew. Morfael smiled as he watched the man drink it. It must have tasted worse than it smelled, judging by his expression.

"What is to be done?" Morfael asked.

"I've no time to explain," Artemas answered. "Please be silent."

Morfael blinked in mild surprise. Had Master Artemas actually said *please*? He crossed his arms and fell silent. This must be even more serious than he had realized.

Artemas began to speak, and the markings in the chalk circles began to glow. Morfael edged away until his back touched one of the misplaced workbenches. He hoped the stranger did not throw another of his fits while Artemas was occupied.

It did not seem likely. The potion must have been a sleeping drug of some type; the stranger slowly dozed off in the chair. As Artemas continued to speak and gesture, a nimbus of light surrounded the stranger's head.

Another began to envelop the sorceror's head as well. Morfael thought that he could discern faint tendrils of light linking the two. He sidled along the workbench, a little further from the pair.

Morfael was not certain how long the ritual lasted. It seemed hours later when Artemas finally stepped out of the circle to collapse into a conveniently placed armchair. Felinor was immediately beside his Nymran master with a goblet of wine. Artemas took it with a quavering hand and drank deeply of it.

"Is he well?" Morfael asked.

"Yes," Artemas replied, handing the goblet back to Felinor. "Return him to his room."

"Return . . . ? How?"

"I would suggest that you carry him."

Morfael did not bother to conceal his sigh this time as he hoisted the unconscious man over his shoulder. With a final glare at Artemas he left for the stranger's quarters.

For the second time Steve awoke beneath the canopied bed. With a sigh he sank back into the bedclothes. Would this dream never end?

"How are you feeling?" someone asked him.

"Horrible," he replied. It was true—he was nauseous and his head throbbed. Hell, he hadn't had that much wine.

"You should feel better in a moment."

Steve suddenly sat up, looking toward the sound of the voice. The man he had nicknamed Sleepy sat beside the bed.

"You spoke English!" Steve said, dumbfounded.

"That is correct. What language am I speaking now?"

". . . Nymran? But how . . . ?" Until Sleepy had asked him, Steve hadn't realized the wizard was speaking in another language.

"Magic," Sleepy replied tersely. "Can you speak it?"

"*Certe*," Steve replied, smiling.

"Excellent. Then I shall leave you in Morfael's charge. Incidentally, Morfael speaks Olvan, which you should also be able to speak. Goodbye."

"Hey, wait a . . ." Sleepy opened the door and left, ignoring Steve's protest. The White Knight came in as the sorceror left.

"Magus Artemas tells me you can speak now?" he asked, closing the door behind him.

"I suppose so." The wizard had been right. Steve spoke Olvan as if it were English. "You must be Morfael."

"That is correct. And you are . . . ?"

"Steve. Steve Wilkinson." Steve extended his hand to Morfael. The warrior took the proffered hand and smiled.

"This will make things much simpler."

"I should hope so. Where the hell am I?"

"In Quarin, the fortress of Lord Erelvar, on the southern edge of the Plains of Blood between Olvanor and Umbria. Does that help?"

"Not really. Thanks anyway."

"My pleasure. Now, you shall have to dress and prepare to meet with Lord Erelvar. The strange garments you arrived in are in the armoire."

"Oh. Thank you."

"I shall await you in the hall."

Steve dressed hurriedly, not wanting to keep either Morfael or this Lord Erelvar waiting. Now that people could understand him, maybe this dream would start making some sense.

Theron watched as Erelvar paced across the council room. This present restlessness was unlike him. Even Felinor seemed unnerved by Erelvar's apprehensiveness. Artemas was, of course, calm as usual. Nothing ever seemed to distress him.

"Why are you so anxious to speak to the stranger?" Theron asked.

"I have certain . . . suspicions," Erelvar replied.

"And those are . . . ?"

"I would rather not say just yet. They are almost too fanciful to entertain. And yet . . ."

Erelvar was interrupted by a sharp rap at the door. Theron frowned. What suspicions could Erelvar possibly have about the stranger?

"My lord," Morfael said as he entered the room, "may I present Steve Wilkinson."

"So, our mysterious benefactor now has a name," Erelvar said. "Please sit, Mister Wilkinson."

"Thank you, your grace," Wilkinson said. Obviously, Morfael had provided some instruction on the way here.

Theron carefully observed the stranger as he sat down at the large council table. He seemed nervous, judging from the manner in which he folded his hands together and rested his weight on the table. Perhaps Erelvar had reason to be suspicious. Theron noted that Morfael took a position by the door.

"I am Erelvar," continued Erelvar, "Baron of Quarin. This is Prince Theron Baltasaros, priest of Lindra and cousin to Regent-Emperor Solon Baltasaros of Validus. Magus Artemas you have already met."

"Yes," Steve replied. Theron smiled and nodded, briefly, at the introduction. Artemas said nothing, but Theron knew that maintaining the spell Erelvar had requested the sorceror to perform required his concentration.

"So, Mister Wilkinson," Erelvar said, "exactly who are you?"

"Well," replied Wilkinson, "I'm a student at New York State University. That's about it."

"Ah," Theron said. "A young scholar." That would explain some of the things Theron had observed about him. A wealthy man's scholarly son might share some of Wilkinson's characteristics.

"How did you come by the weapon you were carrying on your arrival?" Erelvar asked.

"That was just my father's hunting . . . weapon."

"Hunting?" Erelvar said. He sounded almost as shocked as Theron at the concept.

"What in the world do you hunt with those?" Theron asked.

"Ducks," replied Wilkinson.

"Ducks," Theron echoed. That weapon would leave nothing more of a duck than a few scraps of feather. He glanced over at Artemas, who discreetly nodded at him. Theron thought that even he looked shaken by Wilkinson's pronouncement—as he should.

"That's not important," Erelvar finally said. "Do you know why the *Kaimordir* wished to capture you?"

Wilkinson paled a little at that question. He glanced down at the table and shook his head as a brief shudder passed over him. Again, Artemas validated the answer.

"Why did Lord Daemor refer to you as the Dreamer?"

Wilkinson's gasp of surprise echoed Theron's. So that had been Erelvar's suspicion. Theron looked the stranger over more closely. . . .

"Answer me," Erelvar said coolly.

"I . . . that is . . . I don't know."

"He lies," Artemas announced unnecessarily. Erelvar merely narrowed his eyes and glared at Wilkinson who, in turn, glared briefly at Artemas.

Finally, Wilkinson looked at his clenched hands. "This is insane," he muttered. When he looked up again, his eyes held a look of defiance. It seemed a totally different man that evenly returned Erelvar's glare.

"All right, then," he said. "Maybe this is what I need to do, anyway. I am a student at New York State. Yesterday I went to Doctor Engelman's class and volunteered for his experiments in dream research. Tonight, when I arrived, he warned me that I was going to have some very vivid dreams and that this was natural. So there. This is all just a damned dream."

Erelvar's look of anger had been replaced with astonishment. Perplexed, he looked to Artemas, as did Theron and Felinor.

"He speaks the truth," Artemas said, as if betrayed by his own magic.

"No," Theron replied. "He speaks what he believes, but not the truth."

"It is the truth," objected Wilkinson. "None of this is real. Oh, why do I care? You people aren't real either. I just want to wake up; I want it to be over." He laid his head on the council table, cradling it in his arms, and began to weep.

That would certainly explain his fit this morning, Theron thought. He had awakened only to find himself in the same "dream" he had been in for over a sennight now. Theron reached across the table and took hold of the man's elbow.

"Wilkinson . . . Steve, listen to me." Wilkinson looked up, his face streaked with tears.

"This is not a dream," Theron continued. "Something must have gone wrong with this . . . experiment. Artemas's magic has somehow torn you from your home, but this is all quite real."

"There is no such thing as magic," Steve said angrily.

"What?" Artemas said.

"There is no such thing as magic."

"I can understand that this is difficult for you to accept," Theron said. "However, for your own sanity, you must."

Wilkinson muttered something in his own language, looking away from Theron and shaking his head. Theron looked to Artemas questioningly.

"He said, 'Marvelous, now I'm having my psyche analyzed by my own dream,' " Artemas said. "That's a fairly poor translation, I'm afraid."

Theron sighed. "I suggest we allow Mister Wilkinson to return to his quarters, or wherever he wishes to go. I do not recommend any further questioning."

"I agree," Erelvar said. "I think we've learned all he has to tell us. Morfael, escort our guest back to his rooms."

"Yes, my lord."

"No," Theron said. "Let him go where he wills, Erelvar."

"Are you certain that is wise in his state of mind?"

"As long as he is escorted, I think it is essential."

"Very well. Morfael?"

"I understand. Steve . . . ?"

"Right," Steve said. "You get to escort the kook around."

Theron watched as Morfael led Wilkinson from the council chamber. He would have to find some pretense to visit their guest a little later.

"So, now I've a madman wandering the palace," Erelvar said.

"No," Theron replied. "At least, not yet. What are you thinking, Artemas?" His cousin stared at the closed door through which Wilkinson had just left, oblivious of Theron and Erelvar's conversation.

"Just that his story explains some things I had been wondering about," Artemas said.

"Such as . . . ?"

"Well, the summoning I performed should not have summoned a material being. However, if his spirit were wandering abroad in sleep . . ."

"Then his body has been left behind? Will they think him dead?"

"No, the body would probably not die immediately. With care and tending it could probably survive quite a long time—a few fortnights, at least."

"Could he be returned?" Erelvar asked.

"If he were killed here he *might* return, but the shock could kill him. Especially as the other body weakens."

"If he is the Dreamer," Erelvar said, "we are all doomed."

"He is," Theron said.

"How can you be certain?"

"Are you not the Champion of Mortos—the 'Arm of Death'? Did you not 'draw him forth' from the Burning Hills?"

"He bears no sword."

"I doubt the prophecy is *that* literal, Lord Erelvar."

"Undoubtedly. What do we do with him? Daryna has already demonstrated her desire to have him, and, at your own urging, I cannot merely lock him away under guard."

"I have a suggestion that you will not find to your liking."

"Yes?"

"Pledge him."

"What! Take that . . . that madman as one of my *felgir*? What makes you think he would even accept?"

"He may not. If he does, it will solve some of your problems. You will be better able to dictate his whereabouts and you can train him to defend himself. The *Kanir* know he needs it."

Erelvar fell silent for several moments. Theron waited patiently while the baron considered his advice.

"Very well," Erelvar finally said. "I can think of no valid reason not to, though it may slay me to do so."

Theron smiled. "I've seen the way you train your men, Lord Erelvar. It's more likely to kill *him*. Although, I have some suggestions on that as well. . . ."

Steve looked out across the plain. From the battlements he could see the three rivers that flowed into Quarin. Morfael had named them for him—from the north came the Absinthian River, the river to the east was the Foamcrest and to the west flowed the *Lyrmen* or Stonesong. According to Morfael, these three rivers joined at Quarin to form the Bitterwine which flowed south from here, surrounding Quarin by water.

The plain had been dry and arid when they travelled it. Just south of the river dense forest grew, a sharp contrast to the grassy plain. Morfael explained that this was due, in part, to the depredations of the *galdir* and the bitterness of the Absinthian.

"There lies Umbria," he said, pointing at the forest to the east. "To the west lies Olvanor, my homeland."

"Where is Validus?" Steve asked.

"Validus is the capital of the Regency. It lies west and south of Olvanor."

"So Theron had to travel through Olvanor to get here."

"No," Morfael replied. "No Nymran is allowed inside the borders of Olvanor. Theron must take a ship down the Bitterwine and then go by sea to the Regency."

"Why is that?"

"The Regency lies on land that was once part of Olvanor. The Empire conquered it long ago through treachery. When Theron's people rebelled and broke from the Empire, that was the land they claimed."

"Does the Empire still exist?"

"Oh, yes. Occasionally they attempt to retake that land from the Regency. They lie south of the Regency, across the Inner Sea from Olvanor."

"I see. When will the kings you spoke of arrive?"

"Not for some time, if they come at all. King Botewylf has not yet received Lord Erelvar's message and King Arven will wait for news of Botewylf's reply before answering. It could be a fortnight before they arrive."

Steve turned to look across the plain again. He had been half surprised to find it still there. This dream had certainly been consistent. He glanced briefly at the sky.

"I think I'd like to go back inside," he said. He felt a sudden need for the security of a roof over his head.

"As you wish." As they entered the main part of the castle, a page hurried up to Morfael. They conferred briefly, speaking too low for Steve to hear. Morfael nodded to the page and turned back to Steve.

"Lord Erelvar wishes to see you," he said.

"Oh, great."

They found Erelvar in his study. Bookshelves lined one wall. The opposite wall harbored a sitting area with a small sofa, two comfortable-looking chairs and a fireplace. A large, round carpet covered the floor.

Erelvar himself sat behind an immense, austere desk. Another chair faced the desk. If it hadn't been for the stone walls and the oil lamps, it could have looked like any modern office.

"Paperwork, eh?" Steve said. Erelvar looked at him, surprised.

"Always," he replied. "Leave us, Morfael."

"Yes, my lord." Steve watched Morfael leave with a little trepidation. The Olvan was the closest thing he'd found to a friend here. . . .

"Sit down," Erelvar told him. Steve did so.

"I've an offer to make you," Erelvar continued, glancing down at the surface of his desk.

"An offer?" What could Erelvar possibly offer him?

"Yes. I've given this matter much thought and have decided to offer to pledge you as one of my *felgir*."

Steve frowned. The Olvan word meant "sworn warriors." That didn't sound too appealing. . . .

"I'm . . . not sure I understand. . . ."

"You would bear my standard, care for my horse on the field and, most importantly, be trained as a *rega*."

Rega translated in his mind as, literally, "horse warrior" or "mounted warrior." If he understood correctly, Lord Erelvar was offering to take him on as the local equivalent to a squire, eventually to become a knight. Neither "squire" nor "knight" translated back into any language he had been taught, however. . . .

"I'd be an apprentice *rega*," he said, more in question than in statement.

"Exactly. A position as one of my personal *felgir* would also carry some station with it."

"Why me?"

"Whether you believe it or not," Erelvar replied, "you are a figure of some importance to us."

"Morfael said something about a prophecy."

Erelvar nodded. "Yes. It is in our interests to see that you can defend yourself. By making you my *felga*, that would also carry some advantage for you."

"I see."

"Bear in mind that if you accept, you will be sworn to me. Disobey me and you shall wish that this truly were just a dream."

"Uh . . . I don't know."

"I will not have you lying about the castle and growing fat at my expense. You shall have to do something useful here. This offer carries many advantages for you."

Steve considered for a moment. "All right, I accept," he finally said.

"Excellent. Send Morfael in and wait outside."

Steve rose from the chair and turned toward the door.

"Wilkinson!" Erelvar shouted behind him. Steve whirled to face Erelvar.

"W-what?" he said. Erelvar glared at him from behind the desk. "What is it?"

"When I give you instruction, I expect to hear 'Yes, my lord' in response. You do not merely turn your back on me and walk away."

Steve swallowed the lump that had leapt into his throat. "Y-yes, my lord," he stammered.

"Good. Now send Morfael in."

"Y-yes, my lord."

Erelvar watched as Wilkinson left. The first thing he would tell Morfael would be to teach that man some manners. This was going to be a difficult apprenticeship.

Chapter Five

STEVE DOUBTED THAT the shantytown below had ever seen this much excitement. It was almost comical, seeing the crude shacks and tents decorated with bright banners and flowers as the workers scurried about making their preparations for the arrival of the foreign kings.

He watched from his window, enjoying the unaccustomed leisure. The rest of the castle staff, if anything, were even more frantic than the townspeople below. To Steve it was merely a welcome respite from the strenuous activity of his training.

Steve smiled. If nothing else had been able to convince him this was all a dream, the last two weeks would have. He had gained about twenty pounds in that time—all of it muscle. Theron insisted that this was because he was using his healing powers to increase the amount of exercise Steve could withstand. True, Steve was able to work out almost constantly thanks to Theron removing his soreness, but it was still too fast—for anything but a dream.

When the advance scouts had arrived to announce the imminent arrival of the kings, Steve had breathed a sigh of relief. It would be nice to spend a day looking at something besides the floor six inches under his nose while doing pushups. . . .

He smiled again. He wasn't the only one enjoying some time off. The workers below were taking full advantage of their unexpected holiday as well. . . .

"Tonight, then?" Karym asked, glancing up at the fortress. About them the people of Quarin prepared for the arrival of the kings.

"No," replied Mengaer. "They will be too alert tonight. Hold this ladder steady."

Karym held the ladder while Mengaer carried the gaudy banner aloft. How these peasants grew so excited over the most meaningless things was beyond him. Soon Mengaer was back on the ground.

"We must take him soon," Karym said. "Lord Belevairn grows impatient."

"We will have the Dreamer for him tomorrow, Karym," Mengaer assured him. "Shortly after midday."

"During the day?"

"We will be better able to move among the crowd, and there will be other strangers in the palace."

"Escape will be more difficult . . ." Karym began. Mengaer snorted in derision.

"Do you truly believe we can escape this place, Karym? Even outside the palace, where would we hide?"

"True," Karym agreed. Then a sly smile crept across his face.

"Well, then," he said, "if we die tomorrow, shall we hire some women tonight?"

"We'll make them earn their money," Mengaer replied, chuckling. The two Morvir walked away, laughing with the rest of the festive crowd.

Theron had never seen Quarin this festive. The workers lined the short boulevard between the curtain wall and the inner wall of the palace, restrained only by the barricades and men Erelvar had placed there. It wasn't until they were all gathered into one place that one realized how many men there were here.

King Arven and his small retinue rode through the gate onto the boulevard. An enormous cheer rose from the gathered crowd as the Olvan king approached to where Erelvar and Theron awaited, also on horseback.

"Greetings, your majesty," Erelvar called above the roar. "Welcome to Quarin."

"And greetings to you, Erelvar," Arven replied, somehow capable of speaking over the crowd without raising his voice. "And to you, Prince Theron."

"Your majesty," Theron said, bowing slightly in the saddle.

"If your majesty will follow us into the palace, we may escape this din."

Arven smiled. "Yes. I think that would be best. It has been a few years since you were among my court at Mencar, Erelvar. We have much to discuss. . . ." Theron rode beside Erelvar toward the palace, ignoring the covert glares of the other Olvir.

King Botewylf arrived shortly afterwards. The crowd cheered even louder for him, but then most were Umbrian, after all. His retinue was much larger, with many armed men.

"I should have worn *my* armor," Erelvar said to Theron as the column passed the gate. Theron himself had changed from the robes of state he had worn to greet King Arven into his full legion dress uniform.

"The Umbrians are a more . . . coarse people," Theron replied. "One must present an image of strength when dealing with them."

"How are you going to dress when you have to talk to both of them?"

"I shall think of something," Theron replied, smiling.

"Greetings, your majesty," Erelvar shouted. "Welcome to Quarin."

King Botewylf turned from waving to the crowd and nodded. "Greetings, indeed, Erelvar. You have built a mighty fortress here in two short years. I must confess to a touch of dismay at having such a thing on my border."

"Rest assured, majesty—Quarin shall always stand in defense of Umbria," Erelvar replied.

Botewylf's gaze fell on Theron. "No doubt," he replied.

Theron smiled and inclined his head toward the king. "Your majesty," he said, acknowledging Botewylf's attention. The glares of the Umbrians as they rode back to the fortress were not near so well concealed as the Olvir's had been.

Steve poked at the straw mattress, wondering what might live in it. He hadn't expected to get kicked out of his room this morning, but apparently there was a shortage of sleeping space with the arrival of the two kings.

The pillow seemed to be made of straw too. Oh well, it beat sleeping in the stables—barely.

"Think you can stand it, lad?" someone said behind him. Steve turned to see one of Erelvar's *regir*; a young man, probably no older than Steve.

"I've slept on worse," Steve lied. His reply was in Umbrian, which the *regir* himself had spoken in. How many languages could he speak now?

"Hah! When?"

Steve glared at the man. He didn't like the Umbrian's smart-ass attitude. It reminded him of some of the varsity guys he'd known in high school.

"You try spending a night in the Burning Hills," Steve said angrily. "Or the Bog. Then we'll compare notes." Come to think of it, he *had* slept on worse than this mattress. . . .

"Ah, you must have been with Lord Erelvar on the trip to Delgroth." There was a little more respect in his voice.

"No, I was with him on the trip *from* Delgroth."

The man's eyes grew wide. "You are the wizard that the sorceror Artemas conjured forth."

"What? I'm no wizard."

"They say you drove the goblins away with fire and lightning," the Umbrian countered, taking a step back.

"The story has grown some in the retelling, I fear," an Olvan warrior said, joining the conversation. "It is good to see you again, *felga*."

"Uh, right. I'm afraid I don't recognize you."

"I am not surprised. You could not speak when first we met. I am Delarian, son of Arven and prince of Olvanor."

"Oh . . . uh. Forgive me, your highness, I . . ."

"No," Delarian interrupted. "We are all equals in this place. Here there are none but Lord Erelvar's *felgir*."

"Why are you here?"

"I am sworn to Erelvar for a period of two years, as are all the men here, while he teaches us the Morvan way of combat."

"Oh." Delarian's answer made no sense to Steve.

"I must be going. My father has called for me. Good day to you, Steven."

"And to you, my lo . . . Delarian." Steve was relieved once the Olvan prince had left. How many nobles were in this castle, anyway?

"Well, you certainly fell all over yourself," the Umbrian said.

"I'm still not comfortable with all this flowery speech they're trying to teach me," Steve replied. "What say we call a truce here?"

"Yes. I am Arthwyr ap Madawc." The Umbrian held out his hand. Steve smiled, extending his own.

"Steve Wilkinson. Where do I put my junk?" He pointed with his thumb at a pile of clothes on the bed.

"Have you no trunk?"

"Uh . . . no."

"Then leave them there for now. No one will disturb them

while we get you a trunk." The Umbrian was examining the pile of clothing Steve had managed to accumulate in the last two weeks under Erelvar's tutelage.

"Have you no dagger, either?"

"No, why?"

"Have you any money?"

"Well . . . yes." He'd been given some money by Morfael a week or so ago with the explanation that, as Erelvar's *felga*, he was entitled to a small stipend. Steve had wondered at the time what he was going to spend his unexpected allowance on.

"Good. I'll take you into town."

"What on earth for?" Steve couldn't think of any reason he'd want to go into that jumble of tents and hovels.

"To buy you a trunk."

"You can buy things out there?"

"Of course. Are you required elsewhere?"

"No. Everyone's too busy to worry about me today."

"That sounds about right," Arthwyr replied, laughing. "Come along then."

Morfael knocked on Erelvar's door before entering. Erelvar and Theron looked up expectantly.

"The kings send word that they are refreshed from their travels and will see you, my lord," Morfael said.

"In other words, the spies have finished reporting to their fathers and they have questions for me," Erelvar replied.

"You learn quickly, Erelvar," Theron noted.

"Do you think I did not know why Delarian and Aldric *both* volunteered to accompany us to Delgroth? Or you, for that matter?"

"I did have other motives. Delgroth is Validus's concern as well."

"I know. I accuse you of nothing more than loyalty, my friend. Let us go and see what questions my guests have for us."

The town was a mass of confusion. The jumbled tents and wooden shacks somehow managed to withstand the flood of people that thronged the dirt streets. A carnival atmosphere pervaded the crowd.

That wasn't the only atmosphere that prevailed. Several thousand people were crammed into this cramped space, obviously without decent sewage. Steve made a mental note not to eat or drink anything out here.

He watched as Arthwyr haggled with some merchant over a trunk. The Umbrian warrior had been appalled when Steve had started to pay the merchant's first price. Around the marketplace other similar events were taking place.

"Five sovereigns," Arthwyr said.

"That's half the price he asked me!" Steve replied as he counted the silver coins into Arthur's hand.

"That's why you bargain. Let's go."

"What about the trunk?"

"He's going to deliver it. Do you want to carry it around all day?"

"You got him to deliver it, too?"

"Of course. Let's get you a dagger."

"Do you think I need one?"

"Out here it's best to be armed, and you cannot yet carry a sword."

"Oh."

"Here is a poor selection," Arthwyr said as they came up to a vendor's stall. "Still, do you see anything you might want?"

"I have the finest daggers in all of Quarin!" objected the merchant. Steve was beginning to catch on to Arthwyr's tactics.

"I don't know," Steve replied, rubbing his chin thoughtfully.

"Perhaps this one, my lord," said the merchant, displaying a narrow-bladed knife. Steve could believe that the man did, indeed, make the finest blades in town. Before he could say anything, though, Arthwyr interrupted.

"That is a woman's dagger, merchant! My friend happens to be sworn to Lord Erelvar himself—show us a man's weapon! With quillons!"

Steve gaped at the merchant's next choice. The blade had to be a foot long.

"That's no dagger," he said. "That's almost a sword!"

"Yes," Arthwyr agreed. "Something a little smaller."

"This one, perhaps?" The merchant indicated a dagger with about a nine-inch blade. The crosspiece extended past the edge of the blade in what Arthwyr called quillons. Steve had learned enough in the last two weeks to know that one could effectively block an attack with such a weapon.

"Much better," Arthwyr admitted. "Although the blade is pitted."

"Pitted!?"

Steve smiled as Arthwyr and the merchant began haggling over the dagger. One would almost swear that the two were about to use the daggers on each other.

"Seven sovereigns," Arthwyr finally announced. Steve raised an eyebrow—apparently daggers were more expensive than trunks. The dagger was not to be delivered, either. Arthwyr helped him fasten it to his belt before they left the market.

"Now you look like a young warrior," Arthwyr said.

"If you say so."

"I do. And now you can spend some of that money I've saved you and buy me a drink."

"Uh . . . is it safe to drink anything out here?"

Arthwyr laughed. "I don't want water, my friend. What I want to drink is quite safe, I assure you."

"Well then—lead on, MacDuff."

"No, no—*Madawc*," the Umbrian corrected.

"Yeah, right."

"Majesties, I tell you, the Morvir mean to attack," Erelvar said. "That is the only plausible explanation of the presence of so many *galdir* in the Burning Hills. And that attack is surely imminent."

"I do not doubt you, Erelvar," Arven replied. "I only question your assumption as to *whom* is going to bear the burden of the Dark One's attention."

"Who else is there, your majesty? If not Umbria or Olvanor, who can she attack?"

"Quarin."

For a moment Erelvar merely stared at Arven. When he finally spoke, it was one word.

"Quarin?"

Arven merely nodded.

"Surely you cannot believe that Daryna would summon all this effort to attack *one* fortress?"

"I must agree with Lord Erelvar, your majesty," Theron said. "If I wished to attack Quarin I would do so by attacking Olvanor and Umbria, thereby cutting off Quarin's supplies. I would *not* assault the fortress."

"I agree with Arven," Morcan Botewylf said. "This fortress would be a great prize for them."

"Nonsense," Erelvar said. "Quarin could not stand without the support of Umbria or Olvanor. As Prince Theron said, without supplies it would fall quickly."

"I confess," Arven said, "that I wondered what the Dark One's motivation could be. However, I have recently learned something that could explain such attention."

"And what is that, majesty?" Erelvar asked.

"I understand you have a new *felga*, Erelvar."

"Yes. What has that to do with anything?"

"I understand that you rescued this man from the Burning Hills."

Erelvar sighed. "That is correct."

"Surely I do not need to remind the Champion of Mortos of the prophecies?"

"No, your majesty. However, I am far from convinced that this individual is who you seem to think he is."

"Ah, but is the Dark One convinced? That is, after all, all that is necessary for her to fear Quarin and the 'Arm of Death.' "

"What are you people talking about?" Botewylf said, slapping his palm on the table. "What has a mere boy to do with events of this scale? Are you *all* mad?"

"I refer to the prophecies, Botewylf," Arven replied, dismissing Botewylf's anger with an idle wave. "Consult the Book of Uldon if you do not understand."

"This does not lessen the threat to Olvanor, your majesty. I . . ."

Arven raised his hand, silencing Erelvar.

"I recall your fervor all too well, Erelvar. Was it not I who welcomed you to Mencar when you rescued Morfael? Was it not I who took you into my court during your induction into the priesthood of Mortos? Even then your ardor was . . . inspirational."

"Even so, if the Mistress takes Quarin you shall have to venture onto the Plains to fight her, for this fortress shall not fall easily."

"It shall not fall, now. I have brought five hundred *laegir* with me. They camp but half a day from here. They are yours, my friend, to defend Quarin. Additionally, I shall guard this section of my border to ensure that your fortress is not cut off from us."

"My thanks, majesty."

"And I have brought two hundred cavalry," Botewylf said. "They are at your disposal, Erelvar."

"My thanks to you, as well, majesty."

"I should like to meet this new *felga* of yours, Erelvar," Arven said. "Before the feast tonight, if possible."

"Of course. Morfael, summon Wilkinson."

"At once, my lord."

"And perhaps Glorien? I have not seen my niece in some time."

"Of course. Morfael?"

"Yes, my lord."

"I shall retire until dinner," Botewylf said, "and leave Arven to visit his kin in private." Morfael held the door as Botewylf and his guard left the council chamber before leaving as well.

"I think," Theron said, "that King Botewylf just promised to leave his personal guard with you, Lord Erelvar."

"I think so too. No matter; that gives me two hundred more men."

"True." Theron turned to Arven. "As Lord Erelvar already knows, I plan to journey to Validus after this meeting. There I shall request aid from my cousin."

"Yes?" Arven said.

"I would like to march them through Olvanor, your majesty. It would . . ."

"No."

"But, majesty . . ."

"No. I cannot allow the presence of Imperial troops in Olvanor. The last time a legion entered Olvanor under the guise of friendship, it cost many Olvan lives to evict them."

"Your majesty, those were not our . . ."

"I am aware of that, Prince Baltasaros. Regardless of my feelings on the matter, which, I must add, are not favorable, my people would not tolerate such a thing."

"In that case, will you allow troops to be transported up the Bitterwine on galleys?"

"That I will grant."

"Thank you, majesty. Then, with your permission, I shall retire as well. Lord Erelvar, majesty." Theron bowed to Arven before leaving.

"A very honorable man," Arven said once Theron had left. "Particularly for a Nymran."

"Yes, majesty."

"However, I would advise against trusting Imperial forces in your city, Erelvar."

"I never said I would trust them, majesty."

"Good. Now, regarding this *felga* of yours . . ."

The tavern, if one could call it that, was half shack and half tent. The larger, tent portion of it was where the customers were served. Steve presumed that the shack was where the owner lived.

What surprised Steve the most were the serving girls. Up until now, he had assumed there weren't any women in the whole town. Of course, judging from the open fondling and groping that was going on, he had a fairly good idea of why these were here. . . .

Apparently, Arthwyr was well known here. All three serving girls greeted him as he and Steve walked in. Arthwyr forced his way through the crowd as Steve followed in his wake. The Umbrian somehow managed to find an empty table to claim for them.

One of the serving girls came over. Before Steve could order anything, though, Arthwyr had pulled her into his lap. Steve watched while the Umbrian took a long kiss from the woman. He had to admit, she was the best-looking one in the bar—she was plain instead of ugly.

"Two whiskeys, Rea," Arthwyr said once he let her up.

"Yes, m'lord," she said, turning to leave. Arthwyr slapped her behind and she squealed, scooting just out of his reach before slowing back down to a more normal pace. Steve felt his face flush.

"Hell of a woman, that Rea," Arthwyr said.

"If you say so."

Arthwyr laughed. "You might as well forget those pretty things at the palace, Steve. You shan't get far with them—I know."

"I'm not surprised," Steve said without thinking. Fortunately Arthwyr misunderstood.

"Yea—snooty bitches. Ah, here we are."

Rea returned with two cups, which she set on the table. "Four crowns," she said to Arthwyr. Arthwyr merely pointed to Steve. Rea turned to him, palm out.

Crowns were the small silver coins. Steve dug out one of the few sovereigns he had left. She took it and started to hand him the one crown he had coming.

"Keep it," he said automatically.

"Why, thank ya, luv," she replied, smiling. The coin vanished instantly down the front of her dress. She turned, with a final smile over her shoulder, and left. Steve felt his face flush again.

"You tryin' to pick up my woman, here?" Arthwyr said.

"No! I mean . . . no. Really, I just . . ."

Arthwyr laughed. "That's all right, Steve. Rea's everybody's girl. If you want more than just a smile, though, you need to get a little more aggressive."

"I . . . don't think that's my style."

"Ah. Well, your loss then." Arthwyr smirked as he took a sip from his cup.

Arthwyr drank two more cups before Steve finished his first. After the second, though, Arthwyr started buying his own, for which Steve was grateful. The Umbrian looked as though he could drink the tavern dry. Steve had never cared for whiskey, and he doubted they served mixed drinks here. He wouldn't want to drink the beer, either—not enough alcohol to kill germs.

"Finally finished?" Arthwyr noted. "Rea, two more!"

"No," Steve said. "I think I've had enough."

"*One?* Nonsense; I'm buying. Rea!"

"Yes, m'lords?" She was still smiling at Steve. He suppressed a shudder.

Arthwyr grabbed her and pulled her into his lap again. The kiss was shorter this time, at least. Steve studied the bottom of the cup, wondering when it had been washed last.

"That wasn't very long," Arthwyr complained when Rea disengaged from him.

"I'm busy, Arthwyr."

"Ah, I know you women. You're *busy* ogling my friend here. Probably just because he's Lord Erelvar's sworn man, too!"

The level of background noise in the tavern dropped noticeably. Steve looked up from his cup, quickly.

"Wha . . ." Rea said. "Is that true, luv?"

"Well . . . yes," Steve replied quietly. "Do we have to announce it to the whole damned town, though?" The last comment was directed to Arthwyr. Steve hadn't liked the looks of some of the people in here from the beginning.

"Oh. My apologies, Steven."

"Yeah, well, it's been done now. Forget it."

"Right. Rea, two more."

"Yes, my lords."

Arthwyr pulled her down for another quick peck and whispered something in her ear. Steve absently scratched at a stain inside the goblet. Did the man have no couth at all?

"My lord," she said to Steve. Then she actually curtsied to him before she left. Steve wouldn't have thought she would have known how. It looked ridiculous, coming from her.

She returned shortly, carrying the two cups. Steve figured he could nurse this one and leave without drinking all of it, letting Arthwyr drink himself into a stupor alone.

Rea set the cups down on the table, with a smile to Arthwyr. As she turned to go, however, she slipped on something. With a squeal of surprise she fell sideways into Steve's lap.

Steve caught her instinctively. Two weeks ago he wouldn't have been able to—she would have fallen right through his arms. She smiled at him.

Steve returned what he hoped would resemble a sincere smile and started to set her back on her feet. Before he could do so, however, she pressed her mouth against his. He tried to object, almost clamping his jaws shut when he felt her tongue slip into his mouth.

With no idea of what to do next, he just sat there while she kissed him. His face grew hot as she did. It wasn't a bad kiss— practice made perfect, he supposed.

Finally it was over. Steve smiled sheepishly and helped her back to her feet. Arthwyr was paying distinct attention to the inside of *his* goblet for a change. A knowing smirk was poorly concealed by his hand.

Rea smiled and winked at Steve. She swayed her hips suggestively as she walked away from them. At least she hadn't curtsied again.

While Arthwyr's attention was on Rea's backside, Steve took a mouthful of the whiskey. After swishing it around like mouthwash, he swallowed it. God, it tasted horrible that way.

"I think she likes you," Arthwyr said.

"I think you set me up," Steve replied, coughing a little from the whiskey.

"You liked it. I can tell by how red you are."

"Right."

"You know," Arthwyr began, leaning forward on his elbows, "all you have to do is slip her a sovereign and she'll take you behind the curtain over there."

"Thanks, Arthwyr. I like to be able to piss without gritting my teeth, though."

"You have no need to worry about that. Erelvar has all the women in town visit the healers once a month."

"Well, score one for Erelvar. Look, Arthwyr, I need to get back to the palace."

Arthwyr shrugged. "Very well. Can you find your way back?"

"Yes. Stay here. Have a good time." Steve was certain the Umbrian would manage that.

"I'll see you in the barracks later," Arthwyr replied, smiling. "I'll tell you what you missed."

"I can hardly wait." Steve got up from the table and headed for the "door." Rea intercepted him on the way there.

"Leavin' so soon, m'lord?" she asked.

"Uh . . . yes. I'm afraid I'm . . . required at the palace." Steve did his best to sound disappointed.

"Ye'll come back to see me?"

"Yes. But I really have to go, now."

She pouted, then smiled and winked at him. "I'll be waitin' for ya, luv." Steve smiled before hurrying out of the tavern.

Rea strolled over to where Arthwyr sat. The young lord had left his cup half full. With a quick glance toward the bar, she drank it.

"Shy, isn't he?" she said, sidling up beside Arthwyr.

"Yes, but that is his problem." He handed her a sovereign. She smiled and led him from the table, with one last glance back toward the door.

"Is it *him*?" Karym asked.

"Who else?" Mengaer replied, watching as the whore led their quarry's companion off. As soon as the curtain fell closed behind them, he rose to his feet.

"Quickly, before we lose him," he said. Perhaps they would not have to die to capture Lord Belevairn's prize after all. . . .

Erelvar looked up as Morfael entered the council chamber— alone. Apparently he had not yet found Wilkinson. Glorien and her shield-maiden, Aerilynn, continued talking with Arven.

"Where *is* he?" Erelvar asked. He was beginning to become suspicious of Wilkinson's absence.

Morfael sighed. "Apparently he has gone into the town."

"Alone?"

"No. The gate guard saw him leave with one of the *regir*— Arthwyr ap Madawc."

"Gods," muttered Aerilynn.

"Do you know him?" Erelvar asked, turning his attention to Aerilynn.

"Yes, my lord. You shall likely not see your *felga* before morning."

"I shall see him tonight. Morfael, go into town and find Wilkinson. Take Aerilynn with you, since she knows this Arthwyr ap Madawc."

"Perhaps you should take my son as well," Arven suggested. "He does know Wilkinson, after all."

"Yes. And take some men with you—five should do."

"At once, my lord," Morfael replied. He and Aerilynn hurriedly left the council chamber.

"Damn," Erelvar said. "I should have given orders not to allow him outside the palace."

"Surely the town is not that dangerous," Arven said.

"Ordinarily not, your majesty. However, Wilkinson has decidedly nonordinary enemies, as you know."

"But surely he is safe inside your own fortress."

"Inside the fortress, yes. I can not vouch for every man in the town, however. Any of them could be the Mistress's agents."

"I think you overreact, Erelvar."

"I'd rather overreact than not react strongly enough, majesty."

"I suppose so. . . ."

Steve sighted on the fortress, looming above the town. Eventually, he would find a crossway that led back toward it. He ducked into a narrow sideway that looked promising.

Twenty feet, around a bend, the narrow alley dead-ended. Steve stood there for a moment, his fists on his hips. Damn Arthwyr for leading him out here.

As Steve started to turn around, a coil of rope dropped around his arms and was quickly snugged tight. Simultaneously, a coarse sack was pulled over his head. He was being kidnapped!

He began to yell for help, but before he could make a sound, something heavy slammed into the back of his head.

Steve didn't feel the bag being hoisted onto someone's back as they carried him off. . . .

"Any sign of your friend?" Morfael asked.

"Arthwyr ap Madawc is *not* my friend," Aerilynn replied. "And no, I have not seen him."

"I am certain there is no cause for alarm," Delarian said.

"You obviously do not know Arthwyr," Aerilynn said. Some of the guards snickered. A glare from Morfael silenced them.

"Keep alert, all of you." Morfael glanced down a side path between the tents. With the unexpected holiday, the streets were full of people. He saw no sign of Steve, though.

He was just looking away when something caught his eye. He looked back. Two men were walking away from them. One carried a large sack. The other, unencumbered, swung his left arm wider than necessary to clear his side in a familiar swagger.

"You, with the sack!" Morfael shouted. "Hold!" Without looking back the two men began to run. Morfael was after them immediately. He could hear Aerilynn and Delarian close behind him.

The unburdened man gained an early lead. However, the one Morfael was intent on lagged from the weight of his burden.

Just as Morfael was almost upon him, the man dropped the sack he was carrying. Morfael tried to leap the sudden obstacle, but his foot caught on the sack and he sprawled onto the street. Delarian, too, was caught by the unexpected maneuver.

Aerilynn leapt over all of them, nimbly as a deer, to continue the chase. Morfael watched as she rounded another corner, sword in hand. It was futile, though. Morfael was certain the spy had gained too much of a lead.

He cut through the sack with his dagger. As he had suspected, Steve's unconscious form was bundled therein. Erelvar would not be happy with this. He cut through the ropes that bound the *felga*.

"How did you know?" Delarian asked.

"The walk of a man accustomed to bearing a sword is unmistakable, Delarian. Those were Morvir."

"In Quarin?"

"They probably hired on as Umbrian workers. Did you see their faces?"

"Alas, I did not. Perhaps Aerilynn . . ."

"No," Aerilynn replied. "There was no sign of him once I made the bend. And the damned peasants wouldn't tell me where he went." She looked down at the unconscious man. "So this is Lord Erelvar's new man."

"Not at his best, I'm afraid," Morfael replied as he lifted Steve onto his shoulders. "We had best return to the palace quickly. Erelvar will want Caradoc to see to him."

Steve slowly opened his eyes. Where was he? Memory returned suddenly—he'd been kidnapped! He started to sit up, but a firm hand on his chest stopped him. An old man with gray-blue eyes and slate-gray hair sat on the edge of the bed.

"Lie back, boy," the old man said. "You are safe, now. Look about; you are in your own room."

He was. The canopied bed, the fireplace—all was as it had been this morning.

"How . . . ?"

"Morfael, Aerilynn and Delarian rescued you. How do you feel?"

"All right, I guess."

The old man held up two fingers. "How many?" he asked.

"Two," Steve replied. The old man raised another finger, waving his hand back and forth.

"Three. My head hurts."

The old man nodded. "You suffered a minor break in the skull. I was not able to mend quite all of the damage."

"Oh. You must be . . ."

"Caradoc," the old man interrupted, smiling. "I must admit that I have wanted to meet Erelvar's new *felga*. I regret that first meeting had to be in this manner."

"Believe me, so do I."

The priest laughed. "I imagine so. Well, I shall leave you to rest. May Mortos protect you."

"Thank you." Steve was asleep before the priest even left the room.

Erelvar stood by the narrow window of his chambers, looking at the tower he had ordered Wilkinson placed into. Theron was right—the measures he was taking were extreme. What else was he to do, however?

He had thought that the walls of Quarin were ample protection for his charge. He should have realized before today that the Mistress would have agents even here.

"Do not blame yourself so," Glorien said behind him.

"Have you taken to eavesdropping on my thoughts now, woman?"

"No—I merely know my husband," she answered. "Am I not right? Do you not blame yourself for today's mishap?"

Erelvar was silent for a moment. Glorien waited, knowing he would answer when he was ready.

"Who else am I to blame?" he asked. "My own fortress—my own city, and I cannot hold one person safe within it. How can I presume to defend thousands?"

Glorien rose from the bed to stand behind him, touching his back with the lightness of a feather.

"As best you can," she replied.

"And if that is not sufficient?"

Glorien smiled. Men who did not truly know Erelvar claimed

that he feared nothing. She knew otherwise. Her husband lived in constant dread of an enemy he could not face on any field—failure.

"Then we shall die," she said bluntly, "as people have always died. But we shall die well, and generations to come shall sing of your valor."

"I have no concern for that."

"Of course not. There is more troubling you than the fate of young Wilkinson, however."

Erelvar sighed. "Much more," he admitted.

"Come; share it with me."

Erelvar allowed her to lead him from the window; sleep did not come for them until late into the night.

Delarian leaned on the battlements, staring out into the night as if he could still see the forests of Olvanor across the river. He glanced back toward the castle, at the rooms Erelvar had quartered his father in—the windows were dark.

Would that he, too, could find the solace of sleep. After the fruitless argument with his father, however, that solace had eluded him.

He could have believed that his father would dismiss Erelvar's warnings. After all, what would a Morvan know of the defense of Olvanor? He had not believed, however, that his own warnings would have fallen on equally deaf ears.

Like Erelvar, he had *seen* the armies of *galdir* massing in the Burning Hills—knew that their numbers were too great for a simple siege against Quarin. Still, his father would not listen to him. Delarian had always respected his father and king, but now the terms blind and narrow-minded came to the front of his mind all too easily.

What have you made me, Erelvar? he thought. *Once I too would have trusted in the forest's protection.*

"Wiser," his own mind answered him. Delarian allowed his gaze to drop from the forests he could no longer see. When he next set foot in Olvanor, would the land reject him as an alien—an invader?

"Brother?" a familiar voice said behind him.

Delarian turned to his older brother. He had thought him asleep in the quarters assigned to him by Erelvar, next to their father's rooms.

"Greetings, Laerdon," he said.

Laerdon stepped forward into the light cast by the nearby watch lantern. Delarian smiled—Laerdon had always favored their mother more, with his flaxen hair and turquoise eyes, while Delarian's silver hair and green eyes made him a younger image of their father. He stepped into Laerdon's proffered embrace.

"I . . . came to apologize," Laerdon began awkwardly. "Father did not expect you to support Lord Erelvar's views instead of our own. I know you mean well—that you think only of Olvanor."

"Thank you," Delarian said.

"You will see, though, that Father is right, in time."

Delarian sighed. How he wished that could be true.

"No, Laerdon," he said. "Father is *not* right, and I fear with all my heart that the land shall pay for his error."

"But—to fight on the Plains! That is not our way, Delarian. . . ."

"It is the way of the ash to grow straight and tall, is it not?" Delarian asked.

"Yes, but what . . . ?"

"But if an ash tree encounters an obstacle, does it bend and grow around or does it refuse to grow further because that is not its way?"

"It bends, of course."

"And is it still an ash, even though it has left its way?"

"Of course—but we are not speaking of trees here, Delarian."

"No—no, we are not."

"Would you have us throw away our lore every time some outlander comes to us with warnings of peril?"

"Am *I* an outlander?"

"Delarian . . . I did not come here to argue with you. Please, let there be peace between us."

"Very well, my brother. There is one thing I would ask of you, though."

"Ask."

"If Erelvar turns out to be right, and you must lead the tribes in battle against the Morvir, will you promise me that you will at least *remember* what I have said tonight? That you will at least *consider* bending your way so that Olvanor may continue to grow?"

"Yes, Delarian—I will promise you that."

"Thank you."

Chapter Six

"DO YOU THINK you'll be able to make it through the autumn storms?" Erelvar asked.

"Yes," Theron replied. "The river should be calm almost all the way to the sea. Once at sea we'll be able to beach on the Olvan coast if the weather turns bad. The Olvir allow *that* much, at least."

"Good. I wish you a pleasant, and swift, journey."

"Thank you," Theron replied. "I shall return as quickly as possible."

"Hopefully the Regent will see fit to send some men back with you."

"I can almost assure it. Goodbye, Erelvar, Artemas."

"Safe travel, Theron," Artemas said.

"Goodbye, my friend," Erelvar said. Theron smiled and climbed aboard the small boat that would take him out to where the Nymran galley waited.

Erelvar watched as the workers rowed Theron to the center of the river. The galley lowered a rope ladder over the side and some sailors assisted Theron aboard. He gave a final wave before vanishing from Erelvar's sight.

"I must have work begun on the docks," Erelvar said to Morfael.

The workmen began rowing back toward shore. As soon as the small boat was clear, the galley raised anchor and deployed its portside oars. Erelvar watched as the Nymran trireme used the lazy current of the Bitterwine to turn in place before deploying the starboard oars to head downstream.

By the time Erelvar, Artemas and Morfael had crossed the causeway back to the bluff, the trireme was already out of sight. As they rode back to the palace, Erelvar looked at the tower Wilkinson was sequestered in. It was time he sought guidance regarding his new *felga*.

*   *   *

The chapel was deserted when Erelvar entered it. Of course, at this time of day that was not surprising. He pulled the bell cord by the doorway and went to kneel before the altar on the low, padded bench.

Eventually he heard Caradoc emerge from his quarters at the back of the chapel. Erelvar kept his gaze fixed on the surface of the altar, as befitted a petitioner.

"Who comes to petition the Lord of Heaven and the Dead?" Caradoc asked.

"Erelvar, once known as Moruth, and now the Champion of Mortos."

"Then look on me and speak your petition," Caradoc said in response to the ritual answer.

Erelvar lifted his gaze to meet Caradoc's ice-blue eyes. Another set of features almost seemed to lie over the familiar face he knew—features very similar to those on the marble statue behind the priest. Erelvar felt the hairs at the back of his neck rise. . . .

"I . . . I seek guidance regarding my *felga* Steven Wilkinson," Erelvar began.

"The Dreamer," Caradoc/Mortos inserted. "What guidance do you seek?"

"I am . . . uncertain what to do with him, my lord," Erelvar replied. "He seems so helpless. It is as though the only way I can keep him safe is to make him a prisoner."

"Helpless? Yes, I suppose he must seem so to you. I assure you he is neither powerless nor safe."

Not safe? Erelvar could think of no further measures to protect Wilkinson. Unless . . . if he had Artemas ward the tower . . .

"Not even the Nymran's wards can protect him," Carandoc/Mortos said in response to Erelvar's unvoiced question. "My sister *will* have him, despite all your efforts to the contrary."

"Then what hope is there?" Erelvar said bitterly.

"Do not be a fool, Champion," Mortos replied coldly. "You *know* the prophecy of Uldon—having him is not the same as holding him."

"Forgive me. . . ."

"Forgiven. You must strive to *delay* the Dark One, not prevent her."

"How, my lord?"

"As best you can. That is all I can say."

"Can you tell me nothing more?"

Caradoc/Mortos paused as if in thought. After a moment, his gaze returned to Erelvar.

"I can say this and no more—three attempts shall be made to take him and three attempts shall be made to lure him. Ware these, but especially the third of each."

"But . . ." Erelvar began.

"The petition has been heard," Caradoc/Mortos interrupted. This was the ritual ending of the audience. Erelvar bowed his head to gaze at the top of the altar.

"May our Father, Kanomen, grant you the wisdom to find your path in this matter," Caradoc/Mortos continued. Erelvar almost thought he could *feel* the blessing being signed over him. Then, with a rustle of black robes, Caradoc was gone, leaving Erelvar with more questions than answers. . . .

"I'm tired of being a damn prisoner!" Steve shouted at no one in particular. He'd been cooped up in this tower for five days now. You would've thought that *he* had tried to kidnap somebody instead of being the victim. He stared out the window, over the town. He'd even like to see Arthwyr now.

"I understand how you feel," Aerilynn replied. "Neither of us can do anything about it, however. Come, let us return to practice. It will take your mind off it."

Steve could think of better ways for her to take his mind off things—that armor hid a gorgeous, turquoise-eyed blonde. He certainly wasn't going to suggest any of them to her, though. She'd probably break every bone in his body if he did.

"I'm really not in the mood, Aerilynn. I haven't had a break in five days."

"It is not the work that troubles you."

"No, you're right. I hate being grounded."

"Grounded?"

"Locked up, imprisoned, incarcerated."

"Oh. Come practice with me." She poked him in the back with the blunt sword.

"No," he replied. She poked him again—harder.

"Ow! Stop that." That just earned him another poke in the back.

"Dammit!" He blocked the next poke with his shield as he turned from the window to face her. "Cut it out."

The next thrust was more forceful. Steve blocked with his shield, refusing to lift his own practice sword.

"Aerilynn, stop it." He raised his shield to block a downward blow toward his head. The shield jarred on his arm. Before he could object again, Aerilynn's shield caught him in the side, fortunately without as much force as the sword. It still hurt, though.

Steve threw a wild swing at her side. It was easily blocked. If she wanted to play rough, by God, he'd oblige her. He hadn't been able to land a blow on her in the last five days, but he was going to now.

She staggered slightly under a hard downswing. He easily blocked her responding thrust toward his stomach. They'd locked him in this damn tower and pounded on him for the last five days—made him run and fight and work his ass off. He was sick and tired of it.

A hard leftward blow with the sword knocked her a little off-balance. Steve let the momentum of the sword carry it away from her and brought it back hard. The dulled blade rang off Aerilynn's helmet, the force of the blow spinning her half around before she fell.

Sanity returned to him almost instantly. Dropping both sword and shield, Steve knelt beside her.

"Aerilynn, are you all right?"

She rolled from her left side onto her back. With a whoop, she sat up and embraced him.

"You hit me!" she said. "That was marvelous! Oh—I'm dizzy." She leaned back away from him, holding her helmeted head.

"No, you're crazy." Steve helped her up. She was a little wobbly on her feet.

"Come on over to the chair," he said, helping her sit down. "Take off that helmet." Steve winced when he saw the shallow crease in the bronze. How hard had he hit her?

Her silver-blonde hair was braided into a bun atop her head. Steve had wondered how she got all that hair underneath her helmet. There was no blood where he'd hit her; that was good. He touched her head where the blow had landed.

Her hand grasped his fingers and pulled them firmly away from her head.

"You forget yourself, sir," she said coldly.

"Be serious, Aerilynn. Are you sure you're all right?"

She looked at him oddly for a moment and then smiled.

"Yes, I am well," she said. "Thank you."

"What is happening here?" a voice said from behind them.

Steve nearly jumped out of his armor. Erelvar and Morfael had entered unheard behind them.

"Nothing," he replied automatically.

"He hit me!" Aerilynn said. She said it as though she had just won the New York Lottery.

"You should have seen it," she continued excitedly. "He knocked me flat on my . . . back."

Erelvar bent over and picked Aerilynn's helmet off the floor, running a thumb along the shallow dent in it. He handed the helmet to Morfael, who raised his eyebrows when he looked at it.

Aerilynn did not object when Erelvar probed her scalp with his fingers as Steve had tried to do earlier. At one point she winced when Erelvar found the exact site of the injury.

"Go to the chapel," Erelvar told her.

"My lord," Aerilynn began to object, "I am quite . . ."

"Go. Tell Caradoc what has transpired and that I wish him to examine your injury."

"Yes, my lord." As Aerilynn stood, it was apparent that she was still unsteady on her feet.

"Morfael, go with her. See that she does not fall down the stairs."

"Yes, my lord."

As the two left, Erelvar turned to face Steve. Steve braced himself for the chewing-out he was certain he was about to receive—if he was lucky.

"Well struck," Erelvar said. "It pleases me to see you pursuing your training so . . . enthusiastically."

"Huh?"

"You *will* try to restrain yourself in the future, I presume."

"Yes, my lord."

"To land such a blow on Aerilynn displays more skill than I was led to believe you yet possess. You will show me how it happened."

Steve swallowed as Erelvar picked up Aerilynn's practice sword. Until now he had only trained with Morfael and Aerilynn. And he had been complaining *before*. . . .

The pool of quicksilver shimmered in the marble font. Reflected in its surface, a Nymran galley sat on some remote coast. Sailors swarmed over its surface, hastening to lash it down against the pounding surf and rain.

How easy it would be to reach forth and crush that tiny vessel; how easy to let the sea swallow up Theron Baltasaros. To do so would expose her to attack by her siblings, however. No, it was much more prudent to work in subtler ways.

A shadowed hand passed above the silver surface. The image of the galley vanished, replaced with a columned hall. Her agents in the Empire had done well under Daemor's direction. . . .

General Nestor paced in the hall before the gilded doors to the Emperor's rooms, ignoring the whispered rumors that filled the palace this afternoon. The physicians had been tending to His Eminence since early this morning when the Emperor's damned stallion had gone mad.

The horse itself had been put to death, but not before it had thrown and trampled its master. Some had cried poison, some sorcery. Accusations had been leveled at everyone from the traitors of the North to the Emperor's son himself, although *those* had been whispered.

Nestor glanced over to where young Titus Baltasaros waited with his courtesans. Nestor could believe that of Titus. The boy's father lay on his death bed, and the little bastard thought of nothing but his whores.

He had best curtail that line of thinking, though. The "little bastard" could well be Emperor before morning, horrible as that thought was.

The doors to the Emperor's rooms opened and the physicians emerged. Silence fell over the columned hall as everyone waited for the pronouncement. Nestor already knew what it would be. Were the Emperor still alive, at least one of the physicians would have stayed with him.

"The Emperor is dead," the senior among them announced.

Nestor wanted to cut the man's tongue out, ridiculous as that thought was. He wanted to hear anything but that Erasmos was dead—that Titus was now the Light of the World.

Some fool yelled "Long live the Emperor!" Nestor grudgingly turned and dropped to one knee as everyone else in the hall had done.

Gods help us, he thought, even as he echoed the salute.

Steve raised his shield just enough to block Morfael's thrust. His own thrust curved around the edge of Morfael's shield. Morfael blocked it easily.

They circled each other in the small room, each looking for an opening. Steve deliberately pulled his shield too far in front of himself. Morfael had gotten him a few times for that yesterday.

Morfael took the bait, stepping in with a vicious side-swing to Steve's left. Steve, expecting the attack, was able to block with his shield, while delivering a strong blow to Morfael's left leg.

Morfael staggered from the blow and Steve lunged forward, slamming his shield into his opponent. In a din of crashing armor, Morfael fell to the floor.

"Gotcha!" Steve said. This was the first time he'd been able to actually floor Morfael.

"You gave me that opening deliberately," Morfael accused as Steve helped him up.

"Yep. And you fell for it."

Morfael winced. "Literally. If you could fight with your jests instead of your sword, we would all be defeated in short order."

"Except for Lord Erelvar," Steve said. "He's immune."

"We are going to have to bring in some fresh opponents for you. You are learning how to manipulate us."

"I wouldn't mind seeing some different faces," Steve admitted. "Even if it *was* over a shield."

"Perhaps Arthwyr. You and he could reminisce over past lovers."

"Morfael!" The *rega* had teased him about his one day on the town ever since he had discovered how appalled Steve had been by it.

"Gotcha, as you say."

"Yes, you did," Steve agreed, laughing. "Morfael?"

"Yes?"

"Am I ever going to get out of here? I've been locked in this damn tower for almost a month now."

The worst thing was realizing that he'd even be happy to see Arthwyr's girlfriend, Rea, now. That was a sign of how desperate he was getting. If they didn't let him out of here soon, he'd build a hang glider or something.

"I shall speak with Erelvar," Morfael said, placing a hand on Steve's shoulder. "I know this captivity has galled you, and it is not just."

"You can say that again. What's with him, anyway? You seem to know him better than anyone else I know."

Morfael sat down on the floor of the practice room, his back against the stone wall of the tower. This unfurnished practice room and the bedroom above had been the limits of Steve's world for the last month.

Steve slid down the wall to sit beside Morfael. The young *rega* was the only person in the castle that he thought of as anything resembling a friend. Steve was beginning to *hate* Erelvar. . . .

"There are many things 'with him,' as you put it," Morfael finally said. "You know that Erelvar is of the Morvir, do you not?"

"Yeah, I had heard that," Steve replied.

"Yes, but do you know what that truly means?" Morfael asked. After a moment Steve shook his head in reply.

"The life of a Morvan is not a pleasant one," Morfael began. Steve settled into a more comfortable position. This had the sound of a long story. . . .

"Male children are taken from their mothers after five summers and placed in barracks," Morfael continued. "From that day forward they are trained to enter the Mistress's army."

"Good lord," Steve whispered. That would be enough to warp anyone. Something about what Morfael was saying didn't make sense, however.

"But who does all the labor?" Steve asked. "I mean, *someone* has to grow food."

"Aye. When a child reaches the age of sixteen, the officers decide his final fate. Those who excel become officers. Those with exceptional intelligence join the ranks of the *kaivir*, the Mistress's sorceror-priests. Those who are deemed unworthy, the majority, are castrated and become the slaves who till the fields and perform the menial tasks of Morvanor. The women are also expected to perform such tasks."

"C-castrated?"

Morfael nodded. "It helps to make them docile after their many years of military training. Also, only officers are allowed to breed regularly with the women. The common soldier is only allowed to mate if he distinguishes himself."

"My God!" Steve said. "It . . . it sounds like a cattle holding!"

"In essence, that is exactly what it is," Morfael agreed. "The Mistress breeds warriors as we breed horses and cattle."

"No wonder Erelvar's so big. . . ."

Morfael smiled. "Aye. He himself has said that the Mistress 'likes them big, strong and dumb.' I have never seen a Morvan under eighteen hands tall."

Around six feet, Steve thought. *And those are the* runts *of the group!*

"So how did Erelvar fit into this? Did he escape after being judged . . . unworthy?" Come to think of it, he and Glorien didn't have any children. . . .

Morfael laughed. "Erelvar? Unworthy? No, my friend—Erelvar was an officer and was to eventually become Lord Daemor's personal aide before he fled Morvanor."

"But . . . why? It sounds like *he* had it made."

"No one in Morvanor 'has it made,' if by that you mean he had a pleasant time of it. As to why, that is something you shall have to hear from Erelvar—if he chooses to tell you. I can say no more without betraying his confidence."

"Oh," Steve said. "Well, that *still* doesn't explain why he's got me locked up in this damn tower."

Morfael was thoughtful for a moment. He turned to look Steve in the eye. . . .

"Erelvar tends to think in absolutes," Morfael said. "He *must* protect you from the Mistress, and so he has had you incarcerated in the most secure location he can think of and placed in the care of people he can trust."

"Well that's just great!" Steve said, rising to his feet. "Don't even worry how I *feel* about it—just lock me up in the damn tower and forget about me!"

"There is no need to shout, Steven."

"Isn't there? What's he going to do if I go mad in here? What good am I going to be to him then?"

"He doesn't consider you to be of any use to him at all," Morfael replied coldly. "You are an obligation—a burden he must bear. And, as far as going mad, he is not concerned with that because he feels you are *already* mad."

"W-what?"

"Tell me, Steven—do you still think the world around you is nothing more than a mere dream?"

"I . . . I . . ." Steve stammered.

Morfael watched as Steve looked around the practice room. One would have thought he was seeing it for the first time. Steve fell back against the wall behind him and slid down to sit with his head in his hands.

"Maybe Erelvar's right," he said quietly. "Maybe I *am* insane and this is really just a padded cell somewhere."

"Steven," Morfael said, kneeling down in front of him and putting his hands on the boy's shoulders, "you are *not* mad. Not *yet*. But, if you keep denying the truth you may become so."

"Leave me alone," Steve said.

"Steven . . ."

"Please, Morfael. I need to be alone for a little while."

"Very well," Morfael replied quietly. "I shall be outside when you are ready to continue your practice."

"Thank you."

Morfael glanced back at Steve as he opened the door. He was still sitting against the wall, but his shoulders shook as if with weeping. . .

Theron waited impatiently outside the audience chamber. He had arrived in Validus over twenty days ago only to find his cousin away from the city. The Regent had just returned from his mysterious journey late last evening.

It was not like Solon to leave Validus for such an extended period of time. Even more disturbing were some of the rumors Theron had heard during his stay in the palace. He had not added his own news to those rumors—it was best not to fuel the fire.

If the rumors were true, it was unlikely that Lord Erelvar would receive any aid from Validus. He doubted that the Empire was truly marshalling a half-dozen legions against them, but if the rumors were only half true . . .

He heard the herald call him to audience. Theron rose from his seat and made his way through the crowd of petitioners. Those who had not seen him earlier conveyed their greetings and welcome as he passed.

He smiled and thanked them, realizing he had been away from Validus too long. He had not realized how much he had missed civilization until these last few days.

Solon waited behind his desk. As always, Theron was struck by Solon's resemblance to his father and Theron's uncle, Aineas. Straight, jet-black hair, square jaw and broad shoulders. The strongest resemblance lay in the hawk-keen dark eyes, however. That resemblance had grown during Solon's service as Regent.

"Cousin," Solon said, rising to greet him. "Welcome home."

"I should say the same to you," Theron replied, clasping Solon's hands. "You've been away for some time."

"Yes. I wish I had been here to greet you."

"Thank you. I have heard some ugly rumors during your absence. Is there any substance to them?"

"Yes, to some of them. Erasmos Baltasaros has died."

That had been at the heart of all the rumors. If that were true, then the rest was suddenly more plausible.

"How?" Theron asked. "He was barely in his forties."

"Some type of riding accident. His son Titus now reigns in the Empire." Solon gestured toward two chairs near the tall windows that looked out into the garden. They sat.

"That is bad news indeed," Theron observed.

"It grows worse. There seems to be some suspicion that Titus could be . . . responsible for the accident. Sources in the Empire tell me that he plans to move against us to divert attention from the scandal."

"Sources? I was not aware that we had any loyal agents within the Empire."

"Neither loyal nor within. It seems that Erasmos's chancellor is not in favor with the new Emperor. He fled as soon as Erasmos was injured."

"I take it you do not trust him."

Solon laughed sharply. "Hardly. The man is a viper. He crossed the border with enough gold to pave the Plaza, and any fool knows where he got it."

"Does he have any estimate of numbers?"

Solon sighed. "He claims that Titus plans to march against us with four legions."

Theron felt his heart sink within him. "Four?"

"Yes. I do not know how far to trust his information, however, or where he has obtained it."

"I see."

"What news do you bring?" Solon asked, ending their discussion of the Empire. "Does Erelvar respond favorably toward an alliance?"

"He does. Unfortunately, I am here to beg for troops on his behalf."

Solon's eyes narrowed, attempting to read beyond Theron's words.

"Troops? Against whom?"

"Morvanor."

"Morvanor? That is far too coincidental. Tell me of it."

Theron briefly recounted their trip into Delgroth for the Regent, particularly the discovery of large bands of *galdir* in the Burning Hills. Solon listened intently to Theron's estimate of their numbers.

"It seems we both deliver ill tidings," Solon observed once Theron had finished.

"There is more."

"More? What more could there be?"

"Erelvar has rescued the Dreamer from the Burning Hills."

The news shocked his cousin, as Theron had known it would. Solon rose from his chair and stared out the window at the palace gardens. For a long time he said nothing. Finally, he turned back toward Theron.

"How certain are you of this?"

"Absolutely," Theron replied.

"You speak of the final battle—the end of the world."

"Or its salvation. The prophecy itself is a two-edged sword."

"Yes. Lord Erelvar has this person secured?"

"He does. At my suggestion he has taken the Dreamer as one of his *felgir*."

Solon walked back to his desk and sat behind it. For a moment he stared into space, resting his chin on his fist.

"If the Empire is preparing to move against us, I dare not spare any troops," he finally said. "Yet, if I do not aid Lord Erelvar in this, there may be nothing to defend. You have handed me quite a dilemma, cousin."

"I know. As you say, the timing is too coincidental to be mere chance."

"Yes." Solon thought for a while longer. Theron did not envy his cousin this decision.

"Very well," Solon finally said. "I shall send a maniple from the *triarii* of the Veran Guard with you. I know that is almost nothing, however. . . ." The Regent spread his hands out, palms upward.

"Lord Erelvar will appreciate them . . . and our situation," Theron assured him.

"Good. Make apologies to him on my behalf, and promise more help as soon as possible."

"I shall."

"I suppose you must leave immediately."

"I have been away far too long already. Erelvar was certain that attack was imminent."

"Yes. At least we have finally found someone favorably disposed toward us."

"Lord Erelvar is favorably disposed toward anyone who will help him battle the Dark One."

"Hopefully, it is not already too late."

* * *

Steve's eyes fluttered open to see Caradoc's lined face smiling down at him.

"What . . . happened?" he asked.

"From what I hear," Caradoc replied, "you knocked yourself off your horse with your own lance."

Steve winced. That was right—now he remembered being pole-vaulted out of his saddle when his lance-point had struck the ground. He was lucky he hadn't broken his fool neck. . . .

"Thank you," Steve said. He liked the old priest with his smiling, ice-blue eyes. Steve had seen a lot of the healer during his training. Erelvar was fortunate to have Caradoc—Steve had learned that healers were a rare thing indeed.

"May Mortos protect you," Caradoc said before leaving.

Morfael entered as Caradoc left, bowing deferentially to the broad-shouldered old man. According to Morfael, Caradoc had been the Champion of Mortos before Erelvar. Steve could believe it.

"Are you well?" Morfael asked once Caradoc had left.

"Yeah. A little sore, but I'm all right."

"Good. Erelvar wishes me to continue with you on the sword for the remainder of the day."

"What?" Steve objected jokingly. "No rest for the wounded man?"

"Shall I inform Lord Erelvar that the mounted practice is too strenuous for you?"

"No!" Steve replied, sitting up. "No, I was just joking, Morfael." His newest phase of training was the only time he was allowed out of the damn tower. He wasn't about to let them take *that* away.

"As was I, Steven," Morfael replied, concern briefly crossing his face. "I am sorry, I should not have threatened you with that even in jest."

"Oh. I should have realized that—it's not your fault. I guess that fall rattled my brains."

"Then let us forget it and begin our work with the sword."

Steve's heart wasn't in swordwork, however. Morfael defeated him easily in their first three practice bouts.

"I know you can fight better than this," Morfael finally said to him.

Before Steve could reply, the door opened and two of Erelvar's guard entered the room.

"Yes?" Morfael asked. "What is it?"

"Lord Erelvar sends for you, m'lord," the taller of the two replied.

"For what reason?"

"He did not say, m'lord."

With a look of exasperation, Morfael hung the practice sword on the rack.

"I shall return as soon as possible, Steven." He then turned and headed toward the door. For some reason he still carried the shield he'd been using in practice.

Before Steve could say anything, however, Morfael said something to the shorter guard in a language Steve did not recognize. Whatever it was must have been offensive, judging by the man's reaction.

"Morvir!" Morfael shouted through the open door, as he drew his sword. The taller guard slammed the heavy door shut as the shorter one engaged Morfael. Steve heard something slam into the door from the other side as the man dropped the bar into place. The taller Morvan turned toward Morfael, drawing his own sword.

Steve stepped forward, barely in time to divert the attention of the second Morvan to himself. His shield blocked the thrust that had been meant for Morfael's side.

The man turned toward Steve with a wicked smile. He was unhelmeted, befitting his disguise as a guard inside the palace.

"So, the pup wants to fight, too," he said, as he hurled a swing at Steve's side. Steve blocked it easily with the shield, thrusting toward the man's undefended face.

"Lord Belevairn shan't mind his prize a little cut up," the man continued, blocking Steve's thrust with his own shield.

Steve raised the edge of his shield to block a downswing, hurling another thrust toward the man's face. He almost managed to slip the sword past the shield—almost. He wasn't going to do much damage elsewhere with the blunt practice sword.

He heard someone cry out behind him; it sounded like Morfael. Damn! Steve blocked another swing with the shield. The Morvan's sword caught briefly in the leather rim. Steve's smile was hidden by his helmet as he threw a powerful swing at his opponent's side. The Morvan automatically moved his shield to block the swing, exposing himself.

Without pause, Steve stepped forward, planting his right foot in the center of the man's chest. With legs strengthened from weeks of posting in the saddle, Steve kicked.

The impostor slammed into the tower wall with a report like a rifle shot. His eyes rolled up into his head and he slid down to the floor, leaving a trail of blood. Steve bent down to take the man's sword. He rose and turned toward Morfael just in time to see the shorter Morvan plunge his sword through the light practice armor into Morfael's stomach.

"Morfael!" Steve shouted as he charged the assassin.

"Damn you, you murdering son of a bitch!" he screamed, smashing his sword down onto the Morvan's shield. "Damn you to hell!"

Steve hurled blows at the assassin faster than he would have thought possible a few moments before. His shield moved as though of its own will, blocking blow after blow aimed at him by his desperate opponent. Senses Steve hadn't realized he'd developed warned him of every tactic his opponent attempted well in advance of the actual attack.

Finally the Morvan failed to block an attack. Steve's sword sliced deep into the man's neck, stopping only at the spine. Steve wrenched his sword from the man's neck and swung again, severing the head from the body. His stomach threatened to revolt as he watched the twitching body fall to the floor.

"Well . . . fought . . . Steven," Morfael said behind him.

Steve turned and knelt by the wounded *rega*. Blood fountained from the wound in Morfael's stomach. His eyes were cloudy, unfocused. Steve felt tears rise into his own.

He rose and hurled the bar from the door, opening it in time to see Erelvar and several guards bringing up a small hand-held ram.

"Get Caradoc!" Steve yelled. "Quickly!"

He turned back to Morfael and knelt. Morfael seemed to be having difficulty keeping his eyes open.

"Don't die, Morfael," Steve said. "For God's sake, don't die." He didn't even notice the tears that ran down his cheeks.

"I shall . . . endeavor not . . . to," Morfael replied. "Besides, 'tis . . . just a dream—remember? Did you . . . not . . . say . . . thus?"

Steve sat back away from Morfael, shocked. Just a dream.

"The healer is coming," Erelvar said, kneeling beside them. "Hold on, my friend."

"Y-yes, my . . . lord," Morfael replied. "Your new *felga* . . . acquitted himself . . . quite well."

"Silence. Rest."

Steve watched, dazed. Caradoc arrived to tend Morfael's wounds. After a long time they carried the unconscious *rega* away.

"Will he live?" Erelvar asked. His voice was cold as ice.

"Yes," Caradoc replied before leaving.

Erelvar surveyed the room. One man sat against the wall, dead. Another lay on the floor, his head severed from his body.

"Well done, Wilkinson," he said, turning toward Steve who still sat on the floor. The boy merely stared up at him, eyes wide.

"Steven?" Erelvar knelt before him.

"Morfael?" Wilkinson's voice was soft, almost inaudible.

"Morfael will live," Erelvar assured him. "You saved his life."

For no apparent reason Wilkinson began to weep. Erelvar had seen this reaction before, in others. He stood and looked at the crowd behind him.

"Aerilynn," he said, seeing her face in the press, "take him from here. Take him to the room we first quartered him in."

"Yes, my lord." With some coaxing she led Wilkinson away from the carnage.

Erelvar looked around the room again. It was unfortunate that Wilkinson had not left one of them alive.

"Get someone up here to clean this up," he said. "I shall be in Morfael's quarters if I am needed."

Steve stood by the window. He hadn't fully realized that he'd been returned to his old room. The workers below went about their business as though nothing had happened—as though Morfael had not almost died.

Just a dream, Morfael had said. But was it? How long had it been? Over two months? A two-month dream?

Perhaps it wasn't just a dream. Perhaps he was insane. Perhaps . . . it was real. If so, what of the two men he had killed today?

"Steve," Aerilynn said behind him. "Steve, Morfael shall live."

"I know," he replied softly. "Please. I need to be alone."

"Steve . . ."

"Please, Aerilynn." For a moment he could feel her standing behind him. Then he heard her soft tread across the floor—heard the sound of the door opening and closing.

Just a dream. . . .

Chapter
-------- Seven ------------

STEVE STOOD ATOP the battlements staring out across the plain. Since the assassins had invaded the fortress over a week ago, Erelvar had allowed Steve the run of the palace. Steve reveled in the newfound freedom.

The line of people crossing the causeway from the plain into Quarin were anything but jubilant, however. They came with wagons and animals loaded down with everything they owned.

Steve had not realized that anyone lived on the Plains of Blood. Morfael had briefly explained that they were from clan Taran, whose lands were north of the Foamcrest River. They were regarded almost as renegades by most other Umbrians. Now they were refugees—the first victims of the invasion Erelvar had predicted.

Steve went back into the palace. The place was like a stirred-up anthill. The few warriors that had arrived with the refugees were being quartered in the fortress. The remainder of clan Taran had to make what shelter they could outside the town on the barren top of the bluff.

"Wilkinson!" someone called behind him. Steve turned to see Caradoc forcing his way through the corridor. Steve bowed to the priest when he finally reached him.

"It is good I have found you," Caradoc said. "I need some help getting the Tarans situated on the outer bailey. Come along."

"But . . ."

"Lord Erelvar's orders. Come along."

Steve sighed and fell in behind Caradoc. So much for his day off. . . .

According to his watch, it was after midnight when Steve finally stumbled into his room, exhausted. Caradoc hadn't warned him that he was taking Steve out to deal with the Tarans as Erelvar's representative. Steve had thought the priest wanted him to help set up tents or something, but no—he'd been put in charge of organizing the whole damn thing while Caradoc tended the wounded.

He fumbled with the straps of the armor Caradoc had made him wear. There'd been a few times out there when he'd thought he was going to need it. Couldn't really blame the Tarans, though. Not after what they'd been through.

He dumped his armor beside the bed and collapsed onto the soft mattress. For an instant he felt guilty, thinking about the refugees sleeping in their tents on their straw mats, but only for an instant. He pulled the covers over himself and fell into oblivion.

The entire palace slept soundly after the hectic day, save those guarding the walls. The corridors were dark and unoccupied; there were none to see the glowing rift that opened in mid-air in one upstairs hallway.

Belevairn guided his mount into the corridors of the palace. The cloven hooves made no sound on the heavy wooden floor. For a moment he sat, glancing up and down the corridor.

He finally oriented himself with the hastily drawn map he carried. The Mistress had been the only one able to locate the Dreamer after Belevairn's sorcery had failed. Erelvar had somehow managed to ward his guest against Belevairn's magic. It would do him little good.

He silently cursed Karym and Mengaer for making this necessary. He paused outside the door to the Dreamer's room, dismounting. He had not been sighted thus far. It was best to make certain, however.

His hand dipped into the pouch he wore at his side. With a sweeping motion he cast the fine sand around him as he softly chanted the rhythmic calling. The night sounds of the palace quieted as the slumber of those nearby deepened.

The door itself was barred. Still, that would pose little problem for him. His hand dipped into the pouch at his side yet again. . . .

Steve's eyes snapped open. Something burned at his throat. His fingers sought the source of the irritation. It was the amulet Artemas had given him after the assassins had attacked him and Morfael. The thing was hot enough to burn his fingers when he touched it.

As he was about to remove the amulet, he heard a sound from the door. In the light of the almost-full moon he saw the door latch slowly lift of its own accord.

He rolled off the bed onto the floor, throwing the covers over hastily rearranged pillows. He picked up his sword and ducked to where the door would hide him when it opened. He hoped this trick worked—it did in all the movies.

The door swung silently open. In the light from the hall, he saw a black-cloaked figure steal quietly to the bed. When the thing reached for the covers, he saw its skeletal hand and gasped.

The monster spun to face him, red eyes glowing behind its gold demon-mask. Steve turned to bolt out the door, only to find it blocked by an equine torso. He vaulted into the saddle and down the other side in a single, smooth motion. The demon-horse made a single, almost human snort of surprise before turning to pursue him.

Steve didn't know how the damned thing had gotten its horse into the palace, but he knew how to lose it. He ran for the nearest flight of stairs.

He leapt onto the banister as he'd been taught to leap into the saddle. As he slid down toward the floor below, he risked a glance behind him. The demonic horse followed, still just behind him. He'd forgotten the damn things could fly.

He leapt the remaining distance to the floor below. Unfortunately he was now in a large foyer; the horse would have plenty of room to maneuver. Light shone from beneath the double doors to the chapel. With a whoop of delight, Steve ran for the chapel.

He barely made it through the doors ahead of the demon-horse. He stumbled and crashed to the floor just inside the small chapel. Rolling onto his back, he looked out into the foyer.

The demon-horse stood there, snorting and pawing at the floor, its cloven hooves striking sparks on the stone. Steve let his breath out in a sigh of relief. He had been right; the monster could not pass into the chapel.

The door at the back of the small chapel opened. Caradoc stepped out into the sanctuary, apparently just awakened.

"What goes . . . Lord of Heaven! Steven, away from the door!"

Steve hastened to comply, retreating to where Caradoc stood by the altar. The demon stood its ground, blocking the doorway, but was still barred from entering.

"Give me your sword, boy," Caradoc ordered.

"But . . ."

"Now!"

Steve had never heard such command in the old priest's voice. He handed him the sword, watching as Caradoc laid it across the stone altar.

"Mortos, Lord of Heaven and the Dead," Caradoc began, "bless this blade to the destruction of thy enemies."

Steve watched in astonishment as the bronze sword blackened. Once the blade had become fully black, it began to lighten until it shone like the purest silver. Even Caradoc seemed surprised by the extent of the transformation.

"There is a shield in my room," Caradoc said, his tone muted with awe. "Fetch it, boy."

Steve turned and hurried through the door into the priest's small room. The shield was easy to find, hanging over Caradoc's bed. He lifted it from the hooks set into the wall.

"Here," he said, returning to the chapel. "You're not going to fight that thing, are you?" The demon still blocked their only egress from the sanctuary.

"Yes," Caradoc replied, taking the shield from him. Steve watched as the old priest advanced toward the doorway. From within the protection of the chapel, he thrust the sword toward the demon's face. It snarled and retreated to outside the reach of Caradoc's weapon.

Before Caradoc could advance out of the chapel the demon's master stepped into the doorway.

"Foolish priest," he said. "Stand aside, lest I destroy you."

"Never, Belevairn," Caradoc replied. "Your dark sorceries cannot avail you here."

"True. But I hardly think I shall need them against a geriatric warrior and an unarmed boy."

Caradoc retreated a pace, back into the chapel. Steve's heart sank as Belevairn passed the doors into the sanctuary. Apparently its protection did not extend against him.

Belevairn opened the battle with a swing toward Caradoc's head. Caradoc easily blocked the blow, thrusting toward Belevairn's abdomen. The monster blocked it with a shield bearing Erelvar's crest. He must have stolen it from a wall somewhere.

Steve watched as the two battled, wishing for a sword of his own. Caradoc's moves were studied and perfect, but the old man's reflexes weren't what they used to be. Belevairn was sloppy; Erelvar would have cut him in half by now.

What Belevairn lacked in skill he made up for in sheer strength. Several times, Caradoc was literally knocked backwards by the force of some of the blows. Somehow, the old warrior managed to keep his feet during these exchanges.

Steve turned and ran back into the priest's room. He *had* to have a sword back there. Anything Steve could use. The sound of the battle continued behind him.

There it was—hung on the wall opposite where the shield had been. He lifted it from the wall and drew it from the scabbard. It was steel, not bronze. Good.

Steve returned to the chapel just as the priest slipped his blade past Belevairn's guard, grazing the monster's sword arm. Steve heard a hiss like meat in a skillet as smoke drifted up from the wound. Belevairn screamed and slammed his stolen shield against Caradoc's sword.

With the crunch of breaking bone, Caradoc's sword was flung down the aisle to stop by the altar. Steve saw the point of Belevairn's blade emerge from Caradoc's back. The old priest slid silently off the weapon to lie in a crumpled heap on the floor.

Steve's heart turned to ice as the monster turned toward him. He raised the sword to guard as Belevairn advanced down the aisle.

"Surrender, Dreamer," Belevairn said. "You have no shield to protect you from me."

Just a dream, Morfael's voice said in his mind. No . . . it wasn't. No dream; not for the Tarans, not for Caradoc—and not for him. Calm washed over him with the sudden acceptance. Perhaps now he truly *was* insane—it didn't matter.

The blessed sword lay on the floor by him, seeming to glow with a light of its own. He slipped Caradoc's old sword into its scabbard. Belevairn stopped, began to straighten from his fighting stance until Steve lifted the shining blade from the floor. The glow of the sword seemed to brighten. . . .

"Do not be a fool, Dreamer."

Steve narrowed his eyes to glare at Belevairn. "The Dreamer has awakened," he replied. "You shall pay for Caradoc's death, monster." He began to advance up the aisle toward Belevairn.

"Brave words, child. Take care, lest they be your last."

"You want me alive, Belevairn. I have no such limitation."

"Alive, yes, but not necessarily hale."

Steve quickly crossed the last few feet between them, thrusting toward Belevairn's legs. Belevairn lowered his shield to block the thrust while bringing his own sword down.

Steve swung his sword up to block the blow, grasping the long hilt with both hands. The impact jarred every bone in his body. He snapped the sword around in a flat arc, putting all his weight and anger behind it. Belevairn moved his shield to block the strike.

The shield rang loudly from the force of the blow as Belevairn staggered beneath it. Steve followed it with another and another, driving the monster down the aisle, keeping him too off-balance to attack effectively. Rents appeared in the metal of the decorative shield as Belevairn struggled to keep it between himself and the furious blows.

"There!" someone yelled from outside. "In the chapel!"

With a roar of frustration, Belevairn hurled his almost-useless shield at Steve. The impact knocked Steve from his feet. He quickly rolled to his feet, but Belevairn was already leaving the chapel to mount his steed. Horse and rider vanished into empty space just as Erelvar and his men reached the chapel.

Steve walked over to Caradoc and took the old man into his arms. The priest still lived, apparently; Steve could hear the breath gurgling in the old man's throat.

"Caradoc," Steve said. "Caradoc, it's over."

The old priest's eyes opened briefly, locking with Steve's.

"Steven? The sword?"

"I have it."

"Keep it. You have . . . powerful . . . enemies. You have . . . need . . . of it."

"I will."

"Steven?"

"Yes, Caradoc?"

"Never . . . shame it. Never . . . shame . . ."

The old man sagged back, his gray-blue eyes staring at nothing. Steve felt his own eyes mist over with tears.

"I won't," he whispered in reply. "I swear it."

The corridors were still largely empty this early in the morning. What few people Steve passed stared at him oddly, and most gave him a wide berth—news travelled fast in the palace.

Artemas's rooms were in the southeast tower, directly opposite where Steve had been incarcerated for almost two months. He had some questions for the wizard this morning.

Steve rapped loudly on the heavy brass-bound door. Each tower was capable of standing alone from the rest of the palace. That had almost been fatal when the assassins had tried to kidnap him and kill Morfael.

Steve heard the heavy bar lift from the door. Felinor opened the door partway, just enough for his face to be visible. The apprentice looked Steve over briefly, apparently not recognizing him. Steve was not surprised—he'd added about thirty pounds since Felinor last saw him.

"The Magus is not seeing anyone this morning," the apprentice told him.

"He's seeing me, Felinor. Tell him the Dreamer wants to speak with him."

Felinor blinked in surprise. He took a closer look at Steve, who was trying to look as serious as possible after delivering that ridiculous line. Felinor nodded once, and then closed the door. Steve did not hear the bar slide back into place—good.

After a few moments Felinor again opened the door. The apprentice beckoned Steve to enter as he held the door for him. The small room was almost exactly as Steve remembered it. It looked like a chemistry professor's garage sale.

"Magus Artemas is in the sitting room," Felinor said, gesturing toward the door to the stairs. That would have been the exercise room in Steve's tower, one floor above the main body of the palace.

"Thank you, Felinor," Steve said before ascending the stairs.

Steve had thought Artemas's books were kept in the laboratory. He'd been wrong—the dozen or so books downstairs must be what Artemas was currently working on. The entire sitting room was lined with bookshelves containing hundreds of books.

"Good morrow, warrior," Artemas said, rising from the chair he was seated in. "What can I do for you?"

"Good morning, Magus. I have some questions I want to ask you."

"I assumed *that*. Ask them." The wizard poured a goblet of wine from a decanter by his chair and handed it to Steve.

"I want to know how I was brought here."

Artemas stared into his own goblet for a moment, considering. After a time he looked up at Steve.

"I am afraid that I am responsible for that."

"I know that. I want to know *how*."

"Ah. Well, to put it simply, my magic transferred your . . . spirit from the . . . realm of the sleeping to here and, in the process, clothed it in flesh matching your . . . self-image."

"That's not what I mean, either," Steve said, shaking his head. The concepts he was trying to express did not translate well.

"Let me try to be more precise," he continued. "Did you transfer me from another . . . plane of existence or merely across space within the same . . . realm? Is this my universe or another one entirely?"

Artemas looked at him, an eyebrow raised inquisitively.

"I beg your pardon," he said to Steve. "I was not aware that your studies included cosmology."

"Only the basics."

"Indeed. Felinor has not yet mastered what you so blithely call the 'basics.' However, to answer your question, I do not know."

"You don't?"

"No. You see, my casting went awry. I am not quite certain what happened."

"I guess this means that you can't send me back, either."

"Actually, I possibly could. In fact, you possibly could."

"How?"

"Your immaterial self, your soul, has an affinity for your home and its true flesh. If it was freed from this body, by whatever means, it would quite likely return to its own—if not interfered with."

"Interfered with?"

"Steven, you have . . . enemies that want possession of you very badly. I have heard that one invaded the palace just last evening intent on your abduction."

"Yes. Your amulet warned me."

"Precisely as it was intended to. That one in particular could interfere; could even intercept you. Also, if your true body no longer lives, your . . . soul would have nowhere to return to. You would die."

"I . . . see. Thank you for your time, Magus."

"You are quite welcome. Now, tell me—what was your field of study?"

"Ah . . . that would be difficult to explain."

"Please, try. . . ."

"What do you mean, he is not in his quarters?" Erelvar said.

"Precisely that, my lord," Morfael replied. "The guard says your *felga* left his room before dawn this morning. I do know that he has *not* left the palace."

"At least not by conventional means. Find him. Turn the palace upside down and shake it if you must, but find him; before someone else does."

"Yes, my lord."

"If, as you say," Artemas said, "this so-called 'speed of light' is as fast as anything can travel, how is it that I can project my astral self to, let us say, Validus, instantly?"

"Because Validus is so close," Steve replied. Their conversation had long ago converted to English, so that Steve could better express himself.

"You see," he continued, "light can travel from here to Validus in a few milliseconds. If your 'astral self' travels at even a tenth of that speed, you'd never notice it."

"Milliseconds. I cannot seem to grasp how short a time that is."

"I can't quite conceive it, either. As I've told you, I don't fully understand all of this myself. . . ."

They were interrupted by a loud knock from downstairs. Steve could hear Morfael telling Felinor that it was imperative that he speak with Magus Artemas.

"I suppose I shall have to go see what he wants," Artemas said. "Excuse me."

Steve breathed a sigh of relief once Artemas had left the room. He hadn't expected to play physics teacher to Artemas this morning. He had other things he needed to be doing, as he was certain Morfael was here to remind him. Still . . . it had been nice to speak English again.

There was some quiet discussion downstairs that Steve could not hear. After a moment Morfael entered the room. He looked about the room, eyeing the bookshelves suspiciously.

"Lord Erelvar has been looking for you," he said, finally turning his attention to Steve.

"I'm not surprised," Steve replied, rising from his chair.

Morfael turned and walked down the stairs. Steve followed. Apparently Morfael and, of course, Erelvar were upset by his morning excursion. Too bad. Steve was tired of being hovered over—and he had a promise to keep.

Steve paused in the laboratory before leaving to thank Artemas for his help. Morfael waited impatiently, although he couldn't completely hide his curiosity at their exchange.

"Why did you not tell the guard at your room where you were going?" Morfael asked once they had left the sorceror's tower.

"I wasn't planning to be here long," Steve replied. "How was I supposed to know that Artemas would practically tie me to the chair for the last two hours?"

"Erelvar . . ."

"Is upset, I know. I'm afraid that's simply too bad. I had to speak with Artemas."

"I was going to say that Erelvar is concerned with your welfare after last night's incident. Steven, has Caradoc's death upset you more than I realized? You do not seem yourself today."

"No, Morfael, that's not it. I realized some things last night. . . ."

"We shall have more time to talk, later. Erelvar will want to see you immediately."

Steve sighed as Morfael gestured at the door to Erelvar's office. Still, Erelvar was the second person Steve had wanted to speak with this morning. He just hadn't wanted it to be when the man was upset.

Steve opened the door and walked into Erelvar's office, followed by Morfael. Erelvar looked up as they entered, glaring briefly at Steve before turning to Morfael.

"Where was he?" Erelvar asked.

"I found him with Magus Artemas, my lord."

Erelvar had apparently not been expecting that answer. He glanced at Steve curiously.

"My lord," Morfael continued, "Magus Artemas urged me to tell you that he must speak with you on a matter of the utmost importance. He would not explain further."

"Very well. I shall as soon as I am done here."

"He said it would be preferable if you spoke to him immediately."

Erelvar closed his eyes in exasperation. Irritatedly, he rose from behind the desk and started toward the door.

"Lord Erelvar," Steve interrupted.

"What do *you* want?"

"I want to see these prophecies that apparently pertain to me. Do you have them here so I can read them while you're gone?"

Erelvar and Morfael exchanged questioning glances. Erelvar turned to his own bookshelf, which was much smaller than Artemas's. He retrieved a large book from the shelf and handed it to Morfael.

"Show him the prophecy," Erelvar said. "I shall return shortly."

"Yes, my lord."

*   *   *

Erelvar knocked on the door to Artemas's rooms. It was not like Artemas to summon him this urgently. Whatever information the sorceror had for him must be important. Perhaps he had news of Theron's impending return.

Felinor opened the door for him. The laboratory was cluttered, as always. Erelvar wished the sorceror would keep his workroom on a higher floor.

"The Magus is in the sitting room, my lord," Felinor told him.

"Thank you." Artemas had apprenticed the exiled Olvan, Felinor, at Theron's urging. He had argued that a Nymran-trained magus would be a great aid to Erelvar. Erelvar himself suspected that Theron also wished to spread the Nymran practice of formalized sorcery further into the Northern Kingdoms. Erelvar had agreed, however, and Artemas had commandeered the entire southeast tower.

Erelvar didn't begrudge the space. Nymran magi were the only equivalent he knew to the Mistress's *kaivir*. Umbrians shunned magic, and the Olvan lore-masters were nearly powerless outside their own lands. It would be good to have a magus in Quarin loyal to him.

Artemas was seated at his desk when Erelvar entered the sitting room. The sorceror was writing hastily. A small stack of drying documents sat to his right. Erelvar sat down in a chair facing the desk. Artemas had never been one for ceremony.

Artemas laid aside the sheet he was writing on and looked at Erelvar. He got up and poured them both a goblet of wine before returning to sit in a chair near Erelvar.

"Do you have news of Theron's return?" Erelvar asked.

"Hm? Oh, yes. Theron should be here within four to five days. The galley has just now reached the mouth of the Bitterwine."

"Good. Hopefully, he will reach Quarin before Daryna's armies."

"Hopefully. That is not why I wished to speak with you."

"Oh?"

"No. I want to talk to you about Steven Wilkinson. I know why the Dark One wants him."

"Of course. He is the Dreamer. . . ."

"No. She wants his knowledge."

"What do you mean?"

Artemas rose from his chair and began to pace around the sitting room.

"This morning your *felga* came to me, asking how he was brought here. The questions he asked were surprising in the level of understanding they implied."

"I . . . see. What, exactly, is it he knows?"

"A great deal about a great many things. After I answered his questions, I asked a few of my own. In two hours I have learned more about things that I never even considered the *existence* of than I care to imagine. Concepts that I cannot yet translate into my own language.

"The workings of the Universe lie in that man's mind. And he claims that he is largely untrained—a novice, studying only one small portion of a vast store of knowledge. If Daryna were to capture him, it could indeed mean the end of the world."

"You are certain of all this?" Erelvar asked. Artemas stopped pacing and turned to face him.

"Absolutely. After speaking with him at length, I can easily believe they use weapons such as the one he carried to hunt ducks."

Steve closed the Book of Uldon and laid it on Erelvar's desk. It had been like reading *Revelations*—most of it was nearly incomprehensible. Some of it was painfully clear, however. The "arrows fletched with fire" that "melted the hills with a fervent heat" could only be a reference to nuclear missiles. The dragons spoken of must similarly be a reference to other modern weapons of war. Perhaps jets—he had been studying aerospace engineering.

Still, it made no sense. He simply did not know enough to enable a medieval culture to manufacture such weapons. It would take generations—they needed the tools to build the tools to build the weapons. Only a complex industrial society could manufacture such things.

And how was he supposed to shatter the gates of Delgroth? Blasting powder? He didn't know the correct proportions of charcoal, sulfur and saltpeter. He wouldn't even know how to find or recognize saltpeter.

The prophecy had two possible outcomes—the destruction of the world and all life on it or the final defeat of the Dark One. Somehow it all pivoted on Steve—he was the fulcrum. He didn't like this at all.

The door opened and Erelvar entered the room. He walked over and sat down by Steve.

"Have you read the prophecy?" he asked. Steve nodded in reply.

"I understand," Erelvar said. "Return to your room—think. If you go anywhere, please inform the guard."

"I will. Thank you."

"Go." Erelvar watched as Steve left the room, shoulders slightly bowed.

"I believe the Dreamer sleeps no longer," he said to Morfael.

Chapter
-------- Eight ------------

THE ARMY ARRIVED mid-afternoon the next day, driving the last tattered remnants of clan Taran before it. The Olvan archers were able to hold the *galdir* from the causeway as the refugees struggled to reach the safety of the fortress.

Erelvar now watched as the *galdir* made their camp north of Quarin on either side of the Bitterwine. There were few Morvir among them, which meant they were not here to lay siege to Quarin. What Morvir were among them Erelvar recognized as *kaivir*, members of the Mistress's cadre of wizards. Each *kaiva* drove a wagon—odd.

A member of the Twelve led them. Erelvar strained his gaze; he saw no sign of a shield—Belevairn. His gauntleted fists clenched tighter, longing for the monster's throat. He glanced toward Wilkinson. His eyes were on the Dread Lord as well.

The youth had changed since Caradoc's death. He was more . . . serious, more reserved. Erelvar could tell, by the way Wilkinson's left hand held the hilt of the transformed sword at his hip, that the young man's thoughts were also on Belevairn. No doubt he, too, longed for Belevairn's death.

"Twenty thousand," Morfael said, estimating the number camped below. Erelvar returned his attention to the Plains.

"Not enough to assault us," he replied.

"No, but enough to seal us behind the walls."

"Only to the north. They have not yet crossed the river." Belevairn had not even attempted a crossing. Erelvar was certain the *Kaimorda* knew what lay concealed in the forests south of Quarin. Even Umbrian archers could strike *galdir* in the water.

Nevertheless, Belevairn's army carried boats. They intended to cross eventually—somehow.

"What are they doing now?" Wilkinson asked.

The *kaivir* were supervising the unloading of barrels from the wagons. Why the elite wizards should be performing such menial tasks was beyond Erelvar—unless there was something of sorcery in it.

"Morfael, summon Magus Artemas and Felinor," he said. "I do not like what I see."

"Yes, my lord."

Erelvar watched the preparations below closely. Hopefully Artemas could shed some light on these odd proceedings. . . .

Artemas was easy to find. Erelvar had requested the sorceror wait in his quarters should he be needed. Artemas himself opened the door at Morfael's knock.

"Lord Erelvar requests that you join him on the northwest tower," Morfael said.

"Lead on," Artemas replied.

The last of the barrels were being unloaded from the wagons when they returned. A row of barrels lined the northern banks of the rivers for almost a mile in each direction. Morfael watched as Erelvar explained the curious situation to Artemas.

The sorceror closed his eyes briefly. When he opened them, a puzzled expression had appeared on his face.

"There are six wizards," he announced. "Four on the Olvan side of the river, two near Umbria. I do not know what is in the barrels, save that it has a slight taint of magic. Almost a residual amount."

"Could they be planning to poison the river?" Erelvar asked.

"Not with such small quantities. The river would wash it away too quickly."

The last of the barrels were finally unloaded, and the *kaivir* fell back almost a half-mile from the riverbank. For a long time they merely waited, evenly spaced along the length of the line of barrels.

"What do they await?" Morfael wondered aloud.

"Sunset," Artemas replied. "Their power will reach its peak at sunset."

If that were true, they would not have long to wait. Already the sun was nearing the tops of the trees. Sunset was, at most, half an hour away.

"Can you and Felinor defend us?" Erelvar asked.

"Yes, but only because I suspect their full attention shall not be directed at us . . . yet."

"I suggest you prepare."

"Agreed." Artemas led Felinor to the back of the tower roof, away from the others.

"I shall erect the wards," Artemas said to his apprentice. "Then I shall hand them over to you. Do not attempt to strengthen the entire ward, only where you feel an attack. I shall assist, unless I see an opportunity for attack."

"Yes, Magus."

Artemas closed his eyes, invoking the wards. He would have to spread them very thin to cover all of the palace. However, with Felinor reinforcing only specific locations, it should hold, as long as the Morvan wizards did not concentrate their attention on Quarin.

He finished the construction and handed the assemblage to Felinor. His apprentice had enough raw strength to maintain them once built. He maintained his heightened awareness long enough to assure that Felinor had indeed taken control of the wards before returning to the limited awareness of the flesh.

Approximately a quarter-hour had passed. Artemas walked to where the others watched the enemy. He could see that the Morvir had begun their casting. They must be performing a slow ritual if they had started this long before sunset.

Again he cast his awareness outward, onto the fringes of their power. He inserted his consciousness into their construction, ever so gently lest they detect his presence. Their power coalesced into a single effort save Belevairn's. His power rode theirs as the *Kaimorda* himself rode his demon-steed—guiding, directing.

Artemas felt the shape of their calling, felt the mass of cold, wet air they summoned from the northeast. They were summoning a storm.

He withdrew from their presence as carefully as he had entered it. With a sigh, he opened the eyes of his body, once again abandoning his otherworldly vision. He gently touched Wilkinson's elbow, indicating to the youth that he wished to speak with him.

"What was it you told me about . . . electricity?" he asked. "Particularly, how it applies to lightning?" Artemas listened to the young scholar, occasionally interrupting to ask specific questions. By the time he was satisfied he had heard enough, he could feel the first faint breaths of cool, damp wind across the tower.

He returned to where Felinor waited, assuring himself that his apprentice still held the wards intact. Then he launched his soul on the wind.

He found the . . . charges, as Wilkinson had called them, now that he had some inkling of what to look for. Small spots of darkness danced in the air, dropping small tendrils toward the ground. Corresponding motes of light danced in the ground, raising tiny feelers into the air.

Now all he had to do was gather them together. . . .

Morfael squinted into the wind, watching the activity below. The *galdir* had broken open the barrels and were busily hurling spadefuls of some type of powder into the air. The wind caught this and hurled it south, across the river.

Morfael looked south, and his heart fell. The forest, in the full bloom of late summer, had begun to wither and brown. The leaves began to fall from the trees in an obscene mockery of autumn. Across the palace wall, Morfael heard the rising wail of the Olvir as they watched their homeland forests die.

Short reversals of the wind threatened to send the deadly poison back to its source. Morfael knew that the lore-master of this region's tribe was attempting to repel this horror. Sadly, he was not succeeding.

"Defoliant," Steve whispered. Morfael looked at his friend in shock. He actually had a word for this obscenity?

Morfael jumped at the first loud crack of thunder. He spun about, toward the source of the lightning flash. Faster than he could count them, seven bolts of white light snaked from the clouds into the ranks of the enemy. The combined roar of thunder was deafening.

"Way to go, Artemas!" Steve shouted jubilantly.

Morfael looked back to where the sorcerors stood. Three more flashes of light punctuated the continuous roar behind him. Artemas stood in the center of the tower, his hair standing out in a sphere about his head. Little flickers of white light played about the ends of his hair.

Morfael touched Erelvar's arm. Erelvar turned at his touch, saw the fear in Morfael's eyes, and looked toward Artemas. He said nothing when he turned back. Morfael shuddered at the ice-cold smile he had glimpsed.

Two more strokes of lightning flashed behind him. Morfael turned. The enemy lines were in chaos. Another stroke of lightning illuminated the scene, and then another. Morfael closed his eyes—no man should wield such power.

A bright flash of red, directly before him, forced him to open his eyes. A mere score or so yards away sat the crimson-eyed demon-horse of the *Kaimorda* commander. As Morfael watched, a red column of fire snaked toward him.

He ducked as the fire splashed outward against an invisible barrier. Soon, another bolt of fire struck the sorcerous defenses. Morfael fought the urge to flee the tower—his place was beside Erelvar, sorcery or no.

Erelvar had been right, however. This must be Belevairn, the only sorceror to be made a member of the Twelve. No other could have located Artemas so quickly; no other could hurl fire this frequently.

The flashes of lightning had stopped. Morfael looked back to the sorcerors. Artemas lay on the tower floor, unconscious. Felinor stood nearby, his face showing the strain of defending against Belevairn's attack. Would the apprentice be able to defend against Belevairn's sorcery?

Morfael looked back to the forests. Almost a square mile of forest had been denuded. Only the bare trunks of the trees stood to mark the presence of a once-proud forest. The *galdir* swarmed across the river in their small boats as the last light faded from the sky.

The image in the marble font faded. Fortunately, the attack had not been a complete debacle. The *galdir* had established the necessary foothold in Umbria and Olvanor. Only the secondary attack to capture the Dreamer had been quashed.

Four *kaivir* dead, two more spent from the strenuous defensive spells they had hastily erected. Belevairn thwarted, yet again. Although, to his credit, the blame for this failure lay not on his shoulders.

Where had the Nymran sorceror gained such power? Even Belevairn, who had grown considerably in strength when she had invested him, could not generate such destructive might. Admittedly, the lightning had almost consumed the Magus as well, but not before he had defeated six *kaivir* superior to himself.

There could be but one answer—Belevairn had been the first to feel the Dreamer's sword. She must wrest Wilkinson from Moruth's vigilance. Only then could she hope to defeat the prophecy.

The only question was how. Three attempts against him had now failed. And she dare not leave Delgroth to take him herself. . . .

Her smile was hidden in shadow. Perhaps she had been using the wrong approach all along. . . .

Lightning flashed through Steve's dreams, churning up huge clumps of earth. Helicopters flew over the forests outside Quarin, spraying clouds of dust over the trees, leaving only barren desert in their wake. Artemas and Morfael shouted at him, begging him to stop them, to use the Sword—the Dreamer's Sword.

He couldn't find it. Frantically, he searched the palace, but the Sword was nowhere to be found. Finally, he reached the chapel. On the altar lay Caradoc, the Sword held in his dead hands, the point near his feet.

Steve grasped the ornate hilt, and Caradoc's eyes snapped open.

"Never shame it," the dead priest said. "Never shame it."

Steve sat up with a shout. For a moment his disoriented mind did not recognize the familiar surroundings. Gradually, his pounding heart slowed and his ragged breath calmed. It had only been a dream.

Steve climbed from the bed. His nightshirt was damp with sweat. He lit the oil lamp by the bed and pulled another nightshirt from the armoire. Perhaps a small glass of wine would help him sleep.

He changed into the dry nightshirt and poured a mouthful of wine into a goblet. He turned the lamp down to a bare glow and, with a sigh of fatigue, walked over by the window. Outside, on the Plains, dozens of small fires twinkled—the *galdir* camps. He knew that larger fires burned in the decimated forest.

He turned away from the window, halting in mid-turn. *She* sat in the chair by the fireplace—green eyes transfixing him from a face concealed by shadow. His breath stilled as she gazed through him. He had come to believe her nothing more than a dream.

"Good evening, Steven," she said in the breathy voice he still remembered.

"What do you want?" His voice shook as he spoke.

"You know very well what I want." She rose from the chair and took a single step toward him.

"Don't come any closer," he said. His sword was on the far

side of the bed. Of course, it was probably useless, anyway.

"Do not fear. I am powerless; as insubstantial as a vapor." She passed her hand through the mantle of the fireplace in illustration. "I cannot harm you, nor would I."

"Yeah, right." He edged away from the window, toward the bed.

"I have much to offer you, Dreamer. Do not spurn me too hastily."

"Offer?"

"Yes."

"What could you possibly offer me?"

"Anything you desire. Wealth, power, even to rule with me if that is your wish."

"Oh, yeah. Let me guess the rest—'We shall share the wealth and glory of the throne together, making love every night and twice on Sundays.' "

The green eyes widened in surprise for the smallest instant. Then they narrowed, with an accompanying chuckle.

"If that is your wish," she replied.

"What's so funny?"

"That you would dare to make such a statement. You know your value too well, Steven. I must admit, I do want you more than any *mortal* woman ever could."

"For different reasons."

She walked to the bed and sat upon it. It did not yield to any weight.

"True," she agreed, "though unimportant. Is that your desire, then? To love a goddess?"

Some insane part of him was tempted to say yes. He walked around the bed slowly. Her eyes followed his every move. As he approached the bed she moved more fully onto it, her hand suggestively indicating the empty place beside her.

In one fluid motion Steve lifted and drew the sword from where it lay beside the bed.

"No," he said.

"Answer carefully, Dreamer. I could even send you home . . . afterwards."

Home!

"No!" Steve replied. "I don't trust you. In fact, you scare me to death."

She gracefully rose from the bed and approached him. Steve backed away from her until he came up against the side of the armoire. She continued forward, impaling herself on the sword. Steve felt nothing on the blade.

She stopped only inches from him. Had she been real he could have felt her breath on his face.

"My offer stands, Steven. You have but to speak my name and I shall grant your every desire."

She was gone as quickly as she had appeared. Steve slid down to the floor, his back against the armoire. The shaking did not stop for several hours.

The Nymran trireme shipped its oars and quickly coasted to a stop, dropping anchor before the current could carry them downriver. The other two galleys coasted to a stop behind it before dropping their anchors as well.

"We are at anchor, Prince Theron," the captain informed him.

"Thank you," Theron replied, never taking his eyes from the north. Clouds of smoke rose into the early morning sky. Quarin? It was possible—from this distance it was impossible to tell.

"Prepare a boat for me," Theron ordered.

"Yes, highness," the *magister* replied, after a short pause.

"*Praetor*," Kupris, the principal centurion of the maniple, said, "is this wise?" To either side of them lay Umbria and Olvanor.

"Wise or not, I need information. The Olvir do not act hastily, and one man is hardly going to be seen as an invasion."

"Eleven men would not seem an invasion, either, *Praetor*."

"To the Olvir, eleven Nymrans would seem a very large force indeed. No, Kupris, I must go alone."

Theron almost wished he had heeded Kupris's advice when the small boat beached on the riverbank. He had not even debarked before the Olvir made their presence known. A single arrow embedded itself in the prow of the boat.

"I come peacefully," Theron said, making no further attempt to leave the boat.

"You may leave in the same manner, Nymran," came the reply. The voice almost seemed to emanate from the mass of the forest itself.

"Please—I carry men to the aid of Quarin. I only seek to learn what has transpired to the north."

The silence that followed his plea earned him nervous glances from the oarsmen. His own calm seemed to reassure them, however.

"Very well," said the unseen speaker. "We will speak. You, alone, may approach deeper into the forest. We guarantee your safety."

"Agreed," Theron replied. He climbed from the boat onto the riverbank.

"Wait here," he told the oarsmen. "If you value your lives, do not set foot outside this boat."

"Yes, Prince Theron," they replied.

As soon as Theron was beyond sight of the riverbank, he was confronted by several Olvan archers. They dropped silently from the trees around him, surrounding him on all sides. He stopped.

Few Nymrans had ever seen tribal Olvir. Their long, pale hair was braided into two braids. Theron knew enough to know that the cords woven into the braids were not just ornamental, but were actually extra bowstrings.

They were clad in soft leather tunics and leggings. Over that a heavier, stiffer, leather tabard was worn, presumably as some type of armor. The only weapons they carried were their bows and, worn on their belts, the long, backward-curving, forward-weighted knives that they could wield or throw with deadly accuracy.

The one before him was their leader, if he judged the intricacy of the design on his leather tabard correctly.

"May the forest lend its peace unto you," Theron said.

The Olvan's eyebrows raised in surprise. "And to you and yours," he returned. The Olvir about them relaxed slightly.

"What news do you seek?" the Olvan asked him.

"The smoke to the north—what is it? Has Quarin fallen?"

Sadly, the hunt-leader shook his head. "That would be bad enough, but the truth is far worse. *Galdir* have crossed the rivers into both Olvanor and Umbria."

"When did this happen?"

"Two nights ago."

"What are their numbers?"

"Two thousand *galdir* make camp at each corner of the Four Rivers. Six thousand more penetrate deeper into both lands. Those in Olvanor die even as we speak."

"How did they cross? Were there not archers at the river?"

"The Dark One sent a poisoned wind that killed the forest and all within it. An entire tribe perished in that wind, and no forests stand within a mile of the rivers' junction. The *galdir* crossed unopposed and burned what little was left."

"Mother of Wisdom!" Theron could hardly believe what he was being told. A square mile of forest, gone in a single night?

"How many men do you take to Quarin's aid?" the Olvan asked.

"A full maniple of triarii," Theron replied.

The hunt-leader furrowed his brow in thought. "Only a hundred men?"

"The Empire marches against us," Theron replied. He would not ordinarily release such information so candidly, but Olvanor was hardly going to attack them under these circumstances.

"Hm. You will never fight your way into Quarin."

"I could possibly fight my way into Quarin. I would only have a handful of men remaining, however. With your help we could fare much better."

"Our help? How would we be able to help, presuming we were willing to do so?"

"It would involve very little risk on your part . . ." Theron said. As he explained his plan, the Olvir around him began to smile. . . .

Steve found Erelvar in the chapel, kneeling before the altar. Quietly, he walked up behind him.

"My lord," he said softly. Even now he felt strange saying that.

Erelvar did not respond immediately. After a short time he rose from the kneeling bench. He signed himself and then turned to Steve.

"Yes?"

"Artemas wanted me to find you. He said that Prince Theron is nearing Quarin."

"Excellent." Erelvar retrieved his helmet and shield from the floor where he had been kneeling. Every warrior in the palace had practically lived in his armor for the last two days.

Before they had even left the chapel, blaring horns sounded an alarm throughout the palace. Erelvar turned and hurried toward the northwest tower. They met Morfael coming from the tower.

"There is some activity in the *galdan* camp in Olvanor," he reported. "The *galdir* seem to be leaving."

"That makes no sense," Erelvar replied. "But then, *galdir* rarely do. Gather the *regir* for a sortie; meet me at the plaza."

He turned and motioned for Steve to follow him. In the courtyard, grooms waited with Erelvar's black charger and a bay mare.

Steve mounted the bay, and one of the grooms handed him Erelvar's standard. He and Erelvar galloped out of the courtyard as grooms and pages scattered out of their path.

At the plaza an Umbrian guard took the reins to their mounts as Erelvar led Steve into the southwest tower. At the top of the tower, Steve's breath caught in shock.

Morfael had described the desecration of the forest to him in painful detail, but even that had not prepared him for the actual sight. Hundreds of acres of forest to the southwest had been burned into barren waste. Burned trunks, devoid of branches, jutted out of the blackened ground.

Morfael had been correct, though. The *galdir* were moving away from Quarin. Steve thought he could discern occasional glimpses of movement ahead of the *galdir*. He even saw a few of the *galdir* fall, not to rise again. Were the besiegers under attack?

"How many?" Erelvar asked a guard.

"No more than a score, my lord."

"Against two thousand *galdir*? Madness—yet, if they draw the *galdir* away from the causeway, we can sortie to aid them."

"My lord!" another of the guards said, pointing up and to the right. Belevairn rode his mount across the river, to the deserting *galdir*. After a moment, roughly half of the force began to return to the causeway.

So much for the sortie, Steve thought. From the south, the glint of sunlight on metal caught his attention.

A small force of men had emerged from the forest south and east of the *galdir*. They were moving quickly, apparently in an effort to reach the bridge. Steve could see from here that they weren't going to make it. With a group roar that was audible even from this distance, the *galdir* turned to close on the small band.

"Theron," Erelvar said. "We *must* sortie, or he has no chance of making the causeway."

Theron jogged alongside the standard bearer. His first ploy had failed—as planned. There was now no hope of reaching the bridge before the goblins were upon them. He glanced behind them, gauging the distance to the forest.

"Now!" he commanded.

Belevairn looked down upon the field from his mount. The Nymran soldiers were trapped—there was no way they could reach the causeway to Quarin and safety. The *galdir* would intercept them long before.

Had he allowed Prince Theron's diversion to work, that would have been another matter. He had seen through the ruse, however, and Theron had panicked—had finally erred and would pay dearly for that error. Belevairn would probably lose half the *galdir* to the Nymrans, but that was a small price to pay for Theron's life. *Galdir* bred quickly.

On the field below, the legionnaires stopped their advance, halfheartedly lifting their shields into a wall. Fools—the *galdir* outnumbered them ten to one. But then, Nymrans were renowned for their unthinking bravery.

The Nymrans turned and fled. A ragged cheer of bloodlust rose from the *galdir* as they gave chase. Belevairn was not so enthusiastic. Legionnaires did not flee. Retreat, yes, but they never fled in panic.

Angrily, Belevairn drew his sword. The *galdir* were now beyond any hope of control. He would never be able to stop them before they fell into Theron's trap. With an angry curse, he hurled fire down on the Nymran force.

Belevairn had finally fathomed the trap as Theron had feared he would. His hellfires outlined the ward protecting the maniple. The magical standard contained enough gold to empower the ward for over an hour, though.

Another burst of flame silhouetted the maniple. As long as Belevairn concentrated his attack on them, Theron's plan could still succeed. If he turned his fires to the forest, however, that could pose a serious threat.

Theron glanced back at the goblins pursuing them. The beasts were slowly narrowing the distance between them and his men.

"Form up," he ordered. The formation had, until now, appeared to be nothing more than chaos. It reformed as each legionnaire took the necessary step or two to come back into place. The stupid goblins probably had not even noticed. Theron glanced back again—a mere two score feet separated them from the goblins.

"Stand fast!" he ordered. "Wall! Volley!"

The maniple halted immediately, shields rising to form the wall as a hundred javelins flew to meet the charging foe. The second and third ranks then set their spears to receive the goblin's charge.

Even as the spears were hurled, four score Olvan archers fired

on the unsuspecting beasts. Theron smiled. The goblins now had
a choice—fight and allow the Olvir to decimate them, or flee and
let the maniple have the privilege.

He looked up to where Belevairn sat astride his demon-horse.
The battle had long ago proceeded past the point where that
abomination could command the forces it controlled. That was
the weakness of goblins—they knew no discipline.

A man cried out from the front rank. The legionnaire behind
him stepped over him, shielding him from the further attention
of the goblins. He was quickly dragged back into the center of
the square.

Theron used just enough of the Power to save the man's life. It
would not do to tire himself too quickly. If Erelvar did not sortie
soon, he would suffer even more losses.

Another crimson bolt flew from above. This one was not aimed
at the maniple, but at the forest. Now the Olvir must withdraw,
having no protection against Belevairn's sorcery. Theron cursed
as the last storm of arrows flew from the forest.

"Slow advance," he commanded. The maniple began to creep
forward, each step bought with blood. There were at least fifteen
hundred goblins yet before them. Where was Erelvar . . . ?

Erelvar ordered the charge even before the crash of the falling
drawbridge had faded. The hooves of two hundred horses thun-
dered across the heavy wood onto the stone bridge. Steve watched
the small black form of Belevairn high in the air. With dismay,
he saw the distant figure begin to move toward them. They had
no defense that Steve knew of against his sorcery.

They beat the monster to the end of the bridge. As the horses
hit the bank, the column wheeled toward the *galdir* over half a
mile away. From what Steve could see, Theron had done quite
well with his small force. The size of the *galdir* army seemed to
have been cut in half.

Belevairn's fire halted above them, splashing against an invisible barrier. Steve knew that Artemas was still bedridden—this
defense must be Felinor's doing.

The galloping horses devoured the distance between them and
the *galdir*. Erelvar led them west of the battle and wheeled
them hard to the left. The cavalry crashed into the enemy ranks,
scattering *galdir*; some living, more dead. Steve spared a glance
for the Nymrans—had the size of the square diminished? It was
hard to tell.

In seconds they were past the battle and Erelvar was wheeling the column about for another charge. The *galdir* turned to flee, but it was too late. The cavalry slammed into their retreat, driving them into the ground. What few survived the second charge scattered in all directions. Some actually fled into the burning forest to escape the horses.

The cavalry scattered as well, pursuing small groups of the fleeing *galdir*. Perhaps a thousand had escaped the initial cavalry charge. Steve doubted that half that many would reach safety.

Erelvar reigned his own horse about to face the Nymran square. Steve fell in beside him with Morfael as they rode up to Theron.

"Welcome back, Prince Theron," Erelvar said.

"Thank you, Lord Erelvar."

"Is this your entire force?"

"I fear so. The Empire marches against Validus."

Erelvar paused for a moment. He had not expected such news.

"I . . . see," he finally said. "Let us return to the palace. We have much to discuss. . . ."

Chapter
-------- Nine -------------

"IT'S MADNESS I tell you," Erelvar said. "How much time do you think you have to train these men? Most of them have never lifted a sword in their lives."

"That is true of every raw recruit," Theron said. "Erelvar, you have a large supply of manpower with nothing to do. Let me have those who are willing to learn. Besides, we may have several weeks yet. Any training will be better than none."

"How do you propose to equip them?"

Theron sighed. "That is the difficult question. The most important items are shields and swords. The shields we can make from lumber you have stored here for building. As for the swords, I suppose we shall have to obtain every scrap of bronze we can find and put all the weaponsmiths you have to work."

"I have swords."

"A thousand?"

"Approximately. I was expecting to be overrun with refugees— it's what I would have done."

Theron laughed. "You call me mad for wanting to turn farmers into soldiers, and now I find that you were planning the same. These swords of yours—I suppose they are monstrous things. . . ."

Erelvar smiled. "Actually, no. They are almost the same type of swords your men use."

"Truly?"

"They were cheaper to manufacture, and an untrained farmer is less likely to kill himself with one."

"This is too good to be true," Theron said. "I salute your foresight, Lord Erelvar."

"Surely you don't intend to equip a legion with nothing more than swords and shields?"

118

"It would have sufficed. However, since you have the swords on hand, we may be able to manage more."

"How?"

"Confiscate everything of bronze you can find. We can cast breastplates that your armorers may finish out."

"Do you know how long that will take? I have, perhaps, half a dozen armorers in all of Quarin."

"Even if we manufacture only half a dozen, that, too, will be better than nothing. Besides, only the *triarii* shall require full breastplates. The *principes* will be given only a flat pectoral guard."

"What of helmets?"

"They take far too long to craft. I shall simply have to teach the men to use their shields correctly."

"I still think it is a mad plan."

Theron smiled. "Perhaps mad enough to succeed?"

"Perhaps," Erelvar replied. "Perhaps. . . ."

"You want us to do *what*?" Kupris said. Theron's principal centurion wore an expression approaching horror.

"You and Otos shall be promoted to tribune," Theron said. "Promote each decurion to principal centurion. Each principal centurion shall select one man from his decade to be promoted to centurion secundus."

"From legionnaire to centurion in one day. . . ." Kupris muttered.

"All remaining men shall be promoted to decurion," Theron continued. "They shall each recruit nine men from among the refugees and townsmen to be trained as legionnaires. We want no experienced fighters—it will be too difficult to retrain them."

"Is that all?" Kupris asked.

"No, each new centurion is to recruit ten men to be trained as *velites*."

"*Velites*! *Praetor*, such troops have not been used in hundreds of years."

"Since the Empire conquered the barbarians, I know. However, they will again be effective against goblins."

"*Praetor*?" Kupris said.

"Yes?"

"I must confess—when you led us against the goblins, I thought you mad. You proved me wrong. Even without Lord Erelvar's cavalry we would have won through, albeit with heavy losses. But now, when you tell me that we are to build a legion from Umbrian farmers and laborers, with all due respect, I *know* you are mad."

To Kupris's dismay, Prince Theron merely smiled at him.

Steve stared out over the battlements at the *galdan* encampment. On either side to the south lay the blighted and burned forests. Smoke rose on the horizon to the east and west. Presumably, it marked the location of the combined armies of Morvir and *galdir* that had passed Quarin two days ago, only a day after Theron's return.

Each army had boasted a thousand heavy cavalry and five thousand of the apelike *galdir*. The army that had passed into Umbria had also carried siege equipment. Those had delayed long enough to destroy the southern bridges.

Both armies had left behind fifteen hundred *galdir* to reinforce the troops besieging Quarin. Now two thousand *galdir* guarded each of the southern approaches into Quarin while twenty-five hundred watched each of the northern approaches where the bridges were still intact.

Steve's hand brushed the hilt of the sword at his side. He almost wished they'd attacked instead of merely marching past. It would have been a break from the tedium of the siege.

"Standing watch, Steven?" a woman's voice said beside him.

"Hello, Aerilynn," he replied. "No. There's not much else to do, however."

"That is the way of sieges, I understand."

"Yeah, hurry up and wait. Are you on watch?"

"Me? No, Erelvar never puts either myself or Lady Glorien on watch."

"Yeah, he never struck me as much of an equal opportunity employer."

Aerilynn laughed. "Sometimes you say the strangest things. Lord Erelvar should have made you his jester."

"Thanks—a lot. Hey! I've got an idea."

"Oh?"

"Yes, neither of us are busy. Let's sneak off . . ."

"Steven!"

" . . . and find a couple of spare horses. I could use some lance practice."

"Lance practice?" Aerilynn seemed surprised by the suggestion.

"Yes. I haven't gotten to work on my horsemanship since Morfael plastered me."

"I-I'd be delighted," she said, smiling. Her expression became more serious. "Are you teasing me?"

"Teasing you? No—what makes you think that?"

"You *are* serious. Very well, we shall need someone to marshal us. . . ."

"Hm. Perhaps Lady Glorien? Or is she busy?"

"One can only ask. You equip and await me outside the town."

"All right. See you later."

Kupris watched in dismay as the newly promoted decurions tried to teach their Umbrian recruits to march. At least half of them didn't know left from right, he was certain. It had taken several days just to recruit and organize them.

"Take heart, Kupris," Otos said. "Raw recruits are always clumsy."

Kupris glared at Otos. In Kupris's opinion, his former subordinate was being swayed too much by the glamour of his new rank.

"Perhaps," Kupris replied. "But raw recruits have never made up the entire body of an army before now. I only pray that Prince Theron knows what he is doing. It will be at least a month before I would dare take these men against even the goblins."

"We may have a month. A pity the *Praetor* did not think of this ere we left Validus. We could have brought extra equipment."

"Ha!" Kupris laughed derisively. "Why do you think he was so particular about choosing men that spoke Umbrian? We have no equipment only because he knew that the Regent would never have approved such a mad plan."

"You believe he had this in mind all along?"

"Of course. Besides, we do have some equipment. Each man carries a full replacement set of gear, or had you forgotten?"

"Hm, perhaps you are right. Nevertheless, we have a legion to train."

"Aye, that we do, Otos. That we do." Kupris winced as a decade fragmented itself executing a turn. Four of the nine recruits had turned the wrong way. . . .

Aerilynn found Glorien in the armory. She had been slightly unfair when speaking with Steve—Erelvar never set Glorien on watch duty because she had too many other duties. Aerilynn waited patiently while her mistress organized and dispatched a team to retrieve bronze from the townspeople and refugees.

Finally, Glorien turned to Aerilynn, smiling.

"Theron's new troops are like a plague of locusts," she said, "devouring every scrap of bronze in Quarin."

"Is this the armor?" Aerilynn asked. A rectangular plate of bronze a mere one and a half feet long and a foot wide lay on a cooling rack.

"Yes. It hardly seems sufficient, does it not?"

"Hardly."

"You, however, did not come here to ask me about Theron's armor. What is it?"

Aerilynn took a breath. "One of the *felgir* has asked me to spar against him with lances. I have come seeking someone to marshal us."

"Whom?" Glorien's tone was suspicious.

"Steven Wilkinson, my lady."

"Ah, my husband's *felga*. He *is* sadly lacking in horsemanship. And, of course, Erelvar has dropped his training with the onset of the siege. Tell me, whose idea was this?"

"His, my lady. He is the only man in the palace who treats me as a warrior. Other than my lord Erelvar, that is."

Glorien smiled. "And has it not occurred to you that this may well be a ruse?"

Aerilynn flushed. "I-I think not, my lady. I . . . believe he is sincere."

"He may be. Of course I am willing to oversee your practice. I have discharged my duty here. Let us equip and go meet your friend."

"Thank you, my lady."

Steve rode out into the outer bailey. He and Aerilynn would not be the only ones out practicing today, apparently. The area outside the town was filled with Theron's recruits. Space might be a problem.

He rode up to where Theron stood talking with his two tribunes. They looked up as he approached. He stopped a reasonable distance away and dismounted.

"Good afternoon, warrior," Theron said. "Does Erelvar send for me?"

"No, highness," Steve replied. "Aerilynn and I are planning to practice with lances today. I merely wish to find out where we can do so without being in your way."

"Ah. Would over there serve? It looks flat enough and long enough."

"Yes, I think you're right. How are the recruits doing?"

"As well as can be expected after only a half-day's training."

"Well, I'll go and leave you to your work."

"Thank you, warrior." Theron watched as Wilkinson rode away to claim the area Theron had pointed out to him.

"He speaks Nymran extremely well," Kupris noted.

"Of course," Theron replied. "He is the Dreamer, after all."

"Did he say he was going to practice with someone named Aerilynn?" Otos asked.

"Yes."

"*Praetor*, is that not an Olvan woman's name?"

"Yes, it is. I assure you, *I* would not want to face this woman on horseback. They shall be working with lances. You will both want to watch this. . . ."

Steve smiled when he saw Aerilynn and Glorien ride out of the main gate. One thing was certain; no one had ever had two prettier instructors.

Keep your mind on business, Steve, he chided himself, his left hand moving to touch the hilt of his sword.

"Lady Glorien," he said when they had approached. "I'm glad you could accompany us."

"My pleasure. Few of the men are willing to spar with Aerilynn."

"What? Why not?"

Glorien blinked in surprise before replying.

"Because she is a 'mere' woman. They feel there is nothing to be gained."

"Well, I happen to know that this 'mere woman' can currently beat the . . . tar out of me—especially on horseback."

"I would not care to seriously battle you on foot now, Steven," Aerilynn replied, smiling.

"Really? I'd say we're about even. Anyway, shall we begin? I really need the practice. My horse combat su . . . stinks."

Glorien smiled. "I *have* watched you practice. You are no worse than any novice. But yes, let us begin."

Glorien rode alongside him during the first trotting pass. Steve blocked Aerilynn's lance easily, but still could not seem to get his own under control. Aerilynn's lance was as steady as Morfael's had been.

"You have not been taught to isolate the lance properly," Glorien told him.

"I haven't?"

"No. You see, most men *think* they control the lance with their strength. That is the mistake you are making—you try to hold the lance firm. In actuality you must isolate it, moving the arm in opposition to the movement of the horse."

"Ah, I think I see what you mean. . . ."

"Let us try another pass."

Glorien was right. Steve didn't quite get the rhythm down on the next pass, but his control over the lance still improved dramatically. By the third pass his lance was almost as steady as Aerilynn's.

"Spar without me for a time," Glorien told him. "I wish to watch you from afar."

Steve and Aerilynn made three more passes at the slow trot as Glorien watched. With each pass, Steve's control over the lance improved.

Glorien had them quicken the trot for the next several passes. After a dozen more passes she stopped them.

"I think that is enough for today," she said. "It has been a pleasure working with you, Steven."

"Thank you, my lady," Steve replied. "Perhaps tomorrow?"

"I am not certain. Perhaps. For now, Aerilynn and I shall bid you good day."

"Goodbye, ladies."

"Now, what do you think of Erelvar's women *regir*?" Theron said as Wilkinson and the two women rode back into the fortress.

"I still find it distasteful," Kupris replied. "Although she took some blows that would have easily unhorsed a Nymran cavalryman."

"Those stirrups of Erelvar's have much to do with that."

"Such a simple idea. I wonder that no one has conceived of it ere now."

"True. We shall have to introduce them among our own cavalry. . . ."

"You were correct, Aerilynn," Glorien said once they had returned to the palace. "He is sincere; he does respect you as a warrior."

"I knew he did," Aerilynn replied, smiling.

"But I was correct as well."

"My lady?" Aerilynn stopped in the corridor, turning to face Glorien.

"Mind you, I am not accusing him of duplicity," Glorien said. "I doubt that even he realizes the full extent of his feelings toward you."

"Mistress! Steven and I are simply friends. . . ."

"I am certain he would say the same. He was too quick to praise you, however."

"As you said—he respects my skill."

"And your beauty. Consider well, Aerilynn—Steven Wilkinson is an exceptional youth. You could do far worse for a suitor."

Aerilynn blushed and looked away. Glorien smiled—her husband's *felga* was not the only one losing his heart.

Two more armies of Morvir and *galdir* passed Quarin three days later, en route to Olvanor and Umbria. Steve watched from the outer wall with Theron, Aerilynn and Glorien.

"For now they are content to leave us be," Theron noted. "I wonder how much longer that shall last."

"I, for one, wish there were something we could do to stop them," Glorien said. "My husband did not build this fortress to sit within it and watch the Morvir destroy the Northern Kingdoms."

Theron turned to watch his recruits on the training ground. They had made a lot of progress in the last three days. Now they were marching in century formation.

"In another fortnight," he said, "or perhaps a sennight, we should have the wherewithal to emerge. If we can remove the *galdan* foothold in Umbria and Olvanor and then take to the Plains, we could very well break the momentum of the invasion."

"Such a tactic would be suicide," Glorien objected. "Even if you had a true legion, they would not withstand the Morvan cavalry."

"I was not implying that we would survive, Lady Glorien. Only that we would break the invasion."

Steve looked curiously at Theron. That was certainly a cheerful thought. Glorien was right, unfortunately—Theron's infantry would go down like grass in front of a lawnmower when faced by Daryna's heavy cavalry. But there was something about infantry and cavalry—something he'd heard in world history. . . .

"True," Glorien said, agreeing with Theron. "Aerilynn, Steven, let us return to your practice. There is nothing more to be seen here."

*   *   *

Erelvar glared at the maps. He had been imprisoned in his own
fortress for almost a month now, while the waves of Daryna's
invasion flowed past like the rivers below. Just as the bluff on
which Quarin sat could not halt the Bitterwine, he was powerless
to stop the flow of Daryna's armies. The situation had become
intolerable—it was time to act.

"Four waves have passed into Olvanor and Umbria," he said. "A
total of four thousand Morvan cavalry and twenty-five thousand
galdan infantry into *each* kingdom."

"With the addition of a thousand or so artillerists sent into
Umbria," Theron added.

"How are your recruits faring?" Erelvar asked.

"Quite well. We still do not have all the breastplates finished
for the *triarii*, but the *principes* are fully equipped—aside from
helmets, of course. In all other respects, I would say they are ready
for combat."

"How would they fare on the causeway against the *galdir*?"

"Against only one of the garrisons around us, I would expect
minimal casualties. If Belevairn succeeds in bringing the other
three garrisons to bear before we reach the end of the causeway,
I would estimate my losses at approximately two hundred men."

"Perhaps three hundred," Kupris amended. "The men are not
seasoned."

"Of course, these estimates presuppose archer and artillery support from the gatehouse and walls," Theron continued. "Without
them, I could easily lose the entire force if all nine thousand *galdir*
were brought against us."

"Naturally," Erelvar replied. "The main question is this; once
we have cleared the *galdir* from about Quarin, do we again retreat
behind the walls, or do we press on to the Plains?"

"Or into Umbria or Olvanor?" Theron said. "There is something
to be said for striking the invaders from behind, liberating one of
the two kingdoms to aid us in return."

"True," Erelvar agreed. "I had not thought . . ."

He was interrupted by the sound of trumpets. Erelvar's guard
were sounding the alarm. For the last few weeks that had meant
but one thing. . . .

"Surely that cannot be another force?" Theron said. The last
had passed by only two days before. Thus far, there had been
approximately a sennight between the arrival of each invading
army.

"There is but one way to find out," Erelvar replied. "We shall continue this discussion later."

Beneath the cloud of dust on the horizon Theron could barely make out the distant forms of an army on the march. It came from the correct direction to be another wave of the invading forces. There were only troops on the one side of the river, however—the east side, toward Umbria. It also seemed much smaller—perhaps a thousand or two.

"What is your opinion?" Erelvar asked.

"I am not certain," Theron replied. "From here it seems to be infantry. If it is infantry, they are marching in columns, however. *Galdir* do not march well at all."

"They do not *march* at all."

"Precisely. You have told me that the Morvir have gone completely to cavalry."

"They have."

"Then that leaves only one possibility."

"Which is . . . ?"

"Delvir."

Erelvar turned toward Theron. "You cannot be serious," he said.

"I am."

"The Delvir would never side with the Mistress."

"I do not believe they are. We shall see what sort of reception they receive from Belevairn. I doubt it will be a favorable one."

"Why are they here?"

"That I cannot even presume to guess. We may have to sortie out to their aid."

"If we can."

"We can. Belevairn does not know we have a legion. He will probably leave only enough *galdir* to prevent your cavalry from crossing the causeway."

"Yes. The Delvir will probably arrive near sundown. Prepare your men."

Theron stood on the battlements of the northeast gatehouse. Erelvar's estimate had been correct—the Delvir were an hour's march away and it was little over an hour till sunset. Belevairn had gathered his forces from south of Quarin, leaving only five hundred to guard the footholds in Umbria and Olvanor. If only the southern bridges were still standing . . .

They were not, however. If they had been, Belevairn would not have withdrawn fifteen hundred goblins from each to face the Delvir. Theron watched as Belevairn led five thousand goblins against the thousand Delvir. If the legends Theron had heard of the Delvir in battle were true, that would not be enough.

Of course, Belevairn dared not withdraw too many troops from guarding the northern bridges. If he allowed Erelvar's cavalry to gain the field, the battle was lost, and he knew it. As Theron had surmised, however, the Dread Lord did not know of the fledgling legion at Theron's command. It would be good to blood the men in a semicontrolled battle such as this—it would give them confidence when they took to the field.

When the two forces were near to engagement, Theron left the battlements to join his men in the tunnels. They looked like a legion—Kupris had managed to dig up enough scarlet cloaks for all of them. Theron still didn't know how Kupris had managed it. If only they'd been able to do something about helmets. . . .

The crash of the descending drawbridge heralded the end of time for speculation. Theron gave Kupris the command to march. The standard dipped forward, and Theron heard the command to march echoed by the trumpeters.

The miniature legion moved forward along the causeway. Theron led with the heavily armored *triarii*. On the narrow causeway it would have been impossible to withdraw the lightly armed *velites* once their supply of javelins had been exhausted.

The goblins who had begun across the stone causeway paused at the sight of Theron's men emerging from the gatehouse. Theron hoped the raw soldiers would keep their wits about them. They had already won the battle at this point if they did.

After faltering momentarily, the goblins charged—a tribute to their fear of Belevairn. Theron held his troops to a march—let the goblins exhaust themselves. The battle would be joined soon enough without charging across the quarter-mile that separated them, and Theron wanted the goblins within the range of the Olvan archers.

Once the goblins were halfway across the causeway, the archers opened fire. Perhaps a hundred of the fifteen-hundred-strong army fell. The rest of the goblins fell back out of range of the Olvir. Some of them hurled their spears in the direction of Theron's men—they fell woefully short. The legion continued its sedate march forward.

When the goblins were only a hundred yards away, Theron gave the order to charge. The trumpets echoed his command and the men charged. The goblins charged as well, already forgetting the Olvir. Theron had promised these former Umbrians revenge; today he would deliver on that promise.

When they had closed to within a hundred feet, the first ten ranks of the *triarii* hurled their light javelins into the advancing goblins. Theron smiled at the confusion this generated as the goblins in the rear stumbled and fell over their slain comrades. He had reasoned correctly—the *velites* would do quite well against goblins in the field.

The *triarii* crashed into the near-panicked goblins as the second ten ranks launched their javelins. They had slain roughly three hundred of the beasts already. Now began the bloody work of the swords.

As the front ranks of the *triarii* slowly pressed forward, the second ten ranks maintained a constant barrage of javelins. The javelins would soon be exhausted at this rate. Still, they needed missile support. . . .

"Slow retreat," Theron ordered. The trumpeters echoed the command. Perhaps they could draw the goblins back into the range of the Olvir.

As Theron had suspected, the goblins had completely forgotten the archers. Approximately five hundred had already fallen. If they could be drawn within range of the archers, they might very well rout.

The legion retreated, drawing the goblins back along the causeway. Theron's standard bearer signaled for the Olvir to hold their fire—Theron wanted to bring the goblins well within range of the Olvan bows.

The legionnaires retreated further along the causeway. Theron waited until he had drawn the goblins well within the range of the archers.

"Stand fast," he ordered. "Signal the archers."

The trumpets relayed his command to the legion as the standard bearer signaled the Olvir. A storm of arrows sailed over Theron's men to land among the middle ranks of the goblins. Another quickly followed.

The goblins, now cut down to half their original strength, routed. At least another hundred were slain as the panicked creatures trampled each other in their haste to be away from the arrows.

"Charge!"

The legion charged forward, massacring the fleeing goblins. By the time Theron's troops reached the end of the causeway, only a few hundred of the original fifteen hundred remained. Those scattered, some fleeing toward their companions battling the Delvir to the north.

Theron formed his troops up on the far bank as Erelvar led his cavalry across. Only a little over twenty men had been wounded, and those not seriously. He ordered them to return to the fortress.

The legionnaires would possibly not be able to reach the Delvir in time to aid them. That task would have to fall on Erelvar's swifter-moving cavalry. Still, the battle had gone quite well. . . .

Steve's horse stepped gingerly over the *galdan* corpses. Theron's legionnaires had gone through the *galdir* like a hot knife through butter. The legion had formed up just off the causeway. Some men, apparently wounded, were being sent back to Quarin. There didn't seem to be very many of them—maybe twenty.

"Your men did well, Theron," Erelvar said once the cavalry had left the causeway.

"Yes," Theron replied. "I suggest you lead the attack to aid the Delvir. I shall catch up to you as quickly as possible."

"Agreed. Wilkinson, signal the advance."

Steve dipped the standard forward and the cavalry began northward at a trot. After a moment, Steve glanced back. Theron's men were following, losing ground quickly to the faster cavalry.

Steve shifted his attention back to the north. He couldn't be certain from this distance, but it seemed that Belevairn had finally noticed them. Steve smiled. This siege hadn't gone well for Belevairn—unexpected guests kept arriving.

The sounds of the battle reached them dimly. The monkeylike hooting of the *galdir* mixing with the clamor of metal on metal and the shrieks of the dying.

The horses slowly crossed the mile or so that separated them from the battle. As they neared the battle, Steve could see that the Delvir were much like Morfael had described them—short, stocky men. The tallest among them were just about five feet tall. They wielded large, double-bitted axes against the *galdir* with deadly efficiency.

Once the cavalry were within two hundred yards of the battle, Erelvar ordered the charge. The horses stretched into gallop as if eager to reach the battle. Steve could not say he felt the same—this close, he could see nothing but *galdir* to either side.

The cavalry slammed into the rear of the enemy force, spread into a single rank. Their momentum did not carry them far into the huge mass of the *galdan* force. Even so, four or five hundred of the enemy perished in the initial impact.

"Wheel and retreat!" Erelvar ordered. Steve performed the intricate signal with the standard even as he wheeled his own horse about. They would be away before the stunned *galdir* could even react.

Or so the theory went—Steve's horse stumbled on the *galdan* corpses underfoot and went down. Steve was barely able to remove his feet from the stirrups. The body of the horse landed on his left leg, pinning him briefly, before the animal gained its feet and galloped away without him. Futilely, he screamed for it to come back.

He used the standard to pull himself erect, his weight driving the metal butt into the soft ground. Erelvar's cavalry galloped away to the south without him. He was alone—against several thousand *galdir*; he was going to die.

No, not quite alone. Someone else ran toward him through the temporary gap left by the cavalry—one of the Umbrian *regir*.

"Back to back," the Umbrian said. Steve hastened to comply, placing his back to the standard and the Umbrian.

I'm going to die, he thought. *I'm going to die because of a stupid, goddamn horse*.

Another Umbrian made it to them before the *galdir* closed in. How many had fallen here and been abandoned? Steve drew his sword; in the fading light the blade glowed dimly.

Never shame it, Caradoc's voice whispered in his mind. Steve clenched his trembling jaw as the *galdir* closed around them.

He blocked a *galdan* spear with his shield, driving the point of his sword through the monster's frail armor. It fell back with a scream, almost taking his sword with it.

He withdrew his sword barely in time to decapitate another of the beasts before it could skewer him. The twitching body fell toward him, covering him in blood. Steve deflected the corpse with his shield, fighting the urge to vomit. *My God*, he thought, *there's no end to them—I'm going to* die *here*.

Another *rega*, an Olvan, fought his way to their circle, falling into place on Steve's left. Steve recognized the warrior as Delarian before another *galdir* attacked him. He blocked the spear with his shield and amputated the hand that held it. Blood sprayed over him from the severed stump.

The man to his right screamed in agony as a spear was thrust up under the bottom of his breastplate. Steve stepped over the man as he fell to the ground, writhing in agony and still screaming. *Oh, dear God,* Steve thought, *I can't do anything for him. We're all going to die.*

Time ceased to have any meaning—it seemed he stood there for an eternity, killing *galdir* as the dying man screamed beneath his feet. As soon as one hideous *galdan* face fell back, another would replace it.

At some point he realized that the screams of the dying man had been replaced with his own. Yet another *galdir* attacked him. With a shout of rage and horror, Steve shattered its skull with his sword.

The point of a spear slipped past his shield, grazing his side below the breastplate. He screamed, more in anger than pain, chopping through the haft with his sword and slicing back across the owner's shins. The monster fell in front of him, screaming. Steve thrust down through its back, silencing it. Another appeared before him.

He slew a seemingly endless procession of *galdir* before the battle swept past him. Short, heavily armored men swarmed around him, driving the *galdir* back with their double-bitted axes. Shaking from horror and exhaustion, Steve fell to his knees and yielded to his heaving stomach. . . .

Chapter
-------- Ten -------------

STEVE SAT AT the council table, idly rubbing his right eye and trying to stay awake. He had barely had time to clean up from the battle before they'd dragged him in here. At least Theron had seen fit to heal his admittedly superficial wounds first.

All in all it had been a shitty day. He had almost died out there on the field today, *had* watched several men die at close hand. He was weak and exhausted from the battle, and now they were going to keep him up all night, until Captain Tsadhoq of the Delvan Royal Guard was satisfied that Steve really was the Dreamer they'd been sent here to find.

There was more—something about a *galdan* army, ten thousand strong, half a day behind the Delvir. There was also something about gifts. Steve didn't care; all he wanted was two or three bottles of wine, his bed and a night's sleep free of nightmares.

"We cannot, shall not, take any one man's word on this," Tsadhoq said. Steve sighed; the prospect of a night's sleep was almost nonexistent. Tsadhoq glared at him. Steve didn't care.

"What proof do you need, damn it all!" Erelvar said. "We have told you things that match all of the prophecies. I, the Arm of Death, have rescued this man from the Burning Hills. The Dark One has repeatedly tried to kidnap him. She has even tried to *lure* him away personally."

Steve's head snapped up. How in *hell* had Erelvar known that? Steve had told *no one* about that incident. Were there peepholes in his room or something?

"Is this true?" Tsadhoq asked him.

"Yes," Steve replied. "Although I'd like to know how the *hell* Lord Erelvar knows that."

Artemas cleared his throat. "I fear I am the answer to that, friend Wilkinson. The amulet you wear . . ."

Steve leapt to his feet, fists clenched at his sides. "I've been bugged!"

"Bugged . . . ?"

"Spied on. Watched and/or listened to covertly. Had my fucking privacy invaded!"

"Wilkinson, sit *down*!" Erelvar shouted, rising to his feet.

"SHUT UP!"

The room fell silent. Artemas and the dwarf looked at Steve in stunned silence, mouths open. Theron had shifted forward on his seat, watching both Steve and Erelvar intently. Erelvar glared through narrowed eyes, his right fist clenched to the point of trembling.

"It was for your own protection. . . ." Artemas began.

"That's what they said about Big Brother in *1984*, too. You can have your damned amulet *back*!"

Steve tore the amulet from his neck, shattering the fragile chain that held it on, and threw it across the table to Artemas. The sorceror caught it reflexively, immediately dropping it onto the table.

Steve turned and started toward the door to the council chamber.

"Where do you think you are going?" Erelvar said icily. Steve turned to face his "liege."

"I am going to bed, after I get stinking drunk. You people can stay up all night, if you like, and argue about whether or not I'm the 'Dreamer.' I'm going to get some sleep. It's after midnight already!"

He pounded the face of his watch with his forefinger in emphasis. Again he turned to leave the room.

"Excuse me," Tsadhoq's too-calm voice said at his elbow.

"What *now*?"

"May I see your . . . bracelet?"

"Bracelet? Oh, my watch. Why?"

"Only for a moment."

"Sure. Why the hell not?" Steve extended his arm to the dwarf.

"This is a . . . clock?" Tsadhoq asked after inspecting the watch for *several* moments.

"You got it."

"Such workmanship. . . ."

"Yeah, *takes a lickin' and keeps on tickin'*. Now can I *please* go get some sleep?"

"Certainly," Erelvar replied. "Morfael, escort Wilkinson to his room—in the dungeons. See to it that he wears this." Erelvar tossed Morfael the amulet. Morfael stared at the amulet a moment before replying.

"Yes . . . my lord," he said.

Steve glared around the council room before stomping out into the hall. Theron sat back in his chair, allowing himself to relax now that the crisis had passed.

"That was certainly a childish display," he said.

"Yes," Erelvar agreed. "It was. I am beginning to doubt the wisdom of pledging him."

"I wouldn't. He *did* almost perish today in what was, essentially, his first battle."

"That is not sufficient excuse." Erelvar was obviously still furious.

"I agree," Theron replied. "Shall we return to business? Captain Tsadhoq, after this I doubt we shall be able to convince you . . ."

"There is no need. He *is* the Dreamer."

"Oh?" Erelvar said. "What convinced you? His little tantrum?"

"No, that just convinced me he's got guts. No brains, but guts. However, he bears the sign."

"His . . . wrist-clock?" Artemas said.

"Yes," Tsadhoq confirmed, shaking his head. He stroked his leather beard-case thoughtfully before continuing.

"The Book of Vule says of the Dreamer that ' . . . the hours of the day and night shall be bound upon his arm.' No one could have known that save the Delvir."

"Good. Now, why is it you wished to find him?"

Tsadhoq frowned at Erelvar.

"You haven't changed a whit since the day you braved our pass, have you, Morvan?"

Theron raised an eyebrow. He hadn't realized until now that this stocky, black-haired man was personally acquainted with Erelvar.

"We bring gifts for the Dreamer," Tsadhoq continued. "We shall deliver these to him when he is released from your dungeon."

"I . . . see," Erelvar replied. "That may pose a problem. As my *felga*, he can accept no gifts."

"Then invest him, as you call it. We did not travel here from Deldwar to be told our gifts are not wanted."

"He is not ready. . . ."

"Nonsense. I fought alongside him today—the man is a warrior born."

"There are other considerations. . . ."

"Yes. He is the Dreamer. We *must* be allowed to present our gifts in accordance with prophecy. For now, we shall retire. You may give us your answer on the morrow. Good evening."

Tsadhoq turned and strode from the council chamber. Erelvar turned to Theron.

"Now what do I do? Invest him in reward for his behavior here tonight?"

"I cannot answer that, Erelvar. I would suggest you seek an answer in the chapel. But bear this in mind; Mortos has also given him gifts. You must decide between your pride and the prophecies. I think that Artemas and I shall retire as well. Good evening, my friend. I shall pray that an answer presents itself to you."

"Thank you."

Morfael stood guard above the entrance to the dungeon. He had relieved the normal guard—Steven might feel better knowing a friend watched over him. Besides, he would not be able to sleep for the turmoil in his mind.

What Steve had done in council tonight was not right. Neither was the fault totally his, however. More blame rested on Erelvar's shoulders than Morfael's liege would like to admit.

Morfael's gaze fell on the small, round door set in the floor of the tower cellar. He knew why Erelvar had done this; he had to save face before the Delvir—was forced to maintain his authority. Unfortunately, Morfael was certain Erelvar's response would have been similar had Morfael been the only one present. Things could not continue this way. . . .

The sound of a woman's voice brought him fully awake. His gaze swept the cellar—there was no one present.

"Good evening, Steven," the voice said. With a start, Morfael realized that it came from the dungeon. But who . . . how?

"Where are you?" Steve's voice said. There was a level of fear in it that Morfael had not heard from Steve before.

"Right beside you," the woman's husky voice replied. "I see your friends are taking such good care of you."

Morfael's blood chilled as he realized who was in the dungeon with Steve. He leapt from the stool to grab the key from its hook on the wall.

"Stay away from me," Steve said, almost pleadingly.

"Come with me, Dreamer. I shall give you the station you

deserve—not some dark prison to rot in."

Morfael didn't like the pause before Steve's refusal. He drew Steve's sword from its scabbard where it leaned against the wall. The blade burned like the sun.

"Take heart, Steven!" he shouted, fumbling the key into the locked door.

"Morfael! Morfael, get me out of here!"

Morfael hurled the trap door open. He kicked the rope ladder into the cell. Before he could start down, the sword's light illuminated Steve frantically scrambling up the ladder. A pair of green eyes behind him met Morfael's.

"I shall come again, Dreamer," the Dark One's seductive voice said. "Consider my offer well."

The green eyes vanished as Steve scrambled over the lip of the trap door. His eyes were wide and his breath ragged. Morfael placed an arm around Steve's shoulders which became an awkward embrace as Steve buried his face in Morfael's chest.

"Don't make me go back down there," he begged. "For God's sake, please."

"I shan't," Morfael assured him. He angrily kicked the door to the dungeon closed.

"Let us go speak with Erelvar," he suggested. This nonsense had gone far enough.

Erelvar walked to the door. He had heard no alarms—whoever was pounding on the door to his chambers this late had best have a good reason. He was in no mood for trifles—it had not been a good day.

He was surprised to find that Morfael was his late caller. More surprising was the fact that Wilkinson was with him.

"I gave orders for him to be placed in the dungeon," Erelvar said angrily.

"He was," Morfael snapped. "I released him after the Dark One came calling."

Erelvar paused, taken aback as much by Morfael's tone as by the unexpected answer.

"I . . . see. Very well, then. Place him in his quarters under guard." Erelvar began to close the door but Morfael's hand stopped it.

"We must speak, my lord," he said. For a moment Erelvar just looked at him. This was not like Morfael.

"Very well," he said. "Come in."

"Wait here a moment, Steven," Morfael said before stepping in and closing the door.

"What is wrong?" Erelvar asked, closing the door behind his friend. Morfael did not often become so insistent.

"Many things. To begin, I believe you owe your *felga* an apology."

Erelvar turned to face Morfael, astonishment plain on his face.

"Wha . . . !" he shouted. "Have you gone mad? You were in council tonight—you *saw* what happened!"

"I did."

"And you have the gall to tell me that I owe *him* an apology?"

"Yes, I do."

"Never. The man has not one scrap of honor about him."

"Would a man without honor resist the Dark One so steadfastly? Not once, but *twice*! The second time he was imprisoned by the very people she opposes the most, and still he refused her. You are wrong, my lord. Steven Wilkinson is an honorable man—one I am proud to call my friend."

"You expect me to excuse his behavior tonight?"

"Not completely. I do expect you to realize, however, that you are as at fault as he."

Erelvar slammed his fist onto the table beside him.

"*Me!*" he demanded. "How was this . . . outburst of his attributable to me?"

"Have you said one word to him that was not a command? Or an insult? Have you once consulted him as to what action to take with him? Do you wonder why he has no respect for you when you so obviously have none for him?"

Erelvar glared at Morfael for a moment. He finally turned away to sit in a nearby chair.

"I . . . do not understand him, Morfael," he said, staring down at the ornate carpet.

"You have not attempted to," Morfael replied, moving to stand in front of him. "Do you know that before he came here he had never seen a man die?"

Erelvar glanced up.

"Never?"

"Never. He grieved the deaths of the two men he killed to save my life. More accurately, he grieved the loss of his own innocence. Today, he almost died and had to stand over a man as he died of a gut wound. Did you know that?"

"That he almost died, yes. I was not aware of the other."

"Answer me. Would you not expect a child, who had never seen death, to become . . . unstable from such things?"

"He is *not* a child!"

"Is he not? In many ways, he is as naive. In others, he is wiser than all of us. I think it is long past time for you to become acquainted with your *felga*."

For a long time, Erelvar sat and stared into the fire, seeing nothing.

"You . . . are right," he finally said.

"Yes, I am. I shall leave you now, my lord. Steven is waiting outside. I suggest that you have a long talk with him. Good night." Morfael left the room, closing the door quietly behind him.

Erelvar sighed—he had already had this same argument with Glorien. There was also Theron's statement earlier, in council—that he would have to decide between his pride and the prophecies. Was he truly that petty? Was this nothing more than wounded pride? There was but one way to answer that question. . . .

He rose from the chair and crossed over to the door. Steven was waiting outside—bedraggled and weary. How great a toll *had* today taken on him?

"Please," Erelvar said, "come in." Steven walked into the room, sitting, almost collapsing, in the chair before Erelvar's desk.

Erelvar sat down behind his desk, glancing down. What to say—how to begin? Steven spared him the decision by speaking first.

"This is the first time you've ever even *looked* nervous," he said.

"I am not . . . accustomed to having my actions challenged," Erelvar replied, raising his eyes to meet Steven's.

"I know."

Erelvar rose from his seat and turned to look out through the narrow window. For a moment he said nothing as he stared out into the darkness.

"I . . . am a warrior," he finally began, "not a diplomat. Both Morfael and Glorien, perhaps Theron as well, have told me that I have . . . wronged you."

"I certainly agree with that."

"Why?"

"Because you *have*," Steven replied. "Ever since I arrived here, you've treated me like a stray dog. If I cause you the slightest inconvenience, I get locked up, and you never consult me about any decisions that concern me."

"Is that all of it, then?"

"Is that *all*? You mean that's not *enough*?"

"That is . . . not what I meant," Erelvar said, turning to face Steven. The youth had risen to his feet during the discussion. "Is there anything else?"

"Oh, just a few things," Steven replied.

"Then continue."

"All right. How about the fact that you expect me to learn everything in half the time you give everyone else? And God help me if I fail."

"You are exaggerating," Erelvar objected.

"Not according to Morfael," Steven countered. "I haven't even been here a year, yet. The other *regir* have been here almost two and Morfael for half a dozen. In spite of that I can still beat Morfael about one out of three times in sword practice."

"One bout in three? Against Morfael?"

"Yes, and Aerilynn a little over half the time. But do I ever hear any praise for that? No—you just tell me how bad I'm doing when I fail at something."

"I . . . see." Erelvar stepped away from the window to sit at his desk. After a moment, Steven sat again as well.

"Is there . . . anything else?" Erelvar asked.

"No . . . that pretty much covers it."

"Then Glorien and Morfael are correct—I *have* wronged you. As I said before, I am no diplomat—I know of no way to apologize other than to admit that."

"That's a pretty good start, actually," Steven replied.

"I will not ask your . . . forgiveness," Erelvar continued. "I realize that you must hate me for my past treatment of you. I am prepared to . . . release you from my service if you wish."

"I would rather stay on," Steven replied, "if that's all right with you."

Erelvar looked up to meet Steven's gaze. That had been the last thing he had expected to hear. . . .

"I don't hate you, Erelvar," Steven continued. "And, even though you won't *ask* for my forgiveness, you have it—*provided* you promise to consult me before deciding my fate out of hand."

"That is not always possible. . . ."

"When possible, then," Steven interrupted. "I certainly don't mean in the field."

"In that case, you have my word," Erelvar agreed.

"Then I guess it's my turn."

"Your turn?"

"To apologize—I am sorry for the way I behaved in council tonight. You will notice that I didn't list throwing me in the dungeon tonight as one of your problems."

That was true; there had been no mention of that at all. Erelvar nodded.

"Accepted," he said. "I have . . . misjudged you greatly."

"Not really. You judged the boy who fell out of Artemas's portal and into your life fairly accurately—but I am no longer the same person that I was then."

"No, you are not," Erelvar agreed.

"Friends, then?" Steven asked, rising to extend his hand across the table. Erelvar rose and accepted it.

"If you wish," he replied.

"Good. Now, if you don't mind, I'd like to go get some sleep— I really *am* tired."

Erelvar smiled, almost ruefully.

"I am afraid not just yet," he said. "We must discuss the morrow."

"Huh? What about tomorrow?"

"The Delvir have gifts they wish to give you," Erelvar replied. "To do so, however, you will have to be invested."

"But . . . am I ready for that?"

"Yes—you proved that today on the field."

"If you think so," Steve replied uncertainly. "Is that all?"

"Yes. Good night, Steven. Get some rest—morning will come all too soon for both of us."

"I will. Thank you . . . my lord."

Steve knelt before the altar in the small chapel of Mortos while Erelvar performed the intricate investing ceremony. Fortunately, his nervousness had driven the fatigue from him. It would have been embarrassing to stand here yawning while he was being invested.

" . . . the right to bear arms and administer justice in Quarin and the provinces under its protection. . . ."

Of which there were none. Apparently Erelvar had plans for his little kingdom.

" . . . accept this oath?" Erelvar concluded.

"I so swear," Steve replied.

"Then arise, and accept your mantle, *rega*."

Steve rose as Morfael settled the ceremonial violet mantle around his shoulders. He slowly turned to face those assembled in the chapel. Theron and Tsadhoq, Artemas and Felinor, Glorien and . . . Aerilynn. She smiled, proudly, as his eyes met hers. Steve felt his face flush a little.

He proceeded out of the chapel in what he hoped was a stately manner, followed by Erelvar and Morfael. As they entered the great hall, Steve paused; the hall was filled with hundreds of people. Steve felt a lump rise into his throat as the crowd began to cheer. . . .

Steve stayed the wine steward's ewer with his hand. Another goblet of wine and he would curl up under the table and go to sleep. Erelvar rose from his seat—the noise in the great hall vanished immediately.

"Captain Tsadhoq, of the Delvan Royal Guard, has brought gifts to present to Master Wilkinson," he announced. "I think this is the most appropriate time for those to be presented."

A murmur passed through the hall as Tsadhoq's men carried in a large, coffin-sized crate. A gasp passed along the high table as the Delvir swung open the lid to the crate.

Steve smiled. Here was the first suit of fully articulated armor he had seen since his arrival. Even Erelvar's Morvan armor was fashioned of discrete pieces, with mail protecting the gaps. Steve could see no mail on this. He could, however, see the intricate gold inlays that had been worked into the armor.

Am I supposed to wear this into battle? he wondered. It seemed too fancy to actually *use*.

"The finest armor ever produced by Deldwar," Tsadhoq informed him.

"I can believe it," Steve replied. "Steel?"

"Of course." The dwarf almost seemed offended.

"It seems brighter than steel."

"There are other metals added to give it strength."

"Alloys?" Steve was impressed. Apparently the Delvir had steel manufacturing almost to the stage of his world.

"Yes. It will not rust as mere steel does, either."

Steve had to hastily suppress a laugh. Stainless steel armor, no less!

"It must be alloyed with nickel, then," he guessed, digging up a forgotten bit of trivia.

Tsadhoq's eyes grew wide.

"That is correct," he said. "Please, inspect it."

"With pleasure." Steve left the table and walked over to the case. There *was* mail on the armor, but only on the backs of the joints.

"Truly a work of art," he announced. "I am honored to receive such a fine gift."

Tsadhoq smiled, his ornate beard-case lifting proudly. Steve supposed that his unsuspected knowledge of metals lent added weight to the compliment.

Morfael watched as Steven danced with Aerilynn. Glorien was right, it seemed. There was a closeness there that he had not seen Aerilynn allow any other man in the palace. He smiled. Such a thing could only be good for both of them.

A guard entered the hall, walking briskly to the high table. Erelvar exchanged a few whispered words with the man before dismissing him.

"The army pursuing the Delvir has been sighted to the north," Erelvar said, beginning to rise. "We must prepare. . . ."

Morfael stayed Erelvar with a hand on the shoulder.

"Wait for the dance to end," he advised. "A moment more is of no consequence."

"Morfael is right," Glorien agreed.

"It would seem I am outnumbered," Erelvar grumbled, hiding a smile. "Very well. But I must end the ball after this."

Steve turned to Aerilynn after Erelvar's grim announcement.

"From the dance floor to the battlements," he said, smiling ruefully. "I had begun to hope it would last forever."

Aerilynn flushed, glancing toward her feet as Steve realized what he had just said. He glanced away, feeling his own face grow warm. Then he felt Aerilynn's hand lightly touch his bicep and he turned back to face her.

"There will be other dances," she promised.

The autumn wind tugged at Theron's golden officer's cloak as he looked out over the gatehouse battlements. In the early morning light he could see Belevairn and the other Dread Lord on the Plains, supervising the construction of an immense ram. There was no doubt—the siege was over.

There were no hides or other coverings laid over the framework of the ram. Theron wondered briefly how they planned to protect the goblins as they worked it.

"Will they succeed?" Wilkinson asked.

"No," Theron replied. "They haven't the strength to take *this* citadel. They can only hope to hurt us enough to keep us within the walls."

The ram and the siege bridge it was mounted upon began to creep forward. Belevairn sat astride his steed on the prow of the advancing bridge. Surely he could not expect to defend the entire ram with sorcery?

As the goblins drew the ram onto the causeway, Theron heard the catapults fire from the walls far overhead. Flaming barrels of oil raced out to impact the wooden ram and siege-bridges. Before they could strike their target, the barrels struck an unseen barrier and shattered. Burning oil and barrel staves sloughed aside into the river.

A cry of dismay rose from the gatehouse. Theron merely frowned; he had known Belevairn would not simply roll the ram up the causeway for Erelvar to burn. The power it must take to maintain such a ward! It had to tell against him eventually.

"Lord Erelvar," he said, "fire the catapults as quickly as possible. Do not bother to aim them—just fire constantly. Rocks—not oil." Theron glanced toward Artemas. His cousin nodded to him in agreement. Perhaps that ward could be tried beyond its limits.

Erelvar complied without question. Soon the catapults were releasing an almost constant barrage of stones against the ward. Unfortunately, this strategy seemed doomed to failure, as well. Belevairn maintained the defenses seemingly without effort as the goblins pulled the siege-bridge with increasing speed across the smooth causeway.

The prow of the bridge struck the gate with a crash louder than thunder. Foot-thick wood buckled and twisted under the impact, but held enough to deny the enemy access to the gatehouse's interior. That would not last—the goblins rolled the ram across the log bridge. Soon a methodical pounding began against the gate.

"Can we do nothing to stop them?" Erelvar shouted.

"He cannot maintain that ward much longer," Artemas said. "He cannot!"

"Continue the bombardment, Lord Erelvar," Theron advised. "Every sorceror has limits, even Belevairn."

Theron prayed that they could reach Belevairn before it was too late. . . .

Belevairn watched as the ram slowly demolished the gate. Above him, stones, arrows and oil fell against his ward and were harmlessly swept into the river. The strain was beginning to take its toll against him, but the ward would stand long enough.

Eventually, the tortured wood could withstand no more. Huge beams fell aside as the ram delivered a final blow to the gate. Before them lay the killing room of the gatehouse.

Belevairn extended the ward into the gate, sealing the arrow slits and murder holes that would have made the assault impossible. The *galdir* moved the ram into the gate to assault the inner doors.

Unfortunately, his force was not large enough to take Quarin. However, he had seen the Dreamer atop the gatehouse with Erelvar and Prince Baltasaros. That was his goal—with Baltasaros and the traitor dead and the Dreamer in their possession, Quarin would not long stand against them.

Belevairn would prefer to take full credit for this endeavor. Alas, that was not possible; shared glory would have to suffice. He smiled behind the demon-mask.

A warmth, swiftly escalating into searing pain, began in his head—he had overextended! He hastily withdrew into the gatehouse, retracting the ward until it only protected those within. Some *galdir* would die, but he was certain enough would survive to take the gatehouse. Already the inner doors were beginning to yield to the great ram. Soon it would be time for Heregurth to bring the remaining *galdir* across the causeway. . . .

Belevairn's retreat did not go unnoticed. Above, Theron smiled when he saw that the ward had been withdrawn from above the causeway.

"Artemas," he said, "has Belevairn left the gateway unwarded?"

Artemas briefly closed his eyes before answering.

"Yes," he replied. "What good does that do us? He knows we cannot attack from that direction."

Theron smiled slyly before turning to Erelvar.

"Lord Erelvar," he said, "Belevairn has left himself open to us. We shall need several barrels of oil, a large net or piece of canvas, perhaps a tent, and some rope. . . ."

*   *   *

Heregurth waited impatiently while Belevairn's force demolished the gatehouse. Without the sorceror's magic, this assault would have been impossible. Still, he begrudged Belevairn the initial attack. How was he to distinguish himself while the other, older *Kaimordir* relegated him to inferior duties?

He, too, noticed the sudden reduction in the ward's protection. The few *galdir* on the causeway died quickly once its cover was denied them. Ah, well, the *galdir* bred quickly. It was their only strong point.

Still, if Belevairn had entered the gatehouse, it would soon be time for him to charge the causeway. He guided his mount into the air, preparing to issue the command to charge.

A burning projectile launched from the gatehouse. Whom were the defenders firing upon? Nothing alive remained on the causeway.

Inexplicably, the fiery missile halted in mid-flight and arced violently downward into the gatehouse. He watched, stunned, as the gatehouse became an inferno.

Belevairn did not know anything was amiss until he felt the barrels impact against his ward. The interior of the gatehouse erupted into flame as hundreds of gallons of burning oil sprayed over him and the *galdir*. With a shriek of agony, he wheeled his mount about, toward the gateway, as the flames engulfed and blinded him.

On the battlements above, Steve smiled as he saw Belevairn's blazing figure emerge from the gatehouse. The monster's hellish mount seemed untroubled by the flames. As Steve watched, Belevairn toppled from his mount, into the river.

At least something *can hurt the damned bastards*, he thought.

With a curse, Heregurth abandoned his fleeing *galdir*. He must hurry to recover Belevairn, or his husk, before the river carried him into the hands of the Olvir. He desperately hoped that the sorceror was still incarnate—he did not relish the prospect of facing Daryna with this failure alone.

Erelvar glared down at the scene below, sparing only the slightest glance for the retreating *Kaimorda*. Victory was his, but at what cost? Casualties had been minimal, thank the *Kanir*, but the damage to the gate was severe. Ironically, much of it had been inflicted in Quarin's defense. Artemas and Felinor had already begun to assist in extinguishing the fire that raged in the gatehouse.

He clenched his fists in frustration as he glared at the scattering *galdir*. In a few days they would return to besiege him anew with even greater numbers.

"No longer," he said quietly.

"My lord?" Morfael said behind him.

"Prince Theron, prepare your men," he said. "On the morrow, Death rides to war."

Chapter
------- Eleven ------------

HEAVY DROPS OF rain fell against the foliage overhead as Prince Laerdon looked across the half-mile of cleared land to the Morvan camp. He pulled the leather hood more securely over his flaxen hair as his eyes scanned the fort—it was almost complete.

Like all the invading waves before them, this one had finally run out of *galdir* and was forced to wait for reinforcements. The Morvan cavalry did not fare well in the forests, where the Olvir could ambush them from the trees.

Unfortunately, the Olvir did not fare well attacking the heavily fortified Morvan camps, either. And there was no way to recover the loss to the land that their mile-wide swath through the forest caused.

That fifty-mile-long path of destruction was a road, pointing like an accusing finger toward Mencar, the only true city of Olvanor. It had been cut with axes and fire and was proving an effective defense against the tree-borne Olvan archers. The Morvir could travel down its center safe from all but the luckiest shot. If the Olvir won through the *galdir* and ventured out onto the road to attack, the Morvan cavalry rode them down with ease.

Laerdon turned from the earthen fort with its palisade of butchered trees. The birdlike calls of unseen sentries challenged him as he made his way back to the abandoned winter lodge they had camped in. The lodge's owners should have been preparing it for the tribe's winter rest. Most of that tribe was dead, however, its women and children scattered to various nearby tribes.

Still, the underground lodge was well concealed, making an excellent forward camp. As he climbed down into the abandoned lodge he found the lore-master, Nolrod, waiting near the central fire-pit with Adhelmen, chief of the royal guard. Laerdon exchanged grim looks with the *daegir* of the royal guard under his command as he passed. He did not have to coddle or encourage these men—they knew the trails as well as he. . . .

"How long will this storm you have summoned last?" he asked Nolrod. A fire had been built in the fire-pit; with the rain, there was little danger of the smoke being seen. Laerdon stood near it, allowing the heat to steam the dampness from his leather cloak.

"It is difficult to say, highness," the lore-master replied. "At least through the night, and perhaps longer. It was called from the coast."

Laerdon nodded. The storm could continue for days, then. If it were not interfered with, it should put an effective end to the fires set by the *galdir*. Laerdon shuddered—he could almost feel the anguish of the tortured land here. What must it be like for Nolrod?

"What of the Morvir?" Adhelmen asked.

"They camp, as expected. Their fortress is already complete."

"A scout arrived while you were away," Adhelmen told him. "Another army passed Quarin yesterday morning."

"Damn! I presume their numbers are the same as the previous three?"

"No," Adhelmen replied, shaking his head. "The *galdir* number ten thousand. Twice as many as the previous waves."

"And the cavalry?"

"The same as before—one thousand."

Laerdon shook his head. Ten thousand *galdir* and another thousand cavalry to join the twenty-five hundred already here. There seemed no way to halt the slow, inexorable advance of the Morvir. Unless . . . the idea was almost too unthinkable to speak.

"Have they reached the second fort yet?" Laerdon asked.

"They should not have," Adhelmen replied, wrinkling his brow in thought. "The storm should have slowed them."

"How many guard that fort?"

"Two hundred—mostly wounded."

"Can we reach it ere they do?"

"Certainly, if we take no supplies beyond what we can carry." Adhelmen paused for a moment before continuing.

"Highness," he said, "do you mean to take that fort?"

"I do. It will be easier to overcome two hundred men there than two thousand here."

"Yes, but what purpose will it serve? It shall cost hundreds of Olvan lives, and two hundred wounded men are less threat to us than the approaching army."

"You do not understand, Adhelmen. We shall occupy their fort once we have conquered it."

"Occupy it?" Adhelmen's voice betrayed as much astonishment as his features. "But highness . . . we shall be trapped. . . ."

"Are *they* trapped, Adhelmen? No—they sit behind their walls of earth and wood and laugh when we attack them. This is our only chance to stop them. Nothing else has worked."

"But, highness, that is not our way. . . ."

"No, it is not," Laerdon agreed, "but our way has not served us here. When my father and I travelled to Quarin, my brother asked me if it was not the way of the ash to grow straight and tall."

"Of course it is—what of it?" Adhelmen asked.

"That was my response. Delarian then pointed out that even an ash will bend to grow around an immovable barrier and that it is no less an ash for doing so. The Olvir must learn to bend, Adhelmen—before we break beneath the Morvir."

Adhelmen looked to Nolrod, seeking deliverance from this disturbing line of reason.

"Delarian has spoken wisely," Nolrod said.

"Prepare for the march, Adhelmen," Laerdon ordered. "We are going to occupy that fort."

"Yes, highness," Adhelmen grudgingly agreed. Mencar's war-chief did not seem to be overly pleased with the prospect. Laerdon did not enjoy the thought either, but this road had to be denied the Morvir.

The fort seemed almost empty. Only occasional glimpses of movement betrayed the presence of the Morvir within. It had taken Laerdon and his army almost three hours to reach this point. In another few hours the fourth invading army would arrive from the north. Laerdon planned to give them an unpleasant welcome.

The rain was probably at least partly to thank for the reduced activity at the forts. Wounded men did not like the damp. With luck, the overcast skies would also help hide the *daegir* as they moved toward the fortress. Stealth seemed the best approach. . . .

"How shall we attack?" Adhelmen asked. "We have had little success against these forts."

"I think we shall have to come upon them unseen."

"Across the open ground? Unlikely. And then how shall we scale the walls?"

That was a good question. The logs of the palisade had been smoothed beyond the point of climbing. There seemed no way to gain entry . . . unless.

"Tell me, Adhelmen," Laerdon said, smiling, "do you remember how we used to climb onto the palace roof as boys?"

"Yes, but . . . you cannot be serious."

"I am quite serious."

"That will not work against walls with active defenders! We would be slaughtered like a lame buck by a pack of wolves."

"Unless we draw the defenders away from the section we wish to climb."

"With a false attack. . . ."

"Precisely."

Adhelmen thought for a moment.

"Only the *daegir* will know that child's game, highness," he finally said. "The tribesmen will balk at an attack on the fort if we are not with them."

"We shall only need a hundred or so of the guard," Laerdon replied. "The rest shall participate in the assault. Their presence would be missed otherwise. Pick the hundred yourself."

"Yes, highness." Adhelmen left to select the guardsmen that would make the true assault. Laerdon smiled. It was an insane scheme—perhaps that was why it was so appealing.

Laerdon lifted his face and peered out from beneath the deerskin hide that covered him. In the rain and dim light, the mud-covered deerskin blended almost perfectly with the desecrated ground of the road. These hides had once been winter supplies from the abandoned lodge. Somehow, it seemed only fitting that they be used against the Morvir.

Once certain that no one on the palisade was looking his way, Laerdon slowly inched forward another foot. For the greater part of an hour they had crept upon the Morvan fort in this manner; quickly at first, then more slowly as they had neared the camp.

This disguise would not hold much closer to the camp, but then it should not have to. Once the assault was begun, this side of the fort should be clear.

Laerdon heard a sudden commotion from the southern edge of the forest—Adhelmen, leading the diversion. Laerdon risked a glance from beneath the deerskin.

Adhelmen's force carried a crude ram, fashioned, no doubt, from some blighted tree in the forest. Laerdon smiled—Adhelmen had not been idle while he waited for his prince to move into position. This innovation would lend more credibility to Adhelmen's diversionary attack.

Alarms sounded from within the camp as the defenders roused to repel the attack against their gate. Laerdon hurled the deerskin from atop him, whistling to signal his companions. As hoped, the undermanned fort had concentrated all of its manpower on the side toward the attack. Laerdon's men crossed the last few hundred yards to the camp unnoticed.

At the base of the palisade three groups of six Olvir dropped to all fours, facing away from the logs. Five more formed another layer atop the six. All of the children of Mencar knew this game— it was intended to teach them the cooperation and balance they would need during their ten-year fosterage to the tribes. It had always been regarded as impractical once one reached adult-hood—until now.

With a practiced ease, almost forgotten, Laerdon clambered up the living staircase to the top of the palisade. He swung nimbly over the last few handspans of the palisade to land silently on the catwalk behind it. He unslung the short bow from his back and nocked an arrow into it, waiting. It would not do to attack with too few brethren on this side of the wall.

More Olvir gathered silently behind him, awaiting his signal to fire. Once the forty not forming the pyramids had stolen within the camp, Laerdon raised his bow.

"Vengeance for Olvanor!" he cried as forty arrows sailed across the camp. . . .

It was over in moments. The Olvir within the fort were piling the bodies of the Morvir into the center of the camp as Adhelmen led his men through the gate. The victory had not been without losses—a handful of Laerdon's men had fallen, while Adhelmen had lost almost two score of the royal guard and at least twice that many of the tribesmen.

"Well done, Adhelmen," Laerdon said reassuringly. "Without your diversion, we would have lost many more. That ram was a stroke of brilliance."

Laerdon was confused by Adhelmen's almost sheepish smile.

"Well, highness," Adhelmen said, "I had no idea your fool's plan would actually work. . . ."

Daemor rode at the head of the cavalry brigade, the elaborate harness of his *goremka* mount jingling lightly with each step. The steady, monotonous rain made the march difficult on the horses. The swampy mud of the road mired their hooves.

Daemor did not like it. This treacherous footing could prove disastrous if the Olvir decided to attack. Of course, they probably had no conception of the difficulties of heavy cavalry in this weather.

He had little liking for this facet of the war, anyway. The Olvir would hardly be less of a threat if they simply rolled over and died. Now the Umbrians—those people at least had *some* idea of how to wage war. They ought to; they got enough practice on each other. *That* would have been a campaign more worthy of his direction.

The silhouette of the second camp began to emerge from the rain ahead. Half a day's march barely managed in one! He cursed the weather, for all the good it would do. Still, it would be good to reach the fort—the Olvir had already cost him almost a thousand of the *galdir* in brief skirmishes since passing Quarin.

Now, leaving that fortress standing behind them was definitely a mistake in Daemor's opinion. Better to raze it before proceeding further . . . better still to take it. But to ignore it? Absurd. The Mistress had not asked his opinion in this matter, however.

Whooping in cowardly glee, the *galdir* finally sighted the fort. Although they knew they would not be allowed within the walls, it still represented safety to them. The Olvir would not attack too near the forts.

As usual, a few *galdir* began to break ranks to rush to the fort. Daemor began to order them back, but paused. Something was not quite right here. . . .

When no countermanding order was given to the rank-breakers, the remaining *galdir* broke ranks, as well. His sub-commander, Herun, looked questioningly at him, but Daemor merely shook his head, continuing forward at a normal pace. It was better to let the *galdir* test his premonition than the cavalry. Disciplinary measures could be taken later, if necessary.

There was no sound from the camp, he suddenly realized. Not even the sounds of the horses he knew should be there. He could envision the Olvir, with their hunter's tactics, striving to make as little noise as possible while they waited for their prey. He halted the cavalry and the supply train—it was too late to recall the *galdir*.

The thrum of bowstrings and the surprised and outraged shrieking of the *galdir* confirmed his suspicions. Damn, but he should have held them back! Fortunately, the only route the Olvir left them to retreat was back toward Daemor and the cavalry.

Daemor smiled behind his demon-mask. It was beginning to look as if the Olvir were not going to be such easy prey, after all. . . .

"Hold your shots!" Laerdon ordered as the *galdir* fled out of effective bow range. They had slain approximately three thousand of the *galdir*—without losing a single man.

"What do you think of these forts now, Adhelmen?"

Adhelmen scowled at him. "It is still not our way," the guardsman replied. "Unfortunately, it does seem to be necessary, though."

"It is no different than Mencar."

"Would you see all of Olvanor filled with stone cities? One might as well live in Umbria."

"No . . . no, I would not want that. . . ."

"It pleases me to hear that, my Prince," Adhelmen said, his expression softening. "This works for us now, but do not forget the land."

"What are they doing now?" Laerdon said, looking out across the artificial plain. The Morvir seemed to be making camp.

Adhelmen looked out toward the Morvan army. "Preparing to camp," he said.

"Why do they not attack?"

"Who can say? Perhaps they need to make plans. . . ."

"I want the rampart, the mantlets *and* the ram finished by morning," Daemor informed his sub-commanders. "Put the supply train in the center of the camp. I shall expect to see significant progress by the time I return."

"Yes, Dread Lord," Captain Herun replied.

"Be alert. There are undoubtedly more Olvir in the forest about us. Do not let them catch you unawares."

"Yes, Dread Lord."

Daemor mounted and guided his demon-steed outside camp. Once beyond the last sentry, he passed onto the Gray Plain. The Olvir were finally beginning to learn a little something about war. Daemor intended to teach them much more by the time this contest was completed. . . .

The trip to the third fort passed quickly once outside reality. In moments he was emerging less than a mile from the gate. It would not do to arrive too closely and find himself under attack by surprised defenders.

Soon, the wooden palisade emerged from the increasing gloom. It would be completely dark soon—the reinforcements would not be able to begin travelling until morning. Hopefully, he would not even require them. Best to have them on the way, however. . . .

"Hail the fort!" he called as he approached within earshot of the camp.

"Advance and be recognized!" The light from a sentry's lantern was directed at a location to the left of the gate. Daemor rode forward into its glow.

"Greetings, Dread Lord," called the sentry. "We shall open the gate for you. . . ."

"No!" Daemor replied, countermanding the order. "I shall enter in my own manner. The Olvir are about."

"Yes, Dread Lord."

Daemor guided his mount up and over the walls of the fort. A thousand cavalry should be enough for his purposes. That would leave half again that many behind to guard this fort. More than enough. . . .

Laerdon awoke slightly before dawn. He climbed to the catwalk and looked to the northeast. The first faint light was beginning to show over the forest—little more than an almost imperceptible lightening of the night sky. The sounds of axes and hammers continued through the steady rain.

"They are still building?" he said.

"Yes," Adhelmen replied. "I do not like the sound of it."

Laerdon shrugged. "If they attack, we have an ample supply of arrows."

"I suppose so. . . ."

The sky continued to brighten as the sun rose, unseen, behind the clouds. The silhouette of something large and square began to become visible through the receding gloom. Gradually, the sound of hammers and axes was replaced with the sound of horns.

"They prepare to attack," Adhelmen said needlessly. Within moments all one thousand of the Mencar Royal Guard were atop the catwalk, prepared to drive back the attackers.

The large structure began to move forward slowly, along with several smaller things, only now becoming visible. As the day continued to lighten, the night constructions of the Morvir revealed themselves. A large ram dominated the advancing force. Its front was a heavy, wooden wall to protect its users from arrow fire. It moved forward on wheels apparently stolen from the supply wagons.

Other, smaller walls had also been built. These moved forward, apparently pushed from behind by those they protected. Narrow slits in those walls allowed the attackers to fire from behind their protection.

"I like the looks of this even less than I liked the sound of it," Adhelmen said. "How do we fight *this*, my Prince?"

"I'm thinking!"

"Think quickly."

"Fire through the slits," Laerdon said. "It's all we can do!"

"What of the ram?"

"We can do nothing about the ram. When they break through, we shall fight them. That is all I can say."

"Then that is what we shall do."

"Forgive me, Adhelmen. You were right . . . this is not our way."

"We had to try. *Our* ways have not worked well in this war."

The mobile walls finally pulled to within reasonable range, and the Mencar guard began firing. The walls served their purpose well, though. For every arrow the Olvir slipped through the narrow slits, five were embedded harmlessly in the wood.

Slowly the attackers closed the distance to the fort. The wheeled walls stopped within a hundred yards of the palisade. The ram continued forward, arrows bristling from its protective wall like a hedgehog. Laerdon wished for oil, although setting the rain-soaked wood of the ram afire might be difficult.

The ram finally reached the gate of the fort. It struck the gate with a sound like thunder, shaking the entire palisade. Wood cracked and splintered under its impact. The wielders began slowly pulling the ram back for another strike.

The sound of the ram was a signal. From behind their protective walls the *galdir* charged. Now the Olvir had targets! Three thousand died before they reached the fort. Another two thousand died as they swarmed up the sides of the fort. Another crash of the ram sounded as the first few *galdir* gained the top of the palisade.

Laerdon abandoned his bow for the sword at his side as a *galda* scrambled over the wall in front of him. The creature was easily slain, but another had gained the catwalk beside him. Its spear glanced off his mail shirt as he turned to face the monster.

Had they met in the trees, Laerdon would have had no fear of this beast. The *galdir* died easily in the forest. Here, there was no place to flee, however; no place to run to gain the distance to use his bow. Here he must stand and fight.

Fortunately, those in the fort were the Mencar guard. Unlike the tribesmen, they were better trained at close fighting. Laerdon caught the haft of the spear with one hand, as he disembowelled the *galda* with his sword. He threw the spear over the wall, hoping to strike one of those below.

The bar holding the gate cracked and bent as another blow fell against it. Surely the next would see the gates open. The guardsmen would not stand up against the Morvir nearly so well. Laerdon returned his attention to the battle as another *galda* pulled itself over the wall before him.

He thrust his sword into its throat as he deflected its spear-thrust with his wrist. He glanced quickly along the catwalk.

Everywhere the *galdir* swarmed over the wall, faster than the Olvir could kill them. Several Olvir lay slumped against the palisade, dead or dying. More lay at the base of the rampart, having fallen from the catwalk as they died. And still the *galdir* came.

Laerdon brought his sword down viciously on a *galdan* hand as it came over the wall. There was a cry of pain, receding as the beast fell to what Laerdon hoped was its death. He spared another glance for the ram. It was almost ready for another strike.

A line of blue-white fire burned itself onto his vision as a blast unlike anything he had heard before deafened him. Laerdon blinked his eyes quickly, trying to clear his vision before one of the *galdir* came upon him while he was blind.

Something slammed into him from the side, knocking him from his feet. Laerdon fell onto the catwalk, desperately clutching the edge to keep from falling to the ground below. He heard a *galda* squeal in pain before something warm and foul-smelling fell atop him.

"My Prince!" Laerdon heard Adhelmen's voice say.

"I am alive, my friend," he replied. "My thanks."

Around them the sound of battle slowly died. Soon the sound of bowshots began again.

"What has happened?" Laerdon asked.

"The . . . *galdir* flee . . . highness." Adhelmen's voice was weak, quavering.

"Adhelmen?" Laerdon's vision was slowly clearing. He could barely see Adhelmen where he sat, leaning against the palisade. He reached forward to touch his friend. Warm wetness coated his hand.

"Adhelmen!"

"I am well. . . ."

"No, you are not. Lie still." Laerdon rose to his feet. By now his vision had almost cleared. The ram sat against the gate, ruined and burning.

Across the field the bodies of *galdir* were strewn with perhaps a score of the Morvir lying about the ram. The remaining guardsmen leaned against the palisade, exhausted and horrified. Perhaps three hundred remained standing.

"We need litters!" Laerdon shouted. "Get the wounded to the ground!"

Daemor scowled; the ram was lost. The rain would extinguish the fire soon, but most of the structure had collapsed with the bolt of lightning that had ignited it. Daemor cursed as the surviving Morvir withdrew behind the mantlets. If they had not lost every major sorceror in their service at Quarin, *that* would not have happened. Daemor was certain the gate had almost been ready to give way.

Still, it had not been a complete loss. Less than three hundred of the Olvir remained alive to defend the fort. However, less than a hundred of the *galdir* had survived. Had they not fled immediately upon the first sign of sorcery, the fort would have been taken. Damned stupid beasts.

Now he would have to either lead the attack with the Morvir or lay in for a siege. An assault with ladders would cost him many of the cavalry against the Olvan archers. A siege would be safer, although longer. Unless . . .

"Captain Herun, begin work on a ditch and double rampart around this fort. See to it the rampart on the fort side shields the outer rampart."

"Yes, Dread Lord."

"I shall return shortly."

Daemor mounted his *goremka* and rode toward the fort. There was some risk in this, but he doubted that any of the Olvir carried consecrated arrows. Once he had ridden to within a hundred yards of the fort, he stopped.

He could feel the eyes of the Olvir on him, but no arrows flew. Finally a flaxen-haired Olvan appeared atop the wall. Daemor blinked in surprise. Prince Laerdon? It was possible—the royal guard of Mencar would rank such a commander.

That shed a different light on the situation. It would not do to create a martyr, here.

"What do you want, foul one?" the blond Olvan shouted.

"I have come to discuss the terms of your surrender," Daemor replied, ignoring the insult. The Olvan's speech *did* sound like the more formal Mencarian dialect.

"Surrender to the Morvir? Ha! I would sooner fall on my own sword—it would be swifter."

"Not so, Prince Laerdon," Daemor said. The figure on the palisade stiffened slightly. Daemor had been correct.

"I wish only the fort," he continued. "You are free to take your wounded and retreat to the forest."

There was a long pause. Daemor was certain the young prince was consulting with those around him. Foolish—a commander should make his own decisions. But then, what did the Olvir know of command?

"Why should we trust you?"

"Must I explain it to you? I *shall* retake this fort. Less than three hundred of you remain alive. I have almost four times your number, and you are not experienced in siege warfare. However, a siege will be costly to me. I would avoid that."

"By tricking us into leaving so you can trample us in the open beneath the hooves of your horses."

"Believe what you will—my offer is sincere."

"Come take your fort, foul one. You may find it more difficult than you think."

"Very well," Daemor replied. "On your own head be it."

Daemor turned and rode back to his camp, slipping briefly out of reality to shorten the ride. Perhaps the sight of Daemor's reinforcements would change young Laerdon's mind. They should arrive by late afternoon.

Now that the young prince had rejected his offer, though, Daemor could act with impunity. Laerdon would no longer be seen as a martyr, but merely as a fool.

Laerdon watched the sky as the last remnants of the storm slowly scattered on the wind. Silence reigned across the camp except for the occasional moan of the wounded. In the center of the camp a huge pyre burned, fueled by what had been crude shelters built by the Morvir. Laerdon could not take his eyes away from it for long. . . .

So many had died here—much more than would have died fighting the same number of *galdir* in the forest. Adhelmen was right; this was not their way. If Nolrod had not destroyed the ram. . . .

"Water," Adhelmen whispered beside him.

"Yes, here." Laerdon held the waterskin to Adhelmen's lips. "No, not too much."

"Should you . . . not be on the . . . walls, highness?"

"Easy, my friend," Laerdon replied. "No. The Morvir do nothing but dig now. They fight their wars with shovels."

"That is . . . their way."

"Yes, and this is not ours. I realize that now."

"No . . . you were right. This army . . . has gained no more . . . ground toward . . . Mencar. . . ."

"Silence, old friend. Rest now—there will be time to talk later."

"Highness!" someone shouted from atop the palisade. It was Olsande, Adhelmen's lieutenant.

"What is it, Olsande?"

"You must see this!"

Laerdon cursed under his breath. Damn the Morvir! Could they not give them a moment's peace! He reluctantly left Adhelmen to climb to the top of the palisade. Adhelmen's wound was serious, but not necessarily fatal—if treated promptly. Nolrod was in the forest, however. None of the wounded had received proper care—only the best Laerdon and the others could give.

"What is it, Ol . . ."

Laerdon fell silent as he saw what Olsande had called him for. Morvir, apparently from the southern fortress, were just coming into view over the horizon. They were still too far away to estimate their numbers. How many had been left behind in that fort—two and a half thousand?

As they approached, Laerdon was finally able to discern their numbers. There were about a thousand of them. Now the final attack would surely come. The surviving Olvir were already preparing—setting extra quivers to hand, some with an obvious smell of pine tar. At least any fire would not spread to the forest. . . .

The attack did not come, however. Instead, the reinforcements took a position to the south where they began entrenching. Laerdon watched for a moment, stunned.

"Why do they not attack?" he wondered. "They outnumber us seven to one."

"I do not know, highness," Olsande replied. "It is as though we fight a war against badgers. All they do is dig."

"It is late in the day," another guardsman volunteered. "Perhaps they wait for tomorrow."

"Perhaps. . . ." Laerdon did not think so, however.

"Let me know if anything changes," he ordered before returning to the camp below.

By dawn the Morvir had dug a trench completely encircling the original fort. It stretched from the two camps, about half a mile from the fort north and south to within a hundred yards at its closest approach to the east and west.

Even with their digging completed, the Morvir did not attack. They just sat behind their earthen walls and watched. Once, one of the guardsmen was able to shoot a Morvan who raised his head too high above the rampart. After that, no more promising targets were sighted.

They lost a few more of the injured. Adhelmen's wound continued to worsen. Laerdon spent most of the morning sitting by the guard chief, listening to his ragged breathing, giving him sips of water when he roused.

"What . . . is about?" Adhelmen asked during one of his more lucid moments.

"Nothing," Laerdon replied. "They just sit in their ditches and do nothing."

"They . . . wait for us . . . to starve," Adhelmen said.

Laerdon looked at Adhelmen in shock. He was right . . . he had to be. It was so simple. . . .

Laerdon let his shoulders fall. The *Kaimorda* need do nothing but wait to reclaim his fort. Time was on his side—in less than a sennight another army would pass into Olvanor and arrive here.

"I should have surrendered . . ." he muttered. An iron grip closed around his wrist. Startled, he looked down into Adhelmen's glaring eyes.

"The day . . . you surrender to . . . the Morvir, highness," Adhelmen said, "I . . . shall kill you . . . myself."

A coughing fit followed Adhelmen's words. Laerdon gently laid the war-chief back on his palette.

"Easy, friend," he said.

"Water . . ." Adhelmen gasped. Laerdon lifted the skin to Adhelmen's lips.

"Never surrender," Adhelmen told him. "Not for me . . . not for anyone."

"No," Laerdon agreed. "Never."

The next day was no better. More of the wounded had died during the night, and Adhelmen continued to waste away. A fever had set into the wound, sending the war-chief into occasional delirium and frequent unconsciousness. Laerdon feared he would not last the day.

Laerdon sponged precious water over the war-chief's brow. Rain would have been a welcome sight at this point. Most of the fort's water supplies had been spilled or contaminated during the battle with the *galdir*. Now the water that was left barely filled three barrels.

At one point Adhelmen, in his delirium, called for Laerdon by the name they had not used since childhood. Try as he could, Laerdon could not convince the war chief that he was there. He could only weep while his friend called for him.

Adhelmen seemed to become still about an hour before sunset. Laerdon bent over him for fear the war-chief had finally expired. Adhelmen's breath still moved, however weakly.

"He will not last much longer, I fear," a familiar voice said behind Laerdon.

"Nolrod!" Laerdon said. He quickly rose to face the lore-master. The lore-master seemed different, somehow. Older than even his silvering hair suggested—weary.

"The wounded have need of you, master," Laerdon began, without asking how the lore-master had gained the camp. Nolrod silenced him with an upraised palm.

"Of what use is it to tend the wounded who will soon be dead?" he asked. "If I use my power to heal these, I can not save the strong and all shall perish."

Laerdon could not believe what he was hearing.

"But Adhelmen . . ."

"Will soon be dead, highness. I could not save him with all my power."

"Then why have you come?" Laerdon's voice was bitter.

"He was my friend, too, young prince. Or do you presume to have the wisdom to judge me?"

For a moment Laerdon glared at Nolrod. Then he finally lowered his gaze.

"No, master," he replied. Tears hung, unshed, in his eyes. Something foul and bilious rose in his throat.

"I have come to rescue those I can," Nolrod continued.

"Rescue? How? Your power lies in the forest—not in this ravaged land."

"Many of the people have died here. Where the Olvir shed their blood, there too is power."

"What of the wounded?"

"No, them I cannot rescue. You shall learn why soon enough."

"We cannot leave them for the . . ." Laerdon paused. He *knew* what Nolrod would say next.

"Yes, highness. You know what must be done."

"C-can you . . . awaken him . . . ?" Laerdon's voice shook. He wanted to scream.

"Yes, I can grant you that much."

"Let me . . . tell the others first." Numbly he summoned Olsande, passing on the horrible news. The lieutenant paled at Laerdon's words.

"Y-yes, highness," was all he said before leaving.

"Rouse him, Nolrod," Laerdon said once Olsande had left.

The lore-master bent over Adhelmen's unconscious form. Nolrod sang softly over the war-chief, rubbing lavender leaves against his temples. Laerdon watched, clenching his jaw.

After a moment, Adhelmen's eyes fluttered open. Nolrod stepped away from him, allowing Laerdon to kneel by his friend.

"Leave us," Laerdon said.

"As you wish." Without looking, Laerdon knew that Nolrod had departed.

"That . . . bad, is it?" Adhelmen asked.

"Nolrod says . . . you are going to . . . die."

"Do not grieve, my friend. I have . . . no regrets. We have . . . done well, and learned . . . much."

"Nolrod has come to rescue us."

"Good."

"He says that . . . that . . . we cannot . . . take the wounded." Laerdon was close to tears. For a time Adhelmen was silent.

"Better at the hand of a friend," he finally said, "than the Morvir."

"I would sooner drive the knife into my own breast."

"No, my Prince. Let . . . let it be your last gift to me."

"Adhelmen . . . I . . ."

"Silence. Laerdon?"

"Yes?"

"Carry . . . the knife . . . with you. Remember me."

The tears could no longer be held back.

"I will. I swear it."

"Thank you. Do it; I feel . . . myself slipping . . . away again. . . ."

"G-goodbye, my friend." Laerdon placed his knife against Adhelmen's chest. Try as he could, though, he could not bring himself to drive it home.

"Do not . . . leave me for . . . the Morvir. Do it!"

Laerdon clenched his teeth and drove the dagger into Adhelmen's chest. For what seemed forever he stared into Adhelmen's eyes until they finally looked away into nowhere.

Laerdon collapsed over Adhelmen, sobbing like a child, cradling the lifeless body in his arms. After a moment, a firm hand took his shoulder.

"Highness, we must proceed," Nolrod said. "After sunset I cannot work this changing."

Laerdon lowered Adhelmen gently to the ground. He placed the knife, uncleaned, back into its scabbard.

"Give me the knife, highness."

"No!"

"You will be able to carry nothing. If you wish to keep it, give it to me, then remove your clothing."

Reluctantly, Laerdon handed the knife to Nolrod. Part of him wanted to hurl it over the wall instead. No—he had promised Adhelmen. The others had already removed their war-gear. Laerdon followed suit.

"Drink this," Nolrod said, handing Laerdon a wooden cup. Laerdon stared at the yellow-white liquid within it.

"What is it?"

"Wolf's milk. Drink."

Laerdon managed to swallow the contents of the cup around the lump in his throat. It was warm and bitter and lay like a stone in his stomach. Once Laerdon had drunk the milk, Nolrod began to sing again. This song was neither gentle nor soothing.

Without warning, Laerdon's stomach knotted about itself. With a gasp, he collapsed as the cramps consumed his entire body. Pain travelled from his stomach, outward along his entire body—blood pounded in his temples until he thought his head would burst. . . .

Slowly the pain ebbed, and he rose to his feet, blinking his eyes against the memory of pain. He sniffed the air, growling low in his throat.

The smell of death filled this place. He longed to run, to be far from it. Many of the pack had been lost here. He tilted his head back and howled his anguish. The survivors of the pack echoed his cry.

Up they went, to the top of the wooden pit that held them. The drop was long, but the ground below was soft as he landed on it to tumble down the hill. He rose to his feet, sniffing the night air. The wind carried another scent to him—a scent he hated. He howled again, in anger and challenge. Again the pack echoed him. . . .

"In the Mistress's name!" Herun said. "What was that?"

"Wolves," Daemor replied. "Close by. I like not the sound of this. Tell the men to . . ."

Before Daemor could complete the order, a wolf larger than any he had ever seen leapt the rampart to land upon Herun. The captain's scream abruptly ended as the wolf's fangs tore out his throat.

Daemor's sword was through the beast's heart as soon as it leapt from Herun toward him. He pulled himself from beneath the immense carcass. Everywhere wolves, larger than newborn colts, ravaged the camp. Daemor silently commanded his steed to him.

This was an enemy the Morvir were not prepared to fight. There was no strategy to such a battle, only an attempt to survive. There had to be hundreds of them—where had they come from?

The *goremka* arrived, appearing out of thin air beside him. Daemor quickly climbed into the saddle, eager to be away from this mindless carnage.

Before he was seated firmly in the saddle, something crashed into his side. He desperately groped for the dagger in his belt as the flaxen-furred wolf bore him from the saddle.

Had he been mortal, the impact with the ground would have left him senseless. As it was, he barely had the time to catch the wolf's jaws with his hand. As he wrestled the monster's mouth away from his throat, it locked its blue-green eyes with his.

His surprise almost cost him his life. The wolf's muzzle slipped from his grip and plunged toward his throat. Daemor threw up his left forearm to block the attack. With a cry of rage he rose from underneath the wolf, lifting it with his right arm and hurling it from him in a single motion.

The wolf landed upright, crouched as if to spring again. Instead it circled him, as if it knew what the sword he now held was. Indeed it might. . . .

The wolf darted in toward his left. Daemor dodged, swinging the sword about to impale the man-beast. It was already gone. Daemor whirled back to the right, reaching for his dagger with his other hand. But his left hand was gone, along with the arm below the elbow. The empty mail sleeve flopped uselessly at his waist.

Instinct saved him—he laid his sword across the attacking wolf's cheek before the realization hit him. With a yelp of pain, the wolf-prince darted back out of range. It began to circle him again, snarling.

"Now I have reason to hate you as well, young prince," Daemor hissed at the beast.

The monster made one last feint before turning to flee. Daemor watched as it vanished over the far rampart, far faster than he could hope to catch it. The rest of the much-reduced pack followed it. Angrily, Daemor sheathed his sword. He picked his arm up from the ground and wrapped it in a dead soldier's cloak.

All about him the camp was in disarray. He seemed to have lost about two-thirds of his original force to this . . . this attack. Discipline reasserted itself quickly, however. Soon the surviving soldiers were slaying those wounded too far gone to be saved.

"Into the fort!" he ordered. "Leave the wounded!" He would get the men settled into the fort before returning to Delgroth. Daryna would not be pleased by this.

"We shall settle our debts soon, young prince," he said to the empty night. . . .

The pack took shelter in a briar thicket. Whimpering and whining, the injured wolves huddled together, licking each other's wounds. This had not been a good night for the pack. Before today they had been . . . larger. Many had died. The pack leader settled into the press, snarling at any who tried to lick where the walking dead man's claw had cut him. Tomorrow, they would move on. . . .

The morning sun woke Laerdon. All about him the survivors from the fort were rousing. His right cheek burned. His fingers came away from it bloody. Dim memories of last night came to him—dark things filled with blood and hatred. None of the Olvir would meet his eyes—or each other's. Where was Adhelmen?

Dead, came the answer in his mind. He collapsed to the ground underneath the briar thicket, sobbing.

Chapter
-------- Twelve -------------

STEVE WATCHED AS Erelvar pounded the hilt of his dagger on
the council table like a gavel. At least Steve wasn't the cause of
the commotion this time. . . .

"What do you mean, the Umbrians shall not venture onto
the Plains?" Erelvar said, once order had been restored to the
council room.

"Exactly what I said," Aldric replied. "Our duty lies in Umbria.
On the morrow, I shall take the Umbrian *regir* and the royal guard
and depart for Umbria."

"Prince Aldric," Theron said, "a hundred *regir* and two hundred
lesser cavalry shall make little difference in Umbria."

"More there than if they fight on the Olvan side of the river!"

"Then, if that is your intent," Erelvar said, "you are not needed
here. Go and prepare your men."

"Very well. Lord Erelvar, it is not that I do not . . ."

"I understand, although I do not truly have a homeland. I think
you do not see the best way to defend it, however."

"Yes, you have made that clear. Good night, lords."

Erelvar waited until Aldric left the room before continuing the
meeting.

"Damn!" he said. "I was counting on those cavalry!"

"Yes," Theron replied. "That reduces us from over four hundred
to about a hundred and fifty."

"I think that settles it, then—we shall have to press into Olvanor
instead of the Plains. We cannot face Morvan cavalry on the
Plains with naught but infantry."

Steve wrinkled his brow at Erelvar's words. There was something he knew about cavalry and infantry. He'd been trying to
remember it for days. It had been in world history, with Professor
Roland. The man had been absolutely nuts about it. . . .

"You cannot fault the boy for loving his country," Glorien began.

"Pikes!" Steve shouted, slamming his palm on the table. Every eye in the council room turned to him.

"Oh . . . excuse me," he said, flushing.

"What did you think of?" Theron asked.

"Pikes," Steve replied, less enthusiastically. "The 'footman's best weapon against cavalry,' or so Professor Roland always said."

"I have never heard of them," Erelvar said suspiciously.

"No, cavalry here hasn't reached the point it had in our world at that time. The Swiss pikemen were hell on cavalry, though."

"What manner of weapon is this . . . . pike?"

"It's a heavy spear about, uh . . . twelve to sixteen feet long. It had a heavy, spike point and, I think, a crossbar behind the head. And a sharp butt, to plant in the ground."

"Is it used like a boar spear?" Delarian asked. "You ground it and brace it?"

"Yes," Steve replied.

"I don't see how such a thing could work," Erelvar said. "Cavalry are somewhat smarter than boars."

"So what are they going to do?" Steve countered. "Not charge? If so, the pikes will have done their job."

Erelvar thought for a moment. "They could just maneuver around . . . ?"

"The pikes *can* be moved. A lot faster than the cavalry can dodge them."

"I think the boy is right," Tsadhoq said. "I can see how it would work, especially in numbers."

"The Morvir will just use crossbows," Erelvar said.

"You can use the pikes to block arrows," Steve said. It was all coming back to him, now. Thank God, Roland had been such a fanatic on the subject.

"How, in Mortos's name, can spears block arrows?"

"The back ranks hold them up at an angle. It's like firing through a dense thicket. The arrows bounce around and fall to the ground."

"It would require cool heads to use such a weapon," Theron mused. "As well as some practice in handling such unwieldy things."

"Perhaps the Delvir?" Erelvar suggested, glancing toward Tsadhoq.

"Hmm," Tsadhoq replied. "We cannot return to Deldwar until this war is over. Yes, we shall experiment with these 'pikes.' We will need some time to craft them—a day or so."

"Very well," Erelvar said. "Master Wilkinson shall assist you."

The barracks were quite busy when Steve visited them. The Umbrians planned to leave at first light. Steve found Arthwyr sorting through his belongings.

"Hello, Arthwyr," he said.

The Umbrian turned to face him. "Hello, Steven," he said.

"I wanted to talk to you before you left."

"I'm surprised Aldric allowed you back here."

"I offered him a choice—he could let me back here or explain to Erelvar why he and I were dueling in the barracks."

Arthwyr chuckled. "Now I am truly surprised he allowed you back here. Why have you come?"

"To say goodbye. You're one of the few friends I have here."

"I am pleased to hear that," Arthwyr said, squeezing Steve's shoulder. "I owe you my life since that day against the *galdir*."

"What?"

"You did not know? I fought behind you when we were thrown from our horses."

"I . . . had no idea. . . ."

"Yes, had you not raised the standard, I would not have known to find you. I would not have survived alone . . . what is so funny?"

Steve swallowed back his laughter. "That . . . was an accident, Arthwyr. I just used the standard to help me stand up; I had no idea I was creating a rallying point."

Arthwyr smiled. "Still, it saved many of us."

"Must you leave?"

Arthwyr looked away from him. Steve thought that the Umbrian almost looked ashamed.

"It does not please me to desert Lord Erelvar, Steven," Arthwyr finally said. "But I must think of my clan, as well. I am torn by honor—I can desert my sworn lord, or my clan. Do not force me to abandon a friend as well."

"I'm sorry, Arthwyr. Good luck."

Arthwyr led his skittish horse off the raft onto the beach. Ferrying the horses across this way was risky, but they had been fortunate thus far. Once ashore, he mounted. The only gear he carried was in the saddlebags behind him. Prince Aldric wanted to travel as light as possible.

Arthwyr allowed his hand to stray to the dagger at his belt. Steven carried his old dagger now, while Arthwyr carried the one he himself had bought for the strange man he had befriended. He glanced back toward Quarin.

A lone figure stood on a tower of the upper wall, sunlight glinting from its armor. Steven? It seemed likely. Arthwyr raised his hand in farewell before joining the rest of the cavalry. The figure on the wall waved back.

"Goodbye, my friend," he said, knowing his words could not reach across the river. "May the gods bring us together again someday."

Steve watched as the Umbrians departed. The small band of cavalry looked insignificant compared to the armies of Morvir that had preceded them.

One figure below waved. Steve waved back, certain it was Arthwyr. He hoped the guy made it through this all right—he was a lot like Frank Caldwell, back home. Even down to trying to hook Steve up with Rea. . . .

"Goodbye, party animal," Steve said, smiling. "Keep your goddamn head down."

Once the Umbrians had ridden out of sight, Steve descended from the tower. Tsadhoq was probably looking for him. They had to get started on those pikes and, hopefully, get them finished soon enough to have a little time to practice with them. It was going to be a busy day. . . .

Chapter
-------- Thirteen------------

LORD JARED STARED at the maps and papers on the table before
him. Firelight flickering through the window of the ruined manor
cast odd shadows about the room that the lamps could not drive
away. Jared glanced up from the maps as a woman's distant shriek
momentarily distracted him.

Thus far the Umbrians had proven more tenacious than Jared
had expected. The manors at Aberstwyth, Bath and here at
Weyton had fought them to the last man, costing him precious
time. Now it was a race to see who would reach Castle Aldwyn
first—his forces or Botewylf's.

From the maps and the reports of the scouts, it was obvious that
King Botewylf would win that race. Especially considering that
Jared's forces were burdened with the siege engines that would
be needed against Castle Aldwyn.

"Suggestions?" he asked. "How can we reach the castle ahead
of Botewylf?"

"We cannot, Dread Lord," Captain Rashine replied. Jared
looked at him coldly. The man glanced away from Jared's gaze.

"That is obvious, Captain," Jared said. "I have no need of your
counsel to determine that."

"Our main problem is the terrain," Captain Garth interrupted.
"That and the siege engines. Without the catapults, we could
possibly reach Castle Aldwyn ahead of Botewylf's army."

"That would do us little good," Jared replied. "We cannot very
well tear down the castle with our bare hands."

"No, Dread Lord. I was merely observing . . ." Garth leaned
forward to inspect the map more closely.

"Yes? Continue, Captain."

"Perhaps we take the wrong approach, Dread Lord," Garth
said.

"Don't give me riddles, Captain."

"I was merely thinking . . . instead of attempting to reach Castle Aldwyn before King Botewylf, perhaps we should keep *him* from reaching it at all."

"Intercept him en route? How? We would be made to travel even further."

Garth stood up, leaning over to point out locations on the map.

"Send the catapults and supply train on to Castle Aldwyn," he said. "The *galdir* and two thousand cavalry should be sufficient to protect them. The remaining cavalry, with no supply train, could easily overtake Botewylf. Lord Phelandor's forces should overtake the catapults by . . . noon two days from now, giving them additional protection."

"Yes," Jared agreed. His gloved fingers picked up a knotted cord, measuring distances on the map. "We should be able to intercept Botewylf . . . here."

"Assuming we force march the cavalry," Garth said.

"I think that is imperative."

"That is fairly gentle terrain," Garth observed, "for Umbria, that is."

"Yes," Jared said. "If we can avoid his scouts, Botewylf shall not be expecting us. Excellent—Captain Garth and Ulan, your men shall move to intercept King Botewylf. Rashine, you shall travel with the catapults. Garth and Ulan shall rejoin you . . . here, two days outside Castle Aldwyn. I expect to move out at dawn, Captains."

"Yes, Dread Lord," they replied.

"Good. Now leave me." The captains left the manor hall Jared had selected for his council chamber. He rose to stand by the narrow window—Weyton burned as the Morvir scavenged what plunder they could from the battered town.

The fingers of his right hand toyed with the latches of the gold demon-mask. A part of him longed to remove it, but he lowered his hand. He would be dust in seconds. It would almost be worth it, though, to have the damned thing off for the first time in centuries. He removed his glove and stared at the withered hand beneath it.

He glanced up as a woman shrieked in the distance. The same one? It didn't matter. Women were little more than an idle curiosity to him . . . now. Jared turned from the window, back to the table—he had a war to direct. . . .

*   *   *

Arthwyr was silent as the cavalry rode through what was left of the village. Aldric and the others had fallen equally silent at the grisly sight of the corpses that littered the village. It must be particularly hard on the Aldwyns. . . .

There were no unburned buildings in the town. The Morvir had been brutally thorough. No smoke rose from the ruins—this village had been sacked weeks ago. This was the first habitation they had passed since leaving Quarin this morning. Arthwyr feared what they might find further in.

Arthwyr glimpsed movement from the corner of his eye. When he turned toward it, there was nothing there to be seen.

"Aldric!" he whispered.

"I saw it too, Arthwyr," Prince Botewylf replied. "When we pass the next corner, take your clansmen back around this way. We shall see what we can catch. . . ."

"They are probably fellow Umbrians. . . ."

"We need news. Do as I command."

"Yes, Prince Botewylf." Arthwyr didn't like the way Aldric had assumed command of their small force. Still, someone had to command, but he would rather it had been anyone but Aldric.

At the next turn, Arthwyr and his nine clansmen separated from the main group. If the refugees were not warriors, they would probably not notice the ten missing riders. After waiting a moment, Arthwyr led his men back until they found a crossway that should lead them back to Aldric's men.

Five of them went ahead on foot, moving as quietly as possible. The other five kept the horses back to avoid being heard. Arthwyr slowly crept forward, hoping that Aldric had the sense to slow down for them. . . .

Apparently he did. Arthwyr caught a glimpse of the cavalry over a ruined wall. Someone else was also watching the cavalry from behind that wall. It seemed to be a boy, judging by his size.

Arthwyr and the other four crept up behind the lad as he watched the cavalry. Some small sound must have given them away, because the lad suddenly turned, spying Arthwyr.

The boy was fast, Arthwyr had to grant him that. He was off like an arrow, fleeing down the maze of twisted, rubble-choked alleys. He also picked places the horses could not follow him through. Arthwyr was damned if he was going to let some stripling lose him, though.

He finally caught the boy by the collar, barely blocking the knife-thrust the lad aimed at his gut. He twisted the boy's arm around behind him, squeezing the wrist until the knife fell to the ground.

"Calm down, boy!" Arthwyr shouted. "Don't you recognize your own countrymen?"

"Countrymen?" The boy's struggles ceased. Arthwyr relaxed the pressure on the boy's arm before pushing the boy ahead of him back down the alley.

"That's what I said," he replied. "Now, come along. Prince Botewylf wants to ask you some questions, and there are some of your clansmen who would probably be happy to see you as well."

"Aldwyns?"

"Yes. Come along. Here, take this sorry knife back. Just don't try to use it on me again. It would probably give me lockjaw."

"What clan are you?"

"Madawc."

The lad regarded him suspiciously for a moment.

"Well, am I going to have to kick you back there? Move your behind, boy!"

Aldric and Arthwyr's clansmen were waiting at what had once been the village well. From the smell, Arthwyr doubted that anyone would get decent water out of it for a long time.

"What's your name, lad?" Aldric asked once Arthwyr had brought the boy to him.

"Rhys."

"Are you from this village?"

"No, lord."

"I thought not. Where are you from?"

"Aberstwyth."

"Aberstwyth has fallen?" one of the Aldwyns asked.

"Yes, lord."

"I should not be surprised with the number of Morvir and goblins that have passed into clan Aldwyn's lands, Cai," Aldric said to the Aldwyn that had spoken.

"Do you have any food?" Rhys asked.

Aldric scowled in thought. "Our supplies are low," he began.

"We can share one meal with the boy, Aldric!" Arthwyr objected.

"Aye," Aldric agreed. "Do you know where Quarin is, Rhys?"

"Yes, lord. To the northwest."

"There are no Morvir or goblins behind us. You can reach Quarin in a day—they will take you in. If you have any friends here with you, I suggest you take them as well."

"Thank you, lord."

Aldric glanced up at the sky. The sun would set in a few hours.

"Are there any buildings in town intact enough for us to camp in, Rhys?" he asked.

"No, lord. We . . . I have been staying in a barn outside the village. I only came in to look for food. . . ."

"We? Then there *are* others with you?"

Rhys glanced over to the other Aldwyns. Cai nodded to him reassuringly.

"Y-yes, lord."

"How many?"

"Less than a score, lord."

"How far is this barn?"

"Less than an hour away."

"Very well. You run ahead and tell your friends we are coming. We have enough food to share with them tonight."

"Thank you, lord!"

"Run along now, lad. We'll follow." Aldric watched as the youth ran off down the street.

"Cai, do you know this village?"

"No, Prince Botewylf."

"No matter. I don't believe the boy will think to hide his trail, or that he could if he decided to try."

Jared sat astride his mount, watching the lowering sky. This storm had arisen too suddenly—he suspected sorcery. The Umbrians generally shunned magic like a plague, but some few still practiced it. The impending storm had come from the west and had not yet broken. Hopefully it would hold off a bit longer.

"The scouts have returned, Dread Lord," Captain Garth reported.

"Has Botewylf's army been sighted?"

"Yes, about an hour away."

"Good. We shall prepare an ambush behind that hill." Jared pointed to a hill overlooking the road, roughly half a mile distant. "Have your men hit the main body of the force. Leave the supply train intact—we can make use of it."

The men had ridden hard for the last two days to make it here. Still, they seemed eager for the coming battle. Jared sighed quietly. He had seen too many battles over the centuries. Still, one did not wish to disappoint the Mistress . . . .

King Botewylf glared at the threatening sky overhead, as if his displeasure could prevent the imminent rain. If it began to rain, they would have to halt the march—this pitiful excuse for a road would become a miry trap for the wagons of the supply train.

He had hoped to make Castle Aldwyn by late tomorrow. Still, if the weather slowed him, it would slow the Morvir and their siege engines even more. Perhaps they would gain some time on the invaders.

A fat drop of rain fell onto his hand. Another soon followed it. The rain began to increase steadily. Soon this road would become a small river. . . .

"We shall camp atop that hill," he ordered, pointing to the highest nearby hill. "Hurry, before we're all drenched!" The army began to move toward the hill as the storm broke.

Jared lay prone, watching as Botewylf led his force, supply train and all, toward the very hill Jared had selected for his ambush. Was the man not even going to scout it? Apparently not . . . the king was the first to reach the foot of the hill.

"Now, Dread Lord?" Garth whispered from beside him.

"*I* shall order the charge, when I am ready," Jared hissed back. "Silence."

Botewylf's men began to advance up the hill, apparently intent on making camp. Jared smiled . . . the storm was doing most of his work for him—Botewylf had allowed himself to become too hurried. Jared watched—when they were a quarter of the way up the hill, he crawled back down out of possible view before rising to hurry to his mount.

"Order the charge," he commanded. He spurred his *goremka* forward as the trumpets sounded the charge. . . .

Botewylf's head snapped up at the unexpected sound of trumpets. It was an ambush!

"Behind the wagons," he ordered. "Quickly, or we are all dead men!"

The Morvir cavalry crested the hill, their charge gaining momentum as they reached the downslope. At their head rode one of the Dread Lords, personally leading the charge.

Old fool, Botewylf thought. *You should have scouted the damned hill.*

"Hold fast!" he shouted as they made for the cover of the supply train. The panicked horses threatened to send the wagons tumbling down the hillside.

"Kill the wagon horses!" he ordered.

The wagons would break the force of the charge, making it impossible for the Morvir to use those damned lances he had seen demonstrated at Quarin. It was not much of a plan, but it was their only hope at this point.

A few stragglers were caught and overrun by the charging Morvir. However, the wagons broke the Morvir's momentum as Botewylf had hoped they would.

The mounted attackers flowed around the wagons like a spring flood. Some few even leapt the wagons to tumble, horse and rider, down the hill, through Botewylf's men. The area about the wagons became a frenzy of combat.

Botewylf watched in dismay as the Morvir decimated his disorganized men. Perhaps. . . .

"Follow me!" he shouted. A handful of men around him followed as he made his way down the hillside. The force of the initial charge had been broken. If he could rally his men atop one of the other nearby hills, he might still salvage the battle. . . .

Jared blocked an attack from his sword-side, bringing his blade about in a smooth arc, decapitating his attacker. The initial engagement was going well. The unexpected attack had demoralized and confounded Botewylf's army. This was good, since Botewylf's forces outnumbered Jared's by almost five to one.

Where had Botewylf gone? If he succeeded in rallying his troops, he could possibly delay Jared here for several days. That was something that must be avoided. Jared spurred his mount into the air after disembowelling the opponent on his shield-side. Once safely into the air, he surveyed the battlefield.

Roughly half of Botewylf's force had been slain. Jared had lost less than a tenth of his own men. Excellent—that brought the numbers more within his liking.

King Botewylf was halfway down the hillside, accompanied by almost a hundred of his so-called cavalry. As Jared had suspected, the king was apparently attempting to rally his disorganized troops. Presumably, he was trying to reach another of the nearby hills.

Jared scowled. He must not allow Botewylf to reach another hilltop. Jared's cavalry would be almost useless attacking uphill. Botewylf's superior numbers would easily enable him to hold such a position.

Jared held his sword aloft, concentrating. The fires in which the Mistress had forged his mask responded. As the gold warmed upon his face he directed it into his outstretched arm, into the blade of the sword. With a cry of agony, he hurled his arm downward, releasing the pent-up Power onto the battlefield below.

Steam boiled from the sodden ground as the fire-bolt incinerated those few caught within it. The already demoralized Umbrians scattered from the immediate area. Jared's mount hurtled earthward, landing in full gallop as he shouted an order to charge. He heard the hoofbeats of a score or so of the Morvir behind him as he led them toward Botewylf's retreating band. . . .

A red flash from behind drew Botewylf's attention. He looked back to see the Dread Lord leading a tiny band of cavalry to attack him. It was already too late to outrun them. . . .

"Wheel and stand fast!" he ordered. The cursed monster had apparently divined his plan. Perhaps his men could defeat this small band and still reach the next hill.

The Morvir cavalrymen bore down upon them. Despite the uneven, downhill terrain they rode with the heels of each rider almost touching those of the man next to him. Erelvar had been right—Botewylf had never seen such horsemen.

The charge impacted the front rank of Botewylf's own small band of cavalry. Instead of halting at the front ranks, the charge barrelled through his small force. A score of Morvan cavalry slew half a hundred of his men in mere heartbeats. Botewylf was nearly thrown from the saddle of his own mount as he blocked a blow from a passing attacker.

The Morvir halted their charge just below his force, having only lost one or two of their number. Still, they no longer had the momentum of the charge to aid them. Botewylf led his remaining men against them. He still outnumbered this band by almost three to one.

As the battle was joined, it soon became apparent that that was not sufficient. Unlike the goblins, the Morvir were skilled warriors, and the Dread Lord was unstoppable. Any man who came up against him was dead before they had exchanged half a dozen blows. Once, Botewylf saw a good, solid blow glance harmlessly from the monster.

It was quickly apparent that Botewylf himself was the Dread Lord's goal. Botewylf set his jaw, spurring his mount forward to meet the monster. Perhaps his sword, blessed by the priest of Uldon at Weymour, would prove more effective. Perhaps not. . . .

A ramlike blow landed on his shield. Botewylf heard the wood of the shield crack from the impact. The Dread Lord deflected Botewylf's blow as if it were but a child's feeble strike. Gods, but this monster was strong!

Botewylf blocked another sword-strike with the shield, fighting to remain in the saddle. He attempted to thrust beneath the monster's shield. The Dread Lord lowered his shield to block it. The shield drove the point of Botewylf's sword down, scraping it along the flesh of the demon-horse.

White fire trailed behind the sword point as it sliced through the hide of the monster's steed. With a shrill, almost human, scream, the unholy thing leapt into the air, spinning to attack Botewylf with its fangs.

He had barely enough time to interpose his shield between himself and the demon-horse. Demon fangs bit through bronze and wood like leather. Botewylf desperately brought his sword blade across the monster's throat before its jaws could reach his arm.

The thing died instantly, although Botewylf had not thought the wound so deadly. Its weight pulled him from the saddle as it fell to the earth. Botewylf fought to remove his arm from the trapped shield. He gained his freedom just in time to block another blow from the Dread Lord with his sword.

He faced his inhuman opponent across the body of the slain demon. About them his men were slowly overcoming the outnumbered Morvan cavalry. One of Botewylf's men attacked the Dread Lord from behind. It parried the blow with its shield, spinning to slay the man's horse from beneath him.

Botewylf sliced across the monster's back. It was like striking a tree, although a line of white fire momentarily marked the path of the sword. With a cry of agony the Dread Lord turned, slamming his shield into Botewylf with the force of a catapult.

Dazed, Botewylf feebly attempted to regain his feet until some-one grasped his hair and pulled him to his knees. He briefly looked up into the red, burning eyes of the monster as its sword came down across his neck. . . .

Jared turned from Botewylf's corpse, the king's severed head clutched in his shield hand. His back burned where King Botewylf's sword had struck it. Ignoring the pain, he surveyed this small portion of the battle.

Few of the Morvir who had accompanied him still survived. He blocked an attack by a mounted Umbrian with his shield. He drove his own sword up under the Umbrian's breastplate, using the sword to lift the dead warrior from his horse.

Jared clambered into the empty saddle, fighting the horse under control. It had been centuries since he had ridden a true horse. Normally, they would not tolerate his presence. However, on a battlefield, with so many frightening smells already present, he was certain he could control it.

The last Morvan went down nearby. Jared tried to reach the fleeing horse, but the press of Umbrians kept him from it. He blocked a blow with his shield, slicing through the Umbrian's elbow with his own blade. There were approximately a score of them remaining.

The force of his own blow almost toppled him from the sad-dle. Damn these Umbrian saddles! He fought his way aright, once again—a difficult task without the stirrups he had grown accustomed to.

He was surrounded by the Umbrian cavalrymen. Were this his own mount, he would simply take to the air. As it was, he was hopelessly trapped in the press of battle.

Two men pressed in on either side of him, attacking vigor-ously. A sidewise blow from Jared's shield toppled the man on his left from the saddle. The man's horse fled, creating a temporary gap through the Umbrian cavalry. Jared blocked a blow from his right with his own sword and wheeled his mount to the left.

Only one man sought to block his escape. Jared easily dis-patched him as the stolen horse sped downhill. Soon he had escaped the press surrounding him.

The Umbrians were close behind, however. Fools. They prob-ably did not have the means to truly slay him. Unless one of them had claimed Botewylf's sword. . . .

He attempted to turn his mount sharply to the right. The horse's feet slid from beneath it on the wet hillside. Jared felt the bone of his right shoulder break under the impact. Damn! Now that arm would be useless until he could return to Delgroth.

The Umbrians charged past him, unable to stop as quickly. Fortunately, their horses instinctively leapt over him. Some did not recover and sent their riders tumbling into the small river that had once been the road.

Jared pulled himself from beneath the horse and struggled uphill. The Umbrians below could no longer charge him, at least. However, a knot of unmounted men charged him from above. What they did not see, however, was the cavalry unit bearing down on them. Jared stopped, glancing behind him.

The surviving Umbrian cavalrymen fled. Only then did the men above him look back. By then, it was far too late—the Morvan cavalry was already upon them.

Captain Garth rode down to him, leading an extra mount. Jared mounted the skittish horse, fighting to keep it under control. At least the damned saddle had stirrups. . . .

"Take this," he said, handing Botewylf's head to Garth. "Mount it on a lance. Make certain the Umbrians see it."

"Yes, Dread Lord."

The battle was nearly over, as it was. Botewylf's army barely exceeded Jared's cavalry in number—and most of the survivors were infantry. The sight of their king's head on a lance finished it. The survivors who could escape did so. Most were overrun by the cavalry.

"Do not pursue them," Jared ordered. "We do not have the time."

"Yes, Dread Lord," Garth replied. Jared sighed inaudibly. Without his mount it would be a long march to castle Aldwyn. Hopefully he could make it there by the time Rashine and the siege equipment arrived.

Aldric watched the Morvan army march past below. The reinforcements that had passed Quarin four days before Aldric had apparently arrived just before them. His own force of three hundred cavalry suddenly seemed very small, indeed.

Brett ap Botewylf, captain of his father's guard, lay on the hilltop beside him. "Doesn't look good, highness," he said. "Ten thousand or so goblins and almost two thousand Morvir. . . ."

"We'll have to use harassment tactics," Aldric replied. "We

can at least slow those catapults from reaching Castle Aldwyn. The Morvir will not expect an attack from behind." In truth, the Morvir rode at the vanguard of the army. An attack from behind would give Aldric's men time to flee.

"That won't work, highness. Not with the Dark One's demon about. He can follow us anywhere with that damned horse of his."

"Where are the others?" There should have been almost three times the cavalry and at least three of the Dread Lords.

"The demons could be anywhere," Brett replied. "The cavalry, I cannot say."

Aldric continued to watch the scene below. He did not like the absence of so many of the cavalry. The Morvir were scouting heavily. If they had come across signs of Aldric's force . . .

"You have not heard from Lord Jared today?" Phelandor asked Jared's captain, Rashine.

"No, Dread Lord," the mortal replied.

"Has he . . . returned regularly?"

"Yes, lord. However, if all went well, he was to engage King Botewylf today. I would not expect to see him until much later."

"No doubt." Phelandor glanced skyward, unconsciously searching for some sign of Jared. He had tarried overlong here already. The Mistress would expect him back to take command of his next wave of reinforcements. Although why Jared should be in command of the Umbrian war while Phelandor was relegated to shuttling reinforcements was beyond him.

"I must depart," he said to Rashine. "Maintain the patrols. These fool Umbrians never realize when they are outmatched."

"Yes, Dread Lord."

Phelandor turned and urged his mount into the air. He could enter the shadow realms from the ground, but to do so might panic the mortal horses. He paused, glancing about one last time for some sign of Jared before slipping from reality.

Aldric and Brett watched as the Dread Lord vanished. His ascent had driven both of them to seek cover under the low brush covering the hillside.

"Now that was too close for my liking," Brett said.

"Aye," Aldric agreed. "Let us return to the men. We may be able to attack before he returns."

"Yes, highness," Brett said resignedly.

* * *

Aldric watched as the small patrol passed beneath them. There were only fifty riders—his larger force could take them easily, with minimal losses. . . .

The men under you are neither your friends nor your country-men—they are playing pieces, Erelvar had said during their train-ing. *If your opponent has more pieces, you cannot afford the loss of even one. Strike quickly and retreat—let him follow you: only stop to fight on ground of your own choosing. The horse gives you that option. . . .*

Minimal losses would not suffice . . . he must lose as few men as possible, preferably none.

"What lies ahead?" he asked of Cai ap Aldwyn.

"More of the same," Cai replied. "Hills, valleys and bracken."

"We must find a suitable ambush site," Aldric said.

"Ambush? But we outnumber them. . . ."

"Recall how Erelvar said to fight a superior army. This is but a small part of the whole."

Cai looked at him in surprise for a moment. "Aye, I recall. Since when do you speak with Lord Erelvar's words?"

"Since I began to realize how true they were," Aldric replied. "Quickly, before we lose the patrol."

The Morvan scouts were keeping to the hilltops for greater visibility. Aldric placed his force behind the tallest hill along the patrol's path.

The Morvir mounted the far hill, pausing to survey the sur-rounding countryside. For miles there was no sign of human existence. All had fled the invading army. Aldric watched as the patrol started down the hillside, riding toward them. He waited until the first horseman touched the foot of the hill before hastily backing down to rejoin his men.

He mounted silently, taking his lance from Brett. He started up the hillside as quickly as the horse would take him. The Quarin-trained cavalry followed him.

At the top of the hill, the horse's struggling trot became a gallop. The Morvir, halfway up the hill below, paused in obvi-ous astonishment. This was, undoubtedly, the last thing they had expected to see.

Aldric lowered his lance, leaning into the downhill charge. Beside him the rest of the cavalry rode, stirrup to stirrup, forming a line twice deep across the hillside. Brett led the royal guard two horse-lengths back. His larger, less trained force would dispatch any survivors.

The Morvir had recovered by the time Aldric's charge reached them. There was little they could do against the downhill momentum of the horse-borne lances, however. Aldric's lance pierced a Morvan breastplate, hurling the slain warrior from the saddle.

A sword blow rebounded solidly from his shield as he passed another. Behind him, from the corner of his eye Aldric saw another lance take the Morvan from his mount. Then Aldric was through the patrol, turning his horse to the left, slowing its charge.

A glance back showed him the remnants of the Morvan patrol mixing with Brett's men. Though less trained, the downhill charge gave the royal guard enough advantage. The last few Morvir fell beneath the lance heads of Brett's charge, as Aldric circled back.

"Gather their horses!" he commanded. "We don't need them returning home and warning the army that something is amiss!" Besides, the horses would be meat—his small force was desperately low on supplies.

Aldric took a moment to survey his force. Despite the surprise of the ambush, he had lost two of the *regir* and six of the guardsmen. If he had not ambushed the Morvir and had trusted instead to his superior numbers . . .

"My thanks, Lord Erelvar," he said quietly.

Captain Rashine glanced again at the lowering sky. The storm had swept in from the west with an almost unnatural swiftness. If it began to rain, as it seemed it would, the catapults as well as the wagons of the supply train would soon become hopelessly mired.

He was about to give the order to make camp when a commotion began among the *galdir*. Turning he saw a group of cavalry charging from the northern flank. He blinked in surprise—there could be no more than three hundred of them, at most.

"First company!" he ordered. The thousand cavalry of the first company wheeled and moved out to the north. Before they had even begun, however, the enemy cavalry had engaged the *galdir*. Their lances scattered the cowardly beasts like sheep. Where in the Mistress's name had the Umbrians gotten lances? They rode like Morvir—stirrup to stirrup in tight order.

The Umbrian cavalry cut a swath of destruction through the

galdir, toward the supply train. As Rashine watched, they hurled burning missiles into the wagons, turned and retreated. They were back among the hills before the first company could reach them.

"Sound the recall!" Rashine ordered. The trumpeters responded, recalling the charging cavalry. Rashine had no intention of sending his cavalry into ambush.

"Prepare to make camp!" he ordered, glancing again toward the sky. Where was Lord Jared?

"Get the supplies out of those wagons!" he shouted. He doubted there would be much to salvage from the wagons, however. The spineless eunuchs had fled the burning wagons as quickly as the *galdir* had routed before the cavalry.

Ten wagonloads, up in flames. He quickly dispatched his four companies of cavalry to defensive points around the formation. He could afford to lose no more supplies. . . .

Aldric watched from the hilltop. No Morvir pursued them. Apparently the enemy feared ambush. A pity—they would not have been disappointed. Aldric smiled ferally. He had lost no men in that foray and had slain almost a thousand goblins. The damage to the supply train was more vital, though.

"What now, highness?" Brett asked.

Never strike from the same place twice, Erelvar's words said in his mind. *Let them waste time searching where you have been. Keep them confused as to your numbers and whereabouts. Make them increase their patrols—large patrols are simpler to find and avoid.*

"We circle behind them," Aldric replied. "They will search for us to the north. We shall travel south and ambush a few of their patrols. Let's make them think there are more of us than there really are."

Aldric mounted and led his men westward. They might not be able to defeat this army, but they could certainly slow it.

Slow their progress and attack their supplies and you can besiege the enemy as they march. . . .

Chapter
-------- **Fourteen** -------------

STEVE SHIFTED IN the saddle. He had forgotten what a *distinct* pleasure it was to ride a horse all day long. At least he was in much better shape now than he had been the last time he'd ridden this long.

He glanced at his watch—it was just after noon. Lunch would be eaten on the march, cold. Theron and Erelvar wanted to intercept the next wave of Morvir as far north as possible.

The cavalry rode behind the two hundred Olvan archers Erelvar had brought from Quarin. In front of them marched the legion. The Delvan pikemen had been formed up into centuries and incorporated into the legion itself. That way, Theron had reasoned, they could choose quickly between a front line of pikemen or legionnaires.

The Delvir had taken quickly to the new weapons. They definitely possessed the nerve to use them. Steve just hoped the pikes worked as well as Professor Roland had seemed to think they did.

Steve glanced behind them at the supply train. Other members of the cavalry had, for the moment, been delegated as food distributors. They were mobile enough to distribute the cold rations without slowing the army in its march. Of course, if they weren't saddled down with the fifty wagons they could make even better time.

However, one saying that this world shared with Steve's own held true; an army marches on its stomach. Take away those supplies and they would soon be defeated, pikes or no. Steve thanked the Olvan *rega* who handed him his cold rations. Being Erelvar's standard-bearer held some advantages, such as not having to play mounted waiter.

Steve shifted in the saddle again. They had been riding since well before dawn. Of course, Erelvar and Theron expected to encounter the next wave of Morvir at any moment. Another advantage to carrying the standard was that one was able to overhear Erelvar's discussions with Theron and Tsadhoq.

Theron had been given command of the composite army—a decision which had surprised Steve. In truth, the major decisions were being shared between the three commanders, but in battle Theron's word would be final. Somehow, Steve could not imagine Erelvar taking orders from anyone.

"You should not squirm so," a woman's voice said beside him. Steve turned to see Aerilynn's turquoise eyes gazing at him from beneath her barrel-helm. Both she and Glorien had accompanied this march.

"It only makes it worse," she added.

"I'm not used to riding this long," Steve replied. "I'll be glad when we find the Morvir."

"Do you long for battle now?" Aerilynn asked.

"No," Steve said, shaking his head. "In fact, I'm scared to death. I just want it to be over. . . ."

"Then I can agree with you. I too want it to be over."

"You shall both have your wishes granted soon, I believe," Erelvar said. "Morfael has returned."

Morfael had been sent ahead to meet the scouts sent out the previous day. Now he rode back, ahead of the unmounted Olvan scouts. Theron and Tsadhoq joined Erelvar as Morfael rode up.

"Have they sighted the enemy?" Theron asked.

"Yes," Morfael replied. "The same numbers as before, save that two of the Twelve ride with the army on this shore."

"That means they intend for the army on the far shore to proceed despite us," Erelvar said.

"As I suspected," Theron replied. "They outnumber us heavily."

"We can only hope that Master Wilkinson's pikes prove effective," Erelvar said. "Even had we equal numbers, we dare not allow their cavalry to engage ours."

"Oh, they'll be effective all right," Tsadhoq said. "After having had a day to work with them, I'm certain of it."

"How far are they?" Theron asked.

Steve listened as the scouts themselves arrived and the commanders began questioning them. Yes, the armies were of the same size and were composed of the same mixture of *galdir* and Morvir. Yes, two of the Twelve rode with the army on this shore and they were less than a half-day's combined march away. Yes, they had seen scouts from the approaching army, but had managed to avoid them.

"We should meet them just before sunset, then," Erelvar observed.

"No," Theron said. "We shall meet them earlier than that."

"How?"

"By abandoning the supply train. It can catch up to us during the battle."

"That is a dangerous tactic, Theron," Erelvar said. "The supply train will be undefended. . . ."

"Yes, but now we know where they are. I think there is little risk—or would you rather fight during the night?"

"No, I would not. But what of the army on the far shore?"

Theron gestured expansively toward the languid waters of the Absinthian. "They are on the far shore," he said. "They cannot cross quickly enough to be a threat."

"Very well," Erelvar agreed. "Tsadhoq, what is your opinion of this?"

"I'm not certain," he replied, scowling. "I'd hate to lose those supplies, but we need to hit them before sunset. And you both want to catch them as far north as possible . . . I say we do it."

"It is agreed, then. Morfael, instruct the drovers."

"Yes, my lord." Morfael turned his mount and rode back to the supply train.

"I hope this mad scheme works as well as those you have had in the past, Prince Theron," Erelvar said.

"What is your report?" Daemor asked the scout. "Have you sighted the traitor?"

"Yes, Dread Lord," the *rega* replied. "They are two hours' march to the southeast. They follow the river."

"Did you see any of their scouts?"

"No, Dread Lord, we did not."

Daemor frowned. That meant that Moruth's scouts had seen and avoided his.

"What of their numbers?" he asked. If his force outnumbered theirs as much as he suspected, it would not matter if Moruth knew his position.

"As Lord Heregurth reported, there are seven hundred Delvir and a thousand Nymrans. There are also two hundred Olvir. However, we only counted a hundred and a half cavalry."

Daemor paused. "Only a hundred and fifty? Moruth should have three times that many cavalry."

"There were no more, Dread Lord."

"I see. How large is their supply train?"

"They had no supply train, Dread Lord."

"What? That is impossible."

"There were no wagons or pack horses."

"You may go." No supply train? It was apparent that Daemor would have to investigate this personally.

"What do you make of this, Daemor?" Lord Hilarin asked.

"That Moruth is either a fool or a genius. I shall have to determine which myself. Send no more scouts until I return."

"And if you do not return?"

Daemor glared at his counterpart. "Do not count on that overly much, Hilarin. I am *not* a fool like Belevairn. Even if I *am* sorely wounded, the Mistress will return me to battle rather than letting me sit untended out of spite." Daemor turned and led his mount away toward the south.

"I would not be so certain of that, Daemor," Hilarin muttered behind him.

Steve shifted in the saddle. According to the latest news from the scouts, they should be meeting the Morvir in just under an hour. He glanced at his watch—it was about four-thirty. That should give them about three or four hours of light.

A sudden commotion drew his attention. Some of the legionnaires were shouting about the sky. Steve glanced upward and his heart climbed into his throat.

One of the Twelve sat astride its mount, far above them. Steve wondered if Theron had taken aerial reconnaissance into account when he decided to abandon the supply train. . . .

The scouts had been correct, about both the cavalry and the supply train. However, what the scouts had not been able to see from the ground was the cloud of dust that followed Moruth's army. If Daemor was correct, the supply train and the missing cavalry were about a quarter-day's march behind. Moruth had left his supply train in order to gain daylight for battle. . . .

Daemor guided his mount out of reality. The supply train was not far behind. In a few moments, he emerged in the air almost directly above it. Fifty wagons—about two weeks' supplies for an army the size of Moruth's. Perhaps three, if one expected to lose half of one's army in the first week. . . .

There were no cavalry, however. The supply train was completely undefended. Risky but, in this case, effective. Who was going to attack it after all? Still, it was a tactic one should take only when certain of victory. Moruth should know he was hopelessly outnumbered.

Daemor returned to the main body of the traitor's army. He saw nothing that should make Moruth certain of victory—he had almost no cavalry to speak of and only two thousand infantry. He was outnumbered by five to one in infantry and by more than six to one in cavalry.

Of course, the Nymrans and the Delvir would eventually defeat the *galdir*, despite their numbers. However, the Morvir would destroy them easily. Neither group had ever before faced the newly formed Morvan cavalry. And Moruth did not have enough cavalry of his own to stop them . . . it made no sense.

Daemor wondered if he should attempt to maneuver around and attack the supply train. No, that was only necessary when one was disadvantaged. Also, the extra supplies would prove quite useful in Olvanor. If Moruth had truly hoped to deter the war, he was going to be sadly disappointed.

Steve watched as the Morvan army arrayed before them. If he was a gambling man, he would've put his money on the Morvir. *I hope you knew what you were talking about, Professor*, he thought. If the pikes didn't do the job, it was all over but the crying.

The Morvan cavalry were forming up in front of the army. They were obviously going to lead, as Erelvar had guessed. Supposedly the *galdir* would charge behind them. After the initial charge, Erelvar had said, the cavalry would wheel to retreat and attack the flank, leaving the shattered front line for the *galdir*.

Theron had placed the right flank, and the archers, against the river for protection. Erelvar's meager band of cavalry defended the exposed flank. The maniples were still open, in case the enemy led with the *galdir* against expectations.

Now I know how Custer felt. Steve swallowed, trying to dislodge the lump from his throat. This was different from the charge to aid the Delvir—there was no impregnable fortress to retreat into, and a lot more time to get worried. . . .

With the sound of distant trumpets, the enemy cavalry began to move forward. They moved slowly at first, gaining speed as they approached. Steve watched as the rear centuries of the Delvan pikemen moved out and forward, sealing the gaps in the front line. Now Theron had committed himself. . . .

Steve's heart pounded in his ears in contrasting regularity to the avalanchelike rumbling of the charging cavalry. Still, he sat with the others, waiting for the enemy to come to them. . . .

Tsadhoq's heart pounded, as well. It was one thing to discuss tactics and new weapons in council. It was quite another to stand in the field with naught between you and a crazed Morvan war-horse but seven cubits of wood.

He watched as the horses charged. He had never before seen a cavalry charge. It was hard to believe that these frail pikes could stop such an overwhelming thing.

Tsadhoq raised his chin, lifting his leather beard-case. He would have to show no sign of the dread the sight of the charge inspired in him. He must maintain a strong appearance for his men. . . .

He waited, as had been discussed, until the Morvir were barely more than twenty cubits away. Without a word, he set and lowered the heavy pike. Around him the seven hundred surviving members of the royal guard did likewise. Tsadhoq smiled as a wall of spears formed before him. Perhaps this strategy could work after all. . . .

The Morvir in the lead ranks saw the danger, but it was far too late. The momentum of those behind pushed them along like brush before an avalanche. Tsadhoq felt the first shock of a horse impaling itself on the pike.

The impact threatened to tear the pike from his grip. Tsadhoq grimly clung to the weapon as it bent under the strain, lifting him from the ground. He struggled to place more of his weight atop it, lest the wood snap from the shock.

He felt the impact of a second horse. Before him the once-awesome charge was now a seething pile of horses and men. At least as many Morvir died in the confusion of the collapsed charge as spent their lives on the spear points of the Delvir.

A steady rain of arrows flew over Tsadhoq's men to land among the Morvir. The Olvir were taking advantage of the confusion and the lowered pikes. Tsadhoq released his hold on the pike to drop to the ground. With a grim smile he unslung the double-bitted axe from his back. The Morvir owed a blood debt to the royal guard. . . .

Steve sighed in relief; Professor Roland had been right, after all. Between the depredations of the pikes and the archers, Steve guessed that perhaps two hundred of the Morvir managed to escape. This battle was over. . . .

The few surviving cavalry retreated as the Delvir advanced into the wounded that remained. The steady rise and fall of their axes slowly brought a grim silence to the battlefield.

"What now, Prince Theron?" Erelvar asked as Theron rode up.

"That's what I would ask of you, Lord Erelvar," Theron replied. "Among us all, none know Daemor better than you. What now?"

Erelvar thought for a moment. "He has no choice but to retreat," he said. "We can expect an attack by the *galdir* soon."

"I thought you said he would retreat."

"Aye. He shall use the *galdir* to cover his retreat."

"You mean to say that he would waste ten thousand troops to save a mere hundred cavalry?"

Erelvar smiled. "You do not understand, my friend. A Morvan *rega* is trained for years, and the *regir* are precious few. The *galdir* are untrained and do not take well to retreat; besides— *galdir* breed quickly. . . ."

Only nine score of Daemor's cavalry had survived the charge against the Delvir. A thousand of the Mistress's best *regir* defeated by only seven hundred unmounted soldiers. It was unthinkable.

Nevertheless, unthinkable or not, it had happened. The *galdir* remained intact. Although, cowed as they were, they would be even less effective than usual. Daemor suspected they would rout before they had defeated even half of Moruth's army.

Daemor found the prospect of retreating before what had been an inferior force distasteful. The fact that his defeat lay at the hands of the traitor, Moruth, made the shame even less bearable. There seemed to be little choice in the matter, however.

Very well—at least the *galdir* would do some damage before they were slain. With luck, they might even kill Moruth. . . .

"I still think this is a waste of time," Erelvar said. "Such a shallow ditch will afford almost no protection—especially once it has filled with bodies."

"We have the time to waste," Theron replied. The Delvir and rest of the legion had excavated a two-foot-deep ditch around the army. A trumpet sounded from the north side of the incomplete camp.

"No longer," Erelvar observed. "The *galdir* approach."

"And the Morvir retreat," Theron noted, looking to the north. "Artemas?"

"Yes, Imperator," the wizard replied. "Felinor and I shall raise the wards."

"Good. Lord Erelvar, take your *regir* south of the camp. Be prepared to charge the *galdir* once they have engaged us."

"As you wish, Prince Theron." Erelvar turned and rode off. Steve followed, his horse nimbly leaping the shallow trench. So much for any chance of getting out of this without fighting. . . .

Erelvar led them a few hundred yards south of the legion. There he wheeled them about and made them wait. The horses stamped and snorted impatiently, as if they knew as well as the men what was about to happen, and were eager to be done with it.

The *galdir* approached the legion slowly. Behind them, high in the air, rode the two Dread Lords, driving their reluctant forces forward. Steve swallowed—the mere sight of them was enough to chill him to the bone. . . .

As soon as the *galdir* were in range, the Olvan archers began to fire. Now there was no forest of pikes to block them, and wave after wave of arrows fell among the *galdir*. Steve guessed that perhaps a thousand of them died before they even reached the legion.

"Soon now," Erelvar observed as the first sounds of battle reached them. "Do not fall and lose my standard this time," he said, turning to Steve.

Steve blinked in surprise. Was that a joke? It had sounded more like a command. Before Steve could either reply or question, Erelvar gave the order to charge.

They moved to the left of the battle before wheeling to charge the point where the *galdir* were thickest. As they neared the battle, Steve's stomach attempted to twist itself into a knot—the *galdir* had only a quarter of this number in the battle at Quarin. Also, Erelvar had possessed triple the cavalry in that battle.

The charge drove into the *galdan* army, clearing the ape-men from its path. As soon as the momentum from the charge was lost, Erelvar gave the order to wheel and retreat. As they wheeled, Steve saw one *rega* on the edge of the formation pulled down by the swarming *galdir*. Whatever cry the man might have uttered was lost in the general din of battle.

Steve felt bile rise in his throat and struggled to keep the meager contents of his almost-empty stomach down. Now he understood why Erelvar had forbidden them food before the battle.

As the cavalry wheeled about again, a safe distance from the battle, Steve searched in vain for some sign of the downed *rega*.

There was none—he could not even see the man's horse. The mass of *galdir* blocked it from his view.

God, please *don't let my horse fall*, Steve thought. There would be no survivors among those who fell in *this* battle.

Erelvar ordered another charge. The horses' hooves churned the ground, sending scraps of turf flying as they bore down on the enemy. What *galdir* could, fled the charge. Most, however, were too hemmed in by the press of their neighbors to retreat. Steve's horse stumbled as it trampled a *galdan* body, but quickly regained its balance.

Again the cavalry wheeled and fled once its momentum was lost. Steve did not see anyone brought down during this retreat. . . .

Three more times Erelvar led the *regir* into the press before Steve could see that the cavalry was, indeed, having some effect. While the *regir* had been smashing into them from behind, the legionnaires and the Delvir had been holding Theron's ditch, killing any who got within weapon's reach. Of them all, however, the Olvan archers had taken the largest toll.

The *regir* made two more charges by the time the sun touched the mountains to the west. Erelvar readied them for what Steve hoped would be their final charge. He did not relish the thought of galloping through darkness.

"Charge!" Erelvar ordered. Steve tipped the standard forward, and the *regir* began the charge. Only half the *galdir* remained. Soon it would be dark, however, and the cavalry and the archers would be out of the fight. Steve wasn't certain how Theron would fare without their support. . . .

He needn't have worried—even as the charge impacted the *galdir*, something resembling a flare soared into the sky. It burst into a brilliant globe of light, illuminating the battlefield almost as much as full moonlight would have.

That alone was enough to rout the magic-shy *galdir*—or perhaps they realized that this meant the cavalry and archers could continue to attack. Whatever their reasoning, they fled the battle.

Less than four thousand of the original ten survived to flee and, as they fled, the Olvir accounted for almost another thousand of them. Erelvar led the *regir* north in one last charge to "hasten them on their way."

On their return they found the rest of the army arrayed for the march. Theron rode up to them as they approached. Bodies littered the ground in a thick carpet. Already, crows adorned the field like flies, except for one large, burning pile.

"Where did you get the wood for the pyre?" Erelvar asked.

"Broken shields, spears, and such," Theron replied. "Have the *galdir* fled?"

"Yes, they shall not regroup for some time."

"Excellent. Let us be off, then. I want to make camp within the hour."

"Southward?" Erelvar almost sounded disappointed.

"Only a mile or so. We must meet the supply train, after all."

What Theron had called "making camp" turned out to mean fortifying a square area roughly a quarter-mile on a side with a six-foot-deep ditch and corresponding rampart. Within this he erected a small town of tents and makeshift roads into which all of the horses, wagons and supplies were brought.

Steve could hardly believe it had been constructed in less than two hours. Its layout exactly matched Theron's training camp atop the bluff at Quarin. Steve was able to travel from his squad's tent to Theron's command tent with no difficulty at all.

Theron and his tribunes, Kupris and Otos, as well as Tsadhoq, Erelvar, Morfael and Delarian, looked up as the legionnaire standing guard held the tent flap open for Steve. They were seated at a large table atop which maps had been spread. The tent was illuminated by oil lamps hanging from the tent poles.

"Come in, Master Wilkinson," Theron said. "Sit down."

"Thank you." Steve sat in an ornate chair by the large table. Where had they packed all these things?

"As you know," Theron began, "your pikes performed quite well today."

"Yes," Steve replied, smiling.

"What I want to know is, how effective will they be now that the enemy is aware of them?"

"That . . . depends on their number, I would suppose," Steve replied. He should have paid more attention during that lecture. Now he could only recall vague images of Professor Roland's chalk diagrams.

"He does not know," Erelvar said. "I was afraid of that."

"Hold a moment, Erelvar," Theron said. He turned back to Steve. "We know that, if we press northward, we will soon be facing two thousand cavalry."

"Hm," Steve said. "And we have seven hundred pikemen. . . ."

"Five hundred," Tsadhoq corrected. "I lost almost two hundred of my men against the *galdir*."

"Oh. I would say the pikes would be almost useless," Steve said. "If nothing else, they could split into four groups that size."

"Yes," Theron agreed. "And the Delvir could only stop one of them."

"The archers could account for another," Delarian suggested.

"Leaving a thousand to overcome the legion," Morfael added.

"Do not forget our own cavalry," Erelvar replied. "We might be able to hold one group for the Olvir."

Steve snorted derisively. "Even assuming that we manage to stop a third group that would still leave five hundred cavalry against . . . how many legionnaires are left?"

"Nine hundred," Theron replied.

"Hm," Steve replied, frowning. Three hundred legionnaires, lost; only nine hundred left. Damn.

"Not after that charge hit," he said. "Maybe four hundred—if we were lucky."

"Not one of you has so much as mentioned the *galdir*," Tsadhoq said. "You've all but defeated us with naught but two thousand Morvir. What of the twenty thousand *galdir* behind them?"

"It is hopeless," Kupris agreed. "Imperator, we have no choice but to retreat."

"So it would seem . . ." Theron began.

"No!" Erelvar objected. "We cannot retreat. If we retreat now, we will have accomplished nothing."

"I would hardly call turning one wave of invaders away from Olvanor nothing, Erelvar," Theron replied. "We have bought them a week to repel the invaders. . . ."

"And that will do little more than allow them to catch their breath before the next wave strikes. It will not end this war."

"We cannot hope to defeat two combined waves, Lord Erelvar," Kupris objected. "Would you have us throw our lives away for nothing?"

"No," Erelvar replied. "However, we can stop the next wave of invaders from reaching either Olvanor or Umbria."

"How?" Theron asked.

Steve's heart sank as Erelvar described his plan. . . .

Chapter
-------- Fifteen ------------

"THE SCOUTS HAVE returned, Dread Lord," Captain Garth said.

"And . . . ?" Jared asked, looking across at Garth from the high seat of the wagon.

"There is no sign of Rashine."

Jared sat back in the wagon, silently cursing his mount for having gotten itself killed. It had taken three days since the battle with Botewylf to make it to the rendezvous point. Rashine should have been there already. Jared did not like this unaccustomed lack of information.

"We shall proceed to the rendezvous point," he said.

"Yes, Dread Lord."

"I shall proceed on to find Rashine."

"How many men do you wish me to send with you?"

"None. They shall not be able to keep pace with me."

"Lord! Is that wise? The Umbrians . . ."

"Captain Garth! You forget to whom you are speaking!" Jared's empty eyes flamed red with irritation. Garth paled visibly.

"M-my apologies, Dread Lord," he stammered. Jared silenced him with an upraised palm.

"No, Captain. That is not necessary. I am . . . overtense from this unaccustomed . . . impotence."

"Y-yes, lord."

"Proceed on."

"Yes, lord."

Jared settled himself against the wagon's jarring progress as the team again began moving. This mode of travel was demeaning enough, without having to apologize to his own officers. Still, he had invested much time in Garth's grooming and would not stand to have him become like one of Daemor's worthless yes-men.

He glanced over at the *rega* driving the wagon. Should he have the man killed? The *rega* kept his eyes on the team, never once glancing toward his passenger. Jared looked away; it should not be necessary—the man was terrified at what he had overheard. That should suffice.

What had become of Rashine? Lord Phelandor should have met him with ample reinforcements near the very day of Jared's battle with Botewylf. Surely Rashine could not have lost the entire force so quickly?

No, it was much more likely that he had been delayed. It could be something as simple as a broken wheel on one of the catapults.

Jared shook his head. Some instinct told him it was nothing so simple. No, there was something more serious amiss. He would have to rejoin Rashine once Garth's force had arrived at the rendezvous site. . . .

Arthwyr watched as the Morvan army marched past, below. For the last four days they had harassed this force constantly. Arthwyr had, at first, been resentful of Aldric's command—now there was none of their group he would rather follow.

They had slain more than twice their number of the Morvir and at least twice again that many goblins. It was almost nothing compared to the overall mass of the Morvan army, but it was better than he had thought possible.

More importantly, they had delayed the invaders, buying time for Castle Aldwyn. Aldric also wished to destroy the catapults, but that had proven impossible thus far.

He sighted along the shaft in the crossbow, waiting for Aldric's order. The Morvan commander had pulled in his patrols in response to the Umbrians' ambushes. Prince Aldric meant to teach him the error of his ways. . . .

A grackle cawed once, twice and then a third time. Arthwyr smoothly squeezed the trigger of the crossbow, letting the shaft fly. Three hundred other crossbows fired simultaneously. As previously ordered, he loaded once more and fired, wildly, into the army below.

Without looking to see where his last shot had landed he turned and rushed down the hill to where the horses waited. He leapt into the saddle and spurred the horse away as the rest of Aldric's force did the same around him. Arthwyr risked one glance behind as they galloped away—there was no sign of pursuit. . . .

*   *   *

Jared stopped running long enough to survey the road around him. There was no sign of Rashine's passage. That was disturbing—in the last three hours since leaving Captain Garth, Jared had covered a full day's march for Rashine's heavily encumbered force. For what must have been the hundredth time, he cursed his *goremka* for having the stupidity to get itself slain.

With a growl of frustration he again began to run. Following the road entailed some measure of risk, but it also offered his best chance of finding some sign of Rashine. The catapults must follow the road.

Another hour of travel finally brought some reward. The fires of a large camp were visible in the distance. Jared's unnaturally keen vision was able to discern the hulking shape of siege engines—he had found Rashine. So, the worst had not happened. Jared slowed his pace to a walk—he should encounter sentries soon.

He did not—at least, not as soon as he had expected. The sentries were posted much closer to camp than Jared would have thought.

"Hold!" came the challenge. Jared stopped and waited. Shortly, a band of twenty cavalry approached him. Why was Rashine being so cautious? Jared did not like the looks of this. . . .

"Dread Lord!" said one of the *regir*, presumably the highest-ranking. "My apologies, lord. . . ."

"For what?" Jared snapped. "Doing your duty? Do not be stupid. Where is Captain Rashine?"

"In camp, lord. We shall escort you to him."

Rashine managed to look both relieved and anxious as Jared entered his tent. Jared surveyed the man for a moment. He looked haggard. Rashine squirmed under Jared's gaze.

"What has happened here?" Jared asked, taking a seat at Rashine's camp table.

"We have been under attack for the last four days, Lord Jared," Rashine replied.

"Attack? By whom?" Four days ago matched the date of Jared's battle with Botewylf. If only his mount had not gotten itself killed, he would have been here to deal with this himself.

"We are not certain, Dread Lord," Rashine said. "They appear to be Umbrian cavalry. They are as well trained as our own *regir*."

Jared paused for a moment. "How many?"

"Possibly as few as three hundred. Certainly no more than six."

Three to six hundred cavalry. Call it four hundred and fifty cavalry, as well trained as the *regir*. Jared frowned beneath the demon-mask.

"Moruth . . ." he muttered. "Can you not defeat three hundred *regir*, Rashine?"

"We cannot find them, lord," Rashine objected. "They ambush my patrols, or avoid them. This afternoon they ambushed us with crossbows. By the time my *regir* were able to pursue, they had fled. They obviously know the land."

"How many men have you lost?"

Rashine glanced away without answering.

"How many!"

"Over seven hundred *regir* and almost twice that many *galdir*."

"And how many of them have you slain?"

"No more than a handful, lord."

"Have they ever attacked the camp?"

"No, lord."

Jared nodded. He had thought not. To watch the camp, Moruth, or Erelvar, as the traitor now called himself, would have to camp much closer than he would like. More than likely, Erelvar was camping at night as well, catching up with the slow-moving siege train during the day.

If Erelvar had broken Belevairn's hold at Quarin, that meant reinforcements and supplies might not be forthcoming. Of course, if the traitor was campaigning in Umbria, he could not be holding the crossing at Quarin . . . things did not seem right. A student of Daemor's should have been quick to seize upon the frailty of the Mistress's supply lines. . . .

"What news did Lord Phelandor bring of Quarin?" Jared asked.

"None, lord."

That meant that ten days ago Quarin was still under siege. Jared shook his head. He would know nothing until the next wave of reinforcements arrived—if they arrived. Nonetheless, Quarin was the only possible source of heavy cavalry. Erelvar had broken free somehow—apparently without losing too many of his *regir*.

"How many *regir* do you have?" Jared asked.

"Slightly more than three thousand."

"Then give me three hundred. Have them ready to depart within the hour."

"Yes, Lord Jared."

"And bring me a horse, as well. We shall see if we cannot ambush these ambushers. . . ."

Jared awakened his force at the first hint of dawn. He had selected a sheltered valley for his campsite, slightly less than five miles from Rashine's camp. He hoped it was far enough back to avoid detection by Erelvar's scouts.

He dispatched his scouts with instructions to be wary. Erelvar should not be expecting scouts from behind, but it was still best to be cautious. The traitor did not escape Morvanor or break Belevairn's siege by being stupid. If only Jared's mount had not been slain, he could scout safely from above. . . .

"Are their patrols still withdrawn?" Aldric asked.

"Yes, Prince Aldric," Cai replied. "Only the patrols to the front are still being sent, and they stay within sight of the army."

Aldric nodded. They could not attack the forward patrols—it was too risky, that close to the main force.

"Looks like another target shoot today, eh?" Arthwyr observed.

"I do not want to settle into a pattern," Aldric replied. "We cannot afford to become predictable."

"What else can we do?"

Aldric thought for a while. He could not assault the main force; the catapults and the supply train were now well guarded and the forward patrols stayed within sight of the main force. There seemed to be no other options.

"Very well," he said. "However, we shall circle behind them and attack from the south today. Arthwyr, your Madawcs are our best crossbowmen—can they target barrels?"

"If we can see it, we can hit it," Arthwyr replied.

"Good. I believe the forward wagons are carrying barrels of oil. A burning quarrel or two might cause some distress."

"Aye, it might at that." Arthwyr smiled at the thought. Then he frowned.

"We have no pitch," he said.

"Even straw should suffice. The wood of those barrels will be oil-soaked."

"Perhaps. . . ." Arthwyr did not seem convinced.

"The same plan as yesterday. One shot aimed, one shot quickly and retreat. Only one burning quarrel, Arthwyr."

"Aye."

"Let us ride. I would attack before noon."

* * *

The scout sent northward returned early.

"What news do you have?" Jared asked.

"I have sighted the enemy, Dread Lord," the *rega* replied. "They travel southward behind the army no more than a mile from us."

Jared nodded. Just beyond the horizon from Rashine.

"Is the traitor with them?"

"No, Dread Lord. I saw no one in Morvan plate."

Jared straightened in surprise. Surely Erelvar was not scouting personally! Had he been slain while breaking the siege? *That* would be too much to hope for.

"Were there any Olvir among them?" he asked.

"No, Dread Lord. Only Umbrians."

"How many?"

"Three hundred."

Jared thought for a moment. Where had three hundred Umbrian heavy cavalry come from?

"Which clan?"

"Two hundred from clan Botewylf. The others were from various clans."

Jared frowned. A hundred mixed Umbrian cavalry was approximately the right number to match Erelvar's forces. That still did not account for the two hundred more that were present. Unless . . . had not King Botewylf left his personal guard with Erelvar? Jared frowned. Then where was Erelvar? In Olvanor, perhaps? Or simply not yet discovered by Jared's scouts?

It did not matter—now. He would have to lay an ambush for the force he knew of.

"They shall have to cross the road," he announced. "We shall be waiting for them."

"Yes, Dread Lord."

"Any sign of patrols?" Aldric asked.

"The only things movin' out there, highness, are rabbits," Brett whispered, peering at the road from behind the brush. "And not many of those. The Morvir still have their patrols pulled in tight and the main force is four miles from here."

"Good. Let us cross quickly, then. I do not like being out in the open for too long."

"Aye, highness."

They slid backwards down the blind side of the hill. Soon they had rejoined the others behind the next hill.

"The road is clear," Aldric informed them. "We shall proceed apace across it."

He mounted and led his men toward the road.

Jared watched expectantly from the hilltop. He had seen movement behind some brush atop the hill across the road. It could have been game, but he doubted it—there had been too much stealth for that. Besides, the recent passage of the army would have spooked most game away from the road.

He glanced back down the hill where two hundred of his cavalry waited, prepared to charge. The other hundred were scattered across the nearby hilltops.

A mounted rider came into view. Jared recognized the *rega*—Aldric ap Botewylf. That confirmed his suspicions about Quarin.

"You men, target that rider," Jared told the two to either side of him. "Fire on my signal." He raised his arm, alerting the *regir* below.

"Yes, Dread Lord."

Prince Aldric began across the road. There were almost precisely three hundred cavalry with him. Jared would have to commend his scout. . . .

Jared waited until Aldric had almost reached the far side of the road. "Now!" he shouted, letting his upraised arm fall. Below him a horn sounded, relaying his signal to all within hearing, including the Umbrians.

One hundred crossbows fired at the signal. Jared smiled as he watched Prince Aldric fall from the saddle. The surviving Umbrians began to rout just as Jared's cavalry gained the edge of the road and another volley fell among their ranks. . . .

Arthwyr heard the horn even as he saw Prince Aldric stiffen and fall from the saddle. It was an ambush! An arrow flew past, drawing a thin cut across his right cheek.

"Retreat!" he shouted, wheeling his horse to the right. Fortunately, he had been riding on the flank. To the left he saw Morvan cavalry crest the saddles of the nearby hills, charging down toward the road. The Morvir had practically caught them all napping. . . .

It was over in minutes. Less than a score of the Umbrian cavalry escaped, most wounded. Jared had lost perhaps a score of his own men.

"Do we pursue, Dread Lord?" one of the *regir* asked.

"No. We must rejoin Rashine. Twenty wounded men are no threat to us."

Arthwyr rode into the cave where they had camped the night before. If any of the others had survived, they would return here. He led his horse back into the cave and returned to the brush-covered mouth with his crossbow. If the Morvir found him here, he would take a few with him before he died. . . .

The man who rode into the small vale where the cave lay was not Morvan, however. Arthwyr recognized Cai ap Aldwyn. Good—at least someone who knew the area had survived.

"Cai!" Arthwyr called. The Aldwyn stopped, his head jerking to face the unseen mouth of the cave.

"Arthwyr?"

"Aye. Get under cover, man—quickly!"

Cai dismounted and led his own horse back into the small cave. The cave had barely been large enough for the men last night— now there would probably be room for the horses as well.

"Did anyone else make it out?" Arthwyr asked.

"I do not know," Cai replied. "I thought this would be the best place to find out."

"Aye."

Others had escaped, it turned out. There were eighteen in all, mostly Aldwyns—no Madawcs. Eleven were wounded to some extent, although none seriously. Arthwyr listened silently as the others discussed what to do next. Most wanted to retreat to Castle Aldwyn.

"Then we are agreed?" Cai asked.

"Aye," the others replied in unison.

"Nay," Arthwyr said. All eyes turned to where he stood in the mouth of the cave.

"What do you want to do?" Cai asked.

"I say we do what we set out to do—destroy their supplies of oil. *Then* we retreat to the castle."

"Are you mad?" another asked. An Owein, by his dress. "We are less than a score—we haven't a chance!" The others voiced their agreement.

"Has one ambush turned you all to cowards?" Arthwyr said. He ignored the glares that answered him. "Are we going to run to the castle like whipped dogs with our tails between our legs?"

"Would you rather get yourself killed for naught?" the Owein replied. Arthwyr snorted derisively.

"Would *you* rather sit in Castle Aldwyn knowing the Morvir had oil or knowing they did not? You Aldwyns—are you not willing to give your lives for your chieftain? Or shall a Madawc defend your clan holdings for you? I go to set an ambush for the Morvir—who among you is man enough to follow me?"

Again Jared was forced to ride on a supply wagon. Without the excitement of battle, the horses would not suffer his touch. He would be glad when the next wave of reinforcements arrived.

He was fairly certain of that now. Apparently the traitor's Umbrians had deserted to ride to their homeland's defense. That would leave him little more than a hundred cavalry. Jared's guess was that Erelvar himself had ridden into Olvanor. Let Daemor worry with him. . . .

He spun about in his seat at the unmistakable sound of an arrow impacting wood. A quarrel had pierced one of the barrels of oil behind him. Burning oil poured out of the broken barrel into the wagon, rapidly igniting the other, oil-soaked barrels. It was already too late to save the wagon.

He grasped the brake with his good hand. The eunuch driver had already fled. Jared locked the brake and jumped to the ground to free the panicking horses. They did not need a wagonload of burning oil spilled across the road. . . .

He allowed the horses to flee—the yoke would prevent them from going far. Another burning wagon jolted past him, driverless. As it passed, Jared drew his sword and slew the horse on his side. That slowed the wagon enough for him to board and stop it.

He heard a crash and the sound of splintering wood. One of the driverless oil wagons had collided with a catapult, spilling its burning cargo across the siege engine. Soon, flames were roaring up along its frame. The horses pulling the catapult panicked. Jared watched, helplessly, as the burning structure toppled against its neighbor. Both catapults collapsed into a pile of burning lumber.

Eventually, some sense of order was restored. The remaining oil wagons were stopped and pulled to the side of the road where they could burn harmlessly. Jared had lost two catapults and *all* of his supplies of oil.

The burning ruins of the two catapults made an effective road-block. The horses pulling the supply wagons could not be persuaded to travel around them.

"Make camp," Jared ordered. "I want a thousand men to search the area in groups of one hundred. Do *not* come back empty-handed. Follow them to Hell if you must, but bring me those responsible for this."

"Yes, Dread Lord," Rashine replied before leaving to execute his orders. Jared fumed at his own incompetence. Twenty wounded men—no threat, indeed. . . .

Chapter
-------- Sixteen ------------

PRINCE LAERDON STOOD on the catwalk looking over the palisade at the road beyond. They had just barely completed this wall across the Morvan road in time. It had taken the Olvir three days to dig the trench and place the logs. The next wave should be here soon—should have already been here, in fact.

"Have our scouts sighted anything yet?" he asked Olsande.

"As of last report, no, my Prince," Olsande replied.

"How long ago?"

"It is almost time for the next report to arrive."

Laerdon frowned at the road, as if he could discern the presence of the Morvir better than his scouts five miles to the northeast. Even now, the latest report would be on its way, passed from scout to scout. It took roughly ten minutes for news to reach them from the furthest scout—far faster than the Morvir could hope to cross the same distance.

After a few moments the report arrived—no sign of the enemy. Laerdon's scowl deepened. Surely the Morvir did not already know about the wall? If they did, what action would they take?

He turned and looked to the southwest. He could easily see the remains of the first Morvan fort less than a mile behind them. Most of its walls had gone into the construction of this palisade; only the gate remained.

The other two forts were still far from taken, however. The second had the benefit of fresh supplies and men; the third, although low on supplies, still held one and a half thousand Morvir. Each was surrounded by two thousand Olvir. Laerdon had learned the Dark Lord's lessons well. . . .

"Where *are* they?" he asked, turning to look down the road.

"I, myself, am glad they are nowhere about," Olsande replied. "The land has endured enough at their hands."

"No, Olsande. They will not surrender that easily—not as the result of one battle. I just wish I knew where they are, that they are not here. What devilry are they planning now?"

"Nothing against us, my Prince," a voice said at Laerdon's side. Laerdon's hand flew to the dagger at his belt before he recognized the voice.

"That will get you cut one of these days, Nolrod," Laerdon said. "Where have you been and what do you mean?"

"To Quarin," Nolrod replied.

"And?"

"There will be no Morvir today, my Prince. Erelvar has broken the siege and marched northward."

Laerdon frowned and turned to look out over the road. A mile of wooden wall erected in three days—for nothing. Erelvar fought their war for them, against hopeless odds.

"Olsande, gather the royal guard," Laerdon commanded. "Bring me as many of the tribesmen as will volunteer."

"Volunteer for what, my Prince?"

"To march onto the Plains," Laerdon replied. He could not allow Erelvar to sacrifice himself for Olvanor while the Olvir waited safely in the forest. . . .

The Plains, now in the heat of late summer, were even more arid than when Steve had first passed through them. The tall grass was dry and brittle, breaking crisply as the army marched through it, sending up clouds of grass-dust that choked his throat and brought tears to his eyes.

Another, larger cloud of dust followed them, half a day's march behind. They only enjoyed that lead because Theron had ordered the supply train burned and abandoned. The only supplies now were those carried on the backs of the horses and in the men's packs.

They had pursued Daemor north for two days before he joined with the next wave from Delgroth. The forces from both sides of the river had combined, and now the pursuers had become the pursued. . . .

But that had all been in Erelvar's plan. They led the Morvir almost due west, toward the Iron Mountains—away from the Northern Kingdoms. They were buying still more time for Olvanor and Umbria to gain the upper hand. Unfortunately, everyone knew that that time would eventually be purchased with their lives.

Steve glanced over to where Aerilynn walked, head down. Her

silver hair was dirty from the dust of the last few days' march. Sweat streaked the dust down her face in dirty rivulets.

Still, she was beautiful. She glanced up at him and smiled weakly before returning her gaze to the ground below. Steve's horse tugged on the reins, wanting to stop and eat some of the dry grass beside the army's path. He cursed and tugged harder on the reins, forcing it to follow him. He wanted to stop, too, but they dared not.

Steve glanced at the sky, and at his watch. Three hours or so till sunset. Once darkness came, the temperature would plummet. That sounded good now—hot and tired from the march as he was. It would quickly become too cold, though, and tonight there would be no warm tent to take shelter in. If they camped at all, it would be on the open ground.

Steve glanced up at the mountains, noticeably closer now than when they had begun today's march. Theron's goal was to reach the foothills with enough of a lead to entrench atop one. There they would attempt to hold off the enemy as long as possible—hopefully long enough to pull yet another wave away from the Northern Kingdoms. The end result would be the same, however. . . .

Daemor surveyed the forces below him—twenty thousand *galdir* and two thousand *regir*. Moruth was wise to flee, although he fled westward, leading them away from the Northern Kingdoms. The traitor planned his own death, foolishly sacrificing himself for those who continually spurned and distrusted him. Such a waste—such devotion could have been put to fine use in Morvanor. . . .

It was all for naught, as well. Moruth did not know that the war in Olvanor was already lost. The Mistress had said this herself, when he had reported this latest defeat to her. Fortunately she had not blamed him for that shameful event.

"You have been the second to feel the Dreamer's Sword," she had said, whatever that meant.

Even now Daryna wanted that whelp alive. Nothing was more important, she had insisted. Not even the deaths of the traitor or the Nymran prince were as valuable to her as that one man's life.

Very well—she would have her prize. But Daemor would have his revenge as well. . . .

*   *   *

Night had fallen and, with it, the temperature. Steve wrapped the cloak more tightly about him, shivering in the night air. Dinner had been eaten cold, out of his pack, and had done nothing to warm him. Even now, the cheese and bread sat in his stomach like a rock.

Still, it was easier to march in the cold than in the heat. In another few hours they might even be allowed to stop and camp. Then Steve could climb into his bedroll and rest—a heavenly prospect.

Steve's horse tugged on the reins. The animals were becoming more and more reticent. Steve cursed and hauled on the reins, wondering what he would do when the horse refused to yield to this treatment.

His weary legs betrayed him first, however. His right calf muscle knotted just as he put his weight on it. The leg folded up beneath him and he fell heavily to the ground. The pain in the cramped muscle would not let him lie still—with the aid of one of his comrade's arms he regained his feet. It was Erelvar.

"Keep your feet flat on the ground," Erelvar said.

"Sorry. . . ."

"'Tis not your fault. Now, lean forward from the ankles. Straighten that leg."

Steve did so, as Erelvar held his shoulders to keep him from falling. The pain slowly faded as the calf muscle stretched out. Steve sighed in relief.

"Better?" Erelvar asked.

"Much. Thank you, my lord."

Theron walked up to where they were standing.

"We shall have to make camp," he said. He did not sound pleased by his own announcement.

"I agree," Erelvar replied. "More and more of the men are giving out."

Steve glanced at his watch. No wonder! It was only a few minutes until midnight.

"I had hoped to gain more of a lead than this," Theron continued.

"The men are unaccustomed. Particularly your own—they were farmers less than a month ago."

"Yes. The Delvir could march for the rest of the night, I think. We shall camp for four hours." Theron turned and walked away to give the order.

Steve sighed. Four short hours—it would have to do. Word was quickly spread, and the army halted. The infantry were fortunate.

They had to do no more than spread their bedrolls and sleep. The cavalry had to first tend to their horses—tethering them to stakes driven into the ground, removing their saddles and tending their hooves.

Finally, Steve was able to crawl into his own bedroll, after depositing his armor on the ground beside him. For a while he listened to the horses as they stamped and snorted. After a time the animals quieted and the camp was silent.

Steve rolled over onto his back and stared up at the stars. While he had been marching, he had had to fight to keep his eyes open. Now that he was still, with three hours to rest, he couldn't keep them closed.

His mind wandered back over his experiences in this strange world. He had just come to accept his new life here, it seemed. In fact, in many ways, he was more alive now than ever before. It seemed unfair that now it would all be taken from him.

Steve rolled over onto his left side. No matter what position he lay in, sleep seemed to elude him. He heard someone walking behind him. Apparently he wasn't the only poor fool who couldn't sleep.

"Steven?" a whispered voice said behind him.

He rolled over onto his back. Even in the starlight he could see the white sheen of her hair.

"Aerilynn?"

"Yes. I . . . could not sleep."

"Well, that makes two of us, I guess."

"Can we speak?"

"Of course. What's on your mind?"

"Not here—we will disturb everyone."

Steve glanced around him. He didn't see any signs of their having disturbed anyone. He doubted if a bomb would waken half of these people.

"Where?" he asked.

Now it was Aerilynn's turn to look about. There weren't too many places around for a private conversation.

"Do you see that hill to the south?" she finally asked.

Steve peered into the darkness. A small mound blocked the stars south of the camp.

"Yes," he replied.

"Meet me there in a few moments," she said as she rose to leave. Before he could question her further, she was too far for him to whisper. He lay on his back for a moment, wondering what was going on. This cloak-and-dagger behavior wasn't like Aerilynn.

After two minutes, he rose and walked toward the rendezvous. A sentry acknowledged him as he neared the edge of the camp.

Steve walked out into the tall grass, making no attempt to move quietly. After all, someone out to use the john wouldn't bother.

Once he was certain he was out of the sentry's sight, however, he started moving more quietly. He hoped Aerilynn didn't want to talk too long. That sentry might start wondering if Steve didn't show up after a reasonable amount of time.

"Aerilynn?" Steve called in a whisper. He thought he was in the right spot. It was hard to be certain out in the grass, though.

"Aerilynn!"

"Over here," a voice whispered from somewhere to his right. Steve gingerly made his way through the dry grass. Finally he saw her, a vague silhouette in the darkness.

"What's this all about?" he asked once he finally reached her.

"I wanted to talk to you . . . alone."

"Why?"

"I am . . . afraid. We are all going to die out here and . . . and . . ."

With a sob she threw herself into his arms. Steve stood there, not really knowing what he should do. Finally, he brought his hand up to the back of her head and stroked her hair as she cried.

"Forgive me," she said as the crying subsided. "I am behaving like some silly court lady."

"Nothing silly about being afraid to die," he replied. "I'm scared, too."

"I love you, Master Wilkinson."

For a moment, Steve said nothing as his mind absorbed what she had said. Girlfriends had always been something that the other guys had—never him.

"Why?" was the first thing he said. "I mean . . . that is . . ."

"Hush," she said. He did so.

"Do you love me as well?" she asked.

"Oh, God, yes." The quaver in his own voice surprised him. He felt tears form in his eyes and vainly tried to hold them back. Aerilynn's hand touched his cheek where the tears ran.

"That is why I love you," she said. "You are not afraid to cry or to hold a woman in your arms if she wears a sword."

"Aerilynn . . . I . . ."

"Shhh. Hold me."

He gladly complied with her request. He felt her lips brush against his neck and then his jaw. He lowered his face and she pressed her mouth gently against his. How much sweeter her kiss was than Arthwyr's barroom trollop!

All too soon, she stepped away from him, his hands in hers. Then she knelt, pulling him down beside her for another embrace.

"Aerilynn—should we? I . . . I mean . . ."

"Shh. This may be our only opportunity—in this life."

Her lips caressed his as she unlaced the leather garment he wore under his armor. His fingers found the laces on her garment and he eagerly undid them, revealing the soft flesh beneath her leather tunic.

The bitter cold of the evening was forgotten as they slid into each other's arms. Her arms and legs held him tightly to her as they made love.

Soon it was over and they collapsed on the grass, beside one another. Once his ragged breath had stilled, Steve rolled on his side to face her.

"Aerilynn?" he said.

"Yes?"

"If . . . if we get out of this alive . . ."

"Yes?"

"Will you . . . that is, would you . . . uh . . ."

"Yes, my love, I would."

Steve smiled. "I haven't even asked you yet."

"You ask me to be your wife, no?"

"Yes," Steve replied softly. "You know something?"

"What?"

"It's *cold* out here!"

A sharp giggle escaped from Aerilynn's lips, and she clapped her hands over her mouth, shaking in mirth. After a moment Steve was laughing too, although he kept his silence better.

"We had best . . . return to camp," Aerilynn finally said, out of breath.

"Yes," Steve replied. "Before we freeze to death."

They dressed quickly, the leather cold and stiff after having been away from their bodies. It warmed all too slowly—Steve was starting to shiver.

"I shall return first," Aerilynn told him. "Wait a moment before you return."

"Right."

She kissed him one last time before leaving. Steve waited in

the tall grass, rubbing his hands together and blowing into them.
Now he longed for the heat of the morning. . . .

Erelvar waited by the horses for Steve's return. He had yielded
the tent to Glorien for her discussion with Aerilynn.

His initial reaction had been anger that the two of them had
risked leaving the camp. Glorien had pointed out, however, that
Steven had no tent. If he and Aerilynn needed the comfort of each
other's arms, they had no choice but to slip away from the camp.

Erelvar smiled. Glorien was always able to point out the softer
side of things to him—even when it was himself she was speaking
of. He wished that she had remained behind at Quarin and, yet, a
perverse part of him was glad that they would be together when
the end came. As she had said—he needed the comfort of her
presence.

A part of him claimed that that was weakness, but that part was
Morvan and wrong. It was no more wrong for him to need her
than it was for Aerilynn and Steve to slip away to be alone for
what would probably be the only opportunity of their lives.

Wilkinson appeared at the edge of the camp. Erelvar watched as
the young *rega* cautiously made his way back to where his bedroll
had been left. He stepped forward as Steve looked about for it.

"I did not think you would have any further need of it," Erelvar
said. Wilkinson looked up, startled.

"There is, perhaps, a quarter-hour before we rouse the men,"
he continued. "Come assist me with my horse."

"Yes, my lord," Steve replied, looking for all the world like a
child caught at a prank.

Erelvar said nothing while they prepared first his horse and
then Steve's. Soon, however, they were finished and there was
no putting it off any longer.

"Steven?" he asked softly.

"Yes, my lord?" Steve replied. He sounded puzzled. Softness
was possibly the last tone Steven had expected to hear.

"No—there is no one to hear us. Call me by name."

"Y-yes . . . Erelvar?"

"Do you think it is . . . wise to . . . begin something with
Aerilynn at this time?"

"I . . . uh . . . it . . . it wasn't really . . . my idea . . ." Steve replied haltingly. "I mean . . ." he began again, apparently regathering his wits. Erelvar laid a hand on his shoulder.

"I understand," he assured the younger man. "I know that

Aerilynn came to you—and I know that you are a man of honor. I do not believe you would take advantage of her. . . ."

"No!"

"Quiet!" Erelvar whispered sharply. Steve jerked as if slapped. *Damn!* Erelvar thought. He was not adept at this sort of thing.

"I do not want the entire camp to overhear us," Erelvar continued, more softly. "I was merely saying that I know you care for her—I do not know how deeply. However, I must warn you. You may see her die in the next few days; or she, you."

Erelvar waited patiently as Steve made a few, incoherent beginnings before he finally replied.

"I . . . love her, Erelvar," he said, his voice shaking. He looked away, as if shamed. Erelvar placed both of his hands on Steve's shoulders, forcing the young *rega* to look at him.

"I know how you feel," Erelvar told him. "You are not the only man whose woman is in danger."

Understanding slowly crept onto Steve's face.

"Oh, my God," Steve said. "Erelvar—how could you decide . . . ?"

How could I decide to give an order that would kill the woman I love? Erelvar thought, completing Steve's unfinished question.

"I've asked myself that same question over the last few days, my friend," he replied. "The answer still eludes me."

For a moment the two of them just stood there, uncomfortably. Then they heard the sound of the sentries rousing the camp. . . .

"How long ago did they leave?" Laerdon asked.

"Five days ago, my Prince," the scout replied. Laerdon had arrived at Quarin to find the fortress-town defended only by the members of the royal guard his father had left in Erelvar's charge. The Morvan had taken everyone else onto the Plains.

"And you say that, yesterday, another wave passed into Umbria?"

"Yes, my Prince."

That did not bode well for Erelvar. The most likely explanation was that he and the force intended for Olvanor had destroyed each other. Otherwise, would he have not stopped the force making for Umbria as well?

"Olsande."

"Yes, my Prince?"

"Select a thousand men, tribesmen, to venture into Umbria. The Morvir shall not expect to find Olvir guarding Umbrian forests."

"As . . . you command, my Prince," Olsande replied. It was not the Olvan way to defend another's lands—but this war had taught them many new things. Olsande was not about to question his prince now.

"We shall take the remaining thousand onto the Plains. Hopefully it is not already too late to save Erelvar."

Getting the horses up the side of the hill had been no easy task, but then that was why Theron and Erelvar had selected it. Steve pulled on the halter lead to Delarian's mount with three other *regir* while yet another tempted it forward with a green branch stolen from one of the rare bushes found in these rocky foothills. Finally, the animal made it past the steepest part of the slope and gained the crest of the hill.

"That's the last of them," Steve said thankfully, collapsing to the ground. Going last night without sleep and then marching all day had taken everything out of him. *Then* they had had to get the horses up here.

"No time to rest, Master Wilkinson," the Nymran, Kupris, said, handing him a shovel. "We have less than a day to make this hill impregnable."

With a groan Steve rose to his feet, using the shovel for support.

"Where?" he asked.

"Over there," Kupris replied, pointing to where the legionnaires were already digging. "Shovel what the picks loosen over to behind that stone facing the Delvir are building."

Steve walked over to his assigned position. Until now, the *regir* had not been required to assist the legionnaires with their digging. Now, everyone had been put to work.

Steve threw shovelful after shovelful of dirt and gravel behind the low stone wall the dwarves were erecting. Every few feet, the hastily sharpened point of a pike or a spear protruded from the wall. Those Delvir who weren't working on the wall itself packed the dirt and gravel into a solid, flat-topped rampart behind the stone facing.

The army worked all day and into the early evening before the three commanders decided that rest was more important than further fortification. The low stone wall had become a six-foot barrier under the skilled hands of the Delvir. The rampart behind ended three feet below the top of it. Steve could not help but be astonished as he surveyed the amount of work they had done in just one day.

The relatively flat top of the hill was over a hundred feet across. The entire space was encircled by the Delvan wall, the face of which bristled with the points of hundreds of pike heads. Maybe they might live through this after all. . . .

"Hurry, my friend, or you shall miss dinner," Morfael said. The Olvan *rega* was covered in dirt from head to toe—he had obviously been digging as well.

"Do I look as bad as you?" Steve asked.

"Possibly worse," Morfael replied, smiling. "Breathe deeply, my friend—do you not smell something on the wind?"

Steve sniffed the air, and his mouth began to water. Someone had been busy cooking while they were digging.

"Meat?" Steve asked. Where had they gotten meat? The only supplies they had were what could be carried on the . . . horses.

"Aye," Morfael confirmed when Steve looked askance. "I dare say it won't be the last meal of horsemeat we enjoy ere this is over."

Steve sniffed at the air again.

"I don't care," he told Morfael. "Come on—I'm starving."

"Yes, Daemor," Hilarin said over-politely. "A mildly fortified hill will be no trouble at all for the *galdir* to overrun. It is a pity we shall have to attack this one instead. . . ."

"I am in no mood to endure what passes for your wit, Hilarin," Daemor replied. Indeed he was not. What he had expected to find, a hilltop fortified by ditch and rampart, had turned out to be a veritable keep.

A six-foot stone wall encircled the hilltop behind a five-foot-deep dry moat. The base of the wall sprouted spear heads every foot, three rows high. There was no gate—they obviously did not expect to leave.

"We shall have to reconsider our strategy . . ." Heregurth began.

"Silence," Daemor commanded. The junior lord obeyed.

"This changes little," Daemor continued. "We shall circumvallate the hill and besiege them. We shall still attack with the *galdir*; they do not perform well in sieges."

"When do they ever?" Hilarin grumbled.

"Had we not left the catapults on the far side of the river, we would not now be facing this dilemma," Lord Kephas pointed out.

"No, we would not," Daemor agreed. "Erelvar would now be safely at rest in Quarin instead."

*   *   *

Steve watched from the wall as the Morvir below worked on the trench surrounding the hilltop fortress. Soon, all too soon, their work of the day before would be put to the test. The hill itself looked impregnable. However, as Erelvar always said, a fortress was only as indomitable as the men inside it. And there were so *many* ways to attack something like this.

Daemor, who Erelvar claimed was commanding the army below them, had apparently chosen starvation and thirst as his main weapons of assault. Keep the defenders bottled in long enough, and eventually they would leave their fortress in sheer desperation. Simple and effective—assuming time was on your side.

Unfortunately, time *was* Daemor's ally, here. He could defeat Erelvar and Theron without making one Morvan lift a sword. That fit in with Erelvar's plan, however. He wanted to make Daryna's armies waste as much time here as possible.

Despite the siege preparations, Erelvar insisted that they would still have to face an assault by the *galdir*. Neither he, Theron nor Tsadhoq were overly worried about that in their current position, however.

Steve wished that he could share their confidence. Unfortunately, he could still remember his first sight of the *galdir*, climbing unaided up a thirty-foot wall. In the face of that memory, their little stone barrier seemed almost no barrier at all. . . .

"Thoughts of your true home, Master Wilkinson?" a woman's voice said there. Steve turned to see Aerilynn standing behind there. Like him, she was covered in grime from head to toe.

The commanders had forbade washing—food they had in plenty, but the water in the barrels salvaged from the supply train was all they had. Unless, of course, the well the Delvir were sinking actually struck water. Steve had his doubts. . . .

"No, just figuring our odds," he told her, smiling wryly. "If I were a gambling man, I'm afraid I'd have to put my money on Daemor."

"I would not," Aerilynn replied. "Daemor has a reputation for snatching defeat from the jaws of victory. Or so Lord Erelvar has said."

"Oh? Erelvar once told me that Daemor taught him everything he knows about war."

"You misunderstand—I did not say he was not a competent

general. However, he tends to be overconfident."

"I hope you're right, Aerilynn," Steve said. "I don't want to lose you now."

She looked away, but not before Steve could glimpse the flush that colored her cheeks beneath the grime.

"That is why I came," she replied. "I wanted to apologize."

Steve's heart began to beat more quickly.

"What do you mean?" he asked. Had she changed her mind? Did she no longer love him?

"I . . . did not mean to anger Lord Erelvar against you," she replied. "I . . ."

Steve laughed, interrupting her. After a moment the laughter faded. A few people nearby were staring at him.

"What is so funny?" Aerilynn asked.

"Nothing," Steve replied. "Don't scare me like that—I thought you had changed your mind . . . about us."

"Oh!" Comprehension showed on her face. "No, Steven—never. I was just worried. . . ."

"Well, don't be," Steve assured her. "You did not get me in trouble. Erelvar and I had a . . . kind of a father-son chat, is all. He was . . . concerned, is all."

"Truly?"

"Yeah. He's not as cold as people think—including me, sometimes."

"I am glad for that, then," Aerilynn said. She paused for a moment.

"Steven?" she finally said.

"Yes?"

"Do you truly believe that we shall not leave here alive?"

"I don't know, Aerilynn. I just don't know. . . ."

"The trenches are complete, Dread Lords," Captain Osric said.

Daemor looked to the west. The sun sat atop the foothills. Even as he watched, it began to sink below the hills.

"Send the *galdir* up the hill, Osric," Daemor commanded.

"But it is almost nightfall. . . ."

"Now!"

"At once, Dread Lord!"

"It will be difficult to manage the *galdir* at night, Daemor," Hilarin said. "The darkness shall embolden them, and they may well try to escape us."

"That is why I want to send them before we lose what little

light we have left. Once they are in battle, they will be less likely to think of that."

"Very well," Hilarin replied. "You *are* in command."

"Yes, Hilarin," Daemor agreed. "I am."

Steve was off watch when the sentries raised the alarm. Together, he and Erelvar rushed to the site where the alarm had been sounded. Below, on the near side of the Morvan's defenses, the four Dread Lords had gathered the *galdir*.

Steve's heart sank at the sight. The number of *galdir* on the Plains had seemed overwhelming. There were exactly twice that many below them now. Wall or not, there was no way they were going to stop that mass when it came up the hill. Especially in the dark.

The *galdir* started up the hill. Even from here, it was possible to see the reluctance with which they did so. A few well-placed blasts of fire from the Dread Lords increased their pace, however. Steve was thankful that Artemas and Felinor were warding the camp. The army's defenses would fall even faster if the *galdir* had air support. . . .

From behind him, Steve heard the thrum of bowstrings. The Olvir were firing, arcing their arrows high over the defenders on the wall. Soon, a steady rain of arrowfire fell onto the *galdir* from the darkening sky. A few more flashes of fire showed that the *Kaimordir* were having to further encourage their troops.

Steve drew his sword. As the *galdir* drew near, the blade began to shine through the darkness, its light cast back by the luminous eyes of the *galdir*. Steve had not realized until now that the *galdir* were actually nocturnal creatures. No wonder the enemy was willing to use them at night like this.

The first few reached the trench surrounding the hilltop. As the *galdir* got closer, the light from the sword brightened until it shone like a blue-white beacon. The *galdir* began to climb. . . .

At first the sharpened blades protruding through the wall deterred them, as hoped. Eventually, however, several *galdir* were impaled on them by the press of their fellows behind them. At that point, the spear heads were not an obstacle.

The *galdir* climbed with all of the agility that Steve remembered from his first sight of them. A snarling, apish face rose into view in front of him. Steve sliced across it with the shining blade. There was a scream and the monster fell away, only to be replaced by two more.

Steve brought his sword down, smashing the skull of one. As the other hoisted itself atop the wall, Steve thrust through its chest. The monster fell back with a squeal of pain.

Another had gained the top of the wall to his right. Steve sliced his sword through its arm and into its side. The monster fell away, threatening to take his sword with it. Steve desperately tightened his grip on the blade—he did not want to face this many *galdir* unarmed.

Another had gained the wall to his left before Steve recovered his sword. He lifted his shield to block a spear thrust aimed for his head and slammed the edge of the shield down, into the *galdir*'s shins. The monster swayed back, cartwheeling its arms for balance, before tumbling back down into the seething mass below.

The last faint light faded from the sky as the battle progressed. The circumference of the wall was lit only by the flickering torches set into the earth of the rampart and by Steve's sword. The darkness and flickering shadows lent an unreal, nightmare quality to the battle as snarling, fang-filled faces swarmed over the wall.

The man to Steve's left went down, carrying a *galdan* spear with him as he rolled down the side of the rampart. The monster landed next to Steve, having cleared its way past the barrier. Steve blocked the thrust of its spear with his shield and thrust his sword through its abdomen.

Another had cleared the wall to Steve's right while he was occupied. Two more climbed to the top of the wall before him. Steve turned quickly—if they didn't seal this breach soon, they never would.

Before Steve could attack the intruder, Erelvar's sword point emerged from its chest. Lifting the *galda* like a fish on a spear, Steve's lord hurled the twitching body into the two atop the wall. All three toppled away into the darkness.

"You don't have a blue suit with a red cape, do you?" Steve asked, thrusting his blade into the face of another *galda* as it rose over the top of the wall.

"Shut up and fight," Erelvar replied, turning away to clear his own section of wall.

Steve quickly dispatched two more *galdir* as they tried to gain the top of the wall. It was beginning to look as if they might survive this battle with even fewer casualties than expected. The *galdir* were proving surprisingly easy to kill.

Without warning, the blade in Steve's hand doubled in brightness, momentarily dazzling him. One of the Dread Lords sat

before him on its devil-steed. A burning hoof struck Erelvar's
shield, hurling him from the rampart.

The monster pressed forward, and the protection of the ward
became visible as a crackling nimbus of energy surrounded mount
and rider. *Galdir* swarmed past, unchecked around him—men
shouted and yelled as Steve faced the monster.

He knew it had come for him; Daryna still wanted him alive.
The nimbus around the monster intensified, looking for all the
world like the surface of a bubble pushed in by some great force.
It didn't look like it would hold much longer.

Steve stepped forward, lifting his sword. The heat from the
blade warmed his face, as if the sword had just been drawn from
the forge. With a cry, as much of fear as of determination, Steve
drove the point of his sword beneath the demon-horse's throat.

White fire burned around the blade where it pierced the unnatural flesh. The sound of the monster's scream made the hair on
Steve's neck stand up, but he only drove the blade in deeper.

As the monster died, the ward snapped back into place, hurling the beast and its rider like a stone from a catapult. Steve
had no time to exult in his victory—ten feet to either side, no
one manned the wall. *Galdir* swarmed over the unguarded wall
without resistance.

With a single sweep of his sword, he disembowelled three
galdir in front of him. Part of his mind screamed at him to flee—
that he could not hold this much wall alone—but he dared not. If
this breach were not sealed, and sealed quickly, they would *all* die.

He blocked a spear thrust from his left with his shield even as
he parried another from his right with the sword. A snap of his
wrist brought the sword blade down on the *galda's* skull. The
creature fell, twitching, to the ground. Still the *galdir* flowed
past him.

Someone stepped into place beside him—it was Theron.

"You work leftward," Theron shouted. "I shall take the right!"

"What about the ones that got through?" Steve shouted back
as he killed a *galda* to his left. He stepped into the space it had
occupied.

"They are being dealt with! Shut up and clear this wall!"

A legionnaire stepped into the space Steve had just vacated in
time to kill another *galda* that was climbing over the wall. Steve
raised his shield to block a spear thrust toward his face. He sliced
below his shield, across the monster's legs. It fell with a squeal
of pain. Steve did not take the time to dispatch it, instead kicking

it down the slope of the rampart as he stepped forward. Another legionnaire filled the gap behind him.

In this manner, the breach in the line of defenders was sealed until the flow of *galdir* over the wall had been stopped. Steve risked a glance at the camp behind him.

Small battles raged throughout the camp. Some of the tents had been fired, and the flames threatened to engulf the entire camp. Things did not look good.

Of course, they were going to look even worse if he didn't keep his mind on what he was doing. Steve barely blocked a spear thrust at his stomach. He snapped his sword around in a decapitating stroke, slaying his attacker.

Once the breach had been sealed, the battle settled into an almost monotonous routine. The *galdir* kept trying to gain the top of the wall, and Steve kept driving them back.

How long this continued Steve was not certain. It seemed like hours later when the *galdir* finally fled into the night. The fatigue that had been slowly creeping up on him now overwhelmed him. He dropped to his knees, dropping his sword and shield to rest his arms atop the wall.

Someone placed a hand on his shoulder. Steve looked up to see Morfael standing over him.

"Are you injured?" Morfael asked.

"Tired," Steve moaned in reply. "Where's . . . Aerilynn?"

Morfael looked away before answering.

"Aerilynn died defending Glorien," he said.

Steve felt a knot form in his throat. Aerilynn? Dead?

"When the *galdir* broke through, Aerilynn and Glorien were among those who met them," Morfael continued, his voice trembling. "Glorien fell, and Aerilynn took the spear that was meant for her. She . . . she died quickly with little pain. I am sorry, my friend."

Steve didn't hear the last words as darkness gathered about his mind and bore him away to oblivion. . . .

Chapter
-------- Seventeen ------------

THE SENTRIES AT Castle Aldwyn challenged them as they approached. Fortunately, Cai was known here as Aldwyn's nephew. Clan Aldwyn, like all the clans, had sent their best young men to be trained under Erelvar.

Of those sent by all the clans, only eighteen now returned. However, those eighteen had made a good accounting for themselves against the Morvir. Because of their efforts, this castle had some hope of withstanding the coming siege.

Aldwyn himself met them inside the gate. He was tall, like all Aldwyns, and his grizzled features betrayed some of the Olvan characteristics his line was rumored to possess. He gave Cai a brief, but warm, greeting before getting down to business.

"Do you have any news of the approaching army?" he asked.

"Yes, my lord," Cai replied.

"What are their numbers?"

"Scarcely over five thousand cavalry and about twenty goblins."

"That matches what we already know," Aldwyn noted. "What of engines?"

"They have four catapults and no rams, lord."

"Four? Our scouts reported six."

"We destroyed two of them this morning, lord, in the process of burning their supplies of oil."

Aldwyn smiled broadly.

"Well done, Cai!" he said, clapping his nephew on the shoulder.

"Actually, lord, you should thank my companion, Arthwyr. It was his plan that led to their destruction."

Aldwyn glanced at Arthwyr and back at Cai. He turned toward the Madawc.

"Then you have my thanks, Arthwyr ap Madawc," Aldwyn said. "You shall always be welcome in my hall."

"Thank you, Lord Aldwyn," Arthwyr replied. It was safe for Aldwyn to make such a statement—clan Madawc did not border clan Aldwyn. Gods, but he had almost forgotten clan politics while at Quarin! A part of him wished he still could.

"How far behind were they?" Aldwyn asked Cai.

"They should be here before noon tomorrow, lord."

"Then we have much to discuss and prepare before the morrow," Aldwyn said, turning to lead them inside. "They have no oil, you say . . . ?"

The towers of Castle Aldwyn finally came into view over the horizon. The castle was located in a stretch of particularly treacherous terrain, ripe for ambush. Jared's scouts had found no sign of ambushers, however. Apparently the Aldwyns had decided it was wiser to defend from inside the castle. Considering the difference in numbers, they were correct.

Unfortunately, he did not have the force necessary to take Castle Aldwyn—not without the oil and catapults yesterday's attack had cost him. However, Lord Fanchon should arrive with reinforcements today—assuming nothing had gone amiss. That should give him the strength he needed to take this fortress. With Castle Aldwyn to work from, he would be able to bring the neighboring clans down in relatively short order.

That was thinking too far ahead, though. Any number of things could go wrong between now and then. The key to managing a campaign as involved as this was flexibility. The moment one became committed to a fixed course of action, the war was lost.

"Your orders, Lord Jared?" Garth asked, riding up beside the wagon Jared rode.

"Have scouts been dispatched ahead?"

"Yes, Dread Lord. They report that all about the castle is clear."

"Then proceed on. Today and tonight we shall entrench about the castle. Tomorrow we shall begin the assault."

"Yes, Dread Lord."

Jared would have preferred an extended siege rather than a costly assault on the fortress. It would have given him possession of a more intact stronghold. However, time was a luxury he did not have. His scouts had returned with news of reinforcements from clan Owein.

"Look at them," Aldwyn said, "digging in like they had all the time in the world, the bastards."

"According to Lord Erelvar," Cai said, "that is Lord Jared. He is supposed to be very . . . thorough."

Arthwyr watched the Morvir below in silence. As an outsider, his input would only be politely listened to—and that only because of Cai's previous frankness with his lord. If Arthwyr thought the clan rivalry distasteful now, he would not want to attend next year's meeting of the clans. Not with Morcan Botewylf *and* his heir dead.

Of course, that was assuming that there would even be a meeting of the clans. If the Morvir took this castle, which it was beginning to look as though they might, it would be almost impossible to wrest them from Aldwyn's territory. And with their seemingly endless supply of goblins, it would only be a matter of time before the other clans fell.

". . . as thorough as he likes," Aldwyn was saying, "but he'll not take *this* castle."

Arthwyr smiled grimly. "*A fortress is only as indomitable as the men within it,*" he thought. Aldric had been right—Erelvar was more correct than any of them had known. It took only a single, real war, rather than a mere clan squabble, to drive home the truth behind the Morvan's words. The Morvir, like the Nymrans, made an art out of war. Compared to either of them, the Umbrians were like children scuffling in the streets.

Cai's clansmen, and the survivors of King Botewylf's army, had welcomed them all as heroes. They had, under Aldric's command, done more damage to the Morvir, per man, than any other force. This did not bode well for the future of Umbria. . . .

Jared divided his attention between the men circumvallating Castle Aldwyn and the skies above. It was well past noon—Lord Fanchon's forces should have arrived by now. And if Fanchon did not arrive at all? What then? Retreat would be the only option left to him, distasteful as it was.

A mounted figure appeared in the sky above. If Jared had been mortal, he would have sighed in relief. The figure paused in mid-air. Jared waited for a moment, wondering why Fanchon did not descend, before he realized why.

He did sigh as he stepped out to where Fanchon could see him and waved his good arm. After a moment his colleague spied him and descended.

"Greetings, Jared," Fanchon said upon landing. "What has happened to your steed? And to your arm, for that matter?"

"They were both casualties in my battle against King Botewylf," Jared replied. "That is not important. How far is your army and what news do you have of Quarin and the traitor?"

"Your reinforcements should arrive within the hour," Fanchon told him. "As for the traitor—he should be dead by now."

"Should be? Explain yourself." Jared did not like the sound of Fanchon's answer.

"Daemor and Hilarin were facing him on the Plains as I passed."

"On the Plains?" That did not sound right. Why would Erelvar take to the Plains with less than two hundred cavalry? Jared asked as much.

"There was more to his army than that, Jared," Fanchon replied. "The traitor travelled with roughly seven hundred Delvir and well over a thousand legionnaires."

"*What?*"

"Oh, and approximately two hundred Olvan archers."

"And that is all you can tell me?" Jared shouted. "You have not once returned to either Delgroth or Quarin to learn more?"

"What need was there? Come now, Jared—Daemor had them outnumbered by greater than five to . . ."

"Fool! Do you think Erelvar did not *know* that before he ventured onto the Plains? Take me to Delgroth at once!"

"Very well, Lord Jared," Fanchon replied coolly. "Although I think you will find that Daemor has matters well in hand."

"I hope that you are correct, Lord Fanchon. Although I highly doubt it."

The sound of Jared's boots echoed back from the stone walls as he walked down the corridor to the Mistress's chambers. He had always hated this place, with its ever-present shadows and stale air. More than once, he had wished that the mask did not give him a sense of smell.

He emerged from the shadowed corridor into the more brightly lit entrance foyer. The Morvan guards moved to attention as he entered.

"Tell the Mistress I am here," he said.

"Yes, Lord Jared," one replied. Jared watched as the guard opened the door just enough to slip through. Another senseless ritual; Daryna knew very well that he was here and probably knew why—aside from needing a new steed and healing.

"She will see you, Lord Jared," the guard replied, returning from within. Jared nodded and passed through the doorway as the *rega* held the door for him to pass. Once inside, Jared briefly dropped to one knee at the foot of the stairs to the throne.

"Greetings, Jared," the shadowed figure on the throne said. "How fares the war in Umbria?"

"That is what I have come to ask you, Mistress," Jared replied. "I suspect that it does not fare well at all."

The bright, green eyes blinked in surprise. Shortly afterwards, light laughter followed.

"Ah, Jared," she said affectionately, "your lack of subtlety is as refreshing as always."

"Why was I not informed when the traitor broke the siege at Quarin?" Jared demanded. "Why was I not informed that he had ventured onto the Plains with a third of a Nymran legion and half that many Delvir?"

"He hardly has a true Nymran legion, Jared," Daryna replied. "Merely a thousand Umbrian farmers and laborers pretending to be such."

"Apparently they *pretend* well enough to break the siege at Quarin with minimal losses."

"Ware the tone you are using with me, Lord Jared," Daryna said. "I do not think I like it."

"I need to know the current status of things, now that Daemor has been soundly defeated by Erelvar," Jared said, ignoring her remark. The figure atop the throne stiffened.

"How did you know that?" she asked.

"Because you ordered Daemor to attack with precisely half the strength Erelvar was expecting to face. That was not a wise decision, my lady."

The figure on the throne rose, fists clenched at her sides.

"How *dare* you speak thus to me?" she demanded. "Who do you think you are to lecture *me*?"

"I *thought* I was your advisor and general," Jared replied calmly. "If that is not the case, my mask is, as always, yours to reclaim."

"Then do so!"

Jared paused. He had hoped to shock her out of her tantrum. He had certainly not expected her to accept his offer. . . .

"As you wish," he replied. He reached up and undid the first clasp on the mask. As soon as it was loosened, his sight and hearing vanished. His fingers slid up the side of the mask to the second clasp.

"No," Daryna said, snapping the first clasp back into place.

"No, Jared—I cannot afford to lose you this close to victory, my love." As his sight returned, Jared saw that the shadows had fled from about her.

For the first time in centuries he gazed on her features— flame-red hair and alabaster skin. He had actually forgotten just how beautiful she was. . . .

"Victory?" he said. "I see little chance of that, my lady."

"Not this war, Jared," Daryna said, her green eyes sparkling with madness. "I speak of the ultimate victory that shall be mine when I have the Dreamer in my power."

"Beware, my lady. 'For his is the Power to destroy both the Arm of Death and the Palace of Evil,' " Jared quoted.

"Fear not, Jared," Daryna assured him. "I shall bind him to my heart as I have both you and Daemor. Or have you forgotten when you first entered my service?"

"No . . . I had not . . . forgotten," Jared replied quietly.

"The Twelve shall become the Thirteen," she continued. "And he shall lead my armies to their final victory."

"Then you will not mind if I pull my forces out of Umbria?"

Daryna glanced at him sharply, before her features softened into a laugh.

"No, Jared," she replied. "You have my leave to retreat from Umbria. That war is no longer important. Join Daemor on the Plains and assist him in defeating the traitor."

"I presume, of course, that you want the Dreamer alive?"

"He shall not be there," she replied. "He will come to me soon—of his own free will."

"I . . . see. I shall need . . ."

"I am aware of your need. I shall meet you in the stables to summon your new steed. Go now, and I will follow shortly."

"Yes, my lady."

Jared turned to leave, glancing back as he reached the doors. Already, she had regathered the shadows around her. Jared turned and left the audience hall, his thoughts haunted by green eyes and flame-red hair. . . .

Arthwyr stared out into the night surrounding Castle Aldwyn. From the courtyard below, the moans and cries of the wounded drifted up to his self-appointed post.

No one had expected such a vigorous assault on the first day of the siege. It was almost as if the Morvir had thought they had only one day in which to take the castle. As soon as the entrenchment had been complete, the huge Morvan catapults had begun firing.

Apparently a few barrels of oil had survived Arthwyr's assault. Either that, or the reinforcements had brought additional supplies with them. That seemed more likely. Whatever the source, the oil had quickly been exhausted during the first hours of the assault.

Fortunately, the Morvir had been forced to move the catapults closer to fire stones, rather than light barrels of oil. Aldwyn's catapults had then been able to ignite the Morvir's engines. Now, there was nothing left of the enemy's engines but dying embers.

And then, beyond all expectations, the goblins had attacked. They had swarmed up the walls, and only at the cost of much Aldwyn blood had they been held at bay. Finally, however, even they had been driven away.

Spirits in the castle were high tonight, save among the wounded. There was good reason—the siege was essentially over. The Morvir had no catapults and had already exhausted their entire horde of goblins. Now all the survivors of the assault had to do was wait for the reinforcements on their way from clan Owein. From all reports, that should be within the next sennight. . . .

Arthwyr was not so jubilant, however. Something was not right here. This Dread Lord had not conquered half of clan Aldwyn's lands in this manner. Of that, Arthwyr was certain. There had simply not been that large a movement of troops past Quarin. Something was afoot, but, for the life of him, he could not figure out what it was. . . .

Jared glanced up as the sky began to lighten. Soon, the defenders of Castle Aldwyn would realize that they were no longer under siege. Jared had assaulted them heavily yesterday—both to lessen the odds of pursuit and to rid himself of cumbersome baggage.

If it had been a true siege, his conduct of it would have been deplorable. The *galdir* completely destroyed, and all of his engines burned in the first day. As it was, the first would no longer slow his retreat, and the second could not be used against him.

The fires from the engines had also been useful in obscuring the existence of the burning supply wagons. Their only supplies now were those carried on the backs of the draft horses. Jared wanted to escape from Umbria as quickly as possible—before the country could rally against him.

He had, at most, a six-hour lead on those at Castle Aldwyn. Of course, they might not pursue—for a variety of reasons. Even if they did, he could defeat them easily outside their fortress.

There was no point, however. Now his mission lay on the Plains of Blood—Umbria was the concern of the past.

It would take him approximately five days of forced march to reach Quarin. From there it would take another four, at a more leisurely pace, to join Daemor. He would have to check later, to see if the Aldwyns decided to pursue. . . .

"You mean you are just going to sit here while the Morvir make a clean escape?" Arthwyr demanded, incredulous.

"We have suffered enough in this war," Aldwyn replied. "Let them go."

"What of you Botewylfs?" Arthwyr asked, turning to Dryw ap Botewylf. "Are you going to sit back while those who slew your chief and his heir escape?"

"No," replied the commander of the remnants of Morcan's army. "We shall march with you, ap Madawc."

"Very well. That makes us two hundred strong, at least."

"You cannot attack such a force with only two hundred men," Aldwyn said. "It is madness."

"I attacked it with eighteen, lord," Arthwyr replied. "I intend to avenge my countrymen, if not my clansmen, as well as my king and prince."

"We shall side with you as well, Arthwyr," Cai said, ignoring chief Aldwyn's glare. "We, too, desire vengeance."

"Then let us be off. We have lost enough time already."

Arthwyr turned to face the crowd in the Great Hall.

"Is there anyone else who shall go with us?" he shouted. "Have any of you lost family and kin to these butchers? Or are you content to sit back, as your clan chief would have you do, and let these invaders stroll leisurely out of your lands?"

For a moment there was silence as Arthwyr and chief Aldwyn silently watched the gathering. Finally, a single figure stepped forward.

"I lost my father at Aberstwyth," the Aldwyn announced. "I shall march with you."

"Aye," another shouted from the back. "I lost my brother in Weyton. I want revenge, too."

One by one, the defenders of Castle Aldwyn fell in with Arthwyr. About halfway through things, chief Aldwyn angrily stomped out of the Great Hall.

When Arthwyr finally left Castle Aldwyn, he rode out with over two thousand men in his command. . . .

                              *   *   *

"We've three more days to Quarin," Garth observed, gesturing idly at the map spread on the table. "The Umbrians will have almost caught us by then."

"This is ridiculous," Rashine said. "They are only two and a half thousand strong. I say we turn and crush them."

"And how much time will that cost us?" Jared asked in reply. "A day? More than that, surely, if they decide to hold a hilltop. Perhaps two or three—enough time for clan Owein to intercept us."

"Then what are we to do?" Rashine objected. "Let them attack our rear while we attempt to cross the Foamcrest?"

"There are no hills that near to Quarin, Rashine," Garth replied.

"Precisely," Jared agreed. "If they are foolish enough to pursue us that far, *then* we can turn and crush them—in a matter of hours, rather than days. We march on."

Arthwyr awaited the return of the advance scouts. All too slowly, they had narrowed the gap between the Morvir and themselves. Slightly more than a day's march lay between them and Quarin. If the Morvir made it across the river, there would be no catching them.

By his calculations, he should catch them just before they reached the Foamcrest. Of course, that could be changed by one day's good march for either of them. Either Arthwyr would catch them, or they would escape. He tried not to think of the second possibility.

The scouts finally returned to deliver their report. The Morvir lay precisely where Arthwyr had thought—too far to reach tonight. Should he push the men further tonight? They were already near collapse. What if the Morvir turned to attack on the morrow? By all rights, they should have done so long before now. The *Kanir* knew Arthwyr's small force was hopelessly outnumbered.

No, best to camp and take up the chase anew on the morrow. Yes, and the morrow would decide whether or not the Morvir escaped.

"We shall camp here!" Arthwyr announced.

The Umbrians had gained more ground on them yesterday than Jared had expected. Their desire for revenge drove them harder than any commander could hope for. Still, he should reach the field around Quarin before they overtook him. Then he would turn and destroy them before crossing the river.

"Shall we scout ahead, Dread Lord?" Captain Garth asked.

Jared looked at the forest they were about to enter—the first sign of the gentling of the terrain. Ordinarily, Garth's suggestion would be correct. However, the Umbrians were too close behind—Jared did not want to face them in that forest. His cavalry would have much more advantage in the burned fields west of it.

"No time," he replied. "I have scouted it from above already. There are no Umbrians within it."

"Yes, Dread Lord."

Jared glanced behind. The Umbrians were visible now, about two miles behind them. It was tempting to turn and attack—to show those fools what they were dealing with. Jared resisted the temptation. They would learn soon enough. . . .

The canopy of the forest slowly filled in over them as they pressed onward. Light, filtered through many layers of leaves, cast multicolored shadows on the riders and their horses. Moist leaves hissed beneath the fiery hooves of his steed.

A movement, glimpsed out of the corner of his eye, caused Jared's head to snap around. All he saw was a tree bough, swaying in the wind. The tension of the last few days' pursuit was making him jumpy. . . .

The unmistakable *thrum* of bowstrings corrected him. The man beside him fell from his mount, an arrow protruding from the eyeslits of his helm. After the first, a veritable rain of missiles fell about them, finding their mark with uncanny accuracy.

Another, more fully glimpsed, movement confirmed his sudden, horrid suspicion. Olvir! Olvan archers, guarding the Umbrian forest. Another storm of arrows landed among his force with devastating effect.

Jared cursed—the Olvir had cunningly left them with no retreat, drawing them deep into the forest before making their attack. They would never survive to reach the point where they had entered the forest. What few did make it would then have the Umbrians to deal with. . . .

Jared urged his mount into the air, preparing to escape. There was no salvaging this situation—the battle was already over. Before he could leave he saw Captain Garth below, desperately attempting to rally his panicked men. From his new vantage he could also see an Olvan taking aim on the captain from a nearby bough.

Jared's sword arm flung out faster than conscious thought, and both branch and archer were simultaneously consumed in a gout of fire. He then commanded his mount to drop to the ground beside Garth.

As though Garth were a mere child, Jared hauled the Morvan captain from his saddle and laid him across Jared's own. Then Jared spurred his mount forward, immediately slipping out of reality to the safety of the Gray Plain. . . .

Arthwyr's force was perhaps half a mile from the forest when the sounds of battle reached them. Oddly enough, there was no ring of swordplay—just men shouting and horses screaming.

Riderless horses were the first visible signs of the battle. A small herd of them galloped out of the forest. Soon, however, they saw riders, fleeing from the forest as if the trees themselves had risen up against them.

"Ahead!" Arthwyr shouted. "We have them!"

With a cry of vicious glee, the Umbrians charged forward. Perhaps a thousand Morvir emerged from the forest, in scattered, disorganized groups.

Within the space of an hour it was over, and the last of the Morvan invaders had been put to the sword. Arthwyr rode cautiously to the edge of the forest. They had found some arrows, fletched with birchbark in the Olvan style. He had no desire to be taken for a Morvan by the Olvan archers. . . .

"Hello!" he shouted into the forest.

"Yes, Umbrian?" a voice said from above and to his right. Arthwyr glanced up to see an Olvan standing on a heavy bough. He was certain the archer had not been there before.

"Our thanks!" Arthwyr said in a quieter tone. "I am Arthwyr ap Madawc, commander of this force. May we meet on the ground before I strain my neck looking up at you?"

The Olvan glanced behind him, to the left. Arthwyr followed the Olvan's gaze but could see nothing in the leafy canopy behind him.

"Aye," the Olvan replied, once again turning to face him. "We shall meet you and a score of your men a bowshot within the forest. There is a small clearing. . . ."

Arthwyr smiled and nodded. Even after aiding them, the Olvir were as distrustful as ever. Arthwyr did not bother to point out that the land they stood on was Umbrian.

Chapter
-------- Eighteen ------------

GLORIEN PAUSED AT the well on her way across the camp. The
Delvir had been digging here for the last three days. They insisted
that they *would* hit water eventually. The question was whether or
not they would do so before everyone died of thirst. She leaned
out over the shaft, supporting herself on the well casing. Already,
she could not see the bottom. . . .

She glanced to where Master Wilkinson's tent sat. With a sigh,
she left the well—she could put this off no longer.

For two days the young *rega* had not left his tent. Morfael had
retrieved his meals, uneaten, since . . . Aerilynn had died. Had it
not been for the fact that his ration of water had been drunk each
time, they might have feared suicide.

At the entrance to his tent, she paused again before reaching
out to part the flap. She could see Steven, lying on his cot, facing
away from her. His chest rose and fell evenly beneath his leather
tunic. Was he asleep?

"Go away," he said, inadvertently answering her unspoken
question.

"That is no way to speak to a lady, Master Wilkinson," Glorien
replied, stepping into the tent and letting the flap fall behind her.

Steven was on his feet, facing her, before she had even noticed
that he was moving. Instinctively, she stepped back, her hand
moving to the hilt of her sword.

There was no threat, however. In the dim light that filtered
through the walls of the tent, she could see a momentary expression of horror cross his face, replaced with calm and then something that looked almost like disappointment. He dropped back
into a sitting position on the bed, releasing a ragged sigh.

"Please go away, then," he said.

"No," she said, pulling a stool over to where she could sit
facing him.

"You're just wasting your time," he said, lying back down on the cot and turning away from her. "Nothing you say is going to make me feel any better."

"I did not come to cheer you, sir," Glorien replied. "I came that we might . . . share our grief."

Steve turned back toward her. "What?" he said.

"Did you think that you were the only one who loved her?" Glorien asked, fighting to keep the tremor from her voice. "I have lost the nearest thing to a daughter that I shall ever have. She gave her life to save mine, and now I find that I would gladly cut out my own heart if . . . if it would only bring her back. . . ."

She pulled a kerchief from her cloak to wipe the tears that threatened to fall from her eyes. Perhaps coming here had not been the wisest course, after all. . . .

"I've thought . . . the same thing. . . ." Steven said.

"I do not doubt it," Glorien replied. "I . . . I have something for you."

"For me?"

"Aye. I originally took it for myself, but I . . . I think you should have it. . . ."

She reached into the pocket of her cloak and drew out a silver braid. Cradling it in both hands, she held it out to Steven. His expression was shocked as he timidly reached out to touch it— as if it would dissolve into mist were he not careful.

Gingerly, he took the braid of Aerilynn's hair from her, rubbing it between his fingertips. She looked away, and bit her lower lip to stop the trembling. At the sound of the first sob, she looked back.

Steven sat with his hands pressed against his face. The braid lay in his lap as his shoulders shook. She moved over and sat beside him on the cot, unable to hold back her own tears any longer. At her touch on his arm, he looked up.

"I loved her, too," Glorien said softly, her voice trembling as the tears streaked her dirty face. He leaned against her and cried into her bosom. She put her arms around him, rocking him and stroking his hair as they let the tears wash away their grief. . . .

"Your report?" Laerdon asked the scouts.

"Approximately one and a half thousand men went this way, your highness," the scout replied. "Followed shortly afterwards by perhaps twenty thousand *galdir* and two thousand horse."

"How long ago?"

"Three days at the most."

"Then they were alive three days ago, at least."

"So it would seem, highness."

Laerdon scowled as he looked down the trail that led through the grass to the west. What had possessed Erelvar to retreat in that direction rather than toward Quarin?

"Let us be off," he ordered. "We might still be able to save them. . . ."

"Greetings, Lord Phelandor," Daemor said as his colleague guided his steed down beside him. "How far are your forces?"

"Little more than a day," Phelandor replied, eyeing the nearby hilltop. "I do not think they will be enough to overcome *that*, however."

"They shall not have to," Daemor replied. "Thirst and hunger shall take the hill for us. . . ."

Daemor was interrupted by an unexpected sound. From the top of the fortified hill came the sound of men cheering. One word was predominant among those that drifted down to them—water.

"What?" Daemor said, turning to face the hill. "They *cannot* have struck water! Not *that* quickly!"

"Well," Hilarin replied, "there is still hunger, at least. . . ."

Laerdon rose to his feet to look out over the tall grass. Whistled calls had announced the return of scouts from the north. There was an urgency in those calls that unsettled him.

The top of the tall grass waved to and fro in the almost nonexistent wind. It was astounding how much cover it provided. No one passing by, or overhead, would suspect that an army a thousand strong passed by here.

Olsande rose from the grass not two feet away, startling Laerdon by his sudden appearance.

"The scouts have returned from the north, my prince," he said.

"So I have heard," Laerdon replied. "What news do they bring?"

"A large army has been sighted to the north, less than half a day from here. They travel west and south."

A smile crossed Laerdon's face, quickly replaced by a scowl. Erelvar and Laerdon's brother might still be alive, but not for much longer if this army reached them. . . .

"How large?"

"Two thousand horse and twenty *galdir*."

"Can we get ahead of them?"

"Yes, my Prince. They ... greatly outnumber us. ..."

"Yes, but we shall have the advantage of ambush. Direct the army west and north. ..."

Laerdon frowned as he watched the Morvan army march past, less than a hundred yards away. Even with surprise, there was no way his force could defeat so many. The cavalry rode behind, literally driving the *galdir* ahead of them.

"Let us return to the main force," Laerdon said. He would need to discuss this with Olsande. In the meantime, they could easily stay ahead of the Morvir. ...

Olsande, however, had disturbing news for him on his return. Scouts from the west had found Erelvar and his army encamped on a hilltop, surrounded by Morvan cavalry. They had also sighted no less than five of the Dark Lords in attendance.

"How far is this hill?" Laerdon asked.

"The Morvir should reach it shortly after sunset, highness," Olsande replied.

"Then we *must* stop them here."

"Highness, they are too many!"

"Silence!" Laerdon commanded. "Let me think." The terrain had become increasingly rough as they marched westward. There must be someplace they could lay an effective trap. ...

"Are there any ravines ahead?" he asked the scouts. "No matter how small?"

"Yes, highness," one of the scouts replied. "There is a dry streambed perhaps an hour west of here."

"Nolrod?"

"Here, my Prince." Nolrod emerged from the tall grass at Laerdon's right.

"Can you hide that ravine? Make it look like grassland?"

Nolrod frowned in thought.

"The land here is very weak, highness," he finally replied. "However, I think I can manage to fool the eye—for a short time."

"That will have to suffice. Let us hasten to that streambed. ..."

Laerdon waited in the advance group for the Morvir to arrive. The streambed was about a hundred feet behind them. It was barely twenty feet across and half that deep, but it should serve. Finally, Laerdon saw the cloud of dust that marked the passage of the Morvan army.

He whistled the signal back to where Olsande waited with the rest of Laerdon's army. After a moment, the narrow streambed vanished, replaced with grass, slowly waving to and fro in the almost nonexistent wind. Laerdon blinked—even knowing where the streambed was, he could not make it out.

Another whistled command and he moved out, the rest of the advance force following unseen around him. In moments they were within bowshot of the front of the enemy force.

Two hundred bows simultaneously launched a flight of arrows into the ranks of the *galdir*. Laerdon whistled another command and his men dropped back, circling around to the south. He heard the initial confusion their attack had engendered. Another cry went up as they fired again, aiming by the sound of their foe.

They moved back to the fore, a few of his band allowing themselves to be glimpsed briefly in the tall grass. After one more volley, Laerdon heard a sound like muted thunder and knew the cavalry was in motion.

"Flee!" he shouted, turning and running for the hidden streambed. Now the Olvir made no pretense of stealth . . . running for the stream bed. For very short distances, they could outrun the deer in their homeland. They now made good use of that speed.

Laerdon followed the marks that had been left in the tall grass to guide them. Here a tuft of grass had been knotted as a sign. There a small patch of grass had been cut to half its length. Finally he reached what should be the edge of the stream. . . .

He ran out over the edge of the dry stream, involuntarily holding his breath until his foot landed on the rope that had been strung across it. Beside him, other Olvir crossed the stream in the same manner along the dozen or so ropes that had been laid across the streambed. The Morvir were almost upon them. . . .

"Now!" Laerdon shouted, as his feet again found solid ground. Almost a thousand arrows flew up from the grass around him as Nolrod's illusion faded away. Laerdon spun about.

It had lasted long enough. The leading ranks of the Morvan cavalry could not stop in time. They proceeded over the edge of the streambed at full gallop. Those in the back ranks, who could have possibly stopped, were cut down by the storm of arrows that landed among them. Now, only the *galdir* were left.

Mere heartbeats after the Morvir were slain, another flight of arrows took wing. Almost a thousand of the onrushing *galdir* fell. The rest faltered.

They routed when a second flight of arrows landed among them. With no Morvir to force them into battle, the monsters lost their morale quickly. A third and final flight of arrows scattered them. Laerdon smiled at the sight of the fleeing *galdir*.

"Let us proceed west," he commanded.

Laerdon watched the Morvan encampment from atop a nearby hill. The Olvir had been able to gain the top of this hill unseen, once the sun had set. In the moonlight, he could see Erelvar's camp atop the adjacent hill. It was no wonder the Morvir sat and waited for reinforcements.

He smiled wryly. Those reinforcements would not be forthcoming. Now it was up to him to make the Morvir's current position very, very unpleasant. . . .

"What shall we do, highness?" Olsande whispered.

Laerdon smiled at his second. "That is simple, Olsande," he replied. "We dig. . . ."

"Your men should have been here by now, Phelandor," Daemor said.

"Yes," Phelandor agreed. "I shall have to go and see what has detained them. Perhaps one of the supply wagons has broken a wheel. . . ."

"Let us hope it is that innocent," Hilarin said.

"You worry overmuch, Hilarin," Daemor replied. "I doubt the Umbrians have overcome Lord Jared's forces to the point where they are ready to march onto the Plains. Even if they have, they are almost as unlikely to march out to aid Erelvar as the Olvir. . . ."

"Yes, you are probably correct."

"Of course I am," Daemor replied. "I *was* hoping to have the reinforcements ere sunset, however."

"I shall leave at once," Phelandor said.

"Do so," Daemor agreed. "Bring me word as quickly as possible."

"Do you think we can take the hill with Phelandor's reinforcements?" Hilarin asked once Phelandor had left.

"I doubt it," Daemor replied. "Oh, we shall throw the *galdir* at them, of course. But I suspect that shall only serve to wear them down a little. You saw how ineffective they were before."

"True. . . ."

Further conversation died as they awaited Phelandor's return.

Daemor's attention frequently turned to the hilltop fortress. He was uncertain, but he thought that perhaps a foot or so had been added to the walls over the last few days. With stone taken from the excavation of the well, no doubt. Damn the Delvir for their interference. . . .

"What is taking Phelandor so long?" Hilarin asked, annoyed.

"I was just wondering that myself," Daemor said.

Before they could speculate further, Phelandor emerged beside them from nowhere.

"Did you find them?" Daemor asked.

"Aye, about half a day from here," Phelandor replied. "What was left of them."

"*What?*"

"The Morvir were slain to the last man," Phelandor replied. "It looked as though half of them had ridden full gallop into a ravine. Over two thousand *galdir* were slain there as well. The rest have scattered to the Mistress knows where."

"*How?*" Daemor shouted. In reply, Phelandor handed him an arrow—an Olvan arrow. For a moment, Daemor merely stared at it.

"Shall I leave to scout for the Umbrians?" Hilarin finally asked. . . .

Erelvar savored the biting chill of the predawn air. The morning air was crisp and clean—the success of the well had done much to alleviate the stench of the camp. All too soon, the sun would rise and the daytime heat would revive it.

He stood in the center of the path that ran through the hilltop camp. The ring of his sword as it flew out of its scabbard into a flat arc broke the absolute stillness of the sleeping camp.

He had always relished his morning practices—even back in Morvanor when he had been Moruth, Daemor's aide and star pupil. They gave him time to collect his thoughts. . . .

He stepped, left foot forward, bringing the sword down in an overhand smash that would have shattered the clavicle of any opponent. *Step again; complete the arc; bring the sword around into the backhand shoulder strike.* . . . He could hear the sound of the blade slicing through the air clearly in the silent camp.

Erelvar had half expected an attack during the night. Reinforcements for Daemor should be arriving very soon. *Step again; bring the sword to the left in a flat arc. Again—bringing the sword backhand to the right, the blade horizontal.* . . .

The attack had not come, however. Hopefully it was not because those forces were passing this hilltop by to continue on to the Northern Kingdoms. *Arrest the arc; step; thrust forward. Pull the sword back; thrust up, over and down behind the enemy's shield. . . .*

Erelvar thought that unlikely—there were too many prizes on this hilltop. Himself, the Dreamer and Prince Theron should be enough temptation to divert all of Daryna's attention here. She was impatient by nature—she would want those prizes claimed quickly.

Step; thrust backhand: up, over and down—hold position; complete the arc; swing around in a backhand smash to the head. . . . Thanks to the efforts of Artemas and Felinor, she had been foiled thus far. Erelvar did not know how much longer the sorcerers could endure, however. For the last three days they had, in alternating two-hour shifts, bolstered the ward that emanated from Theron's standard. The strain was beginning to show on them.

Step; swing the blade back, down and up to the opponent's left knee. Complete the arc; step; bring the blade up against the right knee. . . . Even if the sorcerers prevailed, there was only enough gold remaining to empower the device for another two days at most. After that it would be reduced to worthless iron, and all of the power of the ward would have to be drawn from the sorcerers themselves . . . or so Theron had told him. And that would not last long, at all.

Step; swing down in an overhand smash to the head. Arrest the arc; step; swing back, forward and up between the opponent's legs. . . . So, they could endure for another two days at the most. If only some substitute could be found for the gold . . .

Erelvar turned and looked back down the path. The March of the Twelve had carried him a good thirty feet from his starting point. He looked back to the east as the first light of dawn began to lighten the sky.

He sheathed his sword and walked toward the wall, feeling a sudden desire to watch the dawn. He mounted the rampart and leaned against the wall, ignoring the nearby guard's deferential greeting. Right now he did not want to be either Lord Erelvar or the Champion of Mortos. Right now, all he wanted was to watch the sun rise. . . .

To the east the hills rolled down toward the Plains. Very high, cirrus clouds glowed pink with the new dawn. It would be a pretty day to die. . . .

Erelvar glanced down. There seemed to be quite a bit of activity in the Morvan camp—perhaps the reinforcements had arrived after all. No—the number of Morvir did not seem to have grown, and there were no *galdir* about whatsoever. . . .

As his eye travelled back up to the horizon, something on a nearby hilltop arrested his gaze. Studying it more closely, Erelvar realized that the top of the hill was ramparted. Morvir? No, the rampart was behind their lines—besides, it was too sloppy. . . .

As the light of day crept into the saddles between the hills, Erelvar saw that a few Morvan bodies lay at the base of that hill. He returned his gaze to the hilltop. As if aware of his scrutiny, the defenders of the other hill raised the standard of the royal house of Olvanor.

"Guard," Erelvar said. For the first time he noticed that the guard was one of Theron's Umbrians.

"Yes, my lord?"

"I relieve you. Go and bring Prince Theron here at once."

"Yes, my lord!"

A smile crept across Erelvar's face as he returned his attention to the Olvan camp. It would be an even prettier day to live. . . .

Steve stood on the wall, watching the other hilltop. Behind him the rest of the camp laughed and cheered in jubilation at the news. Steve did neither.

Where were you three days ago? he thought. Of course that was unfair—the Olvir had undoubtedly arrived as quickly as they could. Still, he could hardly feel festive. . . .

He felt a hand on his shoulder and turned to find Morfael standing next to him.

"Do not blame them overly much," he said. "They are happy to be rescued. They truly do not mean to spite your pain."

"Actually, I was blaming the Olvir for not getting here earlier," Steve replied. "Pretty stupid, huh?"

"Fairly normal, I would say. You are truly blaming fate."

"Yeah, I guess so," Steve replied. "Morfael?"

"Yes, my friend?"

"I really loved her, you know?"

"Yes, I know. . . ."

Daemor surveyed the situation below. Atop one hill was Erelvar's nearly impregnable camp. Atop another was a not nearly so impregnable Olvan camp. With a thousand Olvan archers defending it, however, it might as well have a stone wall twice the height of Erelvar's. If he attacked the Olvir, his two thousand Morvir would be dead ere they were halfway up the hill.

It was warded as well. Apparently Prince Laerdon had brought an Olvan lore-master with him. Their ward would fail long before that maintained by the Nymran sorcerors. Perhaps if they all bombarded it . . .

He was startled when another mount emerged in the air not a hundred feet away. Daemor stiffened in the saddle. Even though Jared faced away from him, Daemor had no difficulty recognizing him. He urged his mount forward.

"Greetings, Lord Jared," Daemor said coolly.

"Lord Daemor," Jared replied.

"How fares the war in Umbria?"

"About as well as that in Olvanor. Of course, you already realize that."

"Yes, or you would not be here now. Do you bring reinforcements?"

"Only myself. I was taking a moment to survey the situation."

"I am in command here, Jared," Daemor said irritably.

Jared's gaze left the ground below to meet Daemor's.

"No longer," he replied evenly. "The Mistress has sent me to assume command."

"Wha . . . ? You cannot . . . !"

Jared calmly returned his gaze to the ground below.

"I have my orders, Daemor," he said. "I do not know why you are so upset. This way, the blame for the final defeat will fall on me."

"Or the glory of the final victory!"

"I doubt there will be any victory here," Jared replied. "Let us join the others. We need to hold council. . . ."

"My lord?" Morfael said through the closed tent flap. After a brief moment Erelvar opened the flap and stepped out.

"Yes?" he asked. "What is it?"

"There is something strange happening in the Morvan camp, my lord."

"Have you sent for Prince Theron?"

"Yes."

"Lead the way."

Morfael led Erelvar to the eastern side of the camp. Theron was already there, looking into the camp below. From the wall Erelvar could see a hundred or so of the Morvir riding away. Below, a single Dread Lord stared up. Apparently spying Erelvar, he raised his sword in a brief salute.

"It would appear," Erelvar said, "that the Mistress is not pleased with Daemor's performance here."

"Explain," Theron said.

"That is Lord Jared below us," Erelvar replied. "He and Daemor are chief among the Twelve. If Jared is here, it means two things—one, he has relieved Lord Daemor of command here and, two, the war in Umbria has been abandoned."

"He was commanding that?"

"Daemor commanded in Olvanor, therefore Jared must have commanded in Umbria."

"I see. . . ." Theron returned to watching the camp below for a moment.

"Where do you think the other members of the Twelve have gone?" he asked.

"There is no knowing," Erelvar replied. "I suspect they have gone where those hundred cavalry are headed."

"What's all the commotion?" Captain Tsadhoq asked, joining them on the wall.

"The force below has changed commanders," Theron replied.

"Well, good," Tsadhoq said. "Maybe now we'll get all this over with. You know him?"

The last was directed at Erelvar.

"I know of him, yes," Erelvar replied. "He has a reputation for being very . . . meticulous."

Tsadhoq snorted, amused.

"Well, no matter how 'meticulous' he is," the Delvan said, "he doesn't have the men to take *this* hill."

"Let us hope not. . . . " Theron replied.

Jared was not at all pleased with the situation here. Erelvar's hill was unlike any field fortification he had seen before. One might as well be attacking a castle. It was no wonder that Daemor had chosen to proceed with siege tactics.

Still, he could have used his *galdir* more effectively. Instead of hurling the entire mass up the hill, he should have sent them in continuous waves of five thousand or so. He would have gotten more effect out of them that way.

But then, as was his wont, Daemor had been overly confident of success. He always made good initial plans, but he got sloppy in the end. This time it had cost him. . . .

When the others returned from gathering what they could find of the scattered *galdir*, they would assault Erelvar's . . . fortress. Unfortunately, there would be neither the numbers, nor the time, for an extended attack. For all Jared knew, the force that had defeated him in Umbria was on its way here even now.

Of course, it would be necessary to pin the Olvir down atop their hill during the attack. Fortunately, that would not be too difficult. The Olvir themselves had left him the means of doing so. . . .

Erelvar strode briskly through the camp, inspecting the preparations for battle. Everywhere, men were inspecting their weapons and armor, making any needed last-minute repairs and adjustments. With Jared having just assumed command of the Morvir, an attack of some type was imminent.

Erelvar stopped, his eyes narrowing.

"You," he shouted, calling to one of Theron's Umbrians. The man glanced about him.

"Yes, you," Erelvar said. "Come here and bring that shield with you!"

"Y-yes, my lord?"

"You cannot use that shield in combat. It's cracked—see?" Erelvar pointed to a crack that ran about four inches down from the top of the shield.

"But, my lord, 'tis only a small crack and . . ."

"That does not matter. We shall be facing not *galdir* in this battle, but Morvan warriors." Erelvar took the shield from the Umbrian and handed it to Morfael.

"Do you know what will happen if you go into battle with that shield against Morvir?" he asked.

"N-no, my lord. . . ."

"This!" Erelvar spun toward Morfael, drawing his sword and bringing it down precisely where the small crack began on the top of the shield. There was a sound of splitting wood and half of the shield lay on the ground.

"We have spares," Erelvar said, turning back to the Umbrian. "Get one."

"Y-yes, my lord," the Umbrian replied, obviously shaken by the demonstration. Erelvar noted that all the men nearby were giving their shields a second inspection.

"Most Morvir do not have Delvan blades, my lord," Morfael said, once they were away from the Umbrians. Erelvar shrugged.

"So they will need two strokes instead of one," he replied.

The sound of alarm horns echoed throughout the camp. Before the sound of the first note had faded, Erelvar was running toward the wall.

The Dread Lords were returning with the Morvir that had left earlier. With them were just under ten thousand *galdir*. It had been a straggler-gathering mission—Erelvar should have realized that. Normally there were not quite so many to round up, however. This would make quite a difference in the coming battle. . . .

"How many did you find?" Jared asked.

"Slightly more than eight thousand," Daemor replied.

"I see," Jared said, shaking his head. Out of twenty thousand. . . .

"We shall gather them on the northwest side of the hill, away from the Olvir. Once they have engaged the defenders we shall send the *regir* up. That should prevent them from coming under fire."

"And what of the Olvir?" Daemor asked acidly. "Are we just going to leave them to attack us from behind? We must reserve enough force to hold them in position."

"No, Daemor. If we pull any men from our attack, it will likely not succeed. There is a simpler way to keep the Olvir on their hill."

"And what, pray tell, is that?"

"The five of you shall take position in the air above the hill," Jared began. "Before we reposition the *regir*, you shall fire these five points around the top of the hill. The grass that the Olvir have so carefully left in place should hold them atop the hill for at least a third of an hour, or so. By then the battle should be over. If it is not, it will not matter."

"How elegantly simple," Hilarin noted.

"Then you will all move over Erelvar's camp and begin bombarding that ward," Jared said, ignoring Hilarin. "We *must* pierce that ward in order to kidnap the Dreamer. That is all we can truly hope for in this battle. . . ."

"You have us defeated before we even begin, Lord Jared," Daemor said.

"You have left me with very little to work with, Lord Daemor.

I am amazed that I have been able to salvage this much. Now, we have a battle ahead of us. Go prepare your men."

Theron watched as the Dread Lords amassed the goblins below. They were obviously going to attack up the northwest slope of the hill. Fortunately, with the Olvir camped so nearby, they would be forced to keep enough of the Morvir in reserve to hold them at bay.

The goblins had finally been gathered at the foot of the hill. These they could handle. Theron worried about the Morvan *regir*, however. Jared could possibly spare about a thousand of them. As unseasoned as his own men were, the Morvir could pose quite a threat. . . .

The Dread Lords rose into the air, heading to the southeast. Theron straightened in surprise. What was afoot here?

As he watched, five of them took position over the Olvan camp. Was Jared planning to attack both camps simultaneously? If so, he was a bigger fool than Daemor had proven to be. . . .

As five columns of fire snaked to the grassy hill below, their intent became painfully clear. Theron watched as the flames quickly circled the base of the hill in the dry grass. Now Jared need leave no one to hold the Olvir. . . .

Steve winced as another splash of fire struck the invisible barrier fifty feet overhead. It would have been better if he were one of those on the wall—then he would not be free to see such things. Erelvar had made a point of him *not* being on the wall, however.

Steve returned his attention to the section of wall under attack. The *galdir* had gained a toehold on one small spot. A lone *galda* had gained the rampart itself. As Steve watched, one of the legionnaires dispatched it and hurled its carcass from the wall. Not bad for someone who was a farmer a little less than a month ago. . . .

His smile faded as he saw the top of a ladder strike the wall. The *galdir* did not use ladders. . . . As expected, the helm of a Morvan *rega* soon became visible. The defenders in that area were too busy with the *galdir* to push the ladder away.

Steve watched, horrified, as the same farmer who had killed the *galda* was slain by the Morvan before the enemy had even cleared the ladder. The ebon-armored figure killed another Umbrian before he was killed from behind. Two more had gained the battlement. Steve began to run toward the wall, his hand reaching for the hilt of his sword.

"Going somewhere, Steven?" a familiar, husky, woman's voice asked.

He spun around. She stood in the shadow of one of the few tents left in the camp.

"Go away," he said. "There is *nothing* I want from you. Nothing!"

"Nothing?" she asked. "Are you so certain of that?"

She stepped from the shadow, and Steve's breath caught in his throat. The fading sunlight shone on silver hair as he stared into her turquoise eyes. He involuntarily took a step toward her.

"Aer-Aerilynn. . . ."

She held out her arms toward him and Steve's hand fell away from his sword to reach for her. Tears streamed down his face. . . .

Then she smiled—a predatory baring of teeth that would never, never have crossed Aerilynn's face.

"*Nooo!*" he screamed, recoiling from her. "Damn you! Witch!"

His sword flew from its scabbard. The light from it was so bright that Steve had to look away—but not before he could see the bones of his hand through the flesh that gripped the hilt.

"Damn you!" he shouted. Daryna stood there, shadows and illusions stripped away. Her red hair framed an alabaster face filled with sudden fear. She stepped forward, raising the blade to strike as she raised her arms to ward him off.

She vanished just as he felt the blade begin to bite into her side. The momentum of his swing spun him around to fall to the ground. He rose to his knees, his fists beating the earth where she had stood as he howled his outrage to the world.

Strong hands grabbed his shoulders to lift him to his feet. Steve threw several blows at his assailant before he finally heard the shouts. . . .

"Steven!" Morfael was shouting at him. "She is gone—it is over."

"Morfael?" he asked, ceasing his struggles.

"Aye, it is I."

"You saw?"

"Yes."

"God, Morfael; she even *sounded* the same. . . ."

Steve collapsed into Morfael's arms, weeping bitterly.

Daryna knelt before the gilt throne, clutching her side. How had the Dreamer's Sword wounded her? She had been nothing more than an image.

Apparently even that was enough to subject her to attack. She watched, horrified, as a pool of blood began to slowly grow at her knees.

"Jared!" she cried. . . .

Jared stiffened in the saddle as the summons ripped through him. He had seen Daryna below when the unearthly light from the Dreamer's Sword had illuminated the hilltop like a second sun. He had thought her safely fled—apparently that was not the case. He turned his mount toward Daemor.

"We must return to Delgroth!" he shouted as he neared the other Dread Lord.

"What? In the moment of our glory? Are you mad?"

"Daryna calls! She has urgent need of us."

"I have heard no such call," Daemor replied, beginning to turn away from him.

Jared grabbed a handful of Daemor's cloak, hauling him over backwards. Before Daemor could recover from the shock of Jared's treatment of him, Jared's sword was at his throat.

"So help me, if you do not return to Delgroth with me at once, I shall kill you here and now!"

Daemor's eyes glowed red behind the demon-mask. Jared was not concerned. If anything, his own burned brighter. . . .

"I . . . see. Very well, Jared. But this had best not be a hoax. . . ."

Erelvar surveyed the aftermath of the battle. The dead were many—the wounded even more numerous. Master Wilkinson lay in his tent, unmarked from the battle, but perhaps the most wounded of all. Morfael had told him what had transpired— Erelvar feared that the man's mind might have been shattered. Mortos knew that such a thing could destroy even the strongest men—even one like Steven.

Prince Laerdon's men had joined them, once the fire about their hill had died away. Without their aid, the battle might have fared much worse. Without their aid and without the sudden disappearance of all the *Kaimordir*, that was. . . .

Erelvar paused at the entrance to Steven's tent. Perhaps he should ask Glorien to speak with him. Or perhaps Morfael. He, himself, had no subtlety for such things. . . .

He stopped himself as he began to turn away. No. Steven was his friend, and as such, it was Erelvar's place to share his sorrow. He could not send another to perform this task for him. . . .

"Steven?" he called softly as he raised the flap. . . .

"Out, all of you," Jared commanded.

"Jared," Daemor began, "we have the right . . ."

"*Out!*"

The others obeyed, filing slowly out of the room until only Jared and Daemor were left. They stood on opposite sides of the bed wherein the Mistress lay. Jared drew his sword.

"Jared," Daemor began.

"Silence. You may stay, Daemor. I have not the right to command you."

Jared knelt by the bed, pulling the sheet from the prone form.

"J-Jared?" she said.

"Hush, Mistress," he replied. "You must release the shadows."

With a shuddering sigh, she did so. Jared and Daemor gasped when they saw the wound and the blood staining the sheets. To see such beauty so marred . . .

"Jared?"

"Be . . . silent, Mistress." He concentrated, and flame licked along the blade of his sword. The pain of controlling the fire like this throbbed throughout his whole body. Daemor gasped again—he knew what this must be doing to Jared.

"Jared—w-what . . ."

"He is . . . going to stop the bleeding, Mistress," Daemor said. "Lie still. Do it quickly, Jared."

Jared lowered the burning blade against the wound. The fire was the Mistress's own Power vested in the Dread Lords. Only it could close this wound.

There was the hiss and sizzle of burning flesh, and Jared's heart was torn at the sound of her anguished scream. Daemor held her firmly as Jared cauterized the wound. Finally, he lifted the blade away and the screams died away into painful sobs.

"He shall pay for this, Mistress," Jared said. "I swear, I shall make him pay. . . ."

"N-no, Jared," she said. "No. He is my . . . only path to victory. . . ."

"He shall destroy you!"

"No. I . . . shall destroy *him*, but . . . not before I have learned his secrets."

"As . . . you wish, Mistress."

Chapter
-------- Nineteen -------------

STEVE PLACED THE ornate cedar box in his saddlebag. He walked around his horse one last time, checking the cinch on the saddle, giving the shoes one last inspection.

Erelvar had come away from the battle on the Plains with two thousand Morvan warhorses. Steve had been touched by his gift of this golden mare. Palomino horses were very rare here.

The Nymrans had done well, too. They had returned to Quarin to find a full legion camped on the north bank of the river—an Imperial legion commanded by a General Nestor, but flying the standard of the Regency. One of those that had invaded the Regency with the new emperor, it had defected at the last moment.

The Delvir, like Steve, had not done well on the Plains. They had come to Quarin with a thousand of the royal guard. A little more than three hundred had marched home last winter.

His horse poked him in the side with her nose. Steve smiled.

"Impatient, girl?" he said. "I understand."

Steve mounted. The body of the horse felt good beneath him. He nudged her gently in the side with his heels, pulling the reins to the right.

He rode through the outer bailey, where the shantytown had once stood. Now, newly planted grass glistened with the morning dew. The shantytown had moved into the main plaza as the focus of construction had shifted.

Steve was stopped at the main gate to the entry plaza by Morfael.

"Good morrow, my friend," Morfael greeted him.

"Hello, Morfael," Steve replied.

"Where are you going, if I may ask?"

"I'm taking Gold Dust out in the forest to stretch her legs. She's been cooped up in the stable all winter."

"Would you like some company?"

"Not today, Morfael," Steve replied. "I'd . . . kind of like to be alone."

Morfael placed his hand on Steve's forearm. "I understand. Ware the forest—the footing is somewhat treacherous."

"I shall, but Goldi watches where she's going."

"Good riding," Morfael said, slapping the horse gently on the rump. She snorted indignantly and trotted off.

Steve rode down the ramp into the underground entry chamber. Quarin's construction still amazed him. Back on Earth this fortress would rank with the Seven Wonders of the World, he was certain.

On impulse, he rode out the new south tunnel to the docks. The gate was still open from Theron's departure this morning. In fact, as Steve rode out onto the stone dock, he could still barely see Theron's galley as it floated away down the river.

This world had been at war since Steve's arrival. He wondered what it would be like during peacetime. He turned Gold Dust around and rode back through the tunnel, nodding as the guards saluted his passing.

The stone from the new tunnel had gone to build the docks and to repair the causeways. Steve now rode out the southwest tunnel toward Olvanor.

The forest was already recovering from last summer's fire, at least on this side of the river. Morfael had told him the Olvan lore-masters were responsible for that, as they strove to heal the land. Ivy shrouded the burned husks of former trees as new saplings eagerly sought the sun. In shady patches, snow still lingered from the winter.

Steve stopped Gold Dust at the foot of a small hill. There weren't many hills on this side of the river. He dismounted and dropped her reins to the ground. Goldi nickered as he drew the cedar box and a shovel from the saddlebag.

"I won't be long, girl," he said, patting her neck. He turned and walked to the top of the hill.

It didn't take long before the hole was deep enough to suit him. He took the cedar box and opened it. Reaching inside his cloak, he drew out the silver braid of Aerilynn's hair and coiled it up inside the box. For a moment he just stared at it. Then he closed the lid and laid it in the hole.

The cedar would keep it safe here. With tears slowly running down his face, he refilled the hole, tamping it down well. What was left of Aerilynn deserved to rest in her homeland. . . .

"Goodbye, Aerilynn," he said. "I'll miss you."

He turned and walked down the hill, back to his horse. He placed the shovel in the saddlebag and mounted.

Steve glanced back up to the top of the hill. It was time to leave. . . . He nudged Goldi in the side and she began to walk off.

"Steven," a woman's voice said. Steve's head jerked up toward the sound of the voice. She stood by an ivy-shrouded tree.

"Flee, my love!" Aerilynn said. "There are Morvir in the forest!"

Then she was gone, if she had ever truly been there. Steve felt the hackles on the back of his neck rise.

He kicked Goldi hard in the flanks. She neighed loudly in surprise and took off like an arrow. After a short distance, he caught his first glimpse of armored riders paralleling his path to the left.

Steve turned his mount sharply to the right, only to find that the Morvir followed him there as well. He lashed Goldi's rump with the reins, and she shot through their line. With a few shouts of surprise, they turned to pursue.

Relentlessly the muffled hoofbeats of the Morvir followed—he mustn't let them catch him. He leapt a fallen, vine-covered tree and turned his mount to the left. New saplings whipped his horse's flanks as he charged ahead.

Unfortunately the dead, ivy-shrouded trees offered little concealment while still impeding his progress. He could not imagine how the Morvir had managed to conceal themselves here.

He risked a glance behind, catching a brief glimpse of ebon-armored riders racing past on the trail he had just left. They wouldn't be misled long, he was certain.

He circled back to the east, toward Quarin. If he could but reach the limits of the forest, he would be within sight of the city's walls. Surely they would not pursue him past that point. . . .

Horn-blasts from behind told him that his pursuers had discovered their error. He leapt another fallen tree, desperately seeking a path through the jumbled ruins of the forest. The chase had already driven him far from familiar areas of the woods.

Ahead, however, a small ridge rose from the forest floor. It seemed clearer than the surrounding terrain and ran in the desired direction. They would undoubtedly realize that he had followed it, but it might take him far enough before they found it.

The warhorse stretched into a full gallop along the ridge, foam coating her golden flanks. The horse wouldn't last much longer—he hoped she would last long enough.

It was not the horse, however, that betrayed him. As he topped a small rise he saw, with horror, that the ridge ended in an abrupt drop to the forest floor. Without thought he threw himself from the saddle—his only chance.

The breath burst from his lungs as he struck the stony ground of the ridge. He tumbled several yards before falling down a steep slope. Desperately, he attempted to slow his plunge down the side of the ridge.

He came to rest amid a shower of gravel. The screams of the wounded horse told him that she had not fared as well in the fall as he. If that didn't bring the Morvir, nothing would. He had to kill the horse and escape before they followed her screams to him. Surely, he must not be too far from Quarin.

He pulled himself to his feet, using the steep, earthen wall of the ridge for support. For a moment the world spun about him. He took a few deep breaths and allowed his senses to settle back into place.

He looked up quickly when the horse's screams came to an abrupt end. One Morva stood by the dead animal, wiping his sword with a cloth. The young warrior doubted that the Morva had slain the horse out of mercy. More likely, the screaming had irritated him.

Five others sat astride their mounts. The breath caught in his throat—he wasn't ready to die.

Grimly, he clenched his jaw, regathering his courage. He would die well. He owed Erelvar that much, at least. Slowly he drew his sword and retrieved his shield from the ground. He doubted that he would be given the opportunity to use either.

Then again, perhaps he would. With some surprise he watched as the other five Morvir dismounted. Their steeds, superbly trained, stood where the reins had been dropped as if hitched there. The six men approached him, slowly and cautiously, as he placed his back against the ridge.

They stopped in a half-circle well beyond sword reach. For a moment they merely observed him, silently.

"Will you surrender to us?" one of them finally asked. So . . . they wanted him alive.

"To Morvir?" he said. "Hah! I might as well fall on my sword. . . ."

*   *   *

Belevairn leaned against the husk of a tree, his mind reeling. There was so much! Until now, he had been a mere child, playing with things he did not understand. But now, the secrets of the Universe seemed to be laid bare before him. . . .

"Dread Lord?"

"Wha . . . ?"

"What shall we do with the body?"

"Uh . . . leave it. Yes, leave it." Belevairn shook his head, pushing the alien knowledge to the back of his mind.

"Depart here immediately," he told the Morvir. "I leave for Delgroth. . . ."

"As you command, Dread Lord."

Belevairn mounted his steed and immediately urged it onto the Gray Plain. He must report to the Mistress at once. . . .

"We have found him, Lord Erelvar," Morfael said, riding up at a gallop.

"And?" Erelvar prompted.

"He . . . he is . . . dead, my lord."

For a moment Erelvar said nothing. Morfael placed a hand on his shoulder. Erelvar knocked it away.

"Take me to the body," he commanded.

They led him to a small clearing at the bottom of a ridge. Steven's corpse was staked, naked, to the forest floor. His armor and weapons lay in a pile by him. The horse Erelvar had given him, Gold Dust, lay dead a few feet away, her legs broken from a fall. Erelvar glanced up to the top of the ridge.

He dismounted and walked over to kneel by the body. He felt his fists clench and his shoulders begin to tremble.

His eye was caught by the sight of a cloven hoof mark scorched into the moist floor of the forest—*Goremka*. And there was only one of the Twelve who practiced sorcery. . . .

"You shall pay for this, Belevairn," he whispered. "With Mortos as my witness, I *swear* you shall pay for this."

"Bring the body," he commanded. "We shall bury him with honors at Quarin."

"My lord?" Morfael said.

"Yes, Morfael?"

"Magus Artemas once told me that Steven was still linked with his body back in his homeland. Might he not still live, there?"

Erelvar looked to Magus Felinor, who sat ahorse beside Morfael. The sorceror sadly shook his head.

"No, I fear not," Felinor replied. "Even if his body there still lived, which I would doubt after this long, the shock would stop his heart. And I once heard him say there were no healers in his world. . . ."

Erelvar nodded sadly. They had taken another friend from him. . . .

Epilogue

"COME ON, TIFFANY," the young intern insisted. "Just let me buy you breakfast when we get off shift this morning."

"Well, all right," the blonde nurse replied, smiling. "There's an IHOP just down the street. . . ."

"Great! We can . . ."

He was interrupted by a scream from one of the patient beds. He whirled around to see number seven sitting up, screaming as if the devil himself were at the foot of his bed.

The patient collapsed back onto the bed and the EKG alarm went off.

"Holy shit!" the intern shouted, grabbing the crash cart and starting over to the bed. Behind him Tiffany was on the intercom. . . .

"Doctor Wright, code six to the coma ward. Doctor Wright, code six to the coma ward."

The doctor arrived by the time Geoffrey had the jelly on the paddles. Doctor Wright took the paddles from him, rubbing them together.

"Clear!" he called, placing the paddles on the patient's chest. The body jerked as the charge passed through it. Geoffrey found himself holding his breath. . . .

The alarm on the EKG silenced as the heartbeat returned, quickly climbing to a normal sinus rhythm. Geoffrey let his breath out in a long sigh. . . .

A cheer went up through the room, and Geoffrey looked around to see half a dozen staff gathered around the bed.

"He's opening his eyes!" someone shouted. Sure enough, the patient had opened his eyes and was slowly looking about, a panicked expression on his face. He said something, but it was just nonsense, not even words.

"Mr. Wilkinson," Doctor Wright said, "can you hear me? I'm Doctor Wright; you're going to be all right. . . ."

"Oh, dear God," the patient said, beginning to cry. . . .

Appendix

The Prophecy of the Dreamer
from the Book of Uldon

IT CAME TO pass that I, Brys ap Owein, was in Weyton during the Feast of Uldon, having journeyed there in pilgrimage to worship and make offering to the Lord of the Waters. On the first morning of the Feast, I went to the shore of the sea with my offering and once there a great slumber came over me.

And in a dream I saw Uldon rise from the sea and he called to me saying "Brys ap Owein, walk with me," and I rose and walked out onto the water which had become calm and smooth, like unto the surface of a mirror.

Then Uldon said, "Behold!" and in the waters beneath my feet I saw a throne and he that sat on the throne wore a crown with seven stars and about him were the Seven Chiefs of the Kanir.

And he that sat on the throne was troubled, for the hosts of the Dark One had gathered on the Plains to lay waste to the World of Man and he said, "Release the Arm of Death."

And Mortos, Lord of Heaven and the Dead, did break a great seal and I saw the Arm of Death rise from the earth and sweep the hosts of the Dark One before it. From the Plains of Blood it drove them and the Bitterwine River ran red with their blood and I rejoiced, saying, "Mighty is the Arm of Death!" and "Who can stand before it?"

And Uldon rebuked me, saying, "Rejoice not, for there is much to be seen," and I held my tongue and saw the wonders he had to show me.

Then the Arm of Death did reach into the Burning Hills to draw forth the Dreamer, and the Dreamer bore a Two-Edged Sword, for his was the power to destroy both the Arm of Death and the Palace of Evil. Then the Seven did cry aloud, saying, "Who is the Dreamer?" and "Which way shall his Sword strike?"

And he that sat on the throne did say, "None may know until the appointed day."

And I looked to Uldon and said, "What is the power of the Dreamer?" and he stirred the waters with his hand, saying, "Watch and learn."

Then I saw the Arm of Death bear the Dreamer to a great fortress, there to shield him from the hosts of the Dark One while he was prepared to smite the Palace of Evil.

And when he was prepared, the Dreamer and the Arm of Death went forth to battle the slaves of the Dark One and the Dreamer's Sword drove them from the Plains.

But, in the midst of their victory, I saw a Great Darkness descend from above and bear the Dreamer to the Palace of Evil. There the Dark One imprisoned the Dreamer and did, herself, take up the Two-Edged Sword.

And the Dark One cast the Sword into the earth, and where she cast it the earth split asunder and there arose a Dragon whose armor was like unto burnished bronze and which spat smoke and fire from its mouth and none could stand before the Dragon, not even the Arm of Death.

And Uldon said, "Here the waters divide in twain," and thrust his hand into the waters and I saw the waters part about his hand, right and left.

And in the waters to the right I saw the Dreamer break his bonds and take up the Two-Edged Sword. With it, he smote the gates to the Palace of Evil and the gates fell and great was the fall of the gates, so that they could not be rebuilt and the light of the Dreamer shone across the land. Then did the Dreamer take his Sword and emerge to do battle with the Dragon.

But the gates of the Palace of Evil had dulled the Sword and the Dragon was unharmed by it and the Dreamer fled from the face of the Dragon.

While in the waters to the left I saw the Dreamer struggle vainly against the bonds which held him, for they were exceeding strong, and the Dragon devoured the Arm of Death, for there were none who could oppose it.

And I said, "Is there, then, no hope?"

And Uldon rebuked me, saying, "Watch and learn."

And in the waters to the right I saw the Dreamer give the

Sword to the Arm of Death and the Arm of Death did take the Sword and smite the Dragon and the Dragon was slain. Then did the Arm of Death sweep all the hosts of the Dark One from the Plains of Blood.

While in the waters to the left I saw more dragons arise from the sundered ground, some like unto the first and some different. And the dragons went forth into the world and slew all manner of living things, for none could oppose them.

In the waters to the right the Seven did enter into the Palace of Evil and do battle with the Dark One and overcame her. Then the forges and smithies of the Palace of Evil were quiet and the Absinthian River flowed clean.

While in the waters to the left I saw the dragons devour all the Beasts of the South so that there were none left to oppose them save the Hermits whom the dragons could not slay. Then the Dark One drew a quiver from the riven earth and the arrows therein were fletched with fire.

And she loosed the arrows into the hills where the Hermits dwelt and where they struck there arose a great fire and the hills did melt from the heat of that fire. Thus were the Hermits slain and the waters of the world became as wormwood and the air as smoke and naught moved upon the face of the world or beneath, nor in the depths of the sea was there any living thing.

And Uldon said, "Go and write what you have learned that all men may know of these things," and I awoke by the sea where I had slumbered.